"...a free-fo
and hugely
held together by a clever storyline. A good read.
Most definitely!"

SF Revu on Quake

"A hard-talkin', hard swearin', hard-fightin' chunk of
military sci-fi."

SFX on Quake

"A new writer who knows what a regular reader
sitting on the bus wants—action. Pure Die Hard,
pure Rambo. This has got to be a film, surely!"

LADSMAG on Warhead

"Non-stop blood-and-guts action thriller."

SciFi.com

"Hard-hitting, galaxy-spanning, no-holds-barred,
old-fashioned action adventure."

The Guardian

"War Machine became my favorite science fiction
novel of the year. Yes, you heard correctly... I loved
every testosterone-fueled second... And the sequel is
easily one of my most anticipated new releases..."

Fantasy Book Critic

Also by Andy Remic

Spiral

Quake

Warhead

BioHell

A COMBAT-K NOVEL

WAR MACHINE

ANDY REMIC

SOLARIS

First published 2007
Mass market edition published in 2008 by Solaris
an imprint of BL Publishing
Games Workshop Ltd
Willow Road
Nottingham
NG7 2WS
UK

www.solarisbooks.com

ISBN-13: 978 1 84416 616 9
ISBN-10: 1 84416 616 3

10 9 8 7 6 5 4 3 2 1

A CIP catalogue record for this book is available from the
British Library.

Designed & typeset by BL Publishing

Printed in the UK by CPI Bookmarque, Croydon, CR0 4TD

This novel is dedicated to Jake "Sgt" Simmo – cycling adventurer, cliffhanger, a man with the look of eagles, purveyor of toxic fish and the most unpopular man at the party.

For all the good times; for Pernod Night and afternoons in The Sangar, Glyder Fach and Crib Goch, the joy of the Mezcal worm and Ein Prosit... and for cooking B&S on The Viking Route. Never have I seen a spuke fight so hard for a sausage!

"How many men have been where we've been? And seen what we've seen?"

No matter what happens, we're not little men.
Hats on!

TERMINUS 5

SHE HATED SCISSORS: their gleam; their simple function. She laughed, and it was a bitter laugh like a tumbling fall of worlds. There within the maelstrom of her mind—a cold constant, like the elliptical spinning hub of the galaxy—was fury. She lifted the scissors to her face; studied her reflected image. Her eyes filled with tears. Her pale fish-flesh face was streaked with crimson shards; her mouth a bloodless slit.

Contrition bubbled, grew, engulfed her.

She sat on the stairs, one hand on the carpet, weeping.

And knew she would never be the same again.

MACHINE GUNS SHRIEKED. Bullets punched the corrugated rust-streaked wall, forcing Keenan to the ground. He grunted, crawling, MPK submachine gun sweeping out towards the sun-dappled tree line of the steaming jungle beyond.

The explosion of noise stopped, leaving a metallic song in the air. Keenan stared out from the skewed doorway, face locked, sweat rolling down his blackened skin; his eyes searched for the enemy.

"I can't believe they spotted us," whispered Pippa, crawling up beside him on her elbows, commando-style. Her mouth was a grim line, grey eyes suggesting something unholy: a single concept.

Trap.

"They must have been waiting." Keenan's voice was a deep smoker's drawl, smooth, calculating, his words clipped and economic. He blinked lazily in the warm damp atmosphere, like a lizard. "Their presence is damned convenient. This shit only happens when the fuckers are expecting you."

The corrugated bunker lay semi-submerged in folds of foliage; huge Splay Ferns drifted around the half-buried flanks in the wake of a tree-fractured breeze. Dangling vines from towering hardwoods dragged rhythmically against the bunker's domed roof. A green half-light illuminated the scene.

Combat-K: proficient in infiltration, assassination and demolition were pinned like butterflies to an entomologist's specimen board. Trapped, the observation post from which they were plotting a meticulous course to the Terminus5 K Series Shield Reactor offered only modest protection. Disabling the reactor would allow a flood of the Quad-Gal's Peace Unification Army to enter the breach and lock down rogue AI weapons, monstrous Proto Vehicles and covert enemy SandSlags.

Combat-K's mission was pivotal, crucial and now—ultimately—compromised. By accident? Keenan shook his head at an internal diatribe. He doubted it.

"I see them." Franco had silent-drilled a hole in the metal compound wall using his PAD laser, and eased free the micro-barrel of his Bausch & Harris Sniper Rifle with SSGK digital sights. The weapon sported a rapid single action fire linked to a hair-line trigger: a devastating gun in the right hands. "There are four of the bastards." He spat on the earth floor, glancing right towards Keenan and Pippa—lying vulnerable and coiled by the warped doorway where fingers of sunlight raped by swirling dust pointed arrows of accusation through the pepper-pot interior.

"Shall I take them?"

More gunshots exploded, shattering the ambient jungle chatter and rattling off the roof, from the left this time, and behind. It was joined by the orig-inal source—a crossfire—which cut more holes through the wall above the trio in a crazy, spitting zigzag. Hot shavings of curled metal sprayed across the group, scorching exposed flesh unprotected by WarSuits.

Above the cacophony Keenan licked salt lips, annoyed now, and lit a cigarette. "Take them, Fran-co." He eased his bulk around the doorway, smoke stinging his eyes, locked his MPK to the tree line and sent a savage sweeping volley of thundering firepower. Bullets scythed the dense jungle smash eating everything in their path. Howls reverberated through deep green. Tracers spat like fireflies.

There came a solitary *crack* as Franco's Bausch & Harris rifle discharged; it was a leaden noise, chilling and final, and it penetrated the din of automatic gunfire. That sound meant death.

A digitally camouflaged figure detached from its chameleon-blended surroundings, head exploding outwards in a snapping mushroom of brain and skull-shards as limbs and torso folded up and over into the air as if in slow motion, then slammed in sudden acceleration to merge with the jungle floor. Keenan's sub-machine gun swung right, targeted by the kill, his bullets cutting showers of sharp chippings from trunks and worming into soft flesh as the hidden soldiers were revealed like a patterned puzzle arranging itself to the human eye.

Keenan crawled to his knees, then gained his feet, and Pippa joined him as they moved across the doorway, weapons juddering, fire blossoming from hot barrels, bullets decimating vegetation with chopping sounds and cutting down the aggressive enemy attack squad in a shower of smashed crimson and pulped bones.

A soldier stumbled forward, gun loose in blood-slick hands, camouflage armour askew and flickering with green sparks of malfunction; he started to raise hands in surrender as Franco's rifle gave another *crack*. The soldier dropped. Lay still.

Silence flooded the clearing. Smoke rose from stagnant gun barrels. Keenan glanced left, nose twitching on cordite, and Franco signalled military instructions with his left hand. *Clear 12. Five 7.*

"If you live by the sword, then you die by the sword," said Keenan, and placed his boot against the compact dirt threshold of the bunker's door-way, looking up, over and back in an attempt to locate the second firing group. His gun came up, stocky, black, deathly serious, held in strong hands that had no right to be that steady in the midst of a fire-fight.

"We've got to get to the reactor. We're fast run-ning out of time!" soothed Pippa, words tickling his ear she was so close. Keenan could feel the ten-sion of her steel-coiled body pressing against his, could sense the pent-up violence of her controlled compression. For a fleeting moment it reminded him of better times, happier times, prettier times, and he glanced at the sweat beading on the flawless skin of Pippa's beautiful face and licked his lips and remembered, and she was beneath him her writhing athletic body bathed in sweat and the smell of her sex in his nostrils the taste of her sweat on his tongue and she groaned a deep needful ani-mal sound...

No! don't go there! Keenan snapped back to real-ity; breathed deeply. *My friend, you can never go there again.*

"Has Franco got the Scatter Bombs?" He forced himself to keep the tremor from his voice.

"Yeah." Pippa passed Keenan a curved bubble of plastic containing fist-sized grenade charges strung along its supporting arc. She was frowning, eyes fixed to his face. She licked salt lips. Keenan, with-out realising it, watched the pink neatness of her tongue; imagined it on his skin. "This was sup-posed to be a fucking covert infiltration," she snapped.

Keenan nodded. "Our stealth op has been flushed down the toilet." He glanced back at Franco. "Ready? It's a good half klick. Standard 4 formation. I want rearward three-round volleys. OK?" He pulled the pin on the Scatter Bomb cluster and tensed, ready for acceleration.

"Aye, Keenan. And Keenan?"

"Yeah mate?"

Franco grinned, strapping his Bausch & Harris to his back and hoisting quad-barrel Kekra machine pistols, one in each powerful hand. "You be damn careful with those Scatter Bombs. You could hurt somebody."

"That's the idea," said Keenan through a haze of drifting cigarette smoke.

A PARADE SQUARE, symmetrical, functional, home to eight thousand soldiers holding stocky MPKs against matt black armoured WarSuits. A bugle sounded, forlorn, wavering, and sixteen thousand boots stamped in perfect unison as the battalion wheeled—a well-oiled machine—and every greased cog saluted officers standing stern but proud on a high fluid compress alloy podium. This was the climax of four years hardcore training. These men and women were not the elite; they were The Chosen.

There were no cheering families, no waving loved ones, no laughter, no joy, no open celebration; and yet, bright at the core of every man and woman assembled for this clandestine Combat-K Class Passing-out Parade burned pride, and strength, and an incredible determination: a commitment to the accelerating Quad-Gal Peace Process, an obligation to end the *horror* of the Helix War.

EXPLOSIONS ROCKED THE dense jungle, eight concussive blasts in quick succession sending palls of oily smoke rolling into the humid air. Machine gun fire rattled from olive darkness; short bursts, tracer flashing through the trees and cutting the scene with scissors. It was a savage, hurried exchange. Combat-K appeared and sprinted through the jungle, boots thudding, Keenan in the lead with his focused machine gun, Pippa second, her PAD set to >SCAN< for navigation and warning of attack; and Franco to the rear, turning every few seconds to send deterrent bursts down their back trail.

"Up ahead?" said Keenan, sweat rolling down his smoke blackened face, dripping from his nose and chin.

"Confirmed. Between that triangle of redwoods. A single entrance." Pippa gestured. "No guards on the PAD. Looks like we have a clear entry, gentlemen."

"Yeah. I'm sure as hell our exit won't be as smooth." Keenan slowed to a walk, eyes searching surroundings, lids blinking away sweat. He hated the jungle; hated it with a vengeance. Too many damned places for the enemy. "You still showing clear local scans, Franco?"

"Yeah boss. But we've got movement two klicks west. Fifty soldiers. They could be ours."

"You're too optimistic. The Quad-Gal boys won't be here for at least another hour, and only if we get this shit done. Come on, time is our biggest enemy. We're moving in."

The Terminus5 Series Shield Reactor—and sixteen others like it—were housed in low buildings forged from single alloy blocks. Each reactor had a protection chamber that was a classified item of military tek held by Terminus5 government, and protected from external scanners by radiation shielding mats. Combat-K's presence on Terminus5—as part of the spearhead of the Quad-Gal Peace Unification army—should have gone smoothly; without discovery. During covert Impact, the Terminus5 government should not have had time to scramble units to protect what was considered planetary low-key targets, such as this global reactor site. A whole planet was a lot of ground to cover. They should have been blissfully unaware of the Quad-Gal's planned incursion...

And yet Combat-K had met resistance. Keenan told himself it was just coincidence, bad luck, but a nagging doubt tugged his paranoia. The compromise had been just too damned neat. Like deviant SPAWS feasting on a Shuttle's ShieldShell.

Once disabled, the seventeen decommissioned reactors would allow a more overt military domino effect as Combat-K squads—and then the REG army—flooded the open gateway and hit fast and hard. Like night follows day, targets would systematically topple, one after the other... with a minimal loss of organic life.

At least, that was the plan.

First, Combat-K—and sixteen teams like it across the belt of the jungle world—had to deactivate the domino reactors. Targets had to fall within a tightly specified time frame.

KEENAN ROLLED OVER, inhaling fresh white cotton mixed with the musk of the sleeping woman, and the aroma of mingled sweat. She lay with her back to him, a rhythm to her sleep, the flesh of her back scarred from an accident when she had been a child. He reached out to touch her—to touch the damaged flesh with innocent curiosity—but pulled back at the last moment as if lazily stung.

Sensing his movement, a sleepy Pippa turned and stared into his eyes. At moments like this she lost her hardness; when the beast withdrew from its cage and allowed a gentle femininity to break free. "You OK, Kee?"

Keenan nodded, but it was a lie, and she could read the guilt on his face like ink; in his eyes like tears; in his every breathing screaming pore. At home he had a wife, Freya, and two young bright stunningly beautiful girls. His guilt was a tangible thing; like a pall of nuclear ash covering his skin.

"This should never have happened," said Pippa, stretching out her frame with a feline yawn, but Keenan could tell she didn't mean it; by her tone, by her eyes, by the way her hand moved towards him and stroked his skin. There was too much tenderness there, too much need. He had become Pippa's anchor, her lodestone. She was a hard woman, a killer, a devastatingly brutal assassin. But within her lurked a core of insecurity, a child in need of nurture, a young girl locked in a room craving nothing more than love and caring, and—ironically—protection.

He had become her protector, her brother, her father, and, against all probability, almost forced by circumstances, he had become her lover.

"You're right, it should never have happened," he said, moving towards her and kissing her. Their lips brushed. Tongues teased. Her hand came up to rest against the side of his face with a tenderness that touched him.

"I could leave," she whispered, nose pressed against his, sweet breath on his lips.

He pulled her taut powerful body towards him, eyes closing, heart accelerating. "No. I need you. I think I will always need you."

And as the minutes rolled by and by, and he tumbled into her, merged with her, joined with her in body and spirit and mind... so a little part of him screamed... and deep down in the crawling stygian tomb of the soul where dark energy created nightmares born and nurtured by horror and hate... so a little part of him crumbled... and a little part of him died.

THE ALLOY DOOR of the Terminus5 Series Shield Reactor was cold under Franco's gloved hand. He planted the explosive with precision against High Grade FF locks, then waved his comrades back, running and leaping into their adopted shelter. "Fire in the hole," he said with a broad grin, putting his fingers in his ears as they cowered behind the fallen hardwood. The *boom* rocked the jungle. A huge chunk of scorched two-foot thick door went whirring over their heads, edges glowing. It clattered off into the jungle like a pinball.

"You don't want that in the back of the head," said Pippa, peering warily over the trunk where black smoke was idly dissipating. "Looks like we have an entry point, guys."

Weapons covering arcs, the trio leapt the hardwood and moved across the rough ground, noses wrinkled at the stench of the explosion. Shards of twisted shrapnel lay scattered. The huge door had been torn from its frame leaving a ragged maw.

Guns poked inside, and the members of Combat-K blinked at the up-rush of ice-chilled air.

"I don't get it. Where's the damn reactor?" Franco's face twisted in a frown as they gazed into the void.

"Down there," said Keenan, gesturing with his weapon. "Initiate your PAD winches. Let's move slow. This wasn't part of the plan. So much for inside fucking information!"

"Great," said Pippa, voice cool, wiping sweat from her creased brow. "This gig just gets better."

Keenan's face was solid stone. "Calm yourself. We have a job to do."

"Yeah, boss. I'm just appreciating the comedy."

Swiftly, Keenan attached his PAD micro-TitaniumIII cable to the battered stonework. He jacked in with a *buzz*, stepped backwards and was instantly gone. The PAD purred as it threw him into the darkness.

Pippa followed, lips a tight compression, and finally Franco swept his gun across the jungle with a scowl, gave a quick look to the sky—as if offering a final prayer—and dropped his armoured body into the void.

Two minutes later, the jungle parted as a camouflaged soldier advanced. He was followed by another—and another—until the jungle teemed with infantry. They formed a staggered semi-circle around the blasted reactor bunker. Guns were cocked, and heavy machine guns expertly assembled on tripods amongst the rough jungle smash.

"You sure they've descended, sergeant?"

"Yes, sir." Salute.

"Don't worry overmuch. The reactor is protected by The Tangled. I can assure you our offensive invaders won't be coming out. And if they do?" He stared at the collective drilled barrels of the silent machine guns. "Well, we'll be waiting for them."

How deep? thought Keenan as the PAD TitaniumIII cable sped through his gloved hands, and light from his head-mounted torch sliced the ink. He had seen this sort of thing before; deep bunkers protecting military installations. This reactor alone could not be considered a massive protection issue; however, it was feasible that below lay a trap, or guard of some sort. At the end of the day, these machines were used for powering a Global Shield, no matter how low their official priority.

A few feet above, Pippa and Franco descended, lights bobbing and dancing as they fell through the vast chamber. Keenan glanced down, slowing his speed as the bulk of the reactor shell came rushing up to meet him.

Something bit Keenan, bit his mind. He slowed to a stop, bobbing for a moment, and pulled free his MPK, checking the 152 round micro-clip. He switched on the beam, and the gun's light swept the interior of the reactor cubicle.

"You see anything, Kee?" asked Pippa.

"Negative. Just... oil, I think. The whole chamber is flooded with oil."

Keenan eased down, so his boots dangled just above the gloss surface. A few ripples swept away and Keenan peered at the reflected slick ebony.

"Affirmative," said Pippa, scanning. "Standard mineral oil; probably used as a coolant of some sort and leaked from a punctured system. The PAD says it's OK to proceed, it's non-toxic."

And yet, still Keenan paused; the serenity around him, the oppressive atmosphere, the glinting glass of the oil; it made him shiver. He got a sudden intuition that something bad was about to happen.

"You sure the PAD says it's clear?"

"All readings zero, boss," confirmed Franco, eyes locked to his own PAD.

Warily, Keenan descended into the oil, which surged up to his knees, crept into his clothing, and invaded his boots. The pool sloshed thick around him, sending ripples cascading to slap the walls.

Keenan's weapon tracked, and his beam danced over rusted metal. He frowned for a moment, noting that around the chamber—set just above the undulating oil line—were holes, like feeder pipes, each about ten inches in diameter. There were eight of them, set symmetrically around the bunker's circumference. Keenan turned his attention to the reactor shell, the reactor's controlling J-UNIT, and unclipped his PAD from its cable.

"I've got enemy activity above," said Pippa. Her voice was a growl. "Looks like they've found us."

"They were shielded from our PADs," nodded Franco, running a hand through his wild hair. He cocked his weapon, the noise loud and intrusive in this hiemal place. He glanced up, sweat beading his brow despite the chill. "Not quite sure how they did that. We're talking advanced kit, mate. And now... Now we're trapped?" It was the question none had wanted to voice: the maggot in the apple, the cancer in the core. It stank like a three-week cadaver; reeked of betrayal and corruption.

"Let's make this mission count," said Keenan, reaching the reactor's J-UNIT. There was a *shring* as a serrated blade leapt from below the evil eye of his gun. Keenan inserted the blade behind the casing and prised the lid free. The buckled alloy panel spun into the oil with a tiny *splash*. Again, ripples eased away from Keenan, lapping rhythmically against the walls; the slaps reminded him of flesh on flesh.

He attached his PAD to the J-UNIT, and the PAD's screen ignited blue. Tiny beams rolled from the PAD, joined like fluid umbilicals ending inside Keenan's eyes. Licking nervous lips, he started a search for the shutdown sequences using pupil movement and controlled dilation.

"There's something else," said Pippa, gun-light sweeping the chamber.

"I've got it too," snapped Franco. "Inside the walls, movement."

Still working, still focused, and through the gritted teeth of concentration, Keenan said, "What's it this time? Rats?"

"Doing a genetic scan now… um… The PAD's reporting ID unknown."

Keenan paused, glancing up at Pippa and breaking laser contact. "What the hell do you mean, 'unknown'? The PAD's got structures on every damned life-form in the galaxy!"

"I've seen this before," said Franco's low voice. There was a tone that made both Keenan and Pippa glance at him where he hung, boots dangling, eyes deadly serious, a soldier puppet on a wire.

And then…

The squirming noise reached their ears, accelerating in activity and volume, a slithering of metal on metal, a soothing sound not too distant from the lull of a mercury sea against a metal shore.

"Keenan, get out of the oil!" screamed Franco. "Get out of the fucking oil!"

Franco was hoisting himself up on his cable, motors droning, and Pippa instinctively followed his lead. Keenan turned back to the reactor shell, spent a few seconds finishing the >TERMINATE< instruction to shut down the core, then pulled free his PAD: as in the darkness something spewed from eight metal holes set in the chamber's walls, a mass of what appeared to be tangled metal cables rolling over and over one another as they ejected from orifices and flooded the oil, bubbling and seething and churning then surging up and out, tumbling and broiling over themselves as they heaved and pulsed and surged at Keenan. He yelped, leaping up onto the reactor shell and clambering up the black ridges of corrugated metal, slipping and sliding, leaving oiled boot prints.

Pippa unleashed a hail of bullets into the tangled mess, but Franco caught her eye, giving a single shake of the head; firing halted, hollow noise reverberating.

"What is it?" bellowed Keenan, as yet more tangled metal mesh spewed and rolled into the chamber. The metal started to thrash, rolling around and over itself, and slopping oil up the walls. It had filled the basin; thin metal threads gleamed in the dancing light of Combat-K's torches.

"It's a metal AI; they called it The Tangled," said Franco over the din of the mass of surging, heaving, thrashing threads. He caught Keenan's eye across the chamber again, and nodded. "Yeah mate, it is lethal. It eats into your flesh, burrows into your bones, then separates its threads lengthways to tear you apart from the inside out. Keenan, you do not want to touch this toxic shit. It's a messy and painful way to die."

"It seems to be calming down," said Pippa.

The Tangled had finished flowing into the chamber, and the writhing had subsided; but still it moved, lethargically, a million tiny metal eels surging and broiling beneath the syrup of oil, weaving and meshing, intertwining, occasionally rearing above the surface with *hisses* as metal rasped metal, surging and slapping the walls, then disappearing from view.

"You've seen this before, then?"

"Yeah," Franco nodded, "on Geeto8. Saw it take out twenty men during a swamp crossing. Nothing works on it; not bullets, not fire, nothing. The stuff is AI—has a shared intelligence—each strand making up a part of the collective brain."

"The PAD didn't recognise it because it's made of metal?"

"That's right," said Franco, "non-organic life. Pretty rare, I think; doesn't even ident as a GG or PopBot."

The three looked up as voices echoed far above in the darkness. Suddenly, bullets screamed from the black and scattered through the oil filled basin, striking sparks from metal walls and the solid bulk of the reactor hull.

Keenan's MPK barked as he returned a volley into the void. Tracer shot streamers.

"I don't mean to be a killjoy, Keenan, but what have you done to the reactor?" Pippa's voice was tinged with panic. Not a nice sound to hear; she was usually unflappable.

"What?"

"You shut down the cooling systems!"

"No, I deactivated the reactor. Once you're in the control menu it takes no great skill."

"I'm telling you Keenan, the reactor is alive... something must have been crossed, or mis-wired; now there's no cooling. That means the bastard will—"

"Meltdown," said Keenan. He glanced down into The Tangled, surging and pulsing around the reactor shell's base; there was no way on earth he could get back down to the J-UNIT without the damn thing eating him. Then his head shifted back to Pippa and Franco, where they dangled, suspended in the gloom. "Once again, my friends, we've been set up. Some bastard has played us for fools. You two get out of here."

"No heroics, Keenan." Pippa's eyes were wide in the darkness. He could taste her concern.

"No heroics," he nodded. "But you're there, I'm here. You get your arses out, clear me a path home, because when I come out I'm going to be moving hard and fast."

"We're on it."

Pippa and Franco glided up into the black and were lost within seconds, torch beams dancing. Bullets screamed above on trajectories of fire, and booms and crashes smashed echoes around the underground chamber. Tracer lit the darkness for a moment with streamers of green. Savagery unleashed.

Keenan glanced down, then stood and removed a long thin liq-N bomb from his pack; he attached this to a firing groove at the base of the MPK's stock.

So, to kill you I've got to kill myself? He laughed bitterly, thinking of Freya and his two girls safe at home, sitting on the veranda he'd built three summers ago looking out over rolling fields that dropped to the valley and spread away to purple mountains capped with hats of snow. His stallions would be there, grazing under a summer sun, and Sprite his dog would bark at Freya's heels as she called to him. Walking from the dense woodland where he loved to explore, he'd head home for a bowl of red-hot chilli, a mound of tortillas, and a fine cold beer.

"And what about me?" whispered Pippa. *"What about my life? What about my love? What about*

the promises you made me you lying fucking whore?"

Keenan blinked, and the echo was lost.

He breathed deep; calmed himself.

Above, the battle halted with alarming abruptness. A voice with heavily localised accent called down. "Mr. Keenan, we have your friends. We have them alive, but I assure you, if you do not immediately surrender they will be executed under Terminus5 Law."

Keenan allowed a slow breath to leave his body, hissing through gritted teeth. He levelled the MPK at the rolling mass of The Tangled, which seemed to come alive as if suddenly recognising the threat, rolling over and over itself, and rearing up out of the oil, broiling violently over the rim of the reactor shell, and climbing in staccato leaps and surges towards Keenan's oil-slick boots... and the soft, penetrable, brittle, tasty bones within.

Nothing works on it; not bullets, not fire, nothing.

Alarms on the reactor started to shrill as it rapidly approached meltdown. Bullets rained from above like hail, kicking sparks from the shell on which Keenan's battered, defiant boots stood.

"Tangle with this, fucker," he snarled, and fired the liq-N bomb into the heart of the heaving, surging mass...

Closed his eyes...

And waited for the explosion to take him.

...Everything is largely faded.

supporting arm of the GREAT CLUSTER, within
which are HEBSOLINA SOD and TREBONCH, the
SPIRAL GALAXIES together; and there is at least
the much smaller PRESIDA ZETA, is exceptionally

being an extract from:
THE HELIX WAR—*A HISTORY*
kv 4788—hv 3792
written by
Professor Marsaal Su b-Kr∂iy∞

TA(Hons), MA''', Tri-G Dip, P~TG ..DL

MANKIND AND HIS other-world organic colleagues (of course, the term "alien" is in itself now "alien", for are we not all familiar cousins in this great soup of the Quad-Gal collective boiling pot?) are to be found in modest concentration around the galaxy cluster of SINAX, the Quad-Gal being the life-supporting arm of the SINAX CLUSTER. Within this bulge, HESOL, THEOD and TRIGON II are SPIRAL GALAXIES, brothers and sister, whereas the much smaller PRAXDA ZETA is a partially unexplored ELLIPTICAL GALAXY of the E07 category. Old and compact, with a mere 30 billion stars, PRAXDA ZETA can be considered the origin of our current Life-Arm, or Sentient Life Bubble. Ironically, it is the least travelled and the least explored.

There are three main theories provided by scholars regarding the origins, the stimuli, the trigger of The Helix War in kv 4788, which eventually came to embrace the entire sweep of the SINAX CLUSTER during its thousand year cycle. The theories run thus:

1. With the development of K5 fuel for FTL travel, and the subsequent mining technologies used in the extraction of K5 at specified points of Singularity, trade channels were instigated in a quad path between HESOL, THEOD, TRIGON II and PRAXDA ZETA. These channels were controlled by a combined force called The Singularity Ministry which imposed taxation on all K5 commerce. When taxation was increased three hundred and fifty percent, the subsequent price increase was passed down to planetary and state level. It affected every living organism in every cluster and made trade expensive to a point of extortion. The theory postulates that an unnamed covert army led by Inspectors from Praxda Zeta attempted a coup d'état over The Singularity Ministry. This failed, and in turn led to retaliations and a rapid escalation towards the state of Cluster War.

2. The President General Viol Vill of TetraF IV at Hesol was assassinated by Yugga Rebels from the

planet Y7 in Praxda Zeta. This led to a quick-fire escalation of events concluding in a Halo Strike on a Hesol sun, which subsequently destroyed four systems and 25 billion souls. Again, events escalated until a State of War was declared across the Quad-Gal and fringe planets were dragged unwillingly into the battle.

3. LEVIATHAN, a benign member of a rumoured GODRACE, and technically dead for nearly a million years, was somehow reborn and instigated the origins of the Quad-Gal Helix War in retribution for a crime that the races of the Sinax Cluster could never comprehend. LEVIATHAN used its superior position [as GOD] to infiltrate governments, ministries, cabal clusters and monarchies, and from thence directed escalation with the outcome of State of War. This supposition is the favourite amongst Theod [Central] University conspiracy theorists; however main flaws are a lack of evidence. Teller's World, LEVIATHAN's supposed home planet, has never been proved thus; however, it does consume any who travel there, and has been classified as too dangerous to approach. Also, by definition, a GODRACE is a dead race; extinct. If LEVIATHAN was extinct, he could never be reborn, and if he could be reborn, would he really trouble himself with such petty matters?

One conclusion can be drawn, however; no matter which theory—if any—originated the events leading to the Helix War, after several decades the start of the war was no longer of consequence.

Atrocity followed atrocity. Escalation led to destruction, to escalation, to destruction in an apparent Catch 22 of spiralling violence. From three possible origins, all time/space strands intercepted and moved along a sequential and singular course... almost written in stone.

And certainly written in the blood of millions.

Some would later say that Life and War were manipulated.

Professor Marsaal Su b-Kr∂iy∞

TA(Hons), MA''', Tri-G Dip, P~TG ..DL

PART I

COMBAT K

CHAPTER 1
GUILT TRIP

KOTINEVITCH EXERCISED NAKED.

Her taut, athletic figure gleamed with sweat as she practised complex yukana sword combinations. The yukana was capable of cutting twelve-inch armoured steel, and had an ugly curved blade formed from a single molecule. She twirled the weapon, which hissed as she danced, pirouetting, cutting, slicing, the chilled blade freezing droplets of sweat from the air to fall, tinkling almost imperceptibly, as ice.

Kotinevitch accelerated.

Moving fast, body twisting, spinning and delivering killing blows to imaginary opponents—the blade a solid black blur at the core of the action—the lithe yet powerful woman completed her Yukana Krell, The Seventh Ritual, and dropped to her knees, head bowed, eyes closed in a simple, calming prayer.

Moments passed. Releasing a deep breath, Vitch stood and sheathed the weapon; then pulled a silver robe of ancient Krell silk over her shoulders. The hem fell to the floor in a series of gathered, neatly stitched folds and the garment cooled her superheated skin.

Pouring a drink, she walked across the marble tiles as a tiny bell chimed and five men entered the vast expanse of the chamber from distant doors carved of white-oak; they were dressed in matching uniforms and marched with the steady, rhythmic step of the military.

Pillars flowed past to either side of the small entourage, and one of the men—the Terminus5 Ambassador General—gazed up at the high arched ceiling where stained glass allowed pastel light to drift like coloured rainfall.

Kotinevitch sat beside a crystal table and pulled the sheathed yukana sword towards her, positioning it reverently by her side. Sipping at her teka juice—which stained her lips a vivid green—she patiently awaited the group that finally arraigned itself before her, Terminus5's Ambassador General slightly to the fore.

"We were shown in." His tone echoed displeasure.

Kotinevitch nodded, brown eyes taking in the five large men one by one, examining, appraising, then returning to the Ambassador General with a look of gentle acceptance. "You would be... Jukan. Correct?"

"That is correct, General Kotinevitch. Ambassador General Jukan. I find it modestly farcical that you have made us wait forty-eight hours for this simple meeting. You think, perhaps, our position in the war is a joke? You think we are a culture to be pushed around? You think your trade embargoes frighten our military might?"

Vitch looked up, then reached behind her and tied back her hair with neat little movements. "The war is over," she said, "or at least it is for the majority of the Quad-Gal. You feel you have a superior viewpoint, an accelerated understanding? Do you really believe we will withdraw from your inter-continental disputes and allow you freedom for total self-rule?"

"Yes. We do believe that. It is no crime to self-govern. And yet you patronise and threaten us with proximity; you have Armoured Infantry Transporters, I-Freighters and Tri-Klags circling Terminus5 like a bad stellar disease. You do not behave like an army in deceleration; you behave like an army ready to invade!" With great effort, he calmed himself. Breathing deeply, he said, "Anyway, to business. We are here regarding the Combat-K situation."

"Yes. It is being dealt with."

"But... not sufficiently."

Kotinevitch smiled with her lips, but not her eyes. "We are waiting for a sign before we progress."

"A sign?" Jukan snorted, shaking his head. "I should have known better than to deal with a backward people such as the Krell; you are obsessed with trivial pagan totems, indoctrinated by a dark pseudo-religion that should have died ten thousand years ago—yes—along with your devil-decimated clans!"

A second man reached forward, placing a hand against Jukan's shoulder: a reminder, a physical note of caution. You go too far, said that humble touch.

Vitch sat, motionless, cool brown eyes watching him.

"I apologise." Jukan composed ruffled feathers. "This land is too warm for my liking. And your arrogance and lack of manners to a superior Quad-Gal officer are far from appreciated in one so..." he savoured the word, "renowned."

Kotinevitch reached forward, lifted a tiny brass bell and gave it a ring. The high-pitched chime sang across the chamber. A small woman entered dressed in a simple black robe and leading a Helk on a short TitaniumIII leash.

The huge beast lumbered uncertainly, hooves clacking on the marble, its triple nostrils snorting under snot-matted grey fur. Small bovine eyes moved in a large cubic skull, surveying the men suspiciously as the woman came to a halt. The Helk shambled to an almost mechanical standstill behind her.

"Ahh," Vitch smiled, "our omen has arrived." She stood, and in one fluid motion the yukana was unsheathed and slammed through the Helk's bulky neck in a shower of sparkling, suspended crimson. Vitch lowered her blade, where blood rolled free of the frictionless surface.

There came a *slap* as the huge shaggy head hit the ground, then the beast's front legs folded, and the creature rolled forward and pitched onto its flank. Vitch glanced sideways, to where the five men were bathed in splatters of gore, their neat uniforms stained, eyes wide in shock. Jukan's hand had gone to his gun, a Penta 8mm nail pistol; one of his companions restrained him.

Vitch shrugged free her robes so that she stood naked and coiled, then moved towards the twitching farm animal. She dropped to one knee and with a single strike opened the creature lengthways down its belly. Dropping to her other knee in the pulsing surge of blood, she placed her sword delicately to one side and reached inside the creature with both hands. She felt around as great swathes of intestine uncoiled, covering her knees and slopping arterial gore over her crotch and belly, until she pulled out a small purple organ trailing muscles and tendons, which popped free one by one. She lifted the fluttering organ to her face.

Vitch stood, skin stained, eyes meeting Jukan's.

"What…" he croaked, "what is that?"

"This is the Helk's usma, similar in function to a human liver. A pure Helk eats grass and baffa, but some cattle become addicted to the Geddo flower, which poisons the usma, and in turn poisons the rest of the meat, creating a food that is highly toxic to humans. If you note, the usma should be pure black. But this? Gentlemen, this is corrupt." She paused. Her smile was sickly sweet, like the stench of putrefaction. "The Krell consider this a very bad omen." Her voice dropped to a whisper. Eyes gleamed. "It reminds us of the Days of Leviathan."

Jukan pulled his pistol, halting the weapon inches from Kotinevitch's face. "In the army," he growled, "they call you Vitch the Bitch. Now I see why. This is the way it's going to work. You move in front of us, very, very slowly, with my pistol in your back. You will lead us to our Hornet. If you so much as piss yourself, I'll blow a hole in you so wide I can climb through it. Do we understand one another?"

Vitch tossed the Helk's diseased usma into the air and dropped and rolled, spinning and coming up with her yukana; from kneeling through to standing, the matt blade sliced Jukan from left hip to right clavicle, exiting on a streamer of shoulder shards and blood mist. His body slid into two discrete pieces, and there came a vision of organic cross-section—spine, meat, yellow fat and peeled flesh—as it slid in opposite directions and left four sub-commanders staring in shocked awe.

"We understand one another completely," Vitch said, glancing towards the remaining men.

One took a step back, both hands coming up in supplication. "Wait..." he said.

Vitch leapt, and in three strikes turned the four figures into butchered meat. She smiled as limbs twitched around her and the stench of blood aroused her.

Through wide eyes set in a gore-splattered face, she licked at her green, salted lips.

She savoured the taste she found there.

"It appears," she said, "Combat-K must die."

KEENAN FORCED STICKY eyes open and stared at the spinning room. Shit, he mused. When the room gyrated just as badly as it had the previous night, a man could be sure he'd drunk too much. But then... he had a reason to drink, right? Surely he was allowed that single concession? Every morning the bitter pill of the murders filled his mouth with a taste worse than any second-hand Jataxa.

Keenan rolled from his bed and moved through the kitchen to the veranda doors, flinging them open and stepping out into early morning Karaya sunshine. Distantly, the sea rolled and crashed against an unspoilt white shingle beach. Karaya was climbing the sky, gold and bright, and her sister Tekana toiled a little way to the right, smaller and fiercer, more red than gold. On the rare occasion when Tekana lit the day alone, the world had a blood ambience—to Keenan's eyes—that always reminded him of war.

He groaned. One sun would have been bad enough, but two? Did Nature have no sympathy for a man with a hangover? Keenan took several deep breaths of sea air, hands on hips, unshaved face lifted with eyes closed tight. Something bumped his leg, and he glanced down at Cam, his Security PopBot. Small and round and black, the size of a tennis ball and with no discernible features on its shell except for a few scratches and dents, the PopBot seemed—nevertheless—to be grinning.

"What do you want?"

"You've got a visitor, down at the office. Been waiting for half an hour."

"Kube reception. Tell him to come back tomorrow when I feel more... alive."

"Tsch," said Cam, continuing to float near his knee. It lifted then, smoothly, until it was at face level. "A man in your position can't afford to turn away business, my friend."

"My position?"

"Bankrupt, gambling debts, heavy drinker. As good with his family accounts as I am at holding a golfing umbrella."

"Amusing, but don't push your luck, Cam. Remember, I can have you dismantled, burned, boiled, magnetised. You get the picture?"

"Keenan, I think you'll want to hear what this man has to say. Call it machine intuition. Trust me."

"OK. Tell reception I'll be there in thirty minutes." He moved inside, to the marble worktop, and lifted his heavy Techrim 11mm pistol, freshly-oiled and with a full 52 round micro-clip.

"But it better be worth it," he muttered. "I ain't in the mood for playing games."

SHAVED, SHOWERED, FRESH pair of shorts and open, flapping blue and white striped shirt, Keenan strode across the crunching shingle to the edge of the sea, and the TitaniumIII mooring. His black metallic Yamaha SeaWarrior jet ski, 380bhp, three cylinder, two stroke and 1800cc of pure muscle with a 10 blade impeller and Titanium glass-alloy panels, bobbed at its mooring against the warp-planked jetty. Keenan waded in knee-deep, unlocked the Yamaha, climbed onto its rolling platform and fired the engine.

The jet ski raced at a fast idle. Keenan settled himself down, fixed his emergency cut-out in place and blipped the throttle. The engine raced on a surge of torque, and Keenan turned the jet ski sharply and headed for deeper water; then down the coast bounding from wave to wave towards the city of Dekkan Tell.

Spray cooled his face. It felt good. And for a little while Keenan could blank out the past.

Despite its nomenclature as third largest city on the planet of Galhari—which itself lurked on the quiet and peaceful fringes of Quad-Gal, and the Sinax Cluster as a whole—Dekkan Tell was in fact a low slung scatter of white stone buildings sporting terracotta tiled roofs, orange doors and window shutters, all connected by wide paved highways and a proliferation of greenery and bright orange scatters of the local Dekka flowers, which gave the area its name. It was illegal to build over two storeys high in Dekkan Tell, and so the city had spread outwards rather than upwards. The modest city had a population of only thirty thousand.

Keenan's office was a stone's throw from the sea and connected by a planked walkway from a mooring jetty. Tying his Yamaha, Keenan peered for a moment down the coastline and the low scythe of white buildings that swept as far as the eye could see. Then his sandals flapped towards his office and the engraved bronze plaque on the orange painted woodwork:

Z. KEENAN
PRIVATE INVESTIGATIONS UNDERTAKEN
—enquire within

He pushed open the door to see an immaculately dressed man of medium build seated on the cream leather reception sofa. The man had jet black hair, heavily creamed and slicked back into a tight bun, a black drooping moustache, and held a small black hat in both hands; hands adorned with a glittering but tawdry wealth of rings. His head turned as Keenan entered, blue eyes fixing the old soldier with a bright intelligent gaze.

"Anne?" Keenan said, glancing towards his receptionist.

"Mr. Keenan, this is Prince Akeez of Jervai Province. He has not made an appointment but was quite insistent on meeting you. He said he didn't mind waiting, however long it took."

Akeez stood, smiling, and the two men shook hands. "Jervai Province?" said Keenan, tilting his head. "Isn't that the old…"

"Earth colony. Yes, Mr. Keenan. You are indeed correct. Shall we enter your office?"

"After you," directed Keenan, and followed the man, who walked with a nimble, almost dainty step. After settling into respective seats on either side of Keenan's warped desk—fashioned from planks of reclaimed sea-timber—Anne brought them both a small saucer of local green Dek coffee, which steamed before them. Keenan leant on his elbows and stared hard at Prince Akeez.

The Prince sipped his coffee; replaced it on the uneven, buckled surface. "A fine distillation."

"You have a job for me?"

"Ahh yes, straight to the point. Your old friend said it would be this way. He advised you were a man of action, no? He said you are a man to walk the mountains with! A man who always gets the job done!" Here the Prince's eyes glittered, and his face lost a little of its plumpness; looked almost... feral. "No matter what that job might be," he added, his voice a low growl.

"And my old 'friend'... would be?"

"Sergeant Ranger."

"You can, of course, confirm this?"

"He said you would be suspicious when I approached." Prince Akeez smiled a knowing smile. "He said you might think I was... the police." The last word was bad; spoken with sour distaste. "He gave me your old password, so you could find some initial trust at this early juncture, and we would not, at least, have to waste precious time exchanging verbal riposte and parry."

"The password?"

"Lakanek. However, I confess I do not comprehend."

"Lakanek was a prison; a long time ago, on another world. It's—kind of—an old joke." Keenan's voice was distant, eyes dark, face hooded. "Do you mind if I smoke?"

"Be my guest."

Keenan pulled free a silver case, unhitched the tiny lock and opened the device. He rolled himself a thin cigarette with evil looking Widow Maker tobacco, lit the weed, and breathed deep the unfiltered drug.

"Some would recommend smoking is bad for you."

"Life is bad for me," coughed Keenan, and sat back in his chair, home-rolled between his lips, hands behind his head, brooding, half-lidded eyes watching Prince Akeez with precision. Suddenly, Keenan was glad of the 11mm Techrim digging into the base of his spine. And he was glad of Cam's proximity, although he was damned if he knew exactly where the Security PopBot would be: on the roof, behind the door, in the bin? That was all part of their working relationship.

Instinct told Keenan the man before him was bad news. No, *bad news.* Ignore the effete ways, the gaudy dress, the slicked hair and moustache. Ignore the modest build and almost ladylike mannerisms. Prince Akeez was a warrior; he was dangerous; and he was definitely not to be trusted.

"Tell me about the job."

"You have heard of the planet Ket?"

"I've heard it mentioned news-side. After the Helix War Peace Initiatives there were a cluster of planets that refused to surrender arms. Ket was one of them, a God-awful place where, I believe, war is a constant, not a means to an end. Apparently, violence and death are a way of life."

"Ket refused to relinquish arms under the Quad-Gal Peace Unification Process. Now, I will be honest, Mr. Keenan, the place is war torn, a veritable hell, in fact. The entire planet is a seething pit of violence, but it contains an incredible prize for those daring enough to see beyond the battered shell."

"What do you want me to steal?"

"The Ket-i's most valuable treasure: the Fractured Emerald."

"Never heard of it."

Prince Akeez shrugged. "Why should you? If your planet contained the most fabulous, incredible, talented wealth of the universe, would you publicise its presence so that every bounty-hunter and treasure-seeker in Praxda Zeta made a bee-line?"

"Sounds dangerous," said Keenan warily, "and illegal, and likely to get me killed. If I agreed to do this, and if I thought success probable, my fee would be high. Depending on my mood, you might never be able to pay enough."

"Oh, you will agree to this venture, Mr. Keenan."

"Why's that?"

"Your family was murdered, was it not? Prior to this, you had sexual relations with a member of your combat squad, a woman named Pippa. Your wife discovered this adultery and you had, shall we say, a violent quarrel, but she died before you were able to speak to her one last time. You are therefore a man torn with guilt and grief; a man who would turn back the clock... if he could?"

Keenan had gone cold. Slowly, he reached back and pulled free the Techrim. He leant forward, placing the weapon on the warped timbers with a solid *clack*. Keenan stared into Prince Akeez's eyes and composed his words with care before opening his mouth.

"I think, my friend," his voice was low, and very, very dangerous, "you over-step the mark."

"I am sorry, Mr. Keenan. I do not wish to offend. Let me explain: I know about Terminus5, I know you were a member of an elite Combat-K squad. I know your mission went horribly wrong and your CK was disbanded. You received prison sentences and were prohibited from re-forming your merry group of killers, with a GroupD prohibition. To meet up again means to die. Yes?"

"Go on."

"After you were sentenced for sending the Terminus5 K Series Shield Reactor critical and putting the whole Terminus5 planet at risk, you—and your comrades—spent eight months in a high security military facility called the Pit. During this time, your wife discovered your infidelity, visited you in prison just prior to your release, and you fought, quite savagely by all accounts; the kind of argument that can never be taken back. Three days later, and a day after your release, both your wife and your little girls were massacred. Police investigation led to a dead end. There were no suspects—except you—nobody arrested or questioned; no clues, no samples, no DJK files, nothing. No terrorist group claimed responsibility. Nobody came forward after reel-to-reel reports on news-side CrimeShows. The case was eventually suspended, which we both know means it was put on an eternal, no-hope hold."

"I see you have access to my military files," said Keenan, finishing his cigarette. His face had changed; no longer did it hold any hint of friendship. It had gone hard, like a brittle shell. His eyes shone with a terrible light.

"I can offer you ten million gem-dollars... if you can recover the Fractured Emerald."

"Prince Akeez, suddenly, I'm not very interested in your money. Now, I'm going to ask you politely, but I'm only going to ask you once. I advise you not to misinterpret my politeness as weakness, nor to assume you are safe here because of your digital Security Device. It was disabled four minutes ago and can be reclaimed in several pieces at a later date."

At this, Akeez went pale, his eyes dropping to focus on the dark Techrim 11mm. The gun was battered, chipped, dented, scratched. If the gun could speak, it would have told a thousand tales.

"Now," Keenan stood fluidly, and stubbed the dead remains of his home-rolled cigarette into a pink seashell ashtray. "Leave, and not just my office. I suggest you exit Dekkan Tell. I would suggest this is no longer a safe haven for a man with your, shall we say, inside information."

Prince Akeez stood. He sat his small black hat on his head, then reached down and placed a metal card on Keenan's desk. Then he met Keenan's steel gaze.

"May I say one last thing?"

"Better be good. My patience wears thin."

"The Fractured Emerald; it is not just an object of lust, of wealth, of power."

"You have five seconds to leave." Keenan looked at his watch, and reached for the Techrim.

"It has psychic abilities. It can look into the future, and it can see into the past. With the right guidance, the right encoding, with a return to full power, it could discover the identity of the person who murdered your family."

Keenan froze. The room seemed to spin into slow-motion. Keenan glanced to the right, where

Cam floated just outside the window, a tiny red light blinking on its black casing. Then his head snapped back to Akeez and his lips formed a snarl as the world sprang back to reality and shock slammed Keenan like a hammer-blow.

"Get out. Get the fuck out, now!"

Akeez half-smiled, but his gaze was black. "You have a Dark Flame burning inside you, Mr. Keenan. It will lead you on the Right Path." Then he was gone. Keenan slumped back in his chair and closed his eyes, rubbing his temples, listening to the distant surge and crash of the sea. Beyond, the city breathed: sounds of traffic, voices in chatter, the clatter of plates in a nearby Dek Restaurant.

Cam glided into the room, spinning.

It hung, waiting patiently, above Keenan's desk.

Finally, the man's eyes opened and he stared at the security device. "I can't believe that man; to invent such a thing in order to gain my services? What a bastard. In my younger days I would have shot him in the face and dumped his body in the sea, just out of principle."

"Keenan, I've just had an exchange with Fortune. Fortune checked the data. The Fractured Emerald does exist, and is indeed rumoured to have psychic abilities. According to local Ket-i legend it can see into the future... and into the past."

"So he was telling the..."

There came a long, uneasy silence. Cam spun on the spot; a sure sign of agitation in the tiny machine.

Keenan reached forward and picked up the metal card. It had an ident-chip contact. Keenan walked towards the window and looked out over the glittering waves.

"It would, of course, be a highly dangerous mission."

"But then, you are a highly dangerous man," said Cam.

"I could not do it alone."

"You could always assemble a small team; you know some nasty cases, I am sure."

"I would need the best."

There came a long pause. Several tiny lights glittered across Cam's black shell. "I think what you're implying would be a terrible idea; nigh on impossible..."

"Why?"

"Since you last had communication, Franco has been locked in a mental institution and is pumped full of narcotics; whilst Pippa has been charged with eight counts of murder and segregated to a terminal security facility on Five Grey Moons. If she tries to escape she is instantly exterminated by implanted logic-cubes in her skull."

"Still, I would need their help. If Pippa doesn't kill me on sight..."

"She did threaten that, yes. I believe she said she would cut out your heart with her bare fingers. Then burn your corpse. Now, my large and violent friend, do you truly want my advice?"

Keenan turned, fixing his gaze on the Security PopBot. He gave a curt nod and waited, head to one side, unreadable look fixed to his mask.

"Let Akeez go. Stay here, run your little PI business and accept that sometimes in life justice is not achieved. Murders do go unsolved. Evil is not always punished. The weak are not always protected by the strong. Sometimes, Keenan, life is a bitch, and there's just nothing you can do about it."

"OK." He turned, stared out to sea. Waves rolled over the shore, crested with a bubbling of foam.

"But you're going to ignore my advice, aren't you? You're going to head off on a mission in the name of adventure, in the name of honour, in the name of justice."

"Yes."

"Why, Keenan? My prediction algorithms show you have a very low chance of survival, never mind success. And that's just breaking out Franco and Pippa, before we even look at finding this psychic lump of mythological junk. There is a 99.97 percent chance that Pippa will rip off your head and piss down your neck. Why do it? Why risk so much?"

"Risk?" Keenan did not turn. His voice was obloquial. "Because I owe it to the memories of the ones I love."

His words were so gentle they merged with the nearby hiss of the surf eroding the shingle beach.

Cam didn't see the tears on the man's cheeks.

Franco Haggis was in a world of pain.

"Get off me, you bastards!" he bellowed as the doctor and five stocky mental nurses squeezed into the Treatment Chamber and backed the swaying figure of Franco towards a row of benches. "I warn you, I used to be in a combat squad! I can kill a man with a single blow!"

"Of course you can," said Dr. Betezh, standing with long powerful arms loose by his sides. His small black eyes were focused on Franco. His white crisp uniform was wrinkle-free, and only a little speckled with patients' blood.

He looks like a shark, Franco realised.

And... a killer.

Franco felt the alloy bench press into his spine and he halted, calming his breathing. His head pounded from imbibed drugs. He felt groggy, senses treacle, limbs responding as if inebriated on the vodka he loved so much. With eyes gleaming like a cornered rat's, he dropped his chin and allowed his hands to fall by his sides.

He would submit.

He would roll over and... die...

Dr. Betezh took another step forward, with infinite caution. He was no fool, and had played this game a million times over, in simulators and in the real world. His arms lifted and he sensed the threatening presence of the nurses behind him; three carried steel truncheons, and Betezh's nostrils twitched at the subtle smell of oiled metal. Curiously, it aroused him.

Another step forward...

One more.

The smile was just spreading to Betezh's lips as Franco sprang, a right hook thundering against the doctor's head with such power that Betezh was spun around a hundred and eighty degrees and dropped to his knees.

There came a rush as the nurses charged Franco, accepting his powerful blows with an air of resignation until within the anarchy of mêlée a slam from a steel truncheon caught Franco across the forehead with a dull metallic *slap*. He went down, and he went down hard.

Dr. Betezh climbed to his feet as the five men (two with black eyes, one with a broken nose, one with estranged testicles) strapped Franco to the nearest bench. Buckles were tightened without finesse; straps levered into position with a weight of anger and pain. The men checked, double checked and triple checked every possible point of weakness.

"All yours, boss."

Betezh nodded, moving to stand over Franco.

"Ahh, Franco." Betezh leant forward, placing a hand on Franco's arm. To an outsider, it would have appeared a gesture of tenderness, but as Franco's eyes flickered open and clouds of red dissipated, he saw the movement for what it was: a frightening dead-zone of calm... before the oncoming rage of the storm.

"I was in a combat squad," said Franco, groggy under imposed violence.

Betezh nodded, smiling kindly, and gesturing for the trolley which arrived with its one squeaky wheel. Franco knew what that squeaky wheel meant. It was the fun trolley: the pain trolley.

"What did you do, in this combat squad?" asked Betezh. He seemed suddenly interested. His bushy eyebrows were raised, and an emotion Franco could not understand had hijacked Betezh's face.

"I was the... detonations expert."

"You used to blow things up?"

Franco nodded, and as the needle slid into his vein he drooled a little, bloody saliva running from the corner of his mouth. He twitched a couple of times as Betezh stood back and without instruction—the nurses were good at their jobs, efficient to the point of bureaucracy—they removed Franco's trousers and pulled apart his legs. They strapped his ankles into heavy steel shackles, buckling them tight.

"Not the green pads," said Franco through a mouth of phlegm.

Betezh sighed, as two of the heavily-muscled mental nurses attached small green conductive pads to Franco's balls, and spooled out the trailing wires to a gleaming machine. The machine looked innocent; functional, but innocent, like a gun without a trigger.

Betezh rubbed at his jaw, which throbbed from the impact of Franco's tattooed knuckles. "Franco... there have been rumours that you plan an escape. At the Mount Pleasant Hilltop Institution, the 'nice and caring and friendly home for the mentally challenged', we do not allow escape. Now, I will only ask you once: what are these plans?"

Franco looked up through the drug haze. He raised his middle finger, shackled as it was, to the bench.

"Sit on this," he muttered.

"As you wish." Betezh's voice was stone. He looked over towards a nurse and nodded. The man flicked a switch and the machine gave a little whine, then a jolt against its restraining bolts as gears meshed and it found its trigger.

"Let me out of here," mumbled Franco, glazed eyes trying to focus. "I ain't mad! I tell you, I ain't mad!"

"That's what they all say." Betezh leaned close with a threatening intimacy. "Now, my friend, I would like to say this isn't going to hurt... but it will." He nodded and smiled. "It's going to burn you inside-out, all the way to Hell."

Betezh took a step back.

He gave a curt nod.

And the nurse turned the digital dial all the way to 10.

IT WAS LATER, much later. Betezh sat in a broad leather chair with Franco's screams still ringing in his ears. The kube buzzed in his hand and he initiated a burst, allowing a globe of light to grow rapidly in his palm. It was a long distance transmission; he could tell by the interference.

"You have news?" said a female voice.

Betezh nodded. "Yeah. Franco remembers."

"Remembers what? I thought he was drugged?"

"He remembers Combat-K, and his position within the group."

"Betezh, you were placed there to control him, to sedate him, to damn well stop him from remembering. If the others ever found out..." She left the implied threat hanging in the air.

"We should have killed him, back on Terminus5. We should have killed them all."

"Maybe." The woman's voice was too sharp. "Well, the time will soon come. Akeez has contacted Keenan; we cannot allow him to proceed down the path we anticipate."

"Do you want me to kill Franco? I can do it tonight."

"Not yet. He knows a lot about our operation, if only he could remember it. What you have told me amounts to shit. His recall is as blurred as his history. However, he could still be useful to us."

"We walk a dangerous wire," said Betezh carefully. He did not want to antagonise.

"What is life without a little danger? Without thrill? Without challenge? It becomes nothing more than a stale and second-hand experience; an armchair performance, a fucking banality."

"It's ironic," said Betezh, voice low, "but sometimes I wonder if you should be the one locked away, instead of Franco. I wonder who is the more sane?"

Kotinevitch's brown eyes narrowed. She smiled, showing neat little teeth. "Insanity is my middle name," she said. There came a long pause. "I have contacted Mr. Max."

She heard the harsh intake of Betezh's breath. "If you play with fire, expect to get burned."

"He is efficient."

"Vitch," said Betezh, voice low and filled with... she tried to place it. She settled on concern. "Mr. Max is unpredictable. I strongly recommend you leave him out of this business. Where Combat-K is concerned, he is not appropriate."

"He gets the job done, when all others fail. That's what counts."

"He is guilty of genocide," said Betezh, voice so soft it was barely more than a whisper. "We cannot trust him. You have heard the rumours? You have heard the dark legend?"

"If you play at being soldier boys," said Kotinevitch, words and eyes colder than frozen hydrogen and billion-mile distant, "then expect to get fucking annihilated."

"And Franco?" persisted Betezh.

There came a moment of consideration; then a sigh.

"OK. Kill him."

CHAPTER 2
EXCISION

IT WAS LATE evening.

Keenan stood on his veranda, a fluted glass of Jataxa in one hand, home-rolled cigarette between his lips, smoke stinging his eyes as he watched three distant yachts superimposed on silver waves.

"You made all the arrangements?"

"Yes." Cam settled beside Keenan and said nothing for a while. Keenan allowed the comfortable silence to extend as a breeze filled with salt ruffled his dark blond hair.

The second meeting between Keenan and Prince Akeez had gone more smoothly, especially with Cam and Fortune as mediators. Five million gem-dollars had been transferred to Keenan's account at Off-World Holdings.

"Night's falling," said Cam finally. "Time to be moving; we don't want to miss our private Y

Shuttle. It'll dock with our new transport 10,000 klicks post-orbit."

"Did you get the Hornet? You said you were experiencing teething... problems?"

"No problem, Keenan. I got the Hornet. Three years old, just had an SMOT. Excellent condition; only twenty billion miles on the clock! Bargain at half the price."

"Hold on," Keenan back-tracked, "what do you mean, 'we'? You said 'We don't want to miss our private Y Shuttle.'"

"I'm coming with you."

"Oh no."

"Keenan," bristled Cam, "I am your Security PopBot. I am a GradeA Security Mechanism with advanced SynthAI and a Machine Intelligence Rating (MIR) of 3150. I have stayed on Galhari because I like you. However, I feel the current challenge has become a little bit... below my future achievement plane."

"You mean you're bored?"

"Well, I didn't like to say anything before..."

"Cam, you're a machine!"

"Even so, an MIR of 3150 actually outranks most life-forms in the Quad-Gal. If you want to be pedantic, you could say I am more human than human, certainly more intelligent than most of the dregs you find knocking about the galaxy these days."

"Christ, Cam. I didn't realise you had such a... a sense of self importance."

"Still, my authentic ownership documentation with dealer stamp is in your name. You do, in fact, own me. As your property, I demand Possession Rights. If you don't take me with you, I will initiate a state of immediate SD."

"SD?"

"Self-destruct."

"Bribery, damn you!" Keenan thought for a moment. "OK, let me think this one through. Answer me this: if we were dragged into a combat situation, separated from our firing team and our shuttle marooned on a hostile planet, would you, and this is important now Cam, would you be able to open a tin of beans?"

"Yes. Ha ha, very droll."

"OK, OK. Would you be able to cook a sausage?"

"My sides are splitting, Keenan. You are a modern day stand-up comic. Now, can we get going?"

"Your loss of a sense of humour's convinced me. What time did you say we were catching the Y Shuttle?"

"Five minutes."

"You sure you've got all the papers sorted? I'd hate to reach Shuttle Emigration and stand there looking like a dick because you'd forgotten our exit visas."

"Exit visas?"

"Only kidding."

"Don't do that Keenan. You'll give me a... a..."

"You can't have a heart attack. You haven't got a heart."

"I was going to say nano-circuit modular burnout, actually."

Keenan flicked his cigarette into the falling darkness, hoisted his pack, gave one last lingering look at the sea, and strode through his house for the last time. As he initiated D:LOCK-down, he thought grimly, *and I hope this isn't for the final time.*

Final, as in: terminal. Terminally not coming back.

Cam followed the big ex-soldier, grumbling bitchily.

FRANCO HAGGIS STARED from the barred window at the rain. It pounded from thunder-grey heavens.

What the hell am I doing here?

His past was a maelstrom of confusion, memories a shower of snow in a snow-globe without continuity or even a timeline. He did remember some things. He remembered Combat-K. He remembered Keenan. And he remembered the Visit—just seven days ago—when Keenan had explained The Plan to a drugged-up Franco.

Yes, The Plan to get free.

God, I wish I had one of those magic rainbow pills.

As night fell, so the patients were allowed their evening "relaxation" in the common room of the Mount Pleasant Hilltop Institution, the "nice and caring and friendly home for the mentally challenged". More importantly, jackets were not required.

The common room was predictably sterile, as benefited the environment for a daily gathering consisting mainly of deranged individuals. The walls were green, a puke and pus derived hospital green, the green of slopped-out cells, the green of plague and infection and rotten dead flesh. Padding lined the walls, and the floor lay bedecked in a faded, patterned linoleum that made it easier to clean up the piss.

Franco ambled around aimlessly, staring out of the high windows at the rain. He was sick: sick of the drugs and the patronising, sick of the loonies, sick of having electrodes clamped to his Roger.

"Hi Franco."

"Hi Monkey."

Monkey was a fat man with a mane of curly black hair and a tiny head that was almost perfectly round. His little head sat atop a distended, chocolate-grown body like a pea on a pie. He was, to all intents and purposes, mad. And he carried a terrible secret, to which Franco held the key.

"Fancy a game of Monopoly?" said Monkey.

"Yeah."

Franco, however, despite the drugs and the rain and the melancholy, found it hard to contain his excitement. Franco had been saving his daily rations as part of The Plan, as explained by a heavily disguised Keenan: The Plan which was to be carried out... tonight.

They set out the Monopoly board. Franco chose the old boot.

"Why do you choose that old boot every time?" said Monkey conversationally.

Franco gave a sly look left and right. The guards, ever watchful with steel truncheons and sprays of laughing gas, were vigilant, narrow eyed. Seeing a friend with a broken spine did that sort of thing. It taught you not to fall asleep on duty for fear of waking up with fewer limbs.

"Luck, mate. I always used to choose El Booto... back when I was in the Combat Squad."

"Ahh yes. The Combat Squad." Monkey had heard the story a thousand times.

Monkey dealt brightly coloured money and Franco leant forward and placed a cube of chocolate, obsessively hoarded from his rations, at the centre of the Monopoly board. It sat, brown and soft, and slightly oozing amidst a scramble of little green houses and red plastic hotels.

Monkey froze, mid-deal, eyes growing wide. His hand moved so fast it was a blur... and the choc had gone: vanished, eaten, dissolved. Monkey continued to deal the money without a word, as if nothing had happened.

Because, deep down inside his head, it hadn't.

Franco delved into the secret lining of the loose cotton sacking that masqueraded as clothing. Carefully, he placed another cube of chocolate on the board.

Once more, like magic, it vanished.

The two inmates started to play Monopoly. Franco, as usual, started to lose, but on this occasion he refrained from his usual whining. And as Franco fed Monkey more and more choc chunks, a gradual change started to transmogrify the peanut-headed lunatic; a red flush flowed across his pimpled cheeks and down his arms, covering his skin with deep red blotches. His eyes went wide—dinner plate wide—and his nostrils flared alarmingly. Then, like the gradual movement of tectonic plates, Monkey began to tremble. This state of illness rapidly accelerated until it was not just a tremble of dehydration, but a severe DT jiggle of a middle-aged alcoholic junkie during enforced withdrawal.

Not perturbed by these esoteric changes in his companion, Franco continued to feed him choc with the merciless evil of a piranha chewing an injured fish. After all, the pond was deep and wide, and Franco was fed up being the one who always bit the hook.

Monkey suddenly halted, one hand suspended over a card which read: Go To Jail.

Franco glanced around, nervous now, but none of the guards seemed to have noticed. Franco continued to play alone, continued to shuffle his old boot across The Angel of Islington and The Old Kent Road, continued to place choc on the saliva-smeared and modestly melting board... and watched with barely disguised amazement as Monkey stuffed yet more and more brown lumps into his frothing, spasmodically working jaws. Chocolate streamers ran down his chin, connecting him gooely to the game board to create one gelatinous pulsating brown salivating whole.

Then, Monkey stood up.

He quivered, frothed and jerked.

With a blink, Franco became aware of his proximity to a primed bomb, and climbing to his feet he eased away as inconspicuously as possible, leaving Monkey twitching an electric-chair shuffle.

The guards noticed.

One groaned. It was a groan of genuine pain.

"Shit, Monkey's gone and had chocolate. Again."

"Jesus wept, don't you people know what happens to this son of a bitch when he gets even a sniff of a fucking Helix Crunchy Bar?"

Franco grinned nervously. He estimated he'd fed Monkey around seventeen huge choc bars, begged, scrounged, borrowed and stolen from other inmates and his own modest stash during the preceding week. Now it appeared Monkey was going to a) explode, b) take off like a rocket, or c) do something unpredictable. Franco shuffled towards the rear of the rearmost guard... in readiness.

Monkey suddenly screamed and leapt onto the table, stamping bare feet over the Monopoly board and scattering green houses and paper money like escaping butterflies. He tore his gown to reveal a rotund, red-blotched and pulsating body with a belly that squirmed like an alien pregnancy... and as the guards edged forward with grim faces and steel truncheons raised in threat, so Monkey started to fart and defecate, reaching ponderously behind his quivering arse-cheeks and scooping up his own faeces. These he launched with unerring accuracy at the gagging, heaving, whining, retching mental nurses.

"Wow," whispered Franco in reverent awe, "so that's what happens!"

He stretched forward, tapped the guard before him on the shoulder. The man turned... into a savage right-hook that broke his jaw and dropped him. Franco dragged the guard towards the large games cupboard, half-closed the doors, and hurriedly removed the guard's uniform.

Dull flesh *slaps* reached Franco's ears.

He peered out from the cupboard's crack.

Two shit-covered guards were laid out unconscious on the linoleum as a whirligig of a shit-flinging, plate-fisted inmate whirled and danced and slammed huge hands into flattened faces with a power that belied his size, if not his girth.

Franco pulled on the guard's uniform, took up the steel truncheon and unclipped the keys from the guard's belt. Franco grinned. The keys felt good: a symbol of freedom. That solid metal in his hand; well, he thought, it smells like... victory!

As the fight whirled behind him Franco calmly walked to the gate, inserted the correct key and let himself out. He walked down the sterile cream corridor. Suddenly, an alarm sounded and Franco's pulse quickened. He forced himself to remain calm as five mental nurses stampeded past him with bloody truncheons raised.

Abandoning composure, Franco ran down long corridors, truncheon tight in his sweating fist. He stopped, panting, by a window and gazed out into the rain. His eyes narrowed as he watched the internal fence barriers slamming into place. That could only mean one thing. They didn't want anybody entering or leaving the premises. Mount Pleasant had entered CLAMPDOWN. That only happened on escape attempts.

"Bugger," he whispered. They had neutralised Monkey. Done a head count. Now they realised Franco had gone. the Mount Pleasant Hilltop Institution had its own helicopter for the transferral of highly dangerous patients. This was Franco's target. He tried to orientate himself to find the roof.

"Hello, Franco." It was Betezh. His voice was smooth.

Franco started to back away. "Go to hell!"

"You did well to get this far. However, you must face reality and come back. Escape is... impossible." The voice was soothing, hypnotic, tuned in to the drugs that Franco so regularly imbibed.

Franco frowned, whirled, and ran.

Betezh cursed. Together with three burly mental nurses, he took up pursuit.

Down corridors they sped, a little man waving a truncheon pursued by the big bouncing bullies of the playground. Franco dragged bins from their cubby-holes, sending them rolling back down corridors. He overturned a trolley filled with kidney shaped steel pans that clattered deafeningly to merge with the shrieking sounds of the alarm. These acts bought him a few precious seconds. But, ultimately, Dr. Betezh and his cronies were gaining. They had longer legs.

Franco rounded a corner in his frantic search for steps or a lift towards the roof—and Keenan's promised airlift—only to find a modest square room mid-way down the corridor. It had chest-high counters and cupboards bolted to the walls.

Franco skidded to a halt, rattled the locked cupboards and cursed. His eye fell on a cardboard box. He ripped the retainers free, tore off a long curling strip, and gazed down at a hundred syringes. "Rasta Billy! Now we're cooking!" He stood up just as

Betezh and the guards slowed their pace, approaching with an inculcated instinct that had kept them alive over the years. They noted Franco's stance. They muttered unhappily. It looked far too business-like…

Like a man on a mission.

Franco pulled free a hypodermic syringe, his arm came back, and he hurled it towards the group. It stuck, quivering like a dart, in the forehead of the lead nurse.

There was a moment of shock.

The nurse screamed.

Franco started to hurl syringes like throwing knives as Betezh and the other nurses fled, leaping into the air with little comedy yelps every time a hypodermic buried its two inch blade into thighs, rumps and unprotected necks.

In an abrupt reversal, the men rounded a corner and were gone. Predator became victim.

Shoving syringes into the pockets of his stolen uniform, Franco turned and sprinted away. Then he saw it. He almost ran past the damned thing, but caught a glimpse of a narrow steel doorway at the last possible moment.

It was a lift, a service elevator. He pressed the button. There came a distant analogue *dring*.

Franco jiggled on the spot. "Come on, come on." Distant gears engaged, followed by a tired aural clanking.

"Come on!"

Dr. Betezh appeared—warily—like somebody who's savagely pulled three hypodermics from his throbbing arse. He saw Franco, spotted the lift, and started to run.

The lift *binged* and Franco fell into its welcoming maw. The doors juddered shut on rusted rails and Franco's finger jabbed at the button marked R for ROOF.

Dr. Betezh pressed his face against the wire-mesh glass. He smiled an evil smile. "We're going to get you. And when we do, Franco, we're going to fuck you up, you little maggot."

Franco gave him a wide grin and pressed a middle finger salute against the portal.

The lift groaned and trundled upwards. Betezh scrolled out of view.

FRANCO STUMBLED INTO the fresh night air. The rain had stopped, and it smelled good. "Keenan?" he bellowed, hurrying forward. "Keenan? Where are you, man?"

There was no sign of life.

Did I get the right time? After all, I am a little... mad. Then Franco's eyes fell on the chopper with a look of apprehension. *Well,* he thought, *if Keenan ain't here to meet me, I'll just have to improvise.*

He sprinted to the chopper, bare feet slapping puddles. Lights strobed the edges of the flat roof, and Franco could hear distant shouts and the deep *throb* from the hospital's alarm.

He opened the chopper's door, climbed into the cockpit and stared in disbelief and relief at the keys dangling from the ignition. *Did Keenan leave these here for me? Was that part of The Plan? Shit. I can't remember can't remember can't remember.*

He turned the ignition, flicked the switch for power, and listened as the rotors began to turn.

Slowly at first, flinging free suspended raindrops, then faster and faster until they became a blur above the tinted glass of the cockpit.

"Yes. Yes! YES!" Franco Haggis grasped the joystick and engaged the drive. Then his head snapped right as Betezh and his entourage stumbled onto the glass-slick roof. They were red in the face from sixteen flights of stairs, mouths contorted as they spat obscenities drowned by the noise of the chopper's engines. They sprinted towards him, size twelve boots splashing puddles.

Franco lifted the chopper into the air, nose dipping a little, and with only a gentle whine of misappropriated power. "Yes!" he shouted, punching the air with glee. "Yes! YES! YEEEEESSSSSSS!" But suddenly the helicopter lurched to one side and Franco peered out with mouth agape. There, hanging grimly from the runners, was Dr. Betezh, his eyes dark glittering pools of hatred. Below, the useless gaggle of open-mouthed guards fell rapidly away and became nothing more than tiny toys.

"Land this helicopter now!" screamed Betezh.

Franco slid open the helicopter's window, lifted his stolen truncheon and smacked Betezh between the eyes with as much force as he could muster. There came a heavy dull *slap*. Betezh blinked. But instead of falling—which was Franco's preferred outcome—Betezh started to climb quickly, ape-arms wrenching open the helicopter's door and reaching towards the befuddled inmate.

The helicopter veered to one side with a warning drone of alarms. Lights flickered dangerously across the console: all red. Below, the landscape swept and swirled with a nauseating lurch. The Mount Pleasant Hilltop Institution spun in giddying circles, distant, a dollhouse, a remote red-brick painting.

The helicopter rocked again as Betezh's boots found grip on the runner. A punch found Franco's head and the escaped inmate fell sideways making the chopper groan and shudder, and then fall into a rapid dive towards the ground.

Engines screamed... and stalled. Slivers of shaved engine spat from exhausts.

Betezh's body flapped like a rag doll in the slipstream.

Franco groaned on the precipice of consciousness.

The ground rushed towards him.

"Keenan, you bastard!" he howled. "Where are you when I need you?"

CHAPTER 3
A VIOLENT INTERLUDE

THE FIVE GREY MOONS described a broad elliptical orbit around Tox12, otherwise known as Toxic
World, or one of the Long Dead Planets. It was the
perfect place for a high security prison, and
allowed for a purely nominal staff. The place was
almost self-governing.

Each moon housed a colony for criminals slotted
neatly into categories rated by severity of crime and
judged on a points basis. One moon contained low-
risk criminals, such as thieves and traffic offenders
on repeat charges. Another was designated for certain species of criminal life-form or AI, yet another
for hardcore criminal elements: tax evaders, murderers, sexual terrorists. The fifth moon had been
unofficially named *Hardcore* by its inhabitants.
This moon housed the worst of the worst: multiple
murderers, the criminally insane, soft-target terrorists, combat AIs guilty of slaughtering large groups

of humans, burned-out tek-soldiers caught AWOL and drunk with stolen nukes; that sort of thing.

Each moon was considered a self-contained unit protected by air and anti-spacecraft (ASPAC) defences. Each moon was divided into compounds ruled over by small squads of Merc Police and Justice SIMs working four-weekly shift patterns—just in case of mass breakout attempts or riot—but, on the whole, prisoners were basically dumped with a few possessions and allowed to get on with it. There were no cells. There was no order... just the Law of the Jungle.

If a prisoner wanted to murder another prisoner? Fine. After all, criminals usually operated within their own frameworks anyway. Better to let them police themselves and form self-governing criminal hierarchies (so the principle went), but in an enclosed and ultimately controlled environment where they could be of little harm to what were considered normal civilized cultures and communities. They were still confined, and, if the worst came to the worst, easily exterminated on a mass scale. This was called Global Scrubbing and usually involved a contemporary version of napalm.

Pippa, having been charged with eight counts of murder, found herself on *Hardcore*—the fifth of the Grey Moons—the most violent, lawless and radically non-policed prison available for the imprisoned criminal element. After sentencing, Pippa was jet-dropped to a desolate outcropping of mountain rock, left crouching in nothing more than canvas trousers, a jumper, a pair of old boots, and holding a kitbag containing a knife, some smokes and basic camping gear. Staring up in hatred as the jet-craft fired a glittering path back into low-slung orbit, her future life expectancy had not looked entirely promising, especially for one so apparently naïve and pretty, with her dark bobbed hair, perfect skin, voluptuous and athletic physique. Only those grey eyes set her apart; they spoke of a soul carrying murder and mayhem.

Gathering her kit, Pippa headed off the mountain plateau and gazed down into the gloom of a distant valley as the wind screeched around her, buffeting her. Firelight shimmered from a large scatter of buildings assembled from local grey stone. Pippa descended with trepidation, shivering as the wind bit through thin clothing.

This was it. This place was home... for life, and death: no parole, no community service, no bit of decorating with tea and scones for Mangy Betty; no spot of gardening for Old Uncle Roger; no cleaning condoms from the local canal. Five Grey Moons was a permanent lifestyle choice; a lifestyle change. Where life was life, and death came far too easy.

Pippa was ambushed on her way down a narrow path by three men, bulky and haggard, with gaunt scarred faces and the air of the desperate. They could see her pretty skin, lusted after pale flesh. They knew she was a Fresh Drop...

Easy meat.

It took five seconds of intensity before the hard-core murderers were dead, skewered and gutted like boneless fish on the blade of Pippa's folding knife. She wiped blood from the blade, searched the attackers' holed clothing, pocketed their weapons and copper money, and in an even, cool, calculating voice, said, "So, it's going to be like that, is it?"

With a frown, she strode purposefully towards the raging fires.

I AM GOING *to die*, realised Franco Haggis.

The ground rushed towards him, chopper vibrating and shaking violently in its terminal plummet. The dash sparkled red with warning lights. Franco's eyes were wide. He could not breathe... could not move...

Then there was The Voice...

Calm, and cool, and gentle: a simple lullaby.

A feeling of euphoria flooded Franco. He felt like he'd taken an afternoon nap and woken into a fuzzy, dream-like, unreal focus.

Hello, said The Voice.

"Hello," said Franco in return.

I am a Security Systems PopBot version 2.8 running entwined ARISTOTLE and HOMER (PARA-OP) parallel operating systems. My name is Cam. I work for Keenan. First, let's get you awake.

There was a jolt, which slapped Franco rudely and painfully from his rabbit-freeze.

Reality slammed him. Squawking, he reached for the joystick and grappled with the helicopter's stalled controls. The machine shuddered, engines coughed into life, and with rotors wailing, Franco lifted the machine's nose as the runners cut the heads neatly from a bank of pink flowers. A trailing Dr. Betezh ploughed a furrow through ripe soil, boots juddering.

The thumping machine soared skywards. It spun like a metal toy. It performed rolls and finally pulled up level with the upper storeys of the Mount Pleasant Hilltop Institution. Patients waved enthusiastically at Franco from the barred windows. Those in straightjackets banged their heads against the unbreakable glass in happy appreciation of his aerial display and escape attempt.

The helicopter, barely under Franco's control, spun in huge, lazy, sweeping circles. Below, trees rushed past. Betezh's boots somehow scrambled and found purchase on the runner, and he growled a stream of expletives, hoisted himself up, yanked open the door and threw another punch.

Franco dodged erratically.

Suddenly the world seemed to slip into treacle.

Ahh, said Cam. *This is so tiresome*. Then Franco could see the PopBot; it fluttered alongside the helicopter in perfect parallel, slammed inside the cockpit—entering through reinforced glass—to hang immobile an inch before Franco's nose.

Let's get rid of the bully boy, shall we?

Betezh tried another punch. There was a *sizzling* sound, and a tiny blue arc leapt from the PopBot's black casing and hit Betezh between the eyes. He slid from the helicopter's runners and disappeared, tumbling into the gloom far below,

"Thank... you," gasped Franco.

"My pleasure," said Cam. "Sorry I was a bit late; got caught up in an argument with a petty extortionist bureaucrat about damned exit visas. Gods, border controls, hey? Now, if you'd just like to pilot this heap of junk over yonder perimeter fence you'll see we've got a lovely Fast Attack Hornet waiting for us. Down there, you see it?"

"I see it," said Franco, enjoying the heady rush of freedom. It was better than any drug.

With groaning engines, he took the battered chopper down.

THE TWO MEN embraced, a tight hug, and pulled apart to stare at one another with barely concealed grins.

"It's been a long time," said Keenan.

"Too long!" said Franco.

"You feel OK?"

"Yeah, I will do as soon as these drugs wear off. I swear, Keenan, that place adds layer upon layer to your madness. It spins you on your head. Not so much a cure, more a technique of ensuring you stay mad. I suppose it's all down to bad management, yeah?"

Distant engine noises raced towards them through the darkness. Franco sighed, and eyed the Hornet squatting amongst the trees, sleek and black, and powerful. "Nice ship."

"There are a few faults." Keenan scowled at the innocently rotating PopBot. "But nothing that can't be sorted on our Fast Jump out of this desolate shit-hole. But hey, after all, it was a bargain."

Cam ignored the sarcasm.

"Fast Jump?" said Franco. "Where we going, brother?"

Keenan took a deep breath. "We're going to get Pippa. We're going to re-form Combat-K. I need your help; I need you both like I never needed anything before. I need the old magic."

Machine guns opened fire. Bullets started to *zip* and *slap* through the undergrowth. Keenan and Franco ran up the short ramp, which consumed them.

The Hornet's engines droned, glowed red, and the ship leapt up into the sky—seemed to hang for a moment—then became nothing more than a tiny red dot, which faded into an enveloping, velvet black.

"TELL ME ABOUT the defences," said Keenan, reclining on a leather couch and closing his eyes.

"Extremely hostile," said the metallic voice of Fortune over the kube, a Rorschach-splash light array sparkling in synchronisation with his words. "Violet laser backed up with standard mechanical rockets to mop up anything that—improbably— slips the LW."

"LW?"

"Laser Web. It blankets each of the Five Moons about twenty klicks above the surface. They react to speed and mass intrusion; it is said nothing entering the moons' atmospheres can escape detection. The LW kicks in and intruders get, effectively, cut into metal blocks. Blocked, as we call it in the business. Ha ha."

"Wouldn't a WorldClass Cruiser have the armour to withstand such a global weapon?"

"Yes," said Fortune, "but a WorldClass Cruiser is so big and heavy it could never exit a planet—or moon's—gravitational pull under its own thrust:

engine to mass restrictions as defined per The Law of Zear. An LW is effective against any vehicle that can achieve self-propelled space travel. *Nihil obstat.*"

Years ago, when Combat-K worked missions for the Quad-Gal's military and Secure Police Services—with the singular aim of bringing an end to the Helix War—Keenan, Pippa and Franco had set up a deal with an illegal mercenary AI. Fortune was wanted by the Quad-Gal authorities—had always been wanted by the Quad-Gal authorities—and travelled from hiding place to hiding place within the Sinax Cluster. Combat-K kept Quad-Gal and combat squads off Fortune's back. In return, Fortune acted as an illegal NMH Bridge when the squad worked deals. In the past, this had meant the difference between life and death.

Currently, Fortune was holidaying in a highly radioactive derelict frigate floating on the fringes of the Hesol Spiral. When contacted by Keenan, Fortune had agreed to take up the role of NMH Bridge: navigator, monitor and hacker. This meant Keenan would have access to the Quad-Gal military Factory Class database.

"Supposing I could get us through the Laser Web, how advanced are the standard SAMs?"

Fortune contemplated for a moment; then his voice rattled through the kube. "The SAMs are pretty standard fare; your Hornet is fast attack, with MGrade armour, and according to manufacturer's specifications it should take quite a few hits. With engines on max you could possibly outrun many makes of standard construct missile. You also have adequate firepower, and an exceptional gunman could shoot them down manually."

"A strong trait of the lady we wish to rescue," smiled Keenan. "Any other surprises?"

"Keenan, down there the criminals roam free. Land, get me a terraform fix and I'll locate Pippa for you. Getting through the Laser Web will pose you the greatest problem. And if you're thinking what I think you're thinking, then you're madder than I think I thought."

"I've done it before," said Keenan.

"But you crash landed," said Fortune, metallic voice little more than a *hum*.

"I'm aware of my mistakes."

Franco groaned. "You're talking about the Doppler Shift, aren't you? No, Keenan, no way. That's damned dangerous, not even the top stream of Central K Academy Pilots could pull that stunt off. You'd have to be mad, or desperate…"

"Or on a mission of truth and revenge," said Keenan, face grim. "Hold onto your seatbelt, Franco. Five minutes to *Hardcore*… and closing. Shutting down external energy sources now."

Cam spun around. "Franco? What's a Doppler Shift?"

"I'll tell you if we make it through alive," grunted Franco, tightening his harness and closing his weary eyes. "Yeah: a big 'if'."

THE HORNET GLOWED against the vacuum of space.

In the distance, strung out like pearls, the Five Grey Moons glided majestically into view.

Keenan began to spin the Hornet until internal anti-gyration alarms shrieked. Faster he spun the war machine, hands carefully balanced on controls.

"I don't understand what he's doing," said Cam, as the small Security PopBot was flung unceremoniously around the insides of the Hornet, trying its hardest to remain immobile. It yelped as it bounced from one of the walls. "This whole process is making my gyroscopes malfunction! I wish he'd stop spinning!"

"This is how it works," said Franco, teeth gritted. "A Doppler Shift applies to radiation waves; the radiation is redshifted when its wavelength increases, blueshifted when it decreases. Do you know what a soliton is?"

"The self-reinforcing solitary wave thing? When a wave is set in motion, and due to perfect environmental circumstances and its own structure, it continues uninterrupted for a distance? Hypothetically, in space this phenomenon could continue unto eternity because in a perfect soliton it would lose no energy during transition: a perfection of non-energy self-propulsion. An Infinity Engine, of sorts."

"Yeah." Franco nodded, as all around them the Hornet started madly vibrating. "Keenan is going to set up a displacement wavelength using the Hornet's mass and speed, and some carefully selected manoeuvres, to set in motion a radioactive soliton. This will preclude our Hornet, and we'll tuck in behind the energy pulse, effectively masked and mimicked by a fist of radiation."

"So when the Laser Web initiates, it will destroy something that is in effect our radioactive foreshadow, our imitative pulse, and we will glide through invisibly behind it?"

"Yes."

"I calculate," calculated Cam, "that due to the size of window one would need between each laser strand, this manoeuvre is in fact highly impossible." He sounded smug, but not too smug. If he was right, he was dead.

"Not so," said Keenan, glancing over his shoulder. "The Laser Web initiates from a single source, a global hub. Like a web, it expands across the moon from this central point, and like a web, the further from the central point you move, the larger the gap between laser strands expand in sequentially increasing steps. If you can successfully hit the moon from the opposite global position to the Laser Web's core projection, there should just be enough space... when combined with the soliton... Hold on, shit... here we go. We'll talk later, yeah?"

"If there is a later," muttered Cam.

Keenan killed the cockpit lights.

The Hornet, sleek and black, hammered behind its own pulse of radioactive energy, a radioactive imitation of the Hornet... a synthetic doppelganger.

The Grey Moon loomed.

The Hornet entered the higher reaches of the atmosphere, streamlined in a shadow of imitative existence. They dropped, faster and faster towards the surface of the grey rocky moonscape, and suddenly there came a splash of violet fire blasting skeins of light before them, a glow of criss-crossing energy beams that lit the inside of the cockpit and made the human inhabitants temporarily blind.

"That is beautiful," said Cam, the violet aura washing lines over its black casing.

"And deadly," whispered Keenan. "Fingers crossed."

"We're getting way too close," said Cam. Alarms started to beep proximity warnings. "We need to slow down... we're going too fast, Keenan..." Cam's voice rose in sudden pitch. "Oh no, we're going to—"

As suddenly as they had arrived, the lasers of the Web were gone, and the Hornet sailed through, plummeting towards the rock and levelling out to cruise at a high whining velocity, before sweeping low into a valley and landing with a crunch on the uneven stone-scattered ground. Hydraulics hissed and Keenan and Franco sat back, wiping sweat from their brows.

"Neat," said Franco.

"I've had some practise."

"At least you didn't crash this one."

"Like I said, practise. Come on, we've got to find Pippa."

"I have her," said Fortune, coming online via the kube. "You can make some of the journey in the Hornet—the first few hundred kilometres at least—but then you're on foot. The awkward young lady is camped underneath one of the largest SAM sites on the whole damned moon!"

"Trust our little Pippa," said Franco.

Keenan nodded. "Yeah, she's attracted to danger like a corpse attracts maggots: a bad news hurricane."

"She's going to rip off your head, compadre."

Keenan met Franco's gaze. He licked dry lips. A curious light shone in his eyes. "You really think so?"

"After what you did to her?"

"I had no choice."

"She didn't see it like that."

"Shit." Keenan lifted the Hornet into the air and cruised down the valley. Grey volcanic walls scrolled by, uneven and sporting thousands of jagged chimneys. "Well mate, she'll have to forgive me, or kill me. We're going in, whether she wants to see my ugly face or not."

KEENAN AND FRANCO climbed the ridge and keeping low, peered down the steep rocky slope that tumbled unevenly to the banks of a lake. The surface of the water was perfectly still. It shone, almost silver, under tendrils of bone-grey witch-light.

At the moss encrusted shore, Pippa sat cross-legged on a huge cubic rock. To her right lay the husk of a battered, rusted HTank with twin barrels and a smash of destroyed panels.

She did not acknowledge their approach as they descended, Franco cursing and moaning, and scattering pebbles that clattered down to the water's edge and sent ripples undulating outwards, concentric circles that shouted his name louder than any megaphone.

As they jumped to the ground from a low natural wall, boots thumping up clouds of dust, still Pippa did not turn; instead, she simply said, "I never did find out how you got your arse out of that bunker, Keenan. After they took us down, we were bundled into a Truk and fired away to separate holding cells. I couldn't work out how you survived that metal bastard... The Tangled? Yeah, that was its name. How did you get out?"

"A liq-N bomb."

"Liq-N?"

"Liquid nitrogen: I froze it, walked across the crackling metal surface, hooked back up to my PAD and hauled my arse to the exit. I never killed the damned thing, although I'm tempted to go back one day and fry the fucker, just out of principle. An evil piece of engineering if ever I saw one; no soldier should have to face that."

Pippa turned. She looked a little older, with a few discreet lines around her eyes. She wore rough, hand-made clothing, bleached of colour through excessive multiple-washings. Her eyes held that same cold, emotionless gaze she reserved for enemies.

"I see you Franco; still as mad as a hatter?"

"Madder, I would have to say, something to do with the mercury. I do like your outfit, Pip; you out on the town?"

"Sort of." She smiled, not a very nice smile.

Keenan and Franco moved to either side of the woman, who remained seated, turning back to stare over the still lake. Keenan glanced at the tank, then back to the water. A breeze ruffled his dark blond hair, and something took his spine in its fist and squeezed gently. It was an extremely uncomfortable feeling.

"What you waiting for?" he asked, knowing he didn't want the answer even as he asked the question.

Pippa gestured towards the expanse, and it was only then Keenan saw the two swords lying at her feet. They were curved slightly, black bladed, hand beaten, primitive and yet still... deadly.

"There's a machine, in the lake. It wants to kill me. I'm waiting for it to surface."

"A machine?"

"AI, old combat model, part of our little Clan War here on the moon."

Keenan stared hard at her. "What the hell's going on? We've come to release you from your prison sentence. We've come to free you. We've come to take you..."

"Home?" She laughed. It was a brittle sound. "I have no home. This place is as good as any... for one such as I. One who betrays, and was betrayed."

"I did not betray you." Keenan's voice was gentle.

"You broke my heart."

"I broke my own heart."

"Well we're fucking even then," she snapped.

Deep below the still water there came a savage meshing of gears. Franco took a step back, cocking his weapon, and Pippa's head smashed round. "No! This is my fight. I am the leader of this Clan, and as such I must answer the Call." She leapt lightly from the rock and took up the two blades, twirling them slowly through the grey light. "You two back off!" She smiled. "If it kills me, feel free to shoot the hell out of it."

Keenan and Franco moved away, leapt up onto the low wall and retreated a short distance up the scree slope. Keenan cocked his weapon, then glanced up behind the two men. "We're being watched, yeah? I take it our little friends have arrived."

Franco nodded. "About two hundred; they came up around the cliffs. Must be her Clan, or the enemy Clan? I'm not quite sure how it works on these prison worlds. Still." He brightened optimistically. "Pippa's done well for herself, ain't she? Well done that girl!"

Keenan gave his head a little shake, watching Pippa move to stand by the water's edge, swords poised. The lake was bubbling, frothing and seething. Something gleamed black and silver close beneath the surface.

"Looks like an old GG model to me," Keenan muttered. "Now, they are tough motherfuckers."

"GGs had human status," said Franco, "which means if one went mad..."

"They'd dump it here. Yeah. Great."

Pippa was pacing along the shore, which lapped her boots. The GG came frothing from the lake, leaping from the calm in a sudden burst of flying droplets to land in a crouch a few feet from where Pippa stood, swords limp, eyes fixed. The machine was humanoid in shape, but very slim, sculpted even. Its mechanical torso and limbs were dull black, enamelled and containing hydraulic joints. Behind its fists were huge retractable killing knives hot-welded to its chassis. Its head was silver and swept back to a sharp point. Eyes were dulled black and it grinned with over-sized mechanical jaws, containing long incisors that could inject a lethal toxo-poison, so deadly a human would be an internal bubbling mush before he hit the ground.

The GG unfolded fluidly, knives springing free as it flexed its arms and tilted its head, surveying Pippa. She swung her swords experimentally—loosening her shoulders—then attacked with blistering speed.

The two clashed, the GG's long knives hammering left then right as Pippa's swords smashed up and sparks showered the stone shore. Pippa whirled away, boots splashing the edge of the lake, but the GG attacked even as Pippa moved, bounding to her on all fours, knives striking fire against rock, fangs homing in on her exposed throat.

She ducked, rolled beneath hissing hydraulic legs, came up behind. One sword slashed across metal with a terrible squealing as the GG swayed, whirled, and a long black knife missed Pippa's throat by a hair's breadth.

Franco's gun wavered. "Let me take it, Keenan."

"No. She was right. This is her fight. We cannot interfere."

"She can't kill that, Keenan, not with a hand-beaten sword! The damned thing can't even be cut!"

Keenan gritted his teeth. "I know."

Pippa backed away, eyes surveying the GG. It, also, seemed to be watching her, weighing up her strengths and weaknesses. They were both fast—inhumanly fast—but Pippa was flesh and bone, easily diced, whilst the GG combat model was hardened TitaniumIII over a core-mesh frame. It could take an HTank on the head and still operate.

The GG stalked forward and halted. It spoke, jaws working in a loose approximation of speech mimicry. "You cannot survive this encounter. Forfeit now."

Pippa grinned, shaking her head, black hair bobbing. "Come and eat steel, dickhead."

The GG leapt, Pippa rolled right, one sword hammering across the machine's metal abdomen as the left stabbed towards its shoulder—where the point struck—and lodged in the opening between shoulder joint and chassis. There was a screech of stressed steel. The GG spun around and Pippa's sword was torn from her grasp.

She backed away, her one remaining blade held in both hands. She looked nervously about, as if seeking exit from a battle she could no-longer win.

The GG looked down at its torso, worked hard to remove the lodged weapon, its free hand fixed on the trapped blade and tugging on steel with tiny crunches of compressing metal. It didn't see Pippa's boots until they connected with its chest, and then it was too late.

The GG flailed back, struck stone in a shower of sparks with Pippa above it and driving down hard, knees on its chest and side, leaning her weight on the gripped and trapped sword, which acted as a lever and pinned the GG to the ground with its arm locked in position. The machine's free arm lay trapped beneath its torso, and Pippa manoeuvred across the GG's squirming body as it snapped at her with incisors, straining to inject her.

With the enemy pinned, Pippa lifted her free sword and hacked viciously at the GG's neck.

Once, twice, three times… the machine started to squeal, a sound of metal raped by metal, thrashing its head and squirming around in circles leaving grooves in the rocky shore. Its legs kicked, splashing in the water as Pippa continued to hack with a determined grimace. Her arm became a mechanical hammer, her sword a guillotine blade.

There came a final *crack* and sparks fluttered silver. Then another, and the GG's head rolled out and away, splashing into the lake where it was instantly swallowed.

The limbs eventually stopped thrashing—slowly, as if reluctant to relinquish life—and Pippa stood and nodded towards Keenan and Franco, and the several hundred convicts lining the ridge with grim faces and glowing, proud eyes. She placed a foot against the GG's chest and started to work at freeing her blade.

Keenan leapt down and moved to her. "Neat. You wedged the sword there on purpose, to use as a lever."

Pippa nodded. "I've fought these before. Their arrogance precludes a need to acknowledge and understand their own weaknesses. However, I did have an ace up my sleeve."

"What's that?"

"The swords; made from TitaniumIV. Not many things can damage a combat GG. Even your bullets would have struggled to drop this son of a bitch. You have to know your enemy, Keenan. Always know your enemy."

"Been a problem for you, this one?"

"Killed sixty of my Clan."

Franco whistled, and watched as Pippa gave up trying to free the sword. She stretched, and gave a single wave to the criminals on the ridgeline. They faded away, like ghosts, and Pippa climbed and sat back on her cube rock to stare out over the still waters of the lake. She composed herself, arranging her body into a precise posture of meditation.

There came a minute of silence; then she said, "So you want me to come with you?"

"That was the idea," blurted Franco, and Keenan gave him a kick on the ankle.

"Yeah." Keenan met her gaze. "I've been given a mission, to travel to the planet of Ket. There I must find the Fractured Emerald, an ancient artefact, which can predict the future... and also see into the swirling chaos of the past."

"And what do you require of it?" Pippa's voice was fastidious, a whisper, her eyes hardwired to Keenan's soul. "Information? Advice? How to avoid the situation we found ourselves in? How to protect your lover from pain? How to save a woman's soul from an eternity of agony?"

"I would find the murderer of my wife and my two girls. I would find the man who butchered Freya, Rachel and Ally. I would seek out this man, and remove him from existence."

Pippa thought for a while; her face unreadable, a blank. There followed a hiatus... and Keenan found his hand tightening on his MPK. He watched Pippa close her eyes and he remembered that face breathing slowly in sleep as his fingers traced lines across the cool skin of her silk neck and she turned and woke and smiled at him, reaching up to kiss him, her lips always soft, her breath always sweet.

Here it comes, he thought.

Why should she help?

She hates me. She wants me dead.

I was a damned fool to come here, a damned fool.

If she attacks, can I truly kill her?

Would I be physically able to kill her?

Pippa's eyes snapped open. She ran hands through her thick dark hair. When she spoke, it was with infinite care. "Your loss... greatly saddened me. Freya was a fine woman, your girls just... stunning." Her eyes locked again on Keenan's; he could read no emotion there. Again, blank, like those of a machine.

"Freya didn't deserve what happened to her, Kee. She didn't deserve any of it. And the children... I agree with you. The murderer deserves to be brought to justice. The killer deserves to die. No crime like this should go unpunished."

"So you'll come?" said Franco, and Keenan glared sideways at him. "Sorry! Sorry. *Sorry!*"

"You know if I leave here I break all codes. I will be sentenced in my absence to immediate death. They will send every hunter in the Quad-Gal after my sorry hide... and that's if the implanted logic-cubes don't melt my brain on exit."

"I know," said Keenan. He held out his hand to her, "But I need you anyway. We need you. Without you, we cannot do this. Without you, my family will remain unavenged."

Pippa stepped lithely down from the rock and took Keenan's hand. Then she stepped forward and kissed his cheek. There were tears in her eyes, tears on her face. Keenan could not read her expression… but it chilled him to his core.

"I will do this, Keenan, but not for you; I do it for Freya, I do it for Rachel and Ally; and I swear, Keenan, if you get in my way then I'll slit your fucking throat and gut you like a fish. Understand?"

"I understand."

She stalked away, down to the barely shifting edge of the lake, eyes on fire and staring out over the stillness. Franco approached and laid his hand on Keenan's arm. He smiled kindly. "Volatile lady, that one."

"Aye."

"Don't worry. She doesn't mean it, mate."

"Oh, she does," said Keenan.

"She'll help us, then?"

"Yeah." He watched Pippa thrust her sword into the rock of the shore, where it quivered and sent ripples cascading over the glossy water. "She will fight for us, and she will die for us."

"We can't ask for more," said Franco.

Keenan smiled; nodded.

"I agree," he whispered.

KINGS OF THE WILD FRONTIER

SCISSOR SISTER WAR STORIES

CHAPTER 4
SCISSOR SISTER

THE CITY.

Retreat and watch in jaw-drop awe as three orbiting suns provide near twenty-four hours of dazzling daylight across the majority of continents; and hence perpetuate a non-stop trade. The locals call it "eternity trade", or to some, just the ability to *breathe*.

The City was a planet, and the planet was a city: a big one. Over centuries it had grown, a fast-consuming virus, a cancer overwhelming its host, a swarm of nanobots intent on bio-molecular rearrangement... and, ultimately, betterment. The City—the planet in its entirety—was a synthetic mish-mash jungle of stone, concrete, alloy, a cacophony of contrasting architectural styles from every human, alien and basic organic life-form Quad-Gal side; it rose, dominated, building upon building upon building, tower looming over tower, bridges of steel and glass spanning oceans and deserts and arctic trade zones. The City had once been a planet; and the city had consumed the planet. Every inch of the world had been terraformed; oceans raged beneath alloy struts, onyx bridges, bone walkways, and diamond skyscrapers. Deserts drifted cool in the shadow of elevated fifty-lane freeways, raging sandstorms muffled below buildings, halls, and apartments as big and as singularly huge as any of the old Earth cities in their entireties. The polar icecaps had been a mere distraction for planetary engineers obsessed with expanding and building, growth and enterprise, dominance and conquest. The City was the epicentre of wealth in the Quad-Gal. Nowhere could come close to the economic and private military might of the City. With a population of 112 trillion there was nothing that could not be bought, sold or exchanged, a situation perpetuated and accentuated by the fact there were no regulations. The City had no written rules, laws, or taxation on immigration, trade, import or export. The City welcomed smugglers, robbers and illegal traders: they were rich. The whole ethos of the City was that of free will, free trade, free speech. It wasn't exactly anarchy, but to the casual eye—and especially to one who had never before visited—it was a damn close approximation, either of Anarchy... or Hell... depending on one's individual standpoint and ethos.

Keenan hated the City, because for a man steeped in a need for spiritual balance, self-imposed internal recrimination, and a search for the meaning to his own existence, the City was, as Keenan succinctly put it, a shit-hole—populated by human insects.

Franco, on the other hand, loved it. He loved the wildness, the unpredictability, the bustle and sheer exhilaration of every single damned minute on this planet of excess and debauchery. There was nothing that couldn't be bought. There were no laws, and, therefore, no police. One couldn't get into trouble on the City, because there were no defining boundaries of what trouble actually constituted. Murder, rape, mutilation, robbery, depraved acts of sexual congress, genocide: all were technically acceptable acts on which the City had based its mammoth wealth and continually expanding growth. It was a haven for criminals wanted in other parts of the Quad-Gal. It was also the major trading post, stop-off holiday spot and refuelling depot for any space-going craft wishing to travel across Praxda Zeta; as the saying went, "You haven't lived until you've walked City Streets." There wasn't a pop star, movie star or politician who didn't have some manner of luxury pad there. It was the place *to be*, to *hang*, to *chill*.

"You know it makes sense," beamed Franco, reclining in the Swallow Couch on the other side of the Chill Bay. "Come on, Pippa, back me up on this one."

Pippa frowned, glancing up from her laptop. Her face glowed with reflected light from the screen. "I've got to admit it, Keenan, and loath though I am to say it, Franco's right. Ket has a bad reputation, and I mean properly evil; it's permanently at war and we need some heavy weapons on entry. We ain't going to pick that sort of military hardware up without licenses, not unless we visit the City."

Keenan gritted his teeth, and ran hands through his short, spiked hair. He shook his head in the negative, yet knew inside he'd already lost the battle even as it began. He had to admit it, should have voiced obvious concerns: but, "it's a dangerous den of depravity down there," would be to miss the point entirely. They were a Combat-K squad. Danger was their middle name... and they needed weapons.

You're going soft, Keenan told himself.

He ground his teeth together. *Shit.*

Franco rolled from his embracing jelly couch and stomped across the Chill Bay. He patted Keenan on the shoulder. "Come on, Kee. It'll be just like the old times. We'll have a scream! It's party time, mate. It's always party time Cityside."

"That's what I'm afraid of."

"Don't be such a spoilsport! You're turning into a boring old bastard, and I ain't just talking about the grey at your temples. All that time on Galhari has transformed you into a dullard! The sun has gone to your head, the wine to your belly and the philosophy bleached from your soul. You're losing your balls, my friend, and your spunk has shot out the window."

Keenan considered this rant, then frowned. "Franco, do I have to remind you that you're a wanted man down there, wanted dead, and not just by one, but by four of the Seven Syndicates. Now, call me old-fashioned, but won't you be pushing your luck just a bit too much by popping up again like a rabbit from a burrow? Hey guys, here I am, remember me, I almost robbed a hundred billion in diamonds, but let's just put that misunderstanding behind us for old times' sake. Let's just be friends."

"Hey," grinned Franco, shrugging, "they don't call me Lucky Franco for nothing."

"Mate, they don't call you Lucky Franco at all. You got shot last time we came here."

"'Twas merely a misunderstanding."

"Six times?"

"I was popular with the ladies."

Keenan stared at Franco, stared long and hard. *Were you always like this?* he thought to himself. *Back in the old Combat-K days? Or is it just the drugs from Mount Pleasant that have scrambled your brain?* Then he realised the truth with that sinking feeling of betting on red and coming up black; Franco had always been like… well, Franco: a little mad, a little bad, a man living on the edge of a razor; a lunatic waiting for sanity to kick in like a teen waits for maturity and that first desperate warm slick fumble.

"Are we going in?"

Keenan stared at Pippa's raised eyebrows. He gave a single nod. "Franco stays on the ship," he said. "Me and you will conclude the deal. Franco is grounded."

"Aww, Keenan!"

"Don't fucking 'aww Keenan' me, Franco. When you're in this sort of mood you're a liability. So get back in your Swallow Couch, eat your crisps, drink your Coke, watch your vids, and shut the fuck up. I'm not ruining the mission before it starts just because you can't keep your cock in your knickers."

"Yeah, boss. And Keenan?"

"Francis?"

"Glad to see you've still got some fire."

Keenan bared his teeth in a grin promising violence and pulled free his Techrim 11mm, which he slammed on the console with a *clack*. "You'd better believe it, you old goat."

PIPPA SET THE Hornet's Sinax Tapes for The City, a few hundred million klicks towards the centre of the Praxda Zeta galaxy cluster. However, even backpacking on an inter-galaxy half-umbilical, in a Hornet it would take the squad seventeen days. Seventeen long days... out in VoidSpace, living in one another's laps.

A K Jump would have been easier, preferable, even. But K Jumps were dangerous and massively illegal, and getting increasingly dangerous all the time. It seemed there was a basic computational flaw in 99.9 percent of all computer chips, which meant sometimes—many times—they got it wrong. And if you got a K Jump wrong, you ended up somewhere else entirely, somewhere not quite right. That, or spread like marmalade across the galaxy.

After Combat-K's accelerated exit from *Hardcore* and a few moments of exhilaration as the group waited to see if Cam really could disarm the logic-cubes implanted in Pippa's skull (the lady herself had looked merely bored as Cam juggled with a billion separate unlocking codes), all three settled down for a large meal, a few bottles of wine and a discussion on their next tactical move. Keenan wanted to set a course straight for Ket; but as Pippa pointed out, it was probably one of the most dangerous war zones in the Sinax Cluster. They needed the right equipment for an infiltration. This had led to Franco—eyes gleaming, lips wet and red—suggesting a visit to The City to tool up. The fact he'd been locked in a sanatorium for three years probably had something to do with it. And yet, despite his reservations, Keenan had to reluctantly agree there was nowhere else within a four year radius where they could so easily put their hands on military grade kit.

"I need some sleep," yawned Pippa eventually.

Franco glanced over. "Need some company?"

"In your dreams, Franco."

"Precisely."

Pippa stared at the intense look on his face; an intensity arrived at due to his right hand as sexual partner for over a thousand days. She studied him for the first time in years.

Franco was small, five feet and zero inches of vertically challenged height. He was rotund, barrel-chested, shoulders and arms stocky and empowered with an obvious and inherent strength; he was supported by legs that could only be described in a generous world as stumpy. His face was long, hardy, swarthy, but could never be described as handsome. It had strength, yes, character, certainly, but beauty? Only the rugged beauty of a fine vegetable. Atop his head grew wiry thick, bushy ginger hair, which Franco sported in a variety of styles. Usually, on ops he had it shaved close to the scalp, fine. However, on certain occasions—this being one of them—he allowed it to grow and expand and bush-out into what resembled an unkempt hedge. Sometimes, by cruel members of Combat-K, this hairy outpouring had become known as "The Monstrosity", named after that millennium-old song by robot rockers The Queen. And so, to finish the visual debauchery, Franco intermittently grew a beard. On occasion, a neatly trimmed goatee affair; more often, a vast and hazardous bush clamped limpet-like to his face and used as a store for crumbs.

Pippa loved Franco to bits; she enjoyed many aspects of his wild and wacky character, and owed her life to him on numerous counts. But take him as a lover? Even for a quick shag?

Franco was staring intently.

Pippa smiled. "I'd rather stab myself in the eye."

Franco shrugged. "You don't know what you're missing, babe. One brothel voted me Most Energetic Punter of the Year. I am, trust me, a considerate and robust lover."

"Franco." Pippa sighed. "We've been working combat missions together, on and off, for what? Ten years?"

"Something like that."

"And in those ten years, you have accosted me for sex, what? I dunno, give me a rough idea?"

Franco shrugged. He considered this. "Probably about five, six... maybe seven hundred times?"

"Have I ever acquiesced?"

"Never."

"So why now? What's changed? You know my history. If anything, my outlook on the male of the species has degraded. I am not what you might determine prime-time totty. And, despite what your insane over-inflated ego might think, I am not in the remotest bit physically attracted to you. Do you hear me?"

Franco grinned. "Worth a try." He yawned and winked at Keenan. "Think I might turn in. You sure you won't reconsider…" His words lingered like a bad smell.

"No!" snapped Pippa.

Franco rose, stretched, and ambled down the corridor towards his SleepCell.

Silence surrounded Keenan and Pippa. Pippa returned her concentration to the laptop, and Keenan moved to a portal and gazed out at the inky blackness beyond. Burners were growling distantly, accelerating the Hornet ready for what was termed, slang-wise as a HalfBack Sinax Ride, or "Half Sin"; one of the faster ways to cross the galaxy.

"Look at it out there."

"Mm?" Pippa glanced up.

"VoidSpace… an eternity of darkness. It's a long way down."

Pippa stood and crossed to Keenan. She looked up into his face, and their eyes met. He wanted her then, urgently, badly, a burning throughout his entire body, his entire core, every atom screaming for her with infinite need in every growling lusting molecule. Pippa was beautiful; from her upturned chin, her thick dark hair, her cool grey eyes, down to the small mole on her left ankle. In fact, as Keenan studied her, he realised she was more than beautiful. She carried a natural elegance, and mixed it with a hint of insanity, and a pheromone outpouring of danger. A natural-born killer. The female of the species, more deadly than the male? Damn. Fucking. Right.

"No," said Pippa.

"What?"

"I can see it in your eyes, Keenan. Those days are gone, they're over. We were together, once. Yeah, and I loved you. But that was a long time ago. Things have changed."

"I still love you."

Pippa nodded. "And your wife?"

"It was complex. I was lonely. We'd grown apart and she... she had betrayed me. We were married in nothing but name; yeah I still loved her, but you know it's possible to love more than one person. Pippa, you know what happened between me and Freya; the things that forced us apart. We don't need to mine that shitshaft again."

"Yeah, but still."

Keenan took hold of Pippa's shoulders. Their eyes locked. "What is that supposed to mean?"

"But? Still? You cast me aside, Kee. You chose to leave, to betray my love, and my heart. You broke me, Keenan, for a long, long time; so long. When we met, it was hard for me... to love... especially after my father, hard for me to find trust in a man, to find understanding. I found it in you. Then you broke me, made me worse than I ever was. When those men raped my sister, I hunted them down. It took them days to die. I'd sit with them, staked out, inject their veins with drugs, peel the skin from their bodies. I cut chunks from their flesh and fried it in oil, fed it to them, watched them self-ingest. I amputated limbs with a hack-saw. I bled them, cut out eyes, tongues, castrated them with a blunt knife. And every moment, every precious sip of that terrible nectar that poured uncontrollably through my veins... well, I was thinking of you, Keenan, thinking about what I would do to you when I met you again."

Keenan watched tears soak her cheeks.

He said nothing.

"When they dumped me on *Hardcore,* I fought and when I fought I pictured you. It was your arms I cut from bodies, your head I caved in with rods of steel."

She stepped forward. He held her. She rested her head against his chest. "I wanted you dead, Kee." She looked up, a child in his arms. Keenan felt his heart melt and run through his veins, mingled with a heady cocktail of fear. "But you had me, had me body and soul. You were the only one I ever allowed through the barriers; the only one I ever trusted, the only one I ever loved. But—ultimately—you rejected my love. You chose her over me. You went back to your wife when you said you loved *me.*"

"I had to, for the girls. Me and Freya, our love had withered and died. We both acknowledged it. Our marriage became an act; a play, stage-bound, a fucking dark comedy if the truth be known. But the girls, Pippa, it was for the girls."

"Until they were brutally slain." Pippa's voice was suddenly cold, hard: a brittle black thing.

Keenan stepped away, looking at her in a new light. "What are you trying to say?" A steel edge lined his words. Need left him. Slowly, carefully, he said, "Is there something you need to tell me, Pippa?"

"Don't be ridiculous. The point I'm making, Keenan, is that I was yours. You turned me away. You played a part in the thing I became. You helped shape me, mould me."

"The thing you became?"

"The monster that stands before you."

Keenan stared at the beautiful woman. "You are no monster, Pippa. You are an angel."

"You never saw the things I did." Pippa rubbed at her reddened eyes, then laughed. "Damn you, I said I'd never cry over you again." She ran a hand through her hair, then moved towards her Sleep-Cell.

Keenan watched the flow of her steps, the rhythm of her hips. His mouth was dry.

Pippa stopped, turned. "And Keenan?"

"Yeah?" His mouth was a desert husk.

"If you touch me again, I'll cut off your fucking hands. Now, that's a fucking promise."

Keenan nodded, and watched Pippa disappear into the gloom of the unlit corridor.

IT'S LIKE THAT dream you have, when a loved one has died. You dream about them laughing and crying, walking and talking, warm eyes fixed on you bright and sparkling; and they are there, concrete, real, breathing, alive. You wake up snug under a warm duvet with a pulsing inner glow, because none of those bad things happened, they're alive again, the world is warm again, and nothing evil can ever touch you again. The waking nightmare of your miserable mourning existence has gone...

But it creeps up on you, gradually, like a disease... Reality. A dawning horror... The world isn't all right, the person you loved really is gone and dead and cold; lost, buried, far beneath the soil, and lost to you, lost to you always forever and ever and ever. Yeah. A-fucking-men.

A fist slams your chest rips out your heart tears it to shreds; because... your life will never be the same, can never be the same. How could it? The pain is too great. And let's be honest, in the cruel dawn light of a slowly dying world with hot tears raping flushed cheeks, your prayers are never truly answered. Are they? ARE THEY?

Keenan dreamt of his dead children.

And in his sleep, hot tears soaked his pillow.

IT WAS HOURS later when the door to the SleepCell opened and Franco found himself staring down the barrel of a locked and loaded MPK machine gun. Franco grinned. Keenan relaxed.

"Touchy, bro."

"I've had better nights," said Keenan, slumping back to his bed. He found his silver cigarette case, rested his MPK on his duvet, and rolled himself some Widow Maker. He glanced up. Franco was still standing in just his boxer shorts, one hand holding a sculpted litre of Jataxa.

"Thought you might like a drink. *Jataxa:* remind you of home, all the good things you left behind."

"I would have preferred a decent sleep."

Franco grinned. "Stop being a grumpy old bitch and get some glasses." He settled himself cross-legged on the floor, and accepted some home-rolled from Keenan.

"So, you have an argument, my man?" Franco spoke delicately. Despite his inner moments of madness, he could sometimes display a subtle apperception that belied his violence.

Keenan nodded, snapping back a shot of the thick spirit. He closed his eyes for a moment, feeling alcohol flood his system. Then he drew heavily on his cigarette. "Let's just say Pippa has not revised her position in joining my fan club."

"She'll come round. You see if she doesn't."

"Hmm." Keenan smiled. "I think I've been junked."

"Talking of junk," said Franco, "where's that little weevil Cam?"

"Recharge chute."

"He needs to recharge? I thought battery technology was good for a thousand years; even against Multi-G?"

"I think he just needed some space. I think I upset him."

"Why's that?"

"I called his choice of Hornet—let me think now—called it a worthless un-space-worthy honking heap of greaseless shit. That's when he started to sulk. Said he'd never help me buy a ship again. To which I replied good, because if this was the best a supposedly advanced AI PopBot could achieve, I'd be better off letting the local Kajunga Kids sort out my annual tax returns."

"So, a lover's tiff then?"

Keenan inhaled. "Yeah, sort of. You know what it's like when the honeymoon period is over. Boy meets PopBot, Boy falls in love with PopBot, Boy blows out PopBot down to shite choice of space-going wreck. How many times have we heard that story?"

They drank for a while in easy silence; the past years of separation no longer existed. The void melted away like butter. They were friends again, brothers again. Then, Franco, voice quiet against the hum of the ship, said, "You know when we touch down on The City; you can trust me, you know. Just because I spent a few years incarcerated and haven't had so much as a sniff of wet pussy, doesn't mean I'm going to turn into a sex-crazed lunatic! Ha ha. Anybody would think my balls are like grenades without pins!" His eyes gleamed. "But they're not!" he added hurriedly. "I am still the professional Combat-K squaddie you knew. So, come on, let me out to play. I'm sick of being confined to barracks."

"I see your wily trick, Franco. A bottle of the old Jataxa, grease Keenan up well and get him to agree to something he might later regret. You're a fox, Franco Haggis, a deviant and cunning one."

"Hey. Wily is my middle name. What do you say?"

"No. Sorry, mate. I really do need you to guard the ship. And it's not just some idle excuse to keep you here; The City's a bad place as well you know. You've seen enough of its bars, brothels and cells to appreciate that."

"Why don't you make Pippa ship-sit? After all, she is... a girl."

"Franco, Pippa knows The City better than any of us. And if she hears you disrespecting her she'll put a cap in yo ass. Now, take your—admittedly welcome—bottle and let me get some sleep. We've got some serious planning tomorrow. Remember, poor planning promotes piss poor performance!"

"Ha! To which I'd retort, arsehole adventurers always accessorise anal articulation."

Keenan chuckled. "That's why we plan. I've seen the spaghetti messes you've made of some missions, Franco, and the Fractured Emerald isn't going to steal itself."

"You got the maps?"

"I got the maps," said Keenan, mood turning sombre. "All I need now is the hardware. But to be honest Franco, even without a gun I'd go in now, right now. It's burning me. I need a name, a single name, and then I'm going to hunt me a killer all the way across the fucking galaxy."

"So... somebody's got it coming?"

"Franco, there's a person out there who's Dead Meat Walking. I swear it, by all the Gods."

THE NEXT DAY saw the Hornet spinning silently through VoidSpace. Frozen hydrogen glistened across the hull as readouts scanned for typical deep space threats.

Franco, with his newly shaved and gleaming head, slouched beside the pilot's chair as Pippa's intense gaze followed readouts and checked for consistency with course plotting. She did not trust the Hornet's navigation systems until she had triple-checked everything. She was a perfectionist.

Franco, however, was far less diligent. He sat with a bowl on his knee, in which something long and slimy glistened.

Keenan stepped through the portal, yawning, and rubbing at his tousled hair. A morning cigarette hung from dry lips and smoke stung his eyes, making him squint.

He stopped dead, eyeing the plate on Franco's knee. "What," he said, "is that?"

Franco glanced down, picked up the quivering sausage, and took a bite. Lumps of fat glistened within the thin skin-walls of the mammoth wiener. Franco chewed with delight. "It's my bratwurst."

"For breakfast? After all the Jataxa we drank last night? You're kidding, right?"

But Franco was far from kidding. He was too busy tucking in to the gleaming excuse for semi-meat. He grinned again, mashed mush caught between teeth and lips.

"What did I say last night, Kee? About you lightening up? I've been in a loony bin for nigh on three years; the bastards fed me on bread and slop. This, my friend, is my beanie, my bowow, my tube steak, my puppy sausage. It's a bratwurst, originates from Germany, Earth. And man, it tastes just fine."

"OK." Keenan seated himself beside Pippa, eyes scanning screens—professionally—despite his dishevelled appearance. "It just seems a shame to put a million dollar InfinityChef through such a painstaking creation. After all, you could have Seechee from Bagdabadad, Triptopus from Hojo, even a damned Old Earth Steak smothered in Pepper Sauce. But that? Franco, even for you it's a fucking abomination."

Cam took that cue to make a reappearance. He glided into the cockpit in what he considered a graceful manner, filled with pride, élan, lissomness and symmetry. He spun slowly, observing the three members of the recently re-formed Combat-K.

"You OK Cam?" asked Franco through a mouthful of sausage.

"Actually, now that you enquire…"

Franco held up a hand. "Stop there. No whining, please. You're a machine, mate, so just stick to making toast and we'll get on fine. No more of this mechanical skulking."

"Why, you, you, you…"

"Cam!" snapped Keenan. "OK. We need maps of The City. Street level, tek level, and the names of contacts that can get us high grade weapons, bombs, the best Permatex WarSuits, the lot. Can you do that?"

"Of course. After all, I'm a GradeA Security Mechanism with advanced SynthAI and a Machine Intelligence Rating (MIR) of 3150. I am, as has already been pointed out on numerous occasions, more human than many humans. I'm certainly more human than most of the aliens you see walking the four corners of the Cluster. Thus, I postulate…"

Franco lifted his sausage, and smacked the foot long glistening tuber across Cam's case leaving a long greasy smear. "Go on, beat it, we've got stuff to discuss."

Cam rotated and disappeared down the corridor.

Laughter followed at a discreet distance.

IT WAS LATER, much later.

Over a bottle and shot-glasses of vodka Keenan and Franco pored over the maps. The maps were Realtime TuffMAPS™, maps on rectangles of plastic that folded and shifted like a simple puzzle, but were almost indestructible, and moved and updated in real time from a million different deep-galaxy satellite relays.

"I'm telling you Keenan, I know my way round The City like a junkie sniffing out a dealer."

"For the hundredth time, no."

Pippa entered, rolling her neck and rubbing at tired eyes. "Is he still moaning?"

"Yep."

"Not this time, Franco." She smiled a sweet smile. "You've got the very important task of keeping our ship alive. Within ten minutes of landing at a FreePort we'll have all manner of Scavs crawling over us. You'll have to be a Big Man to sort out the little shits. No offence meant."

"None taken, but it strikes me that a brain-fried gun-toting chick is better suited to this sort of hard-core menial job; no offence meant."

"None taken." She accepted the glass of vodka and killed it. "OK. We're packing, so if you want a Long Sleep the Bays are free. I, for one, am not sitting here for another sixteen days while you two squabble over sausages and map tactics, especially as I know for a fact both of you are better off warside on the ground. Little correlation between the map and the world outside, if you know what I mean. I've seen it before. So, I suggest you get some much needed kip; and Franco, if you so much as try to creep into my SleepCell while I'm on a longways, well, I'm going to warn you, I've rigged an intruder circuit for serious electrocution, with an encore of possible maiming thrown in."

"I wouldn't dream of trying to take advantage," said Franco, looking hurt and shocked.

"Why not? You've tried it before."

"Just that once."

"No-o." Pippa smiled tartly. "I believe I caught you trying, shall we say, a covert infiltration on no less than seven occasions. I broke your ribs on that last one."

"Oh, *that*," said Franco. "I was just, you know, showing a bit of crewmate solidarity."

"You're a sexual deviant, and you should learn to keep your pickle to yourself. So, gentlemen, I will bid you a long goodnight. The ship's advanced enough to deal with SCAVS, Tickles, SPAWS and Blay Stars if the need arises; anything more serious and it'll dredge us up from whatever deep and miserable hells our consciousnesses have conjured."

"Tickles?" Cam had entered, black case gleaming and prissily devoid of sausage grease.

"Yeah," said Pippa. "When you use any umbilical there are risks, because you're touching on VoidSpace. That's where these things live. The SCAVS are like giant octopuses floating on the fringes of real space; they're black, practically invisible, but sometimes certain breeds will pulsate with blue glimmers through their trailing tentacles. They have long bulbous arms, and teeth that can eat through hull armour."

"Can't you just blast them out of the way?"

"A single tentacle would encircle this craft about ten times, Cam, and their armour plating is legendary. They'd eat us for lunch, then spit us out and look for dessert. Not something I'd mess with. And Tickles are swarms of high density, high concentrate coreolic acid; starts off sounding like rain on a ship's hull, but in reality it's the little bastards launching themselves at hull armour in tight choreographed formation dives. Eventually—quicker than you'd think—your spacecraft is like a sponge, you get hullbreach, decompression and you've got a craft full of exploded organisms. These things are not too bright, though; they have a vegetable sentience, but that's about it. They're not forcefully aggressive; just kind of aimlessly destructive, in a nice way."

"How come you don't have these files, anyway?" said Franco, waving his shot-glass wildly in the air. "I thought you had..." he affected an effete voice, "'a Machine Intelligence Rating of 3150.'"

"I do not have Eternity Memory, I am a PopBot. I tend to be more specifically functioned. I was destined for the Galhari market; my mem-mods were area specific."

"What about Pippa's logic cubes? In her skull?"

"Algorithms supplied by Fortune. I have the intelligence, just not the data. With the right codes you would be amazed at how dangerous I can actually be."

"Woo-hoo," said Franco. At that point Keenan and Pippa exchanged a glance, and Pippa took the near-empty bottle from the table and screwed the cap firm with finality.

"Too many years in a sanatorium," said Keenan gently. "He just wants to live it up a bit. Yeah?"

"However, we have agreed a mission," said Pippa. "A certain amount of professionalism is expected."

"But it's a mission that won't, technically, begin for another fifteen days. I think it's definitely time we got some sugar coma-time. Come on, let's put the maps away. We've plenty of time for planning when we're fucking dead."

Keenan and Pippa carried a fast-failing Franco to his SleepCell and rolled shut the door. He began to snore immediately. Keenan leant against the wall, laughing.

"Just like the old times," he grinned, face suddenly youthful and filled with a boyish charm.

"Yeah, just like the old times."

There was an awkward silence, and Keenan felt the avalanche rush between them, like a mammoth crevasse widening with every passing breath. He licked his lips, was about to speak, but Pippa gave a single shake of her head. She moved off down the corridor, and with a silent curse Keenan followed.

WITHIN HOURS, KEENAN and Pippa had arranged their kit, checked one another's navigation data, and entered their private SleepCells. Cam switched into the digital void: the world of offline. The Hornet powered down.

In the darkness of Franco's SleepCell, his eyes flicked open and gleamed against the artificial night. He sat up. Everything was quiet. He pulled out a small bottle from his clothing, opened the cap, and shook free a blue pill. He stared at it for a while, then swallowed.

Moments later, Franco left his SleepCell and moved warily, unobserved, around the downtime ship.

THE DAYS TICKED down.

Twenty hours from The City, the sleeping inhabitants were slowly brought round using KT injections. Pippa was the first to rise, and stood in front of the sink gazing at her reflection and examining the myriad of tiny lines that creased her face. Getting old, slowing down, soon be fish food. She smiled, opened the inset cupboard above the small ship sink, and stared hard at the scissors that sat there, lengths of inconsequential metal.

Scissors. Damn.

She breathed deep.

Pippa stared at the scissors for a long time, but made no effort to reach out, no effort to touch this simple item of gleaming steel. Pippa didn't touch scissors. She had vowed never to touch scissors until the day she died.

Aged nineteen Pippa had been the most skilled killer her Combat-K instructors had met. She was fitter, stronger, more agile, more lethal than most recruits who passed the hallowed hallways of The Silver Academy. She'd been chosen outright, not for standard K Class infantry infiltrations; no, they had special instructions for this little lady. After all, her mentor, the late great General J. K. Cameron, had rescued her from a hostel for teenage criminals at the request of his niece, one of the kind-hearted incarceration officers there, and somebody who recognised an esoteric quality within Pippa's cold moody atmosphere, which she believed could be nurtured, developed and engaged.

Brought up by her father—Daniel—after her mother's early departure, Pippa had led a sheltered life. She remembered little of this premature maternal severance; only it had something to do with alcohol, and a lot to do with violence. Daniel had been a heavy drinker even from the early days, working hard-labour in the shipyards of a rapidly expanding human empire glorious against the backdrop of new stars. He earned good money completing dangerous work on the external fitment of Class G cruisers, the testing of military lasers, and occasional Mechanical Integration, one of the most highly paid and hazardous vocations in the exploding Sinax Cluster. However, his good money was spent at a spiralling rate on the Ijak, Twaz and Jataxa he loved.

Pippa would arrive home from school. If the apartment was quiet, she knew it would be an OK night. But if, as happened five times out of seven, music was blaring from four open windows, the apartment ablaze with violet anti-insect light, the door ajar by just a few inches; well, Pippa knew she was in for a bad gig.

When her mother had lived at home, it would begin with drinking. Father drinking, and her mother, Anna, drinking as a basic cushion of absorption for the abuse inflicted on her unworthy soul: the digs, the mistreatment, the poking of the finger. Yeah, Daniel was good at that, emphasising his point with a jab of the index to shoulder, chest or abdomen. It would deteriorate into arguments about money, food, clothing for Pippa. The arguments would sometimes fizzle out with Daniel too intoxicated to climb from his dominant chair in front of the vidscreen. Other times they would rage around the apartment like a hurricane. Pippa would flee to her room, hide under her covers with either her music turned on full so that it rattled the walls and blanked out the screaming, or a simple pillow over her ears to block out the hate. It was normal. This was all normal, right? Everybody had a home life like this; all those other kids at school and the academy, there was nothing wrong with it, and Pippa dragged herself through a miserable existence unable to speak, unable to communicate her angst, unable to simply *scream*.

Then—mother left. Pippa was hazy about the circumstances. But she remembered the huge purple bruises on her mother's face; remembered Anna holding her ribs, words wheezing through black pulped lips, eyes frightened and darting around the apartment; a woman scared for her life.

It changed the dynamic of their little trio. Suddenly, Pippa, aged a delicate twelve, had been forced into the position of lead female and matriarch. Despite her youth, Daniel's attention had transferred to her—the new victim on the block—for his evening onslaught. Verbal at first, cursing the government, cursing his job, cursing his lack of wealth pissed down gutters and urinals of tek-bars and, when exceptionally drunk, pattering golden over the contents of his wardrobe. But then, as night follows day, so physical violence followed rhetoric: a stinging slap, to arm, or thigh, just to emphasise the argument, you understand love, just to highlight a particularly important point. And the finger—Pippa called it the Finger of Justice—pointing, stabbing, accusing; and hurting, always hurting. But it was all right; surely everybody went through this, didn't they? It was normal, all about growing up. All her friends must be experiencing the same. It's what parents did. Just the way it was.

Pippa did grow up, introverted, sullen, moody, she kept herself to herself and did her work as best she could until a group of seven girls decided she would become the next victim and target of childish playful schoolyard bullying... smug, slimy, peroxide perms and orange tans, long and leggy and as beautiful as cadavers. They attacked, and in the whirlwind that followed Pippa left three maimed and six in the hospital, one in intensive care. Nobody fucked with Pippa after that. They left the quiet demure sullen girl with the grey eyes and the black bobbed hair alone; just the way she liked it.

Back at home, Daniel got worse. His pay increased, and so his drinking increased. He managed to drag himself into work every day but it was suffering, until a disaster on a high-gantry left four colleagues without limbs, and Daniel was dismissed facing public social charges of technical incompetence.

Instead of improving Pippa's life, it made it far, far worse. Instead of starting to drink in the evening, Daniel used his dollarcard and began when he awoke: that first crack of the bottle and a cigarette before climbing from decadent soiled sheets. Pippa endured all agony of depravation, obloquy, humiliation. She was dragged across the floor by her hair, denied TV, food, clothing; even electric. She was forced to wash in cold water and endure a winter without heating, and was locked from the house when she was a minute past her curfew. She was kicked unconscious, scratched, gouged and punched; but worst of all was that finger, the Finger of Justice: prodding, poking, stabbing, highlighting the arguments of an inebriated arsehole. And slowly, slowly, slowly, Pippa began to hate every look, every touch, every word, every breath. Hatred grew and festered, and built until every single second of every single day she felt she would explode.

One day, everything changed.

Mother came back. She looked good, healthy, hair a glowing sheen, eyes bright. Daniel was on the verge of unconsciousness in his chair, nodding like a lobotomised monkey. "Come on," she said, red lips smiling at the look of sudden hope in her bruised daughter's face, "you're coming with me, princess."

"But what about..."

"Him?" she snarled. "He can rot in a hell of his own creation."

Pippa ran to her room, packing meagre belongings into a small case. As she was struggling with the latches she heard raised voices, and a cold dread settled like cancer over her heart. She ran back to the living quarters, just in time to see Daniel strike Anna down, a brutal right hook that broke the woman's nose, twisting her head at a savage angle as she struck the liquor-stained carpet. Anna lay still. Her neck was broken. Blood trickled from her eyes.

Pippa stepped forward. She did not feel anger or hatred, did not feel a rush of hot blood, did not pass through seasons of building rage. She was cold: as cold as the tombstone, as cold as the Void.

"Father, what have you done?"

"Fucking whore, fucking bitch," he slurred, slumping to his knees and staring with the feral look of the alcoholic: no compassion, no empathy, no understanding of his poison, of what he was, of what he had become: a slave, a slave to the piss, a willing victim of the demon in the bottle. "Who does she think she is? Take you away from me, will she? I don't fucking think so! TAKE YOU AWAY FROM ME?"

Pippa stepped forward as Daniel's stabbing finger came up. Pippa's gaze locked to that finger. To her it embodied everything: the hatred, the stupidity, the abuse, the violence. She smiled. It wasn't a real smile. It was a release.

Her hand dropped, scrabbled on the table. She found something there: long, metallic, unyielding.

In silence, her fingers curled around the slender form of the scissors.

And her eyes went hard.

PIPPA GASPED, STARED up at herself in the mirror as if coming up from the depths of unconsciousness. Hands shaking, she took a deep breath and closed the cabinet door. Nobody knew about her past: not her Combat-K instructors, not her team, not even Keenan. To some extent her father's abuse explained the ease with which she dispatched those of the male sex. But she knew it went deeper, far deeper to a place she did not want to revisit... a bottomless well of a simple nightmare. Her father had created a demon, and often that demon walked the world. Meeting Keenan, loving Keenan, she had been exorcised of the cancer in her soul. But in casting her away, in rejecting her love, Keenan had brought her wrath and her violence back tenfold.

And yet... she blinked, realising the truth, meeting her own accusing stare. She still loved him, still loved him with a passion greater than life. But she would rather die than acknowledge that love; for her father was always at the back of her mind, the extended index finger jabbing at her in mockery and a prelude to execution, of mind and spirit, and soul.

Pippa moved to the shower and stood under a stream of hot water, wishing it could wash away her bad dreams, her dark thoughts, her evil past. But it couldn't. Nothing could do that.

KOTINEVITCH WORE A tight black suit with the rank insignia of General gleaming against one sleeve. She crossed the massive cargo bay, glancing up at distant roof struts a kilometre above her, then around at the ranged display of cargo ships gleaming black and gold in the vast freezing interior. Her breath came in short smoke bursts. Her boots crushed ice crystals on the steel walkway mesh.

Vitch approached the docked ship alone as Loaders and Plutonium Cranes buzzed around her, many automated, but several hundred manned by stocky crewmen. The docked ship looked out of place; no Cargo Hulker, but a slim slip of a vehicle, dull white and grey, sleek and designed for speed, for infiltration. No name adorned the ship's flanks, but Vitch knew the model well; it was an illegal outlawed one man stealth-fighter; an Interceptor.

She approached the ramp. There was no visible sign of life within.

Touching a hand to her scabbarded yukana sword, a movement of instinct, of reassurance, she placed a boot on the ramp, and looked up into black eyes. He was a small man, slim and wiry, head bald, features rough under heavy black eyebrows. He wore a short pointed beard peppered with grey. His torso was naked, legs enclosed in baggy black trousers, and tight boots shining with a military gleam. His body was powerfully muscled and heavily scarred, arms, chest, belly, neck, some scars evidence of knife or sword fights, some indicative of previous bullet wounds; some were neat, some ragged. All were worn with pride.

Vitch moved slowly up the ramp, her eyes drinking in the man. He was drying his hands on a towel, and stepped aside to allow her entry to the craft.

She stepped wordlessly inside, turned, and with delicate fingers unbuttoned her tunic. In seconds she stepped free of her uniform and stood naked, skin gleaming, eyes bright as the scarred man approached and hit a switch. Doors kissed shut.

"Mr. Max," breathed Kotinevitch.

He moved to her, his mouth on hers, hand dropping instantly between her legs. She groaned, green lips parting as his fingers entered her and he kissed her strongly, tongue in her mouth, hand moving instantly, frantically slick with her eagerness, her want, her lust. Vitch's hands tugged down his trousers with an urgency she had forgotten; and he entered her hard, her legs coming up over his hips to accept his harsh thrusts, needy as her head lolled back, hair falling free, and for a few minutes she lost herself to this hard brash primal brutal animal fucking. She climaxed first, he a few seconds later, and they stayed like that, against the Interceptor's console for a few long lingering moments as reality tumbled and drifted back to slot neatly, precisely, into place.

Eventually, chewing her lower lip, she glanced up into black emotionless eyes.

"I needed that," said Vitch; her voice was music.

"It's been a long time," said Mr. Max.

"I have a job for you," said Vitch.

Mr. Max nodded, and they dressed slowly under the blue light of the ship's interior. Outside, the

Plutonium Cranes buzzed and laboured, hydraulic arms hauling and lifting and depositing; huge freighter caskets were heaved into the sky and dumped on stacker racks with deafening *clangs* and the clatter of steel on steel.

Mr. Max moved to a tiny bench and poured two drinks, handing one to Vitch who smoothed out creases in her uniform and buckled her yukana in place.

"Assassination?"

"Yes." Vitch sipped her drink. It was smooth and warm. It caressed her throat like silk. "I've sent Betezh to mop up his own mess; but the game is bigger than we first thought. We believe the squad carries a Dark Flame with it. Clever, ingenious of our enemies, in fact. This Combat-K squad in particular has re-formed despite a government imposed GroupD prohibition order. Betezh was sent to bring back one escapee, not to take out a Combat-K squad. However, now our contact loop has been detached I can't call him for a further sixteen hours. He's on his own, and way out of his league. One drugged-up prisoner is one thing; a full squad?" She laughed a cruel laugh. "I don't anticipate his return, not in one body-piece, anyway."

"So I lock on when I can? Finish the job?"

"Yes."

Vitch moved close, slid her hand down the front of his trousers. Her fingers curled around him, felt him harden immediately despite recent ejaculation. She smiled in appreciation. She kissed his neck, tasting salt.

"You want me to kill all three?"

"I want you to fuck me again."

"And then you want me to kill all three?"

"Yes. Keenan is the leader."

"The others?"

"Pippa, and Franco."

"I know of Keenan, and I know the squad. I worked with them once, a long time ago; although they will not remember me. I was a... different man."

"You accept?"

Mr. Max smiled a thin smile. It looked wrong on his face. His dark eyes were unreadable, but glittered with insect amorality. "Consider them dead," he said.

"There is another problem."

"Yes?"

"They seek the Fractured Emerald."

"Big problem," agreed Mr. Max.

"You can stop this?"

Mr. Max considered the situation. "You are talking of Leviathan?"

"I am."

Mr. Max tutted. "I will do what I can," he promised.

KOTINEVITCH RETURNED TO her personal quarters aboard the Class Q Cruiser, *The Sickness and the Cure*. She felt satisfied, deep down inside: satiated to her core.

She kicked off boots and allowed her long elegant toes to revel in thick syrupy carpets, liquid fibre that washed over her feet like gentle surf. She slumped onto her COMBO bed, at ease, and for a few moments was just a normal, everyday flesh and blood woman: no general, no war-commander in charge of a billion heavily armed soldiers, a war fleet and a corrupt maverick view on how a government should discipline its subordinates. For long moments she revelled in this simplicity; she felt young again. Sex usually did that. But, like the best of drugs, the effect was short-lived: a clit-tease, a come-on.

Vitch gave a deep sigh and closed her eyes in the moment of total physical satisfaction. She allowed the COMBO bed to massage her with nano-electric insertions.

Mr. Max, she thought, and shivered; a little in delight, a little in memory of his touch, a little in fear. She had known him for fifteen years, and yet he was still deliciously unpredictable. Twice he had tried to kill her, and twice she had bought him. A mercenary to the core, money was the only currency he worshipped: no honour, no code, no loyalties; and yes, they enjoyed a needful sex, a union of personal necessity, but even this tenuous link of love—lust—was something Kotinevitch refused to acknowledge as anything other than feral. A meeting of convenience, but then, that was the way she preferred it. And Mr. Max?

Mr. Max did not love. He was an automaton: a killing machine.

Max by name, max by nature, she thought. When he got drunk, he drank to be sick. When he fucked, he fucked till he bled. And when assigned to murder...

Mr. Max would not stop.

Period.

CHAPTER 5
CITYSLICKERS

"Freeport 557 ahead," said Pippa. "Bringing her round."

The members of Combat-K braced themselves as jets howled and the Hornet slowed, slamming down through the atmosphere and into the middle of a storm. Thick grey clouds rolled, engulfed them, swathed them, grey and black and bruised, and lit internally by horizontal *cracks* of lightning. Several bounced off the Hornet's hull, and Keenan and Franco exchanged glances. It reminded them of a previous mission, years ago, when they'd been struck from the sky. It had resulted in seven dead. Not a pleasant memory.

"OK. Down we go."

More jets fired along with a vertical turbine; the sound of metal spinning against metal droned distantly. Then they were free of the clouds, storm rain pounding the Hornet, and The City spread before them like an infinite neon nightmare.

"Wow baby," said Franco.

"Yeah," said Keenan. "I always forget how crazy it looks, until I come back. What a dump."

"Ready to touch, boys. Make sure you're buckled in."

Franco winked at Keenan. "That's what she always says to me, when's she's in her kinky mood."

"In your dreams, Little Man."

"Often," grinned Franco.

Lights and lasers flooded the sky, lighting the interior of the Hornet with iridescence. Below, The City was, well, a city spreading off unto infinity. It consistently reminded Keenan of a kind of kamikaze version of Hong Kong or Tokyo, only much wider, much taller, with tiers sporting buildings built on gantries above other buildings, giving an impression of architectural anarchy, which it surely was.

"We've got clearance," said Pippa. In fact, no identity or registration had been requested, just a technical report on the ship for safety reasons. The City welcomed everyone. However, it was safe to assume the Freeports of The City were constantly observed by a myriad of spies from a fistful of different factions, some of which may even have been friendly.

The Hornet caressed steelconcrete, suspension dipping and engines sighing. Rain drummed on the hull, running in rivulets down the cockpit. Combat-K unbuckled.

"Nice landing," said Cam, spinning into view.

"Why thank you," smiled Pippa, climbing from her seat. "Nice to see that at least one of the crew has some manners. Come on Keenan, let's get this show on the road. We're on a tight budget. Who knows what shadowy bastards have clocked us."

Keenan nodded. "Kit's all packed. Fortune gave me a contact via kube: Rebekka Kobayashi. She's a gun runner, knows The City, can take us to a variety of dealers depending on what hardware we need. Franco, you finish that shopping list?"

"Just uploaded it to your PAD. Everything we discussed plus some specials that might come in handy: tank killers, some new forms of explosives, that sort of thing."

"They teach you that in Mount Pleasant?"

"Let's just say I had a lot of reading time," said Franco testily.

Keenan and Pippa headed for the ramp, shouldered their packs, and checked their discrete holstered weapons. Keenan carried his Techrim 11mm, and both were carrying Makarov 3mm Microbore pistols and spare magazines. Just in case of "trouble". Trouble they didn't expect, but then, muggings and casual murder were seen as collateral damage on the streets of The City.

"Keenan?"

"Yeah, Franco? And I hope it's not that same damn question."

"It is."

"Then the answer's no."

"Come on, Keenan, just one pub, one bar, one beer. I've been locked up for three years, my man. My throat is dry. My loins are choked. I need a release."

"Plenty of time in the SIM SUIT on the way to Ket."

Franco, scowling heartily, said, "You have no soul, brother."

"On the contrary, I have too much. That's why you're staying put. I don't want you dead."

"Cam?"

"Yes, boss?"

"Make sure the Ginger One doesn't leave. If he does, sting him."

Cam, spinning slowly with a blue light blinking, seemed to turn to face Franco. Franco's mouth had opened. Then it closed again and he frowned. *It's grinning,* he thought. *The little bastard is grinning!* He watched Keenan and Pippa clump down the ramp, out into the leaden rain, which soaked them instantly.

Pippa turned and smiled. "See you later, deviant."

Franco cursed.

Then, with a tiny *whirr* of motors, the ramp sealed and trapped him inside the Hornet's belly.

KEENAN AND PIPPA jogged across steelconcrete until they were under a shelter. A thousand people jostled on the walkways and ramps, the escalators and personal two-man flyers, the skeetboards and air-cycles. With his back against a neon plastic wall Keenan checked his PAD while Pippa, nervous now, watched their surroundings.

Rain pounded. Thunder rumbled ominously. Salescreens barked and laughed, chattered and crackled. The people were a throng, jostling and jarring, and inter-mixed were what Keenan—old fashioned to the point of pedantry—still called aliens. Proxers, human in form except they had bright, bright eyes displaying silicon origins walked freely, practically without differentiation. Scattered in the mix were GGs and even more modern, much rarer and far more lethal, GKs: advanced AI systems, some humanoid in appearance, but several taking the forms of chassis blocks or spheres. There were also kajunga, who always appeared—to Keenan anyway—as small fat children, only with orange skin and a nasty vicious temperament that could never be matched by any human. Slabs lumbered in the throng, huge muscled war machines bred a hundred thousand years ago in VATS for amoral war games on a planetary scale; but now a discrete race in their own right under Time Equality Laws. There were SIMS, biomechanical humans, proxers or kajunga ranging from one of three classes: Servile, Justice, and Battle. It was all part of the upgrade service.

"That's a lot of guns," said Pippa, moving close and tense beside Keenan. Like him, she preferred open country; The City, to her, was a stifling place, a place of claustrophobia, a warzone without law or justice.

"Don't think about it."

"I don't have to think about it, I can damn well see it!"

"Just give me another minute, then we'll jump a FLEET. We're meeting Kobayashi in... ahh. There, it's Downside West of Titanium Towers. Good neighbourhood, wealthy, not much trouble. Fortune has arranged a meet in a hotel bar."

"Name?"

"*All That Glitters.*"

"Sounds like a brothel."

"Don't be like that, Pippa. It's a high class area. I've been around that sector before. Come on, let's get away from the rain; over there, there's a queue of FLEET cars."

Pippa followed Keenan. The crowd took some effort to part.

IN THE SHADOWS of a drugstall behind a curtain of draining rainfall that poured clattering from an alloy fabric roof, a hunched figure watched Keenan and Pippa vanish into the crowd. The face was broad and brutal, and hidden a little under a tight-fitting black hat. Scars lined one cheek, and the eyes set deep in the face were small and black. His head turned left, eyes fixing on the distant Hornet. Dropping his cigarette, and crushing it under a heavy boot, he headed out into the rain.

FRANCO SAT IN a comfortbubble, face set to scowl, eyes focused on—but not watching—a City broadcast. It showed golden-limbed women running naked into a lapping sea. Behind, towers speared the sky. The turquoise sea lapped along a gold shimmering beach. "*TOX FILTER,*" came a soothing voice. "*DON'T LET THE LACK OF AN ATMOSPHERE SPOIL YOUR FUN! MAKE SURE YOU COVER UP... BEFORE YOU THROW UP!*" One of the women screamed, her perfect body bending and folding, and slowly bubbling away in the toxic sea as a poisonous sun pulverised her unprotected flesh.

"Charming," muttered Franco. Then he eased from the bubble. "Shit. Bastard. Son of a bitchy bitch." He stomped down the corridor and paused before the InfinityChef, but didn't really feel like eating. His imprisonment had removed his appetite. This experience was just too damned close to his Mount Pleasant incarceration.

"Are you really asking the Chef for shit?" enquired Cam, hanging immobile by Franco's head.

Franco started. "You little bastard, sneaking up on me like that. I've a good mind to give you a thrashing. Damn tennis ball."

"Really?" said Cam, voice soft.

There was something about that voice that made Franco wary, something basic, and primitive, which spoke to Franco in terms of his own survival. He shivered. "Anyway," he said, trying to act nonchalant, "what is a sting, anyway?"

"A sharp jolt of electricity. I usually deliver it to a criminal... ha, did I say criminal? I meant person's rectal area. That way, pain spreads out in an uncomfortable web arse-first; it also has the added comedic value of making it hard for you to go to the lavatory."

"Yeah," said Franco, giving a huge grin, "but you wouldn't do that to me, right? I mean, would you?"

"I think," said Cam, voice still a gentle hum, chassis still immobile, "that I might."

"Ye-eeees," said Franco, shuffling a little closer. "But, I mean, after all, you're an AI and I'm a human. That means me, well, my forbears, built you. That must surely mean I outrank you, in terms of—well— *life*. Yeah?"

"Actually," said Cam, "I have an MIR rating of—"

Cam didn't finish the sentence, because with surprising speed, incredible agility, and the force of a natural born pugilist, Franco caught Cam with a vicious right-hook. Cam bounced off the wall, clattered spinning on the deck, and on the rebound Franco delivered an almighty penalty-shootout kick that sent Cam bouncing and juddering down the corridor to disappear into the gloom of the cockpit.

"Ha!" gloated a triumphant Franco. "Sting me on the arse now, you little bugger! You don't mess with the Man on Medication!"

He slammed the control. The ramp descended.

And with a gleam in his eye, Franco jogged down into the rain.

THE AREA WAS surprisingly quiet, and, as Keenan had piously claimed, a considered upmarket zone of The City. Buildings were tall, sporting high security fences and electrified gates; most were built from a high grade smooth stone, marble, alloy, steel and glass. Everywhere seemed clean and well maintained; there were even trees, although as Pippa pointed out, they were grown from recipes. You could see the genetic trademark.

Keenan halted on a street corner, with Pippa close behind. She was watching her PAD closely.

"We OK?"

"So far," said Keenan, hand over his weapon beneath his coat. He was reassured by the Techrim's bulk. "How far to the rendezvous?"

"A klick, northeast. What does this Rebekka look like?"

"She's a proxer, so humanoid, bright orange eyes, long black hair. I kind of got the impression Fortune found her attractive. Said they went back a long way, and she was totally trustworthy."

"But he's AI. What would he find attractive about her?"

Keenan shrugged. "Come on."

They walked through the rain. On the horizon, patches of blue were beginning to show, and the downpour lightened as Pippa called a halt and waited for a group of hooded screamagers to pass.

"Across the road."

Keenan's eyes fixed on the sign. *All That Glitters.* A doorman stood outside, and as they watched a long purple eighteen-wheel limousine pulled up and ejected five giggling glitter-smeared young women. They collided, one dropping her glass of champagne, and they all giggled some more. Keenan blinked. He realised that glitter was, in fact, all they were wearing. They gibbered in a fast-talk local yoof language Keenan didn't recognise; and gradually mauled one another inside. The limousine pulled away, and, with a sigh, the doorman pulled a brush and pan free, and swept up the broken glass.

"Enjoy the show?" asked Pippa.

"Entertaining," admitted Keenan.

"Looks like a rich bitch hotspot all right."

"No need to get touchy. It's not a personal affront."

"I just hate these people," said Pippa in a relaxed snarl. "Fucking moneyheads, wine in their veins, coke in their brains, pissing away their lives and refusing to do anything of damn worth with themselves. I warn you, Keenan, when we step foot through that doorway, if I so much as smell a footballer's wife I'm going to put a bullet in her dumb-ass fucking skull. I just cannot help myself."

Keenan grinned. "The one thing I love about you, Pippa, is the prospect of random chaos you bring to any mission. We're here for weapons, suits, kit. Focus on that."

Pippa nodded.

"And if we do see a professional glamour model; well, let *me* shoot her instead."

THE HOTEL WAS opulent to the extent of farce. The floor was one continuous flowing plasma screen. The walls were edible. The fountains ran with... Keenan dipped a finger. "Champagne," he said, with a pained look, "and it's vintage."

"How do you know? Are you fucking James Bond?"

"Am I *fucking* James Bond? Not recently. I'd remember, it'd hurt."

Pippa stared at the topless whoretress who passed carrying a tray full of glasses; the hermaphrodite smiled dazzlingly at Keenan with gold teeth. Each tooth had a screen set in its surface. They could be tuned to a myriad of pornographic channels.

"Damn this place," snapped Pippa, scowling as the whoretress passed.

"You're just pissed she didn't smile at you."

"I've had better. It's so tacky in here, I'm stuck to the floor."

"So you'd prefer the jungle?"

"Anytime, Keenan, anytime."

They approached the desk, where a young man, a deskjanitor in a stiff suit, smiled a false smile with fake steel teeth. "How can one help sir, madam." He beamed. It wasn't even delivered as a question.

"We have a meeting with Rebekka Kobayashi. I believe she's expecting us?"

"Indeedy she is," grinned the young man. He held out his hand. Keenan stared at it.

"Yes?" he said politely.

Pippa nudged him.

"What?"

"Tip," hissed Pippa.

Keenan pulled out his Techrim and pointed it at the young man's face. The steel gleam faded. "She's through this way, sir. If you'd just like to follow me, sir, to the lounge, sir. Yes, sir. That's where she is, sir."

They followed the now bumbling deskjanitor through a series of swaying organic corridors, past crystal pillars encapsulating rare frozen life forms, over treacle carpets and finally into a spacious lounge with tinkling music and small cubic robot waiters.

"Over by the bookcase, sir, madam." The deskjanitor smiled again. This time he did not hold out his hand. He departed swiftly.

Keenan felt Pippa's glare.

"What? *What?*"

"I thought we were keeping a low profile?"

"In The City?" Keenan snorted a laugh. "You know a gun in the face is low profile."

"Not the gun, dickhead. I meant the tip."

"So you think I'm a skinflint?"

"I think not tipping in a place like this could bring unwanted attention. It's expected."

Keenan nodded. "OK. You're more familiar with this place; I'll let you communicate from now on. You also have the added benefit of..."

"Yeah?"

"The female touch," smiled Keenan.

They moved across the purposefully sticky carpets, down more steps, and across a football pitch sized lounge. It was dotted with tables, chairs, bookcases and trees: small glass trees growing from pulpmud. Several old gentlemen snoozed in comfortwraps, their little pink whiskered faces poking rat-like from folds of velvet with cigars trailing lazy smoke. Occasionally, a cubic waiter would extend an appendage and neatly trim the ash.

They passed a circular couch where the giggling young women from the limousine were shelled in a silencefield; the only way in and out of the couch was to climb; at least Keenan and Pippa were spared a cacophony of horse-like chortles.

"Over there."

"I see her."

Rebekka Kobayashi saw them coming and rose from her suite with fluid grace. She wore a long, simple, black dress and boots. Her hair was, as

Fortune described, long and black, with a lush sheen like the pelt of a panther. Her bright orange eyes sparkled with intelligence. Pippa kicked Keenan on the ankle.

"Fortune sent us."

Rebekka nodded and smiled. "Would you like to take a seat?"

They sat, and Rebekka pulled out a small grey PAD. "You have a list to transmit? I'll forward it to our supplier so they can assemble your shopping items while we enjoy a few relaxing drinks. Half an hour will see our business concluded."

"Your code?" said Pippa.

Rebekka, with long fingers, activated her signal. "Switching to quad bandwidth. Accelerating."

"Received," said Pippa. "Reciprocating."

"I have your list. There're some... interesting items here."

"Can you get them?"

Rebekka looked down her nose. "I can get anything. The price will be..." Rebekka typed fast, then used a stylus built into her index finger to tap out and trace patterns on the PAD. "Seventeen K."

"Transferring."

They waited. Rebekka smiled, and pocketed her PAD. She seemed to relax, settling back in her plush red leather Queen Anne chair and steepling her fingers before her face.

"So you know Fortune. You are honoured. His contact is rare, and his help never given lightly."

"Let's just say we did him a favour, once, a big one."

"Drink?" Rebekka gestured to the cubic waiter.

"I'll have water," said Keenan.

"Lemon tea," said Pippa, and the waiter buzzed and floated away.

"You come a long way?" asked Rebekka. Her orange eyes shone, and Keenan found himself—for a moment—transfixed by that beautiful—*stunning*—gaze. He kicked himself internally; he knew enough about the proxers to understand, despite their outward humanoid appearance, they were actually very, very far from human in outlook, psychology and mental state. Their emotions were a dilution of human; in one account from back during the war Keenan had read that proxers were practically insectile. Physically, they could fight on after the loss of multiple limbs; but more than that, they showed little or no honour towards comrades, even in wartime where situations dictated the greatest of cooperation. Proxers always, always fought independently. In the proxer lexicon there were no words for "team", "unit" or "squad". The proxers lived and died alone.

Drinks arrived.

Rebekka had caught Keenan's stare. "You like what you see?"

Keenan coughed. "Sorry. I didn't mean to appear rude. I was just admiring your... ahhh, eyes."

Pippa gave him a sideways smile. "Lame," she mouthed.

Rebekka took a sip from her own drink, something thick and blood red, and ran her tongue along her teeth. "When our business is concluded, if you have the time, I could show you some of the highlights of The City."

"Another time," said Keenan, feeling his cheeks colour. It had been years since such an offer had been made; back on Galhari, he had become somewhat of a recluse, a hermit; and he had to admit, he liked it that way.

"Where do we pick up this shopping?" asked Pippa, emulating Rebekka's clipped trading style.

"I will take you down to the GeeSide Docks; we have warehouses and safedepots dotted around. It's a good place for a transaction: discreet, not overlooked, and we have secure compounds without right of entry for locals."

Keenan sipped his water, eyes scanning the surroundings. There were few places from which to be observed, but he was painfully aware of the high technology tree in The City. Just because he couldn't see it, or hear it, didn't mean it wasn't there. Despite their high-tek PADs, there was always a superior technology.

Rebekka and Pippa chatted for ten minutes, and Keenan allowed himself to sink into a comfortable ease. He finished his water, and kept his hand on his Techrim, and his thoughts most definitely away from Rebekka and those piercing eyes.

But why not? said a little demon in his mind. *Why not leave Franco and Pippa behind, just for one night. Head out on the town with this babe, after all, it's been a long time my friend, a damned long time, and God only knows you deserve some happiness after some of the scrapes you've been through. Go on compadre... she made you an offer. Take her up on it. Proxers are supposed to be... different than human women:*

fewer inhibitions, more animal, more... violent...

Keenan shivered.

"You OK?" smiled Rebekka, staring hard at him. For a moment he feared she could read his mind.

"Yeah. Yeah, I think so."

Pippa gave him a strange look.

There came an acknowledgment *blip* from Rebekka's PAD and she stood, smoothing out her long black dress. "My flyer's up on the roof. It has enough cargo hold to transport your shopping back to..."

"Freeport 775," lied Pippa easily, blinking away the questioning glance from Keenan.

"If you'd like to follow me."

They crossed the lounge, headed for the stairs and the bullet-shaft elevators beyond. "Six hundred floors," chatted Rebekka as they walked. "Each one based around a different theme. I don't know about you, but the designers must have had some imagination! Six hundred different themed zones? They must have consumed serious drugs in the design phase!"

As they stopped by the lift, Pippa leant close to Keenan. Her hand touched the back of his leg and she slowly pressed a military signal against him: *We're being followed.*

Keenan rested his hand loosely around Pippa's hips, a casual gesture between casual ex-lovers. *I know,* he replied.

Set-up?

Possibly. Continue. Be ready.

OK boss.

They stepped into the lift and ascended to the roof.

FRANCO STOOD ON a street corner and breathed deep the foul polluted air of The City's natural depravity. He squinted through the grey, half-toxic downpour, through the crowds, through the concrete and alloy. There, he could see a man bent over performing fellatio on some kind of stumpy little dwarf alien with yellow skin. And there a woman was being robbed at *serraka*-point; she pulled free a 27mm pistol and blew the robber's head off, quite literally. For a few moments, chunks of skull rained down amongst the heavy fall. Then the corpse collapsed and the woman looted it. And there, two small dog-type creatures were copulating in a puddle. The noise roared, filling his head. The stench invaded Franco's nose, almost making him vomit: food, piss, shit, decay, disease, and entwined, a metallic smell, like a hive of busy insects. Franco licked his lips, savouring the taste that settled on his tongue like Halo Strike fallout.

"Mamma, I'm home!" he said.

AS THE LIFT doors opened and something like a tongue deposited them on the slick roof, Keenan was tense, Techrim ready for action and an uncompromising death. A brutal wind scoured him, blasting across a vast empty expanse of marble and concrete. The sky was a copper bruise. The rain had stopped. Wind whipped water from large standing puddles and speckled the three new arrivals in unholy baptism.

Rebekka's flyer was bobbing against its glass mooring chain. The chain tinkled in the wind's tease, dragging against the concrete platform and growing taut, then slack, taut, slack, in an endless musical rhythmical charade.

Keenan stepped free of the plush lift tongue in unconscious military formation with Pippa; both were checking for snipers, checking trajectories, and checking their own arcs of fire. Rebekka seemed not to notice, but Keenan smiled sombrely. How professional was she? Really? Was she just an arms dealer or... something more?

She led the way to the flyer.

Cautiously, Keenan and Pippa followed.

The roof of the *All That Glitters* was high, and around them The City spread out and beyond, scrolling away over an undulating landscape for ever: buildings on buildings on buildings, patches of greenery, zones of skyscrapers. In the distance, Keenan could make out stacked housing bloks rearing into the heavens for a good kilometre, and apparently blocking out the storm. *Must be a million people live there alone,* thought Keenan, *like sardines. Jesus, what a place.*

Far below, too distant to see, gunshots echoed. Then the rain started again, pounding the roof, and they hurried to the shelter of the flyer. Rebekka started a whisper-quiet engine and disengaged the mooring chain, which whipped back into its housing. They floated swiftly up into the advancing storm.

"How long?" asked Pippa, The City invisible for the moment as they cruised through charging clouds. Lightning crackled along the flyer's flanks. Rebekka's face was a bright blue glow in the reflection from the instrument panel.

"Three minutes. All your gear should be assembled."

They swept down from the sky, back into reality, and the world unrolled beneath them. A huge tidal river swept from east to west, around which rose mammoth cranes and towers, and a nightmare of dockyard buildings and freighter depots. They dropped low, skimming a million waiting containers. Huge FreighterBulks bobbed laboriously at anchor. Even through the protective PlastiGlass screen they could hear the cacophony of this giant insect hive. The City was busy. It was a place that never stopped, never slept.

Lights flickered beneath them. The flyer swayed, circumventing half-klick towers and cranes almost as big. Keenan's eyes were wide. He'd visited The City before, but it had been years previously and the... the scale had grown during the intervening time. Whereas once it had been just big, now the whole essence of the place was truly, awesomely titanic: an aberration, a spaghetti slum of insanity, a concrete abortion.

Rebekka dropped the flyer to ground level, and they chased their shadows through a criss-cross of container lanes. Huge steel boxes hammered by to either side with drumbeat rhythm.

"You're confident," said Keenan, leaning forward over her shoulder.

"I'm good."

"I hope so. Or we'll get squashed."

"Trust me." Rebekka turned and smiled only inches from Keenan's face. He could smell her perfume, see the wetness of her proxer lips, and he inhaled her scent without restraint. He could almost feel Pippa's eyes drilling the back of his head.

They suddenly decelerated and Rebekka brought the flyer skimming right, along a narrow dark alleyway lined with unlit crates. They touched down beside three twelve-wheel BMW limousines, which gleamed, black gloss, in the storm-lit gloom.

Men were waiting, with guns. Keenan felt Pippa tense as Rebekka stepped free, boots clacking on the steel road. She leant back in, wind whipping her hair about her face. "Come on. It's freezing. Your kit is ready."

"We on?" hissed Pippa.

"Yeah. Let's do it."

They stepped out, wary, and stared hard at the men. Most were big, stubbled and wearing expensive suits. At the end of the row of muscle stood—

"Shit. Look," grinned Keenan, "Slabs."

Slabs, genetically modified humans bred in VATS for the game of war. Many centuries ago they had enacted battles on planetary gameboards, their flesh as expendable as the billionaires who bet on the outcome. War had, for a period, become an unfashionable way of settling disputes. Why should millions die when diplomacy, political guile and backhand monies do the job instead? But some races, bloodthirsty and decadent, had taken war to another level on backward fringe planets where nobody policed and nobody seemed to care. No longer an act of aggressor and victim, no longer an activity of technology versus inferiority, (after all, when did an invader actually invade when the odds were stacked against them? Oh no. Only when victory was assured was a head placed under the guillotine. History had unveiled that particular fallacy with a series of guerrilla wars that had left countries and even whole planets reeling in the aftermath of ill-thought out invasions and dumbfuck politics) war was accelerated to the next level: that of game. Hell, why watch little simulated figures on a gamescreen or playwall when you could breed up your commanders, sergeants, infantry, pilots: breed them all up in a VAT in their hundreds and thousands and millions, choose your battlefield over a glass of port, then set these genetic creations against one another in a scrum of real actual violence that left a huge splat of organic soup at the end of the day? After all, Slabs were only genetically bred defects—right? Huge, muscular, far more physically powerful than their cerebrally superior breeders, yes, but created life, unworthy life, a creation that could not think, could not achieve the higher plane of existence where life became deserving of its place. After all, who listened to the screams of a pan of frying mushrooms? Who cared when lettuce was mushed in a frenzy of salad massacre?

But the Slabs had rebelled. Slabs were not as stupid as their masters first thought. And the C *Class*, as it became known, masterminded the Christmas Uprisings where a hundred thousand Slabs in full battle dress, armed with 2070 Kalashnikovs and driving tanks given to them by their masters, turned on and slaughtered nearly sixty thousand settlers, gameplayers, reviewers and (some would say deserving) hypocritics. It was a day of blood and hell: a day of retribution that left the Slabs with their own democracy, government, and seat on the Galactic Parliament.

Now Slabs were used throughout the Quad-Gal as hired muscle. They were powerful, awesomely aggressive, but didn't really think too much, which suited many employers down to the ground.

"I hope they're friendly," murmured Pippa.

"So do I. They're a bastard to put down."

Both remembered Franco emptying a full fifty-two round clip into one crazed Slab professor from the University of Central-Quad during a pleasure cruise through the Orgas Cluster; Combat-K had been on covert ops, in place to protect a rich Quad-Gal senator, his wife and seven (multi-ethnic, multi-alien) concubines. Somebody had put chemicals in the Slab's B&S during a tuxedo dinner, which in turn sent the pumped-up steroidal lunatic on an insane rampage. Franco had to cut the Slab's damn head off before it would stop its terrifying onslaught.

"Don't worry," smiled Rebekka, attempting to disarm a rising tension that greased the air, "they are for our protection—especially the Slabs—and not here to rip you off. We're carrying a lot of expensive stock. If we assassinated every prospective buyer then we'd never get any return business, would we?"

The rain had stopped again, but still clouds bunched like gnarled hardwoods, brown and grey, and swirled with copper. Keenan breathed deeply, eyes scanning the line of mercenaries and criminals; they were a rag-tag band and Keenan didn't trust them as far as he could spit.

Rebekka approached a huge man with an Uzi II.

"I don't like this," said Pippa from the corner of her mouth. "This amount of hardware is way too convenient."

"We're buying illegally: stolen military kit. Be patient."

Keenan approached Rebekka, as a huge mercenary turned cold dead eyes on Keenan. His instinct was to put a bullet in the man's skull. "Come on." Rebekka smiled encouragingly, and moved to a large steel container lit by bare bulbs from ceiling ridges. Keenan glanced around, breath frosting for a moment. A strange silence settled over the place. It reminded Keenan of... a tomb.

He followed Rebekka inside, where the container was lined with shelves and stacked high with weapons. Pippa, her gun held in the open, stayed close.

Rebekka moved to a low table on which a small computer flickered. She typed fast, and text scrolled up the screen. "Your shopping list," she said. "I hope we can do business again. Please feel free to check every item. There is no hurry. We are quite secure here."

Keenan glanced around. The walls were lined with pistols, machine pistols, machine guns, bombs, grenades, mines, heavy mortar weapons, technical rifles, sniper rifles, flak suits, KJ suits, electronic WarSuits, packs, boots, clothing, and a hundred items of military minutiae right down to the EBH: the Emergency Bobble Hat. Keenan stalked the shelves, eyes scanning the stock of equipment. He smiled at Pippa.

"Looks good," he said.

She gave a nod, but did not return his smile. She was tense; too tense.

Does she sense it too? thought Keenan.

Suddenly, guns roared outside the steel container, deafening even within its confines, and Keenan, Pippa and Rebekka all flinched, dropping to defensive crouches. Keenan shot Rebekka a scowl, just as bullets scythed through the container's walls, screaming through steel, cutting shafts through the dust and leaving tracers of pale evening light.

Keenan turned; Pippa's Makarov touched the back of Rebekka's head and jabbed, hard.

"Bitch."

"It's not what it looks like," hissed Rebekka through gritted teeth.

"Slow down!" snapped Keenan. A chopper smashed overhead. More automatic guns roared; then came the distinctive *whine* of miniguns. Keenan launched himself across the chamber, hammering into Pippa and Rebekka and taking all three of them to the ridged ground. Bullets screamed through the container punching fist-sized holes in the steel on streams of superheated air. Keenan scrambled towards the doors, just as a Slab cart-wheeled past the opening, body torn open spraying blood, suit holed, head exploding in a shower of bone and brain gristle. Screams echoed. More guns whined and then came several double blast *slams* of a shotgun. Keenan swallowed, throat dry, trying to work out what the hell was going on, and where the enemy was.

The container doors slammed shut, and bolted from the outside.

"Shit."

"This isn't part of the plan," said Rebekka. Her face was ashen, staring up from the floor. Her fine long dress seemed suddenly tattered, abused. "Please believe me, it's none of my doing!"

"I say we kill her," snarled Pippa, gun still covering the prostrate proxer.

"No."

Keenan, cool now, brain ticking fast and with Techrim in his fist, moved to one of the holes in the wall. Outside, he could see nothing. He glanced up, hearing the smash of the chopper in the distance. It banked.

"He's coming back. You two move to the corner, away from the explosives." Pippa cursed, suddenly realising the vulnerability of their predicament. If a stray shot hit a grenade, mine, cluster-bomb or HighJ, they were, quite literally, going to be blown apart: dog meat, porno spaghetti, as they said in the squads.

"Kee, what we gonna do?"

Keenan was at the container doors. They were locked, and he rattled them. Overhead, the chopper howled, and again they heard the whine of charging miniguns. Keenan paled. They would be cut in half within an eye-blink!

There was only one thing he could do.

Blow their way out...

He sprinted to the shelf, grabbed a Babe Grenade and within a second was wedging it between steel planks.

"You'll kill us all!" hissed Rebekka, orange eyes wide.

Keenan gave her a sour lop-sided grin...

And pulled the pin.

THREE MINUTES INTO his freedom, Franco entered the nearest Irish bar with a proud sign in Gaelic green. The sign read: *A LONG WAY FROM LIM-ERICK*. It was, apparently, the Irish bar's name, and part of the irrefutable truth that no matter where you find yourself across any world, universe, or galaxy, the first bar you'll always stumble across is an Irish one, which will no doubt serve a fine pint of creamy headed Guinness.

Franco savoured the atmosphere: the warmth, the aromas, the *craic*. He ambled over to the bar, struggled for a moment to find purchase on a high bar stool, placed both elbows in puddles of Tox1C lager, and grinned at the frowning barman.

"A pint of your finest black stuff," said Franco.

"You any ID?" sniffed the barman.

"ID?" Franco was aghast. "I'm forty-two years old!"

"Not for your age. Your import papers."

"No."

"That's OK. It's a pain in the arse filling them forms in anyway, so it is." The barman poured. Franco beamed, licking his lips in anticipation of his first proper pint in years. The Guinness was duly delivered. Franco supped, allowed himself the luxury of a cream moustache, and sighed as several dregs of memory from the Mount Pleasant Hilltop Institution, the "nice and caring and friendly home for the mentally challenged" were washed away on a river of warm fuzzing alcohol.

"You new around here, mister?" asked a clanging metallic voice from his left. Franco turned, head tilted, eyes taking in the old GE model robot. The machine—or AI as it would have preferred to be called—would have probably been a top-end machine in its day. Now it looked as if it had been in the wars; all panels were dented, scuffed, scratched and battered. One arm had been welded with an irregular emergency repair, and one leg was slightly longer than the other. The GE's head was not quite straight, listing effortlessly to one side. The bright purple eyes hissed within its head-shell, and Franco rubbed his bearded chin.

"I thought everybody around here was new," he said, cautiously.

"Could be so, could be so." The old GE picked up a small glass that contained what looked like used engine oil, complete with iron-filings and sludge.

"Why, are *you* new around here?"

"Been here a week. Waiting for an old friend to show up," said the GE amiably. "The name's Louis. I'm an old Razor-droid."

Franco raised his eyebrows. The Razor-droids were indeed an old breed, but were also as tough as they came, from before a time when the great Japanese Robotics Corp, VWAS and NanoTek introduced legislation to tone down the inherently violent and awesomely destructive capabilities of some of their top-end models. Razor-droids were built for off-world war. They could survive in any climate. They could adapt most household items into terrible weapons of mass destruction. And they had no empathy chips, which meant their grip on AI status was tenuous; which in turn also made them twitchy, and tetchy. Back in barracks during Combat-K training, Franco's old instructor, Sergeant DDB, had once commented, "Don't ever underestimate a Razor-droid. Tough little bastards, they are. Skewer you with your own pencil as much as look at you." Franco had never met one, until now.

"Nice to meet you, Louis." Franco shook the robot's metallic appendage. "Can I buy you a drink?"

"I'm OK for now. Thanks for the offer. Very much appreciated."

Hmm. Seems polite enough, thought Franco, and sank the rest of his Guinness in one; he ordered another, and made a dent in it with a single gulp. "By God that tastes fine," he said, slapping his lips. "Makes me glad to escape from prison!"

"Prison, you say?"

Franco coughed. "Just a manner of speech. More of a, y'know, mental institution."

Louis laughed, a tinny metallic sound, and watched Franco finish his second Guinness and order two more. They were delivered. They were devoured.

Franco grinned, some would say, like a maniac.

* * *

THIRTY MINUTES AND fourteen pints of Guinness later, Franco was swaying on his stool as he recounted his break from the Mount Pleasant Hilltop Institution, the "nice and caring and friendly home for the mentally challenged". He swayed left and right, and mimed the act of thumping several times in close rhythm. "Yeah, I punched that bastard Betezh in the mush, and he squealed like a chicken, and I said, I said, I did I said, 'Take that you dastardly Dr. Betezh bastard, that's for all those electrolicles on my testoids', you hear what I'm saying?" The surrounding group of entertained punters nodded, indeed hearing exactly what Franco was saying. It would have been hard to ignore the ginger tornado.

The door to the bar opened at that moment, allowing a free flow of toxic air to rush inside. A figure stepped through the portal dripping with rain, and the interruption broke the flow of Franco's considerably exaggerated retelling.

Franco squinted towards the door. It was filled by a stocky figure, silhouetted against a background of clover leaf. The figure shook rain free of a leather cape and hung it on a nearby peg.

Franco suddenly realised Louis the Razor-droid was by his side. Close, intimately close, like a lover.

"My friend," said Louis, by way of explanation.

And into the light stepped the bullet shaved head, the shark gaze, the powerful pendulum arms... of Dr. Betezh. Franco gasped. Betezh smiled: a nasty smile, a shark's grin, in fact.

"Said we'd find you, didn't I, you little maggot," breathed Betezh. And suddenly Franco was in the grip of the GE Razor-droid, Louis. Steel claws locked Franco's arms more effectively than any police handcuffs; his arms became rigid within a simple, elegant, robotic cage.

The circle of punters widened. It was turning into quite an entertaining evening.

"I'm not going back," said Franco.

Betezh pulled free a long hypodermic. A tiny squirt of amber fluid ejected from the tip.

"Oh, I think you are, my boy," he said.

And advanced.

CHAPTER 6
RED ZONE

KEENAN SPRINTED FOR safety, grabbing a pile of flak jackets and diving towards the two women. They huddled in a heap beneath the protective clothing as two things happened simultaneously. Instead of an unleashing of mini-gun rounds, there was a solid *clank* from above the container and it shuddered, like some great creature in the throes of extinction. Then the Babe Grenade detonated. Fire billowed and screamed, and shrapnel smashed out in all directions. Behind their huddle of flak jackets, Keenan, Pippa and Rebekka heard a pattering of thuds as the shrapnel was absorbed. Chemical heat washed over them, scorching hair and searing little bits of exposed flesh. The container shuddered again, and Keenan kicked free the protective jackets, holed and smoking, and was canted forward as the container lurched, picked bodily up and hauled high into the neon sky. The container's ridged floor suddenly tipped to become a violent slope, and the doors—now blasted open—swung wide revealing a fast disappearing landscape. Everything on the shelves began to slide, and Pippa grabbed Keenan, hauling him back with a grunt so he could grab a steel strut. Then the chopper righted itself, the container levelled, and the world disappeared in a swathe of heavy cloud.

Wind blasted inside, chilling them.

Hailstones smashed the flying container.

"What the hell is happening?" growled Keenan, rounding on Rebekka.

"I don't know! I swear!" She held her hands up in supplication. "We've been attacked! They must have been scoping us, checking us out for a heist. Why would I want to have my own damn men killed?"

"Or maybe you led somebody to us?" snapped Pippa.

"Why, who the fuck are you? I don't know you!" There was pleading in Rebekka's voice and tears in her eyes. Her flesh was pale. Her hands were shaking.

Pippa prodded her with the Makarov. "I say we waste her."

Keenan shook his head. "No. If this is a gang rape then she may come in useful; after all, she brought us to this place." He gave a smile, full of teeth. "If she is party to any conspiracy, then she may be a useful bartering tool."

Rebekka grabbed Keenan's arm. "I swear to you. I had nothing to do with this. I carry out five or six deals like this every month; three times in the past we've had criminals try to take us down. Or maybe this is the work of rogue terrorists from one of the Syndicates in need of a few free weapons. My men are—were—good men, tough. Out there, they were cut down like wheat."

"Not easy to fight off a mini-gun," observed Pippa dryly. Her Makarov still targeted Rebekka's head.

Rebekka turned, dark hair whipping. "Hey, let me tell you something. They may have looked like scumbag mercenaries, but they were loyal to me and they did their jobs well. Some had wives, families, so don't be flapping your mouth like a bitch just because your man was making eyes at me."

"My man?" Pippa snarled.

"If you took care of things at the home nest, his hand wouldn't be sliding up my leg. You understand what I'm saying?"

"Keenan is not my man."

"Then your chemistry lies."

"Girls, girls! Calm down." Keenan waved them into silence, and ignored Pippa's menacing looks. Overhead, the chopper clattered and they dropped in a series of jerks, the floor of the suspended container rocking violently, until they fell from the pall of heavy cloud cover, and below spread the ocean, or what would have been the ocean if it hadn't been industrialised. A fifty lane highway soared beneath them, a glittering crescent of emerald steel-tarmac a hundred feet above the waves. It swayed gently, rippling almost like a slow-motion snake, altering its floatation stance with the undulation of the waves. Around this tributary stood buildings, skyscrapers; some were built down into the roots of the ocean, and rose like glittering fingers of glass pointing accusingly at the heavens. Myriad squat blocks of tenements and shops, car parks and malls all spread like some frothy scum across the ocean surface. As night had started to fall, lights glittered through the dusk. The one obvious omission from the surface of the ocean was, well, the ocean itself. The City had spread and conquered, even across the sea.

"Do you recognise our location?" asked Keenan.

Rebekka nodded, hair floating around her head in the slipstream of their travel. She shuffled forward, peering carefully from the flapping, banging steel doors. Her boots trod crushed blackened shrapnel. Her eyes were filled with a sadness that made Keenan lick his lips. *I thought proxers had diluted emotions?* he mused.

"Yeah, Red Zone. Home of the Razor Syndicate."

Across the sprawling metropolis that was The City, seven ruling underworld factions fought for supremacy in—whilst not exactly illegal trade— what could sometimes be considered immoral business. The Seven Syndicates were notorious. From gun-running to prostitution, child smuggling, off-world bleeding, extortion, designer drugs, piracy and hacking, espionage, digital embezzlement; if there was money to be made, one of the Seven Syndicates had it covered. They had ranks, they were so large. They had players. And if The City had possessed such a thing as a stable government, the Syndicates would have bought it. The fact that there were seven, all battling for ever-increasing slices of the pie, meant a sort of equilibrium had developed; and although it was a violent equilibrium based on guns and death, the Syndicates had become a kind of self-policing criminal justice system, only without the legality (farcical though it could be) of the courts, and a 9mm round as the only agreed sentencing tactic.

"I thought the Syndicates were spread thinly across the entire planet?" said Pippa.

"Yes," nodded Rebekka, "but each has a core, or concentrated core that not even police or SIMS would venture into. It looks like we're heading to the central offices of Razor; for you, and me, this is not a good proposition."

"I think she knows more," said Pippa.

"About the Syndicates?" Rebekka laughed a cold laugh. "Oh yeah, I know enough to understand that once you enter this place, it's rare you leave again, as a free person, or as a live one. They must have been watching us; watching our deals for some time. Shit. I thought we had this angle covered."

"What do you mean?" asked Keenan.

"Every transaction has to pay an unauthorised fee to a Syndicate for—ha—protection. You know the score, standard mafia extortion bullshit. We were operating an illegal outfit; we paid no kickbacks, and had a floating centre of operations; fuckers didn't even know we existed. Or so I thought, until now."

"Penalties?"

"Extermination," said Rebekka, eyes locked on Keenan. Then her gaze moved to the stacks of hardware that lined the shelves, sliding and moving, jiggling and rattling during this swinging, pendulous journey. "I could always fight my way out."

"Trained soldier, are you?" Pippa's voice dripped poisoned honey.

"I've done my bit," said Rebekka. "I know how to slot a hundred and fifty-two round micro-clip into an MPK. And I know how to put a round in the back of a venomous bitch's cuckolded skull."

"I'm the one with the gun," said Pippa. Her Makarov nudged, aligning with Rebekka's eyes. "And I don't take kindly to your insinuation. So shut your mouth before I shoot you through the teeth. I won't warn you again."

"Pippa!" snapped Keenan, "Focus. We're coming in to land."

A huge skyscraper, a kilometre high, reared from the surging ocean, which frothed and churned at its base. No roads or walkways led to the edifice; the walls were slick silver alloy without windows. The building gleamed in the rising gloom.

Rebekka gave a little sigh of fear, of resignation. It convinced Keenan of her innocence. She wore defeat like a cloak.

The chopper carrying them started a long lazy spiral of descent towards the skyscraper's rooftop. Below, they could see a wide platform; around the edges of the tower were arched panels, all converging towards a central point. Several of these had slid back revealing a temporary hole and landing area for the chopper. Men with guns stood in ranks, neat and to attention. Keenan squinted, but did not recognise their military-style uniforms. As they closed, Keenan's eyes also picked out mounted Mercury Cannons, a single shot from which could disintegrate the steel container in which they were, effectively, trapped.

"You see them?" said Pippa.

"Oh yes," smiled Keenan. "They have us well covered."

The container lowered through the gap and touched down with a *clang,* first one edge, then slowly lowering to a level platform. Keenan's nose twitched. He could smell hot oil, and burnt metal. He had counted perhaps a hundred men—soldiers?—on the descent.

A voice boomed. "Mr. Keenan, Pippa, so nice of you to join us. Please, step out of your cage."

"That answers that question," said Keenan.

"They were after us," nodded Pippa.

"And no funny business, please," said the booming voice. "After all, I am sure you were witness to our awesome firepower on your rather uncouth descent. Please, do not be alarmed. We proffer no immediate violence."

Keenan stepped free, and tossed his Techrim onto the smooth black floor. A wind howled distantly. Keenan looked up at the sky as the chopper disengaged from the container, lifted, banked, and disappeared into the falling gloom.

Huge arched panels slid smoothly back into place. The sky vanished. They were sealed, as if in a tomb.

"Welcome to my humble abode," said the man, stepping forward. He was tall, with a slender frame. He looked to be early sixties, white hair thinning against the prominent skull of a pointed face. He had bare feet, and loose, baggy, black clothing, and he carried a pistol levelled at Keenan's face.

He smiled.

"Keenan," he breathed, "it's been such a long time."

"I don't know you," said Keenan.

"You do, although I looked different back then. A billion dollars of surgery have worked their wonders. But it was you who killed my brother," said the man, simply, eyes glittering with a reined-in malice. "And it would be my pleasure to return the favour."

FRANCO'S GAZE WAS fixed, immovable, on that simple hypodermic. Within that glistening tube of psycho drugs lay the queuing horrors of Franco's worst demons, worst fears, worst living nightmare hell. Franco had been incarcerated in Mount Pleasant because of these drugs; it would take a miracle of strength to return him there.

Franco went slack. It was a trick he had used often at Mount Pleasant, something the guards and mental nurses had become familiar with. The GE Razor-droid, however, was not a guard, nor a mental nurse, and had no experience with the subtleties of deranged patients; even after they had quaffed a bucketful of Guinness.

Louis, feeling its prisoner relax, loosened the rigid grip. After all, what good was a prisoner when you'd cut off the blood supply to his arms, promoted necrotic flesh and necessitated amputation? Not the desired effect... unless torture was on the cards.

Betezh came so close that Franco could smell garlic. Franco's eyes swivelled up. The needle descended.

Flexing, Franco's boot lashed up and the hypodermic flew from Betezh's hand, up into the air, and Betezh looked back just in time to get the flat of Franco's boot square on the nose. Betezh gasped, stumbling back, scattering stools. The syringe spun, end over end, droplets of fluid dripping and pattering to the floor. Then, like a rocket returning to Earth, it fell, point first, again to connect with Franco's well aimed boot-strike. It shot true as an arrow and entered Betezh's open howling mouth, embedding at the back of his throat.

Betezh gagged.

Franco threw a backwards head-butt, which had little effect on the old GE Razor-droid; however, some locals, deciding this was something of an unfair fight, had picked up pool cues and advanced on the GE. Louis heard a rattling sound of quick successive strikes, and with a blink realised it was four cues pounding his battered cranium. He released his grip on Franco. Never one to fail to capitalise on a situation, Franco charged with a scream. Betezh, still choking, threw his arms up in defence as Franco delivered a thundering right, straight to Betezh's groin, and felt testicles compress agonisingly under his great flat knuckles. Dropping to one knee, again he pounded Betezh's groin, then kicked out, cracking Betezh's left knee-cap with a *snap* of dry wood.

Betezh fell, sending the remaining stools toppling to the floor. His hands grappled to pull free the syringe embedded in the back of his throat. He curled into a foetal position, gurgling, as Franco danced around drunkenly, cheering himself on.

"I win! I win!" cheered Franco, as something flat and metal struck the back of his head, lifted him from the ground and sent him crashing over the bar, where he rolled and cannoned into stacks of whisky bottles, bringing the whole shelving system raining down, around and on top of him. Bottles clonked and smashed off his head. Broken glass scattered like confetti. Franco groaned, but even in red-hot poker-searing agony his fingers somehow found a fifty year-old single malt and popped the cork. He took a long, long draught. He shook his head, and tenderly probed the back of his skull where a lump the size of a tennis ball was rising.

"Son of a bitch."

He climbed to his feet, frowning. The Irish bar was in a state of devastation. The pool table was a broken V, with four unconscious locals draped untidily across torn green felt. The GE, Louis, stood with metal hands on metal hips. Betezh was whimpering in a ball amongst tinder.

Franco threw the bottle, which Louis dodged, then another, and another, and a fourth. The GE's arm flashed up to deflect the whisky vessel, which shattered, showering the robot in finest malt.

"I only wanted a quiet drink!" howled Franco. "Why can't you bastards leave me alone?"

He threw another bottle, groping around in the broken glass behind the bar and slicing his fingers, and then another, which also smashed, allowing amber to wash over the Razor-droid.

"It's going to be a pleasure squashing you, little man," said the battered old droid.

Franco shrugged, eyes dropping to the counter where a cigar burned steadily in an ashtray. Franco reached forward, almost casually, lifted the cigar and took a long casual puff on the fine Trigon II smoke. Then, almost lazily, he flicked the brown weed at Louis... who realised a millisecond too late that he was soaked in Scotland's finest fifty year-old flammable.

WHOOSH!

Flames roared up and over and about the Razor-droid, and Louis turned and sprinted for the rain, straight through the door, leaving splinters and twisted spirals of smoking steel in his wake. Franco heaved himself onto the bar, and then dropped to the floor with a simple thud. He was deflated, weary, his bout of Guinness and a good rumble leaving him ready for a sleep. Then he saw Betezh, still whimpering. The man had withdrawn the syringe and held it in baby fingers. Franco dropped to his knees and stared into Betezh's eyes.

"You hurt me," said Franco, simply.

Betezh nodded. "It was my job."

"You fucking Nazi bureaucrat. What kind of answer is that?" he slurred. "We was playing a game: I try to escape, you try to stop me. It's the comedy game prisoners have played for centuries. There was no need to get so... personal."

Betezh scowled, anger and brute-force stubbornness seeping through his agony. "It's personal,

Franco, because it had to be personal. You weren't just a job, no, you were an assignment!"

Franco grabbed Betezh's arm and dragged up the tight sleeve. There, tattooed on the doctor's wrist, was the tiniest of military script symbol: the mark of Combat-K. Franco reeled, stunned more than any alcohol or violence could deliver. "You're one of us!" he screamed, shock battering him like a hammer. Then, more quietly, more focused, "You're Combat-K."

Betezh, although in pain, allowed a glimmer of triumph to shine through. "You were betrayed," he spat, "condemned by your own. So stop fucking whimpering and accept the fact that you were never wanted. You were an embarrassment. You became expendable."

"Expendable?" growled Franco, feeling a rage well within him greater than anything he had ever felt. Here was another Combat-K special forces soldier removing every shred of honour Franco had ever possessed; here was a brother telling Franco he was no longer a brother; here was a fellow CK squaddie telling Franco he *did not belong*. "I'll give you fucking expendable." He wrenched the syringe from Betezh's fingers and lifted it high in the air.

The Irish bar's punters, those still conscious, watched with held breath. Their eyes were fixed on the hypodermic. The needle fell, slamming Betezh's skull and punching through bone.

Franco injected Betezh with the drugs, direct to the brain.

He watched light dance in Betezh's eyes, which faded to a slack, meaningless nothing.

A hush descended on the public house.

Franco's nostrils twitched. He could smell scorched steel.

He glanced right, to where a small hunched man with a flat cap and chunks of hair sprouting from his nostrils still held his pint of Guinness in rough working-class hands. The man gave Franco a weak but rugged smile.

"That droid. It's behind me, right?" said Franco.

The hairy man gave a single nod.

"God, I need my tablets, especially the yellow ones!"

The hairy man said nothing.

Franco whirled… into the *smack* of a pool cue.

And he remembered no more.

"I KNOW YOU. You're McEvoy, aren't you?" said Pippa, pushing past Keenan. She still held her Makarov, but submissively. That could soon change.

The old man smiled, showing square coffee-stained teeth. "Yes, Pippa my dear."

"Oh." Keenan's face had tumbled into a frown. "McEvoy. That piece of unholy shit." His eyes fixed in an iron bar stare. "I remember you, mate, you were prettier before the blade."

"Yeah," Pippa nodded. "He's been on the cover of *TIME* magazine. Regular media chaser, aren't you McEvoy? The sort of maggot who likes the sound of his own burrowing. Especially into rotten meat."

"You do flatter me so, Pippa. *Drop your weapon.*"

Behind him Keenan suddenly became aware of sub-machine guns raised. The private army was no longer dormant; it was active. A clanking echoed across the hall as a GG AI strode purposefully forward, metal feet ringing, hands flexing almost uncontrollably as if in some parody of a human ailment.

There came a *shring* and the GG held a Sliver Sword, forged from a single molecule and deadly enough to cut armoured hull steel. The GG halted beside McEvoy, blade tip towards the ground and unnaturally still. Pippa's eyes had followed the tip of that blade, then locked on the black eyes of the robot.

She dropped her gun with a clatter.

"Good girl," said McEvoy. He seemed to relax a little, although he had not seemed unduly apprehensive. The tension in the air settled like ash. Keenan looked squarely at Pippa.

"How can you know him?" asked Rebekka, voice soft.

Pippa nodded. "When we pulled that job in New Prague helping the refugees after their fifty-year civil war; this fucker supplied TASK-K with the seeding apparatus. Only it was untested, a pirate-breed concoction of alien toxins that didn't help the people, but instead caused a mass poisoning of millions. We were sent after the bastard. He fled in an ASP Fighter, which Keenan shot down. It ploughed into the city, pulping its inhabitants like mashed cat food." She glanced from Rebekka back to McEvoy and smiled sweetly. "I hear they had to scrape your brother from the floor with a shovel and pile him neatly in a bodysack. They incinerated the worthless piece of garbage as an act of cleansing; after all, he was nothing more than a diseased avatar."

McEvoy disengaged from his casual air. Sobriety etched his face like acid. "So, Mr. Keenan, you see my motive for wanting a little chat. Although I am under no misconception that Pippa here is just as guilty; guilt by proxy, shall we say?"

He glanced to the GG; it was a new machine, black matt alloy and gleaming. "Did you find him?"

"Yes." The AI spoke in the usual clipped format of the AI; trying to be human, but not quite getting it right. "Too human to be human", ran the marketing motto, and they were probably right. "We have him targeted. Will bring him in when the moment is right. He's in a politically unstable region and with the upcoming Magu Elections we don't want to stir up trouble in different zones. We'll do it with discretion."

"Good lad." McEvoy glanced at Keenan, and waved to Rebekka who was peeping out from the battered container. "Ahh, my little Miss Kobayashi, so nice of you to join us. Our timing was not quite right; you were supposed to die with your crew. Your underground illegal exploits have not gone unnoticed by the Syndicate, and your slap on the wrist is long overdue."

Rebekka visibly paled. She said nothing, just stood with arms limp by her lithe sides.

Three tiny prisoners came out of nowhere.

All three were struck with liquid darts; within half a second their legs folded beneath them and they collapsed. McEvoy strode to stand above Keenan, staring down at his drug-slack features. "It'll be a shame to exterminate you," he acknowledged. His eyes moved to Pippa. "And you, my pretty little bag of damaged goods."

But then, he mused, a dark smile touching his lips as he considered the incurable cancer that was eating parasitically through his own bones... death comes to us all, does it not?

FRANCO OPENED ONE eye and peered beadily about. Everything was quiet. That was good. Nobody was inflicting violence on him, even better! *And* he wasn't covered in vomit! Rasta Billy!

Then he tried to move his hands. He was tied to a metal chair.

"Bugger."

A quick succession of command scripts rioted through his brain. Where am I? What happened? Why can I taste sour Guinness? Then he remembered: Cam, right-hook, rain, bar, Louis, Betezh, violence, skull-injection, pool cue. Ahh, he thought.

"Bugger."

The hotel room—and it was quite obviously a hotel room—was nice, in a kind of cosy, middle-class, flowery wallpapered Sunday-afternoon sort of way. Outside, the binary rain had stopped and beams of sunlight filtered through chinks in the curtains. Franco tried to rock the chair, but it was immovable. He tried to free his hands, tight behind his back, but the raze-wire dug deep and he stopped immediately. A man could sever his hands with that evil shit. The more you pulled, the more it bit. And, like a rabid bulldog dangling from your tackle, it wasn't coming off without a fight.

Franco examined his surroundings with more care: flowery thick carpet, in need of a vacuum; flowery faded wallpaper, in need of a sponging; bed, wide, crumpled, in need of fifteen naked whores. Calm yourself, he thought. Gods, too long in Mount Pleasant! Ironically, the thing Franco *most needed* was a pleasant mount.

Instead, he got Betezh.

The door clicked shut, and Betezh limped forward, composure regained, leg strapped tight with bone-bolts. A tiny red dot on his forehead indicated Franco's previous skull violation. Betezh looked to be in a foul mood, truly bad tempered.

Behind Franco there came a *click,* a *hiss,* and a hydraulic *whirr.* Franco realised Louis the Razordroid had been sitting behind him all the time, probably with a gun to his head. Franco strained to see, but couldn't make the turn. An owl, he was not.

"Well, well, well."

"Betezh," said Franco, "you are not an über-villain. Only über-villains say 'well, well, well'. What you are is a sad old doctor, balding, plump round the middle from far too many jammy donuts, you never get your little Roger into mischief, and—let's be totally honest and upfront here—you've probably started looking at young boys, like the sad old paedophile fuckwit you are. Now, be a good lad and take off the raze-wire, will you?"

Despite the insults, Betezh smiled. He looked sombre. Franco took this as a bad sign.

"Franco, lad, I've got a few simple questions. No threats, this time. Just give me some simple answers."

"OK," nodded Franco, warily, wondering when the pain would begin. He had played this sort of game before, many times.

"How much do you remember?"

"Well, I did have fourteen pints of Guinness," began Franco but Betezh waved him into silence.

"No. Let's regress. Do you recall your entry to Mount Pleasant?"

"No. You pumped me full of toxic shit, don't *you* remember?"

"Ahh. So you don't remember…" He glanced at the GE, and seemed to consider his next words with utmost care. "You don't remember receiving any… visitors?"

"No."

"Good."

"Except for that woman."

Betezh sighed. "Go on. Describe her."

"Small, athletic, well-dressed, nice tits."

"Is that all?"

Franco tilted his head. Memories were hazy.

"Other than nice tits?" He thought hard. "She had green lips," he said at last, "and I remember having seen her before, on TV. Some kind of politician, I think. Scumbags the lot of 'em. Only interested in lining their own personal bank vaults."

"So you *do* remember." Betezh seemed concerned. "Shit."

"Yeah. I dreamt about her, a lot. Had some really good dreams about her, God, what a screamer she was, clawing me like an animal... Then she had me perform a series of missions; after all I was in a Combat Squad, I was Combat-K and I was the best, yeah? She had me do all sorts of stuff, infiltration, assassination, bomb-planting; shit, they were good dreams, the best, mate. I forgot about those. They used to get me through the long nights at Mount Pleasant; those fantasies stopped me from going—aha—insane."

Franco glanced up, but Betezh wasn't looking at him, he was gazing out between the slitted curtains. He sighed, a deep sigh, shaking his bullet head.

Betezh looked down at Franco. There were tears in his eyes.

"And you don't remember us, do you?"

Franco frowned. "Well, quite frankly I'm flattered, but I don't remember you leaving flowers or chocs, if that's what you mean. And I certainly don't remember any incident of rearward entry, and if you're going to try and tell me we are long lost gay lovers then I need to inform you I've had a severe case of piles and it must have been quite an unpleasant experience." Franco beamed, in a nasty kind of way. His eyes were gleaming. He could sense fast-approaching danger.

"You never stop joking, do you?"

"It's what keeps me sane, dickhead."

"I trained with you, Franco. We were mates."

Franco frowned. "No, I..."

Fog clouded his past. He swallowed, and realised his throat was dry.

"I've tried hard to keep you alive. God knows, I tried, with the drugs, and the treatment. They were supposed to work. But you remember; you remember too much."

He nodded past Franco. The Razor-droid pressed a gun to the back of Franco's head.

Franco's eyes met Betezh's; and he was shocked, truly shocked, to see compassion there: hurt, pain. A memory sliced Franco's brain with scalpel precision: a pub, a million miles away and a billion light-years ago. Laughing, drinking, lounging over a high bar of waxed wood after a... mountain climb, that's right, a rescue mission against the side of a mammoth hulking squat mountain of death; then, drunk, glancing right at the pretty girls, gee they're looking real fine in their tight blouses and short skirts with legs all the way up to their bottoms then back; left, to the two men, two men in the Combat-K squad and they were heroes: heroes to the local people heroes to all the local girls, and one of them had a bullet shaved head and shark eyes, and he slapped Franco on the back and roared with laughter and it was Betezh...

"No," whispered Franco. His head tilted.

Strangeness injected his veins.

"Goodbye," said Betezh, and gave a single, curt nod.

IT WAS A good dream, the best dream, the sort of dream you wish was never over, and the sort of dream far more real than real could ever be: too perfect. A white sand beach rolled away for eternity. A turquoise ocean lapped tentatively and deposited pink shells like gifts offered from a submissive God. Palm fronds tickled the edge of the beach, and the place was untouched; perfect, intimate, a holy place. Pippa ran towards him wearing just shorts and a white T-shirt. Her long tanned legs shone, her face was a picture of happiness, her shoulder-length black hair was tied back with twine woven from tree bark and she...

She sparkled.

"Kee!" she was shouting, "I found some, look, I found some!" In her hands she carried a collage of small fruits—rare through the Quad-Gal—known as Rainbow Fresh. She collapsed in the sand, giggling, and Keenan gazed into her face, and it was that moment, there, then, that click that connection when he fell endlessly in love with her; or realised that he was in love with her... finally allowed his feelings to force their way through the mesh of guilt, and angst, and denial. He stared at her radiance; stared at her purity. And wondered why he hadn't allowed himself to fall for her before.

The answer was clear; as obvious as sin.

His wife... his daughters... but they were a long way gone, billions of miles across emptiness and spiral trails of frozen hydrogen; and yet, it was deeper, despite the physical distance. Freya had become cold since the birth of their daughters, cold and strange, almost alien to him. A different woman; a different person to the one he had met... and fallen in love with. Had it been merely age? A progression of years? A diversifying of personalities as time passed? Or had it been more? Some other, more subtle (or maybe obvious, only Keenan was too damned blind to see it) trait that hid away from him deep down in a dark place, punishing him with his own stupidity? Whatever the reason, he and Freya had grown apart, far apart, and by mutual consent. They no longer shared a bed. It was a cold bed since the birth of the girls, no longer shared intimacy, and no longer acted effectively as man and wife... even lovers... *Yeah and that makes it all right does it fucker? Find some new meat new skirt, new pussy and watch the dribble roll down your fucking chin. Yeah, just like a sniffer dog with a foot long erection poking from your stained pants as you go on the hunt for fresh fuck flesh...*

But... Freya had her own new love interest: discreet, distant, occasional. But there, all the same. Like a family shame: hidden. Hidden, but known. That had been a hard pill to swallow, that knowledge, that information. He had kept it quiet; kept it to himself; for the sake of his family, for the sake of the girls.

Keenan stared into Pippa's eyes. She stumbled into silence.

She reached out, and touched his cheek.

He felt himself fall into her, and some devil took away his control and the situation was lost to him. He fell into Pippa, on that beach on Molkrush Fed, dived into her, and they were kissing, lips brushing, tongues teasing, and he had her head in his hands, kneeling before her in that purity of white sugar, and his heart pounded like an adolescent's and he was lost, lost, lost.

"I didn't expect that," she said, pulling away from his kiss. Sand stuck to her golden skin. Her eyes sparkled.

"Neither did I."

"What is this, Kee?"

"What is what?"

"Stop being evasive."

He grinned. "I'm not evading anything," he evaded.

She slapped his thick bicep, and leant forward, part of her fringe dropping across her forehead. Her hair was slightly damp from a recent swim; her lips were rimmed with salt.

"Do it again," she said.

"What, evade you?"

And they were kissing, touching, easing gently down to the sand. In the distance behind them, the escape pod from the war-destroyed Hunter lay disguised by huge Splay Ferns, which they'd dragged, giggling like children, over the polymer hull. That had been a month ago, followed by a panicked escape after a detonation of rogue AI missiles had taken out their ship. Their entry to the S3 planet had been tense, their landing violent. And now, it would appear, their distress beacon was being either ignored... or worse, the Helix War was lost. They were lost: alone.

Pippa suddenly pulled away. "We might have to spend our lives here," she said.

"OK."

"Together."

"That's fine."

"That would be like... a dream to me."

Keenan looked at her, really looked at her. Deep into her cool grey eyes; eyes he had so long considered the disconnected gaze of a killer. Only now he read the gentleness there, the need, the longing. He saw the love in her eyes and wondered how long he had ignored it. Or suppressed it? After all, there were certain protocols to follow. Combat-K squads were not encouraged to fall in love. They were comrades, brothers-in-arms, no matter what their sex, creed, religion or even species. They were encouraged to think as brothers; even indoctrinated to some extent, the mental stimulations, exercises and drugs reinforcing that effect. Then, of course, there had been his wife... despite her infidelity.

Keenan kissed Pippa. Her response was incredible and he felt wanted, needed, loved. It was something that had been gradually diluted from his life, a colour drained away into bone-bleach black and white without his knowledge, without even his consent. *When had it gone so wrong?* he wondered idly, as Pippa's hand traced down his chest and his hard belly, and rested lightly, teasingly, lingering on his inner thigh. Such thoughts were pulverised from his mind as her hand, moving snail-slow, soothed up the leg of his shorts, undid the button, slid down the glass zip and took him hard. Keenan groaned. His head rolled back. His past, his present, his future; none were of consequence as Pippa gave him the simple thing that all people—ultimately—craved...

The knowledge that he was wanted, needed... and loved.

CHAPTER 7
SYNDICATE WARS

FRANCO TENSED, WAITING for the bullet he knew would come. Everything was in focus; minutiae exploded into mainstream. Beads of sweat trembled on Betezh's forehead. The man's shaved head gleamed. Tiger-stripes of sunlight jigged across his black clothing. Distantly, a kube rattled. Somewhere in the street below, a child laughed, and Franco cringed as he felt life slip between his fingers, like sand draining from the hourglass of time and life, and trickling its last few grains, which pitter-pattered onto the pyramid, sum of all his dreams and ideas and aspirations... and he realised with a massive sadness that there was so much left for him to do: so much to explore, so much to drink, and so much more he could give.

The roof exploded.

Detonations crackled and screamed, spitting chunks of alloy and concrete. Dust poured down in a desert storm like a flood. Fire lashed the sky. Betezh was knocked like a doll across the room by flying masonry, and Franco didn't see what happened to Louis but there was a heavy final clunk. Then the roof, in its entirety, lifted into the air, and only then, Franco heard the *whine* of a stealth-modded industrial chopper. Franco blinked up into falling dust and debris. Huge chunks of H-Section steel twisted and groaned, dangling from the twisted, deformed, detached roof, which shifted and moved to allow watery sunlight to pour through the raining dust. Franco choked, eyes blinking furiously; he tried to nudge and shuffle to safety on his chair.

Rescue! screamed his brain. I'm being rescued! Thank the Lord!

Exo-S clad figures appeared around the jagged concrete rim of the battered hotel, MPK submachine guns pointing into the whirlwind chaos interior. Franco cheered as they leapt onto churned carpets and cut the raze-wire fastening him to the chair.

Franco grinned into chrome-plated masks, seeing the humour of his own face reflected a million times.

"Thanks guys! Who sent you? Keenan? Pippa? Fortune?"

A gun poked viciously in his ribs.

"The human is to put its hands on its head," said the false mechanical voice of the Battle SIM. "Or I shoot it through skull."

"Hey, I thought this was a rescue?"

"No rescue, pep. This is reintegration. Somebody like to see the human, somebody important. It is not to speak. It is not to attempt escape. It is not to be funny wise-guy, OK? Or I will shoot it without prejudice."

Franco stared at the chrome mask. The SIM's mechanical eyes clicked. There was no emotion there, no empathy. But then, how could there be? This was a SIM: a simulant, a false human.

"Shit." He put his hands on his head. "Don't shoot!" He'd seen these trigger happy characters in action; they had no concept of empathy or grades of violence. Their brains were binary. Everything had two states. So: humans were just living... or dead.

They led Franco past the unconscious, slumped body of Betezh, who the SIMs ignored as if he were merely inconvenient crumpled furniture. They led Franco down the hotel stairs and out onto the pavement where a flyer was bobbing.

"Get in."

"OK boss."

"Don't refer to me as boss."

"Are all SIMs so anal?"

There came a long pause. The chrome mask locked on Franco. The gun wavered, moving to an inch in front of Franco's eyes. He could smell cold cordite.

"Hey! Hey, chill out boss! I was only fuckin' witcha!"

"Don't refer to me as boss."

Franco breathed a deep sigh. If only they had worked on the SIM's personalities instead of their physical prowess, maybe they could have made a positive contribution to society.

The flyer hissed, and lifted vertically into a darkening night sky.

KEENAN CAME ROUND to the sound of voices, irate, bickering, and he remained still and silent for a few moments trying to solidify his dreams and thoughts and memories. Razor Syndicate, skyscraper rooftop: *Shit.* Metal bands were fastened tightly around his wrists, and he rubbed them uncomfortably as he listened.

"I don't know what you're talking about."

"It's obvious. You have feelings for him."

"Go to hell."

"You can deny it all you please, but I see it in your actions, your face, your eyes. The way you talk to him, the way you respond to him: your mouth moves and hot air emerges to deny it, but Pippa, you don't even convince yourself."

"When we get out of this cell," spat Pippa, "I will kill you."

"Why?" It was such a simple, innocent response, for a few moments Pippa was lost for words.

"Just keep your damn opinion to yourself."

"Would you object, then, if I took him? Caressed him? Kissed him? Held him? Stroked him? Would it pain you to see me with him? Naked, writhing, oiled under a cold orange strip-light?"

Keenan opened his eyes and sat up. He blinked, shocked by his immediate surroundings, like waking into a nightmare. This was no normal cell; it was a GRILL. "Great," he muttered, not really knowing if he referred to the cell or the audition of two bickering women.

"Back to the land of the living," said Pippa, her voice rimmed with ice.

Keenan nodded.

Rebekka moved close to him, placing her hand on his arm. "Are you OK? You've been out for some time. We were starting to get worried the insta-drugs had penetrated too far. They do that sometimes; leave you in a coma, vegetate you."

"Yeah. I'm fine. I lay for a while. I was listening to your worries."

Pippa reddened, and gestured with her hand. "How the hell are we going to get out of this? This shit? I admit it's kind of you to rescue me from *Hardcore*, Keenan, but at least I had some semblance of freedom there, albeit within controlled boundaries. I could go where I wanted, kill whoever I desired…" She cast a glance at Rebekka, "I could fuck anybody who crossed my path."

Keenan stretched his cramped, aching shoulders. "Girls, girls, save it for the playground, for Christ's sake. Retract your claws. Reclaim your handbags. Shut up."

Uneasy silence filled the cell. Keenan stood and looked carefully about. They were still in the vast rooftop chamber. The floor was gloss black. Above them arched the panels of the retractable roof shields. The GRILL hung, suspended by thick cables from a distant gloomy interior, and within the GRILL was a gently swaying platter. Electronics beneath the platter created bars of almost invisible heat forming the walls of the cell. To cross this threshold would cause a human to be sliced into thick flesh chunks, ready for any BBQ. Hence, GRILL.

The chamber was the entirety of the skyscraper's roof. Although a large clear space occupied most of the centre—a wide chopper landing site—around the rest of the space there were strange angular machines, shrouded in shadows, row upon row of computer workstations, several vehicles with tarpaulins covering their vaguely military shapes; and three gleaming new attack helicopters, dark and foreboding, silent and still. Their guns gleamed with grease. The tinted cockpits stared like insect eyes. Keenan lingered on them for a while, then turned to watch the two women.

"You're a bastard, Keenan." Pippa gave a sardonic smile.

"I'm just the way the world made me." He patted his pockets, and was delighted to find his tobacco case. "God, I need this," he muttered, and rolled himself a thin cigarette with evil black Widow Maker tobacco. He lit up, breathed deep. Nicotine infused his system with toxin. He relaxed, and rubbed again at the metal bands, fashioned from what looked like copper with a dull sheen.

"OK. What's the situation?"

"We're not dead," said Pippa, moving closer and sitting cross-legged before him, "which means they want, or need, something from us. I don't accept they knew we were coming, which means we were either clocked when we landed, or the unthinkable happened."

"Fortune?"

"Yeah. He could have turned us in." Pippa waved away smoke.

"He's always been reliable in the past."

"He may have his reasons. After all, we know where he is, and he'd do anything to avoid detection and subsequent arrest; Fortune is one of those rare AIs who will never die. Would you want to spend an eternity in a Black Hole Holding Cell? A real eternity?"

Keenan nodded. "Let's skip the shit. What can we do now?"

Pippa shrugged, head tilted to one side. Keenan met her gaze coolly. "You're the boss, boss. You work it out."

A hiss of alloy emanated from the other side of the chamber; the GG AI from earlier entered, dragging a small unconscious man. Hydraulics thumped their way across the hall, and the GG stood on a pad, which lifted from the floor, extending on a thin alloy arm to the GRILL cage where they sat, Keenan smoking, eyes appraising the scene with the detachment of controlled anger.

"One of your comrades," said the GG. He did something with a small control, and some of the heat haze from the bars died. Franco was tossed inside and the bars re-emerged instantly.

Pippa rolled Franco to his back. Blood stained his lips and teeth, and bruises painted his face. One eye was swollen. Franco groaned, opened his good eye, and beamed.

"Hey hey! Pippa! Things are looking up!"

The GG retreated, stood for a moment staring strangely at their suspended cell, then disappeared into a brightly lit corridor beyond. Doors slammed. Silence invaded the chamber on a mission.

"Did they get the ship?" said Keenan.

Franco orientated, and sat up with winces and groans. "No. No, I don't think so."

"What happened to Cam?"

Franco winced again, then looked shiftily from side to side. "Hmm... I'm not quite sure, Keenan. I'm a little concussed; don't really remember what happened. But hey did I put up one mean fight! And that bastard bugger Betezh..."

"From back at the hospital?" said Pippa.

Franco nodded. "Yeah. Yeah, that dude. I gave him a proper pounding." He chuckled. "He won't be electrifying my testicles in a hurry!"

"I think we're gonna need some help on this one," said Keenan quietly. He finished his cigarette and flicked the butt at the superheated bars, where it flashed for a nanosecond, disintegrating into nothing.

"Neat," said Franco.

Keenan reached into his mouth and began to fiddle.

"What you doing?" asked Franco.

"He's got a transmitter and micro-kube fitted in one of his teeth," said Pippa. "The only problem is, once activated the criminals may well detect the frequency. Or maybe the roof above us blocks all signals, even military. Either way, it's a calculated risk, but we seem to have little option. It also has integrated files and army DBs on criminals and data through the Quad-Gal."

"So, it's his wisdom tooth?" Franco congratulated himself.

"Yeah yeah, quick, Franco, quick."

There was a tiny click. "Cam, you reading me?" said Keenan, voice low. "Cam, come in, we're in the shit and could do with assistance. Over."

They waited.

Nothing.

"Maybe I was right," said Pippa. "This place looks like a fortress from the outside; proper high-spec polymer alloy shells. Last thing the Razor Syndicate needs is prisoners radioing for help from the outside world. They seem to be the controlling factor here on The City and they're not amateurs; they must have the tek to render us incommunicado."

"This is the latest hardware," said Keenan, rubbing his forehead. "It's not usually cracked for at least three months, and even then the hackers sometimes screw it up. And—believe me—I'm regular with updates, to an anal degree."

"Maybe they captured Cam, then?"

Keenan nodded. "Or maybe the damn thing's injured, or something?"

Franco kept strangely silent, staring at the floor. He coughed, and started to hum a little tune.

The GG returned, carrying a sheaf of metal papers. "Here we go," muttered Pippa, as the platform lifted smoothly and glided through the vast chamber towards the cell.

The GG, dark eyes glowing, eyed the captured group.

"Pippa," it said, simply.

"Yeah, fuckwit?"

"I thought I knew of you. You were a prisoner on *Hardcore*. News of your exploits has reached me.

Many of my friends—from my production batch—ended up on *Hardcore*. I believe you have... met, many of them."

"Met them, danced with them, slaughtered them," smiled Pippa easily, moving from her cross-legged position to standing. She scraped back her hair and tied it. She licked her lips, making them wet. "I just hate the stink of your metal skin, if the truth be known. I can't stand your arrogance, your base stupidity, and your aspirations of superiority over the humans who created you."

"So you hate my kind?" said the GG. The metal face, swept back into a hook above the long metal head, was emotionless. Tiny pistons moved the jaws but no sounds emerged. The GG relaxed its stance with a hiss of hydraulics.

"Yeah, dickhead, with extreme prejudice."

"Funny, really," said the GG, "because the feeling is reciprocated."

There was a *buzz* and Pippa's metal wrist-bands locked together. The bars shimmered and the GG gestured to her. "Come here, my pretty." Pippa's arms extended before her, and she stumbled—was dragged—towards the opening and out onto the pad. Slowly, she looked up at the GG looming two feet over her. He was a large model with tiny swirls of white military script acid-etched down his arms, chest and face plates. That meant only one thing: Combat Model.

Keenan lunged for the opening, but the bars fizzed into existence and he recoiled from a sudden broiling heat.

The platform eased away, gliding through the vastness until it touched down on the black ground. Pippa glanced at her squad, high above, then looked back to focus on the GG.

"You have a score to settle?"

"Yes."

"You want revenge?"

"Yes, little one. I have long heard your name. I have long savoured a moment like this, but never dreamed it would come to pass. Now a gift has been placed in my lap, and I do not intend the opportunity to escape me."

"Does McEvoy know?"

The AI tilted its head. "What could he understand of my needs? This does not concern him. This is a matter of AI pride. This is a matter of machine over flesh. You are a scourge to my kind, human." The GG spat the word with such venom that Pippa cringed. "Killing you is nothing more than an exercise in necessity."

Suddenly, it flexed backwards and withdrew its black Sliver Sword. The blade, incredibly thin, shimmered in the gloom of the roof bay as Pippa backed away, uncertain whether this was a fight… or an execution.

"Give her a weapon you metal piece of coward shit!" screamed Franco, battered face glaring down from his imprisonment. "Or are you merely indicative of your mercury-bowelled chickenhead kind?"

The GG paused. He glanced at Pippa. Then back up to Franco. With a *click* Pippa's hands released. The GG gestured to the wall where consoles lined every inch of available space. "Over there. You will find your weapon. Choose with care, little lady."

Pippa sprinted, as above her Franco sat back on his haunches.

"Indicative?" said Keenan, staring hard at Franco.

"Yeah, yeah, I know. It must have been the beating; released some rogue verbs into my slopstream." He smiled, a little shamefacedly. He scratched his ginger, recently shaved head. "But it got her a sword. Look!"

"Well done, Franco." Keenan's voice was soft. Worry etched his brow. His eyes were dark and hooded.

"Hey, well, they don't call me Mr. Smooth for nothing, you know?" Franco's optimism was a crazy thing.

Below, Pippa was whirling an identical single-molecule Sliver Sword. It hissed and screamed, slicing air as she spun and, apparently satisfied with its balance and edge, she turned to face the AI.

"I know you," said the GG, readying its weapon.

"Come and eat this," hissed Pippa, and charged to the attack.

Swords clashed, Pippa spun and swayed back as the GG's blade nearly took her face clean off. She retreated, the GG advancing, sword a blur of spinning dark death.

Again Pippa attacked, blades clashing, smashing together, grating and ramming up to the hilts. Their faces grew close. The GG's dark eyes dilated. "You're going to die a long hard death," it snarled.

"That's what they all said," smiled Pippa sweetly, "just before I hacked their heads from their junk-top necks."

With a grunt, Pippa kicked away, the GG's sword following. It sliced a narrow line across her calf and she flipped, landing lightly with a pattering of blood. Her head snapped up. The GG grinned with black hydraulic jaws.

"Sloppy," said Pippa.

The GG growled, stalking forward.

Again they clashed in a whirl of blades, which saw Pippa backing madly away. She was quite clearly outclassed. Her back slammed against a group of consoles, she ducked right, and the GG's sword cut a glowing line through steel and exited in a shower of high-voltage sparks. Pippa rolled, sword hacking at a knee-cap, but the GG flexed and side-stepped, its sword nearly decapitating the woman.

She paused, a tense coil, down on one knee, face lifted. Sweat traced a fine sheen on her brow. A touch of uncertainty etched her cold grey eyes.

This was a fight, she knew, she could not win. And yet, what other option did she have? To run was to die, and to leave her friends to a patiently drawn-out execution? Never.

Yet to fight? Well, she was giving the GG exactly what it desired: an easy execution, a playful retribution.

The machine attacked, metal feet scouring the floor. Pippa rolled fast, her sword lashing out only to be carried by the GG's flashing blade, rolled from her sweating grip, and sent spinning and sparking across the glossy ground. Pippa backed away, snarling, then turned and sprinted for the three dark, insect-like helicopters.

It took a moment for the GG to focus. It made a *cracking* sound, possibly of annoyance. The last thing it needed was to chase a lithe woman on a long sprint around the indoor arena. It would catch her in the end, superior stamina. But depending on her speed, it might take a while.

Pippa sprinted, then veered, slamming the catch on the nearest attack chopper. The door slid silently, and Pippa was ducking and squeezing into the narrow functional alloy confines before it was even halfway open.

The GG chuckled, a nasty metallic sound. It strode forward, almost nonchalantly, swinging its sword. "You can't hide in there for ever, my pretty," it said, dark eyes glowing. Hydraulic thumps echoed through the chamber. It halted, spinning its sword. It could taste the kill. The taste, even for an AI, was sweet, a metal chemical cocktail.

Pippa looked up. The GG could just about see her silhouette through the tinted cockpit windshield.

She looked… triumphant?

The GG frowned, tiny metal scales sliding into place.

"Who said anything about hiding?" asked Pippa. There was a *shring* as quad mini-guns slammed down and locked; then a turbo-whine as the barrels accelerated and spun up, and Pippa squeezed both triggers.

The GG was turning to flee in sudden horrified realisation as a thousand heavy calibre rounds tore into its frame, its shell, pulverising it limb from limb in a violent bright flashing scream of hot metal shavings, molten alloy and disintegrating panels. The GG was massacred, decimated, crumbled. The Sliver Sword spun across the black ground. Metal pieces shot out and scattered. The guns roared. The GG's head bounced, scarred and dead, against the skyscraper floor, then was chased spinning by a line of flashing bullets.

The guns whined down. Smoke poured from barrels. Pippa leapt down and waved up at Keenan, who dazzled her with a smile. "Good girl," he whispered up on the platform, as Pippa jogged to the consoles and activated the lift to the prison GRILL cell.

"Easy come, easy go," said Franco amiably.

"Does nothing ruffle you?" said Keenan.

"Plenty, mate. I'm just good at hiding it." He winked.

"She's a very dangerous lady," said Rebekka, voice quiet, eyes hooded, face pale.

"More than you could believe."

"I'll be careful around her." She placed a hand on his arm. "And thank you, again, for saving me, for keeping me... alive. I am not a part of this madness. I am not your nemesis."

Keenan nodded.

As they waited for the lift, Pippa moved back to the attack chopper; it was an Apache K50, military grade, bearing full armaments. She played around with a few controls, and started warming the engines. The Apache whined, growled, spat exhaust fumes, and slowly the rotors began a lethargic rotation.

The lift deposited Keenan, Franco and Rebekka on the ground. Keenan leapt into action.

"Rebekka, go to Pippa. Do not leave her side. Franco, with me."

"Where we going?"

"To tool up."

"Now that's a good idea."

They jogged through the gloomy space. Distantly, alarms sounded and Keenan threw a glance at Pippa. She gave a thumbs up, and the Apache lifted slightly, gliding across the vast interior of the chamber and settling down, guns and rockets focused on the main doors to the room's interior. Any soldiers who came through that entrance would end up mashed mince-meat.

The grenade-blasted bullet-riddled container bearing the kit they had originally purchased from Rebekka and her team nestled in the shadows to one side. The doors, blackened and charred, swung open easily with buckled groans, and Keenan and Franco hurried inside and armed themselves with MPKs. They pocketed magazines. With a smile, Keenan reclaimed his battered Techrim.

"They're coming!" screamed Pippa across the chamber. Her screens were alive with activity.

"Franco, get the roof open: then load up the chopper. I want all this kit with us. When we get to Ket, I've a bad feeling we're gonna need every last shell."

"OK boss. Where you going?"

Keenan grinned. "I have a score to settle."

* * *

KEENAN POCKETED SEVERAL items from the inside of the container, then sprinted away into the gloom. Free of constraints, he felt his senses vibrating, humming with adrenaline. This was it! How it used to be in the old days before the squad, when Keenan had worked MILintel missions alone: infiltration, demolition, assassination, sometimes protection, but more often than not the cessation of life. That had been a long time ago, before he'd met Pippa, before he'd met Freya: the women who changed him, shaped him, moulded his life, exorcised his darkest demons and laid them to rest.

Now, however, the demons were creeping; they were back. And once again Keenan felt the talons of a dark soul creeping into him, turning him from human into... something else.

Keenan moved along the wall, eyes glinting in the darkness; he checked his location and found a low narrow access door leading to a utility corridor. He slipped inside, amongst the pipes and cables, supports and bare concrete walls. His hand touched the rough surface tenderly; he guided himself along the stretch to a junction. He stopped, listened. Muffled gunshots hammered from the chopper's mini-gun. Keenan smiled grimly. Pippa would hold well; would do her job. He could trust her to do that.

He switched to another corridor, and padding along with his Techrim up by his cheek, moved through the almost complete darkness. Steam shifted around his boots. Somewhere, through solid-merc wire-work grilles purple lights strobed and flickered tiger-stripes of shadow across his face.

Keenan stopped, his entrance blocked by a concrete wall. Beyond this lay the corridor through which soldiers moved to the rooftop chamber: their prison. He pulled a neutral PAD free and drilled a hole through the concrete, slowly, easily, carefully, using its cool laser. The wall was a metre thick; Keenan inserted a tiny digital spy mirror and gazed down onto the ranks of soldiers that were advancing, heavily armed, towards their rendezvous with Pippa's mini-guns.

"Where are you?" muttered Keenan. He shifted the mirror subtly, altering its angle, scanning the wide steel corridor. There: McEvoy, face twisted in a grimace of fury, finger gesticulating and lips spitting as he instructed his soldiers, drilled them with command, and spat curses at advancing heavy artillery SIM support. His white wispy hair was more unkempt than before, as if he'd been dragged from sleep. A light sheen of sweat bathed his brow.

You might be the leader of one of the Seven Syndicates, thought Keenan, but you're just as human as the rest of us: just as weak, just as flappable, and just as fucking expendable.

He set the five tiny Pebble Charges and moved five steps back down the narrow corridor; at the flick of a thumb-switch the directed detonation howled, fire flowing out into the corridor like magma, and half the wall caved in, crushing, compressing and instantly killing ten SIMs. Dust rolled out like atomic fallout. Keenan leapt free of the sudden opening, smashed a right hook against McEvoy's jaw, stunning him, and took the man's gun like candy from a child. Slowly, he pushed the

barrel of his Techrim under the old man's chin.
Keenan slammed his back against the wall amidst
sounds of choking. He grinned. It was an evil
expression, without humour.

"I remember you," said Keenan, voice soothing,
mouth touching McEvoy's ear. "It's all come flooding back like a bad dose of syphilis. I tracked your
exploits until intel missions got in the way. You've
been responsible for everything from gun-running
to child pornography, you deviant piece of shit."

McEvoy said nothing. His breathing rasped on
the dust. His face twitched nervously.

"Tell them to lay down their guns and back
away, or I'll shoot your jaw bone through the top
of your fucking head."

"Weapons down!" screamed McEvoy. Keenan
could feel the man's sweat slick under his grip.
"Retreat to Central, I repeat, retreat to Central."
Slowly, the soldiers and SIMs started to withdraw.
Their looks burrowed with fury and hatred into
Keenan. He shrugged away their animosity like
dandruff and jabbed his weapon tighter against
McEvoy's flesh.

"Good boy," he growled.

He walked McEvoy towards the roof chamber,
stumbling at first over the debris from the chan-
nelled explosion, then past a litter of bullet-riddled
corpses surrounding the entrance in a cadaver arc.
The steel doors were pock marked, dented, buckled
by the fury of the Apache's mini-guns. Keenan
peered cautiously through the smoke.

"Coming in, Pippa," he bellowed.

"All clear, boss."

The chamber stank of cordite. Franco had just finished loading the Apache as Keenan, keeping close to McEvoy—like a lover—inched forward. "Found me a pretty plaything," he said.

"We need to go." Urgency raped Pippa's voice. "They're regrouping."

Keenan nodded. "Franco?"

"We're on. Rebekka's in the chopper. Let's move."

Franco boarded the ramp, grabbed McEvoy and hauled him up, and Keenan kicked away the steel, which clattered. Pippa flicked several switches and motors jerked, whining.

She turned to stare at McEvoy, whose eyes glared malevolently at his captors. "What are the codes? To unlock the roof?"

"Go to hell."

"I could strap you to the front of the mini-gun and try to ram our way free?"

McEvoy considered this; he stared at her for long seconds, then relinquished and gave her a stream of digits, which she punched into the Apache's console. Above, locks made slick grinding noises, like iron filings in grease, and the roof began to fold open, revealing a fresh spread of black sky. Stars glittered, crystals of frozen hydrogen sugar.

The Apache lifted, engines roaring and fire flickering from underbelly jets. It escaped the confines of the chamber as a flood of soldiers burst in, submachine guns roaring, and shot vertically into the great black, banked, and disappeared like a ghost into the night.

* * *

THE APACHE HOVERED at three thousand feet above an expanse of cold black sea. Far, far below tiny tracers of white chased one another over the waves. Keenan slid open the door, pushed McEvoy roughly to the edge and placed a short black blade against his throat. Behind him, Pippa and Franco exchanged glances but said nothing; something was burning Keenan, and they knew better than to step in from a position of ignorance.

"I found out all about you," said Keenan, at last.

McEvoy had lost his cockiness; a man realising death was staring him full in the face, and that none of his billions of hoarded gold and jewels, and dollarcards, ultimately, mattered. None of his arms and armies could help him here, in this place, at this time. No GG AI was there to protect him; no PopBot to pull him back from the dangerous brink. For probably the first time in fifty years McEvoy was totally alone.

"I have money, Keenan, more money than you could ever imagine! I could give it to you! All of it!"

"Dirty money," snarled Keenan. The knife jerked savagely, and a thin trickle of blood appeared at McEvoy's throat. It bubbled around the knife-blade, then ran in twin rivulets, creating glistening trails of guilt. "Money made from selling kids to perverts, you sick little fuck."

"All flesh is a commodity," said McEvoy stiffly. There was no point in denial. Keenan had worked the files; he knew what he knew and there was no denying the Syndicate's appreciation of the pae-dophile trade. It was one of its claims to fortune.

"If I could hunt down every sick little bastard, and cut out their hearts, I would. I know, I understand, we live in a sick place. I have acknowledged the way things work, but I will never comprehend, McEvoy. How can you seek to understand the workings of a deviant? By definition, it is corrupt."

"I am not a deviant," said McEvoy, voice made hoarse by the pressing blade.

Keenan increased the pressure. Blood flowed. His eyes were dark coals. His sanity teetered on the edge of a razor. "The human organism is like any other organism," said Keenan, "and sometimes it becomes wounded, diseased, deranged. Sometimes, the human grows on a diverted path; a place where it can no longer be classified as human, no longer be classed as life. That's where the paedophiles belong: the deviant, non-human, non-life. And then there's you, fucker, the bastard who makes their dreams come true."

Keenan heard Pippa's intake of breath. But it was too late: too late to stop the murder.

He pressed hard, felt the blade cut through skin, muscle, tendon, windpipe. It cut deep and savage in a bright fountain of crimson, the tip slicing right down to the spinal column. And as McEvoy's head lolled back with a gaping crimson mouth Keenan kicked the body from the chopper. It toppled, tumbling end over end, and was consumed by the sea.

Franco peered after it, and shivered.

"You'll have the Seven Syndicates after us, now," he said.

"Fuck 'em."

"You'd fight every last one?"

Keenan's eyes gleamed. "The baby abusers? I'll fucking kill them all. Burn them. No problem."

Pippa moved forward. She placed her hand gently on Keenan's shoulder. The man was lost to anger, to hatred, was deep in a bad place filled with a dark violent energy. Gently, Pippa reached up and rubbed speckles of McEvoy's blood from Keenan's cheeks. "Killing this scumbag won't change anything."

"I know that!" Keenan pulled away, moving into the Apache's interior. Rebekka shrank in the shadows, horrified by this apparent... insanity. This was something she had never seen: a base primal animal logic; a primitive need to kill, and to kill, and to keep on killing until all the bad men were dead unto dust. "I can put a spanner in the machine. I can slow it down, and by slowing it down I hit them where it hurts most: financially." He gave a bitter laugh and rubbed at weary eyes. "Come on. Let's get out of this depraved shit-hole. The City." He snorted a derisory laugh. "What a fucking toilet."

Pippa retook the controls and the Apache banked, dropping towards the rolling sea, and hugging the waves for protection so the moving water could mask their digital signature. It sped towards Freeport 557 and the waiting Hornet.

THE HORNET GLEAMED slick in the cold night air. Despite the late hour, people moved in thick streams down walkways and roads, huge snakes of living moving flesh, human mixing with slab and alien, proxer and kjell. The Apache helicopter came in discreet, low from the Tekkajemnon River, skimming the bulky concrete buildings of hydra-turbines and touching down with minimum fuss on the deserted outskirts of Freeport 557. Slowly rotors died, thumping rhythmically to a halt. In the gloom of the cockpit, Franco glanced nervously at Keenan, his face albino in the glow of the consoles.

"What's the matter?" he asked, almost reverently. Since McEvoy's murder, Keenan seemed to have adopted an invisible mantle, an aura of quiet but dreadful respect.

"I'm not sure," said Keenan. His voice was a low growl. He lit a home-rolled, and the ceiling air-filters clicked on. The glow of the cigarette turned his eyes amber.

"It's clear, as far as I can see," said Pippa. "All the scanners ID. The Hornet hasn't been tampered with. Anti-intrusion detectors are fine."

"Let's just wait it out for a while."

They sat in the gloom, in silence. The rain started again, sheeting across the landscape. Lightning crackled distantly, illuminating a nightmare sky-line: a skyline from the spastic brush of a mad artist. Towers bristled like spikes. Lights glimmered neon against a surreal staccato landscape.

Franco stared hard at the back of Keenan's head. *Shall I tell him?* he thought. Then: *Naaah. It's irrelevant. Anyway, he'll find out soon enough.* Franco chewed his lip, worried a little.

"I'll recon. Watch for my signal; then bring in the Apache so we can transfer the kit."

"Yes," said Pippa.

Keenan stepped out into the rain, and was instantly gone. Pippa watched on the scanners, and glanced up, realising Rebekka was staring hard at her: a focused, intense stare.

"What you looking at?"

"You said you'd kill me." Rebekka was shivering a little. Pippa felt herself deflate.

"I... apologise. Those words were said in anger. Don't take it too personally; I've had a kind of hard life." She smiled. "Maybe we could be friends?"

"That would be... better," smiled Rebekka uncertainly.

"It's a long time since I've had a friend," said Pippa with a deep sigh. She saw Keenan's signal. "Come on, the boss says we're good to go."

"Thank God for that!" blurted Franco.

Pippa spun up the rotors, and gave him a sideways glance. "You sound very relieved, Franco. Something you're not telling us?"

"No, no. No! No! Well, yes, yes, maybe, possibly, but that's the whole damn point. I'm not telling you." He grinned with the smugness of the deranged.

KEENAN PEERED INTO the darkened interior. "Cam?"

"Yeah, Keenan, I'm here."

"You OK?"

"Hmm, sort of, except for a pounding at the fists of that ginger lunatic."

"Ahh, so that's how he got out."

"Yes." Cam spun slowly, a grey light blinking. "Bastard gave me a right hook, sent me bouncing down the corridor like a ping pong ball. Let's just say he caught me unawares."

"Never underestimate the insane."

"Believe me, Keenan, I won't make the same mistake twice."

"Everything else OK?"

"As far as I can ascertain. The rain has been driving me mad with its incessant pounding. I didn't realise we were putting down in the tropical season."

Keenan nodded, watching the Apache skim low over the landing port and touch down nearby. Donning Gore-tex jackets, which soon glistened, Keenan and the others began transferring weapons, WarSuits, ammo, flak-armour, bombs and other kit from the belly of the Apache into the Hornet's bomb-proof hold. They attracted little attention in the bustling surroundings; FukTruks roared and flyers hummed overhead. All around the noise was a magnification of chaos. Combat-K worked, with the help of Rebekka, loading and checking equipment.

"Where will you go now?" asked Keenan, during a lull where he lit a cigarette. Under the canopy of the Hornet's low wing, he watched heavy raindrops rolling and dropping with a fast *tick tick tick*.

"I'll build a new life here," said Rebekka. She smiled; it lit up her face. "I'll just have to keep a low profile, away from the Syndicates."

"Will you be safe?"

"As safe as any other gun-running Syndicate-hunted proxer on a human-run cash-only lawless non-policed world." She grinned. "So, things haven't got any worse, then. Looks like the Syndicates were on to me; shit. I thought I was too clever for them."

"Never underestimate the enemy," said Keenan. He looked down, blowing smoke to his boots.

"The enemy?"

"Yeah, I think the Syndicates have earned that tag from me... for sure. I was in my own little world of pain. I'd forgotten such... scum still existed, still operated, still abused the weak and the poor. When I've completed my current mission—if I'm still alive—then... hell yeah, I'll be back." He rubbed his forehead with the heel of his thumb, leaving a smudge of machine gun oil. "I'll be back, and I'll be packing nukes."

"Come on Keenan, you lazy bastard, these cases are heavy!" As if to emphasise his point, Franco allowed his to thud against the ground, and he leant on it, panting, sweat sheening his face.

Keenan stood, and with Rebekka close behind, moved back into the rain, which clattered against his Gore-tex. Only then did he see the dark-swathed figure standing, almost nonchalantly, with a long, barely disguised industrial molecule stripper—or IMS—in both hands. Water gleamed against the deadly, terrible weapon. It lifted and pointed at the group. Keenan swallowed.

The figure threw back the hood of the thick black coat. A battered, bruised face glared at them; one eye was swollen shut and ringed with thick purple flesh. The nose was twisted. Lips, smashed to a pulp, were stuck together with tape.

Franco gave a wave. "How's it going, Betezh?"

Betezh growled something incomprehensible. The hydraulic footfalls of Louis the Razor-droid stomped behind him, through the rain. The battered AI halted, metal hands on metal hips, staring at them.

"Kill them all," it hissed.

Betezh nodded, refocusing the IMS. The charge whined, and Keenan tensed; when the gun ignited it would take out him, Combat-K, half the Hornet and possibly a ten metre cube of concretealloy runway beneath their feet. An IMS was not, technically, a weapon; they were used in the building trade for construction and—more importantly—destruction. A man with an IMS could demolish a skyscraper single-handedly. A drugged maniac could rearrange half a city quite competently.

Keenan felt his Techrim dig in his back, hard, real. But there was no time to draw, to fire. It was as useless as deadwood… and all his dreams, his nightmares, of a needful revenge, a necessary hunt, a joyful murder, would disintegrate, spiralling down as his skin, his muscle, his bones, his shell powdered into dust and tumbled into nothing. His girls would lie cold in anodyne graves, unloved, tainted spirits, victims of a non-justice. It tasted bad in his mouth: tox, nuke-ash. His hand crawled towards his gun as he saw the muscles writhe and contract in Betezh's beaten face… and realised with a dawning horror there would be no words, no reprieve, no simple parody of parole…

Just brutal extermination.

* * *

JULIAN X WAS a SIM. And it was a bad day.

With the others—SIMs and human soldiers alike—he helped load float-carts with the corpses of his dead companions, mown down by the mini-guns of the Apache helicopter on the roof of the Syndicate HQ. Although he felt few emotions—they had been efficiently machined out of his skull—he felt something as his gloved bio-mechanical hands dropped and closed, lifted and scattered corpses and body-parts onto the low-walled titanium trailers. Here lay Hugo VV, head caved open, brains, skull and tiny mechanical clusters fighting for precedence in the blood and grey mush soup. There, DickFish XII, both arms severed and mechanical eyes smashed into black holes by the onslaught of whining mini-gun bullets.

To top it all, the top dog big boss dude in charge—McEvoy—had been taken by the escapees. Kidnapped! Abducted! It was unheard of, a disgrace. Julian X wondered idly what time they'd let him into the feeding VATS. His hunger was gnawing. And he thought about his mother; in a distant, abstract manner. After all, he had been young during severance from umbilication. And, like most SIMs, he thought about his mother when the hunger came.

"What is this? Human intruder?" The voice was the mechanical clicking of Justice D. Justice D was renowned for having very, very little sense of humour. He was, in fact, ideal for hunting REBs out in the DREGS. Julian X had seen Justice D mow down a whole platoon of unarmed female protesters with placards; then head home for chilli beans on toast. Justice D was legend.

Julian glanced up. A tiny grey-white single-person stealth jet was hovering above the open roof. Strangely, none of the auto-Z Turrets had locked on and blasted the hell out of the craft, which was what normally happened to unidentified vessels behaving suspiciously.

"Must have permission," said Julian X, pausing to glance down at a severed face in his gloved hand.

"No. There is no registration blip," snapped Justice D, checking a chart on his arm. His mechanical eyes clicked and whirred. "The craft is an Interceptor. This craft is not known to us. Sound an alert. We must shoot it from the skies!"

But even as Justice D was announcing his far from eloquent appraisal, the small craft dropped, suddenly, circled the chamber low over the soldiers' heads with a blast of exhaust, then tipped its nose to the sky and disappeared instantly.

"This a strange day," said Julian X.

"A bad day for no umbilication," confirmed Justice D.

They nodded in unity, and went back to loading the dead.

MR. MAX STARED at the stars, caught himself in time, and paused, the Interceptor hanging suspended, as below, lazily, The City turned. Why travel when you can fire your ship vertically, wait for the planet to spin, then drop in on a designated target? Mr. Max found it an economical way of traversing any planet.

It saved him energy for what he did best.

He licked thin lips.

His black eyes stared like cold dead cobalt. With a click Directional finders locked to Freeport 557.

Mr. Max dropped silently out of nowhere.

PART

STATE OF THE ART

STATE OF THE ART

CHAPTER 8
CRASH AND BURN

KET WAS A hot and humid planet fed by twin suns; one cool and orange, one older, larger, a white fish eye nailed to the heavens. With both suns heating the tumbling ball of jungle, there was perhaps only an hour of night between the two of them, depending in which latitude one happened to be standing.

The planet's regions ranged from savage equatorial jungle, a mass of stinking rotting vegetation wreathed in steam, and suffering ten hours of rainfall every eighteen; to salt deserts so vast and dune-raked there was no possible crossing for water-based organic life without machine support. Through the jungles and deserts tore mountains, staggered staccato ranges machine-gunned from the buckled earth a hundred million years previously and constantly changing thanks to the planet's violent and apparently random seismic activity. Many mountains, when not rumbling in quake mode, towered over ten thousand metres high, their summits and the majority of their upper flanks permanently wreathed in snow.

Ket had originally been "discovered" and tagged as an Adventure Planet, back before the War. Whether your particular fetish was hunting strange spiked reptilian beasts through the vast million year-old steaming jungles, adventure motorbike racing over sweeping hardcore seas of salt desert, power-boat exploration across the Milk Oceans, which often suffered from violent whirlpools and sudden storms; and again thanks to seismic intrusion, mountain climbing, ice climbing, crevasse exploration, desert survival, and the reasonably new sport of caving in seismic rifts, Ket was the perfect location for those with a very large screw loose and the need for an adrenaline injection.

Rugged, wild, dangerous; and when one factored into the equation the prospect of meeting one of the fiercely territorial tribes of Ket warrior clans that roamed the planet in a state of constant battle, conflict, war, it added that extra *zing* so many thrill-seekers needed to enjoy their lives back home at the bank, insurance company, management hierarchy.

Then had come Unification, and the integration of Ket into the mainstream of Quad-Gal politics, economics and social acceptance. Ket's government won their votes, put in a bid to Quad-Gal and was accepted with open arms into the Whole. QG offered an umbilical giving access to SPIRAL port technology, and Ket was linked—like so many planets—at the end of a SPIRAL dock. It made life easier for visiting tourists, trade, and political negotiation. Once spacecraft integrated with the SPIRAL dock it was a matter of a few short minutes before the person, or cargo, was dropped down the SPIRAL to a series of anodyne land-ports at SPIRAL's End. This technology had helped Quad-Gal open up the Galaxies; it was also a badge of social acceptance, of civilisation, of trade unity, hell, even humanity.

The problem with Ket was a three million year history of war. The clans and tribes were natural warriors, larger and stockier than humans; the most ferocious had killing blades gem-grafted to the bones of their forearms. Manhood initiation rituals included this bone-grafting surgery without anaesthetic (a process that killed thousands) followed by immediate combat. The Ket-i were close to seven feet in height, stocky, heavily muscled, nearly entirely black and hairless, thanks to the proximity and mixed radiation of the planet's dual suns. Many wore traditional iridescent green-skin war tattoos with pride; it was usual to find tribal markings squirming across torsos, arms, necks and faces, often with lists of script naming the Ket-i warriors bested in battle. Most went naked, and shunned technology and more traditional projectile weapons. Although the Helix War had brought a massive influx of said technology and the planet was awash with guns and bombs, missiles and tanks, traditional Ket-i found this battle technology abhorrent to the point of sacrilege. Mechanical weapons brought impurity, they argued. It was like introducing a deviant to the gene pool.

After the Quad-Gal Peace Unification—which effectively brought the Helix War to a necessary end—Ket refused to surrender arms, quoting a catalogue of war crimes committed against its people, which meant that due to ancient esoteric Honour Laws it could not, in fact, surrender until all parties were totally annihilated. Thus, in breach of Quad-Gal law, the SPIRAL docks were subsequently decommissioned, leaving Ket to regress into a shadow of its former social and diplomatic self. The Quad-Gal saw further breaches of law, and, in further escalations, more and more sanctions were imposed.

Ket, in turn, saw this activity as a betrayal and announced war against all representatives of Quad-Gal. War, in fact, against every living organism that did not reside on Ket.

They did not see this as an act of madness (which it surely was); just an act of necessity as befitted the contractual obligation of their quite insane and logistically impossible honour code.

KEENAN, TEETH BARED, breath frozen in his throat, waited to die. Then, everything happened so fast it was a blur of incomprehension, which saw Keenan on his knees, hands over his head, wondering why the hell he wasn't a corpse.

Cam, spinning slowly as he watched events unfold, *clicked* into battle-mode. For a PopBot this was a simple sub-routine, which routed all power and instruction sets into the art of destruction/survival. The only indicators were black lights glittering on the PopBot's casing, and a quicker turn to its spin.

Cam shot from the shadowy hold of the Hornet using Keenan's bulk as a mask, veering at the last moment, with only a millionth of a millimetre between its case and Keenan's skull, to strike Betezh a crashing blow to the centre of his forehead. Betezh reeled, IMS pointing at the sky and discharging with a *crackle* that flickered like lightning for a half-klick radius. On the rebound, Cam whirled in a low *thrumming* arc under the belly of the Hornet, swinging wide, then smashing back as if attached to an invisible elastic cord to deliver a second, skull-crushing blow to the back of Louis's head. The GG dropped instantly, its IMS discharging with fizzles of electricity to neatly remove its own legs.

Louis lay there, twitching and examining its destroyed anatomy. Runs of metal streaked the concrete like fluorescent mercury blood. Gradually, the GG lay back and was still, the IMS clattering to the ground and dark eyes closing in finality.

Cam moved to hover near Keenan.

"I'd get that second gun if I was you. Betezh looks stunned."

Betezh was, indeed, stunned, sitting on the concrete with a confused and childlike look stamped on his features. A lump the size of an egg hovered above his eyes, blood-red and decorated with webs of burst purple veins.

Keenan hurried forward and prised the IMS from slack fingers. He stared hard at Betezh.

"Ain't this your mate, Franco?"

Franco grunted, and dropping to one knee he bound Betezh's hands with a loop of raze-wire.

"What you doing?"

"He's coming with us."

"Why?"

"Interrogation."

Keenan met Franco's gaze. "What's this about?"

"Believe me, Keenan, he said some stuff back at the hotel—I know, I know, I'll explain later—but he said some stuff that is important for all of us: important for Combat-K."

Keenan stared down. "I suppose we can always dump his carcass in space, later."

Suddenly, Rebekka was there. "I don't mean to be a killjoy, but there's a lot of interest coming this way."

"Interest?" said Pippa.

"The Syndicates."

"They found us," snapped Keenan. "Pippa, get the engines started. Franco, drag this heap of offal to the Medical Hold. And Rebekka..." Keenan glanced over her shoulder. "Shit, I can't leave you here with those." A storm of soldiers appeared a half-klick away, mostly SIMs; they started to fire, bullets whining and humming across Freeport 557. Close by a flyer was struck multiple times. It rattled, then exploded. A ball of blue gas screamed into the sky. Other people, aliens, were cut down by stray shots. Bullets crashed up the flank of the Hornet as beneath engines glowed hot, and Keenan grabbed Rebekka's arm. She did not resist. "You're going to have to come with us."

Rebekka smiled. "I'll be OK, really." She glanced nervously behind.

"No. Come on. They'll crucify you."

Together they sprinted up the ramp, which slammed shut behind them. The attack had gone from a rattle of stray bullets to a *roar*. Machine guns howled. Fire blazed from hot barrels. Tracer streamed, illuminating the Freeport. The SIMs advanced on the Hornet with the stoic bravery of the half-mechanical.

The Hornet suddenly glowed, leapt into the sky with a fighter's agility, and was gone in a shimmering of heat haze.

The SIMs halted, some still firing aimlessly at the screaming crowd, simply to shut them up. Never masters of diplomacy, it took a while for a SIM to wind down from a violent encounter, and even longer to turn off its gun.

Julian X looked down at his smoking weapon, then back to the pounding rain clouds. He holstered the gun, and without a sound turned, mechanical eyes clicking, and disappeared into the heaving broiling mass of The City.

PIPPA JUMPED THEM into fast orbit, then kicked free, and they cruised the cold expanses of space. The City wavered in a flicker of darkness and was gone; just another coloured blip against a backdrop of infinity.

Keenan came up beside her, slumped into his seat at the console and rubbed at reddened eyes. He looked bone-weary, and Pippa reached out, hand touching his arm.

"I thought you were going to cut my hands off," said Keenan, voice thick with exhaustion.

Pippa sighed. "Maybe I'm mellowing."

"What, so now only my fingers are forfeit?" He laughed hollowly. "Pippa, I think I'm getting too old for this running around shit. What am I doing? Risking all our lives—and the lives of others—and for what? For petty, personal retribution that, ultimately, counts for naught."

"That's not true," said Pippa. Her eyes were shining. "It's a noble cause, Kee. Nobody deserves to die like that, and believe me, that crime does not deserve to go unpunished. The Law is a fickle creature, and a joke most of the time. Sometimes it feels like the whole of our race stands for nothing, absolutely fucking *nothing*—if good men stand by and ignore atrocity."

"That's the problem, though, ain't it? It's why we evolved. What we were bred for. The slabs used to amuse me so much. Bred in VATS for the sole purpose of war, they seemed to me to be the perfect pinnacle of our evolution, something we, as a race, aspired to; the ultimate end-point for a sad and pathetic evolutionary trajectory. We created the ultimate man, and he was nothing but a destroyer. We're a doomed race, Pippa. We're a species destined to die."

"Hiya!" beamed Franco, bounding in. He stared at the two morose faces, glum in the blue glow of the console. "Christ, you two've been sucking happy pills, haven't you? Lighten up! We got away! We were the winners! We won! We succeeded against insurmountable odds! We—um—surmounted those insurmountable odds! We won! Time for a drink, hey, I'm thinking!" Franco beamed again, head twitching from Keenan to Pippa and back again.

"Actually, Franco, I need a word," said Keenan.

"Yeah?"

"I never did ask. When that GG dragged you limp and bloody into the Syndicate HQ, how did you end up there? I kind of assumed you'd been taken from the Hornet."

Franco looked suddenly shifty. "Well, 'twas a tale of honour and bravado and derring do! You see, I'd just nipped down the shops for a copy of *The Sporting Chronicle,* when..."

"You were instructed to stay aboard the Hornet!"

"Aww, come on Keenan, I needed a damn pint. OK? All right? I gave Cam a good right crack, legged it, found a rather grand Irish bar and sank a few pints of Guinness. The least I deserved, I reckon, after all that time banged up at Mount Pleasant. Did I ever mention they used to electrocute my testicles? The one up side is that my testes are like twin bags of marbles, and can take any amount of physical abuse." He grinned again. His optimism was a painful thing.

Keenan sagged. He was tired, too tired. "Franco," he sighed, "just tell me this one thing. Have you got it out of your system?"

Franco nodded like an eager schoolboy. "Yes. Yes, yes."

"I can do without nasty surprises when we get down to Ket. It looks like a proper hell-hole."

"I'm a good boy now," said Franco, "a reformatted character."

"Reformed."

"Whatever."

Franco made for the doorway.

"And Franco?"

"Yeah boss?"

"Absolutely no torturing the prisoner."

Franco looked crestfallen. "Aww, *boss!*"

"No, Franco, not until I've had some sleep and had time to question him myself, properly."

"And then I can torture him?" Franco sounded hopeful.

"No!" sang Pippa and Keenan in unison.

Franco disappeared to the music of their laughter.

PIPPA SET THE Hornet on its course for Ket, and after a few sociable glasses of wine, they all turned in for some much-earned sleep. Keenan injected Betezh with a large dose of Sleep-o. The man was obviously seriously concussed, and also in no small amount of pain at the hands of Franco, then the SIMs, then Cam. You could say it wasn't Betezh's century. After checking the razewire securing Betezh to his Medical Hold bed, Keenan retired to his quarters and crawled under a soft white duvet.

It was one of those moments when a fresh bed feels like instant orgasm. Tiredness infused every single atom, and the pillow tasted of nectar; Keenan sank into a loving embrace. His eyes closed thankfully. And then he heard the click of the door. "Pippa?" he said, before he could help himself.

"No, it's Rebekka."

Keenan sat up and watched her close the door behind her. She wore a simple black nightdress.

Her hair tumbled behind her, glowing under the quarter's night-lights. Her eyes buzzed orange, alien.

"What can I do for you?"

"I cannot sleep."

"We have some drugs in the..."

"I need company, Keenan. Not sex, nothing like that, just somebody to hold me. Could you do that? For me? Just tonight? I think I've been shaken to my core. I'm just glad to be alive." She smiled. Fear edged her features like a ghost.

Keenan pulled back the covers and she climbed in, lying beside him. She was long and sleek: a panther. She pulled the duvet over her body and snuggled in against Keenan's chest. He could feel her smooth skin against his legs, under his hands. He banished thoughts of sex with a savagery that surprised even him. Then he pushed his face into her hair and inhaled the fragrance. It picked him up, spun him round, and tumbled him down into a well of sleep, and very pleasant dreams.

KERJUNK.

"Wahhh!"

KERJUNK.

"Wahhhhhhh!"

KERJUNK. KERJUNK. KERJUNK.

"Wahhhhhhhhhhhh!"

Thuds reverberated throughout the Hornet. Keenan came violently and suddenly awake, and wondered why his face was engulfed in hair. Beautiful orange eyes peered up at him sleepily. "Ahh," he said, trying, for a moment, to work out if he'd done the unthinkable. His unintentional erection pressed against Rebekka's leg.

"Shh!" said Rebekka, and put her finger against his lips.

KERJUNK.

KERJUNK. KERJUNK!

Pippa burst into Keenan's quarters. "Keenan, I think it's... Oh." She stumbled to a stop, staring. Keenan followed Pippa's gaze down to Rebekka's muffled form curled beneath the duvet. Even the thickly cosseting linen could do nothing to disguise her shapely, deeply feminine figure.

"Oh," she said, again.

"It's not what it looks like," said Keenan, recognising the cliché.

Pippa disappeared, and Keenan followed with Rebekka close behind. They sprinted down corridors, all the time Keenan's brain screaming, *what's happening? Is the ship under attack? Guns? Lasers? SPAWS eating through the hull? Have we wandered into a field of Blay Stars?*

KERJUNK. KERJUNK. KERJUNK. KER-JUNK. KERJUNK.

"Wahhhhhhhhhhhhhhhhhhhhhhhhhhhhhhhhhhhh-hhhhhhhhhhhhhhhhhhh!"

They burst into the Medical Hold and slid to a halt, stunned for a second by the sight that greeted them. Betezh, still on his back, was strapped to the bed. Franco was kneeling over him, straddling him in a parody of sex, and in one sweating grip he held an Industrial Bone-Staple gun, as used in hospitals throughout the Quad-Gal. It was used—normally—to repair broken bones under a general and very deep anaesthetic. You didn't want to be on the receiving end while sober. Franco grinned at the group weakly.

"Hi."

"What the *fuck* are you doing?" hissed Pippa, eyes glaring.

"Well," gabbled Franco, "Betezh here, lovely nice Dr. Betezh... well he just had a few minor wounds, and I was just facilitating his recovery by... just stapling them back together again. Can't have him bleeding all over the place now can we?" He grinned with bared teeth. "Just doing my bit for the mission, so to speak. So sorry to disturb."

"Get off him," snapped Keenan, and moved forward. Betezh had indeed received a few minor wounds, which Pippa had repaired using steri-strips of Titanium Weld. Over this fine repair—including a four centimetre gash down one cheek—Franco had followed the original line of the wound, injecting huge black U staples with considerable energy and enthusiasm. Betezh's face resembled something from the slab of Dr. Franken-stein. It was not a pretty sight, although, acknowledged, it had been far from a pastel land-scape in its original state.

"You lunatic!" said Pippa, dragging Franco down by the scruff. "Look what you've done to him!"

Franco shrugged, and placed the Industrial Bone-Staple gun back in its chrome recess with all the other neat surgical implements. "I never said I was anything else," smiled Franco.

"Betezh? Can you hear me?" Pippa was leaning over Betezh.

Betezh opened his eyes. "Keep that little ginger fucker away from me!" he screamed into Pippa's face, showering her with foul spittle. His eyes twitched and his hands flexed beneath raze-wire. Pippa nodded, turned, and slapped Franco across the face; a vicious, stinging blow.

"Dickhead," she snapped, and stalked from the room.

Franco looked to Keenan, who merely shook his head in despair, turned on his heel, and left. Rebekka followed without a word, and Franco glanced up at Cam, who had made a sagacious entrance towards the end of the charade.

"You as well?"

"What a muppet," said Cam, and disappeared on a steady stream of ionised air.

Franco considered his position for a moment: this sudden ostracism, this open hostility, this naked aggression. He shrugged, rubbing his blood-speckled hands enthusiastically. "Right, time for some breakfast," he said. He grinned, and added, "And one of those right tasty blue pills."

KEENAN AND PIPPA spent most of the day poring over charts of Ket. They worked their way through maps, both civilian and military. They read up on the history of the planet, and the Ket-i people in particular; a warrior race, they took little understanding as to motivations, but a lot in terms of sheer incompetence when it came to

Galaxy-wide diplomacy and a sheer obstinate belief that they could take on the entire Quad-Gal, and win.

The atmosphere was frozen and uncommunicative between the two ex-lovers. Occasionally they would share information, but exchanges were short and to the point. Both reeled with inner emotions and both were trying, in their own ways, to navigate through a minefield of past problems.

At one point Rebekka entered the room, bringing a steaming drink for Keenan. No words were spoken, but Pippa threw the proxer such a look of hatred and open contempt that Rebekka retreated without a sound. Keenan stared at the frothing hot chocolate as if it was rabid.

"Drink it, then."

"What?"

"Your lover brought you a drink. The least you can do is drink the fucking slop."

"She's not my lover."

"Not what it looked like to me."

"Pippa, grow up."

"What, grow up and shut up? Actually Keenan, we're a long way past the days when I'd smile sweetly, innocently, trustingly, and obey your every last whim."

Keenan laughed. "You never obeyed my every last whim."

"It felt like it."

"How's it going, children?" Franco grinned from the door, a huge sandwich in one paw, mustard—or at least, something thick and yellow—smeared around his mouth and crusted in his beard. He took a bite, chewed, swallowed, and made appreciative mumbling noises.

"Not so bad, mutilator."

Franco nodded. "Mutilator, heh? Quite good. Quite good. I love this witty repartee, this funky exchange of comedy insults. It's what makes us a team, right?" He cackled and mooched over to Keenan. "Big place, ain't it?"

Keenan looked up. "So you've done your research?"

"Aye," nodded Franco. "After all, they don't call me Mr. Photographic Memory for nothing."

"Franco... they don't..." Keenan shook his head. "It doesn't matter."

Franco took another bite of his huge sandwich. He dribbled mustard on the map. "Sorry. Sorreeee!"

"Franco," snapped Pippa, "what the hell do you want?"

"Just wondered when we were going to question Betezh. The bastard has been a pain in my throbbing arse for these last few years. Thought it might be time we got some answers."

"Is it that important?"

"Well, he did say he used to be in a Combat-K squad."

"WHAT?" It was a joint exclamation by both Keenan and Pippa.

Franco shrugged. "That's what he said."

"I thought he was a 'doctor' from your happy little insanity station?" Keenan was frowning, hard.

"He was." Franco grinned amiably. "I get the feeling he was planted there, to keep an eye on me, or something."

Keenan rolled his eyes. "Right. Get your shit together. We'll meet in the Med Bay in five."

"Rodgah that!" saluted Franco.

"And Franco?"

"Sah?"

"Stop fucking about, there's a good lad."

THEY FORMED A semicircle around Dr. Betezh. The lights had been dimmed. The operating table, which had become Betezh's temporary prison, was lifted to the near-vertical; Betezh did not look a happy man. He stared at them suspiciously.

"OK," said Keenan, "talk."

"About?"

"Combat-K."

"What would you like to know?" Betezh gave a nasty smile: the smile of a man who knew a lot, but did not intend divulging. He gestured to Franco. "What has that insane dickhead been spieling you?"

"Less of the insane," growled Franco.

Keenan narrowed his eyes. "I'll start at the beginning. Franco says you know about Combat-K. You know about us. That figures, even if you were only a doctor at Mount Pleasant. Now, what I want you to consider is this. If you know more about me, then you know about some of the things I've done, the places I've been, the missions I've carried out." Betezh's face paled a little. "If so, you'll know I worked with this squad, but before… yeah, before there was a lot of stuff I'm not proud of. I was not a good boy."

Keenan pulled his chair a little closer, became more of a conspirator: intimate. Outside, the chill of idle space flowed by, and Betezh felt the hours of his life slipping through oiled fingers.

"You need to talk," said Keenan. His voice was gentle. "There are things I need to know."

Betezh nodded. "I do know about you: the three of you, Combat-K. I know about the Terminus5 reactor incident; I know about your subsequent trial and incarceration."

"You were Combat-K?"

"Originally," nodded Betezh. "Then I went K-OPS."

"A spook?"

Betezh nodded again. "I worked military assignments: spy work, infiltration, gathering evidence, watching suspects, the usual shit."

"Wait, wait, wait," said Pippa, standing up, eyes blazing. "You mean he's—like—internal fucking affairs? Sent to spy on the good old boys of Combat-K? Make sure we're doing our fucking jobs?"

"Every organisation has its internal agencies," said Betezh, voice dripping poison. "Because every organisation has its naughty players: those who embezzle, defraud, commit crimes of atrocity. My job was simple: root out decay blossoming at the core of Combat-K and excise with a precision scalpel."

"Now I hate him even more than traffic wardens," interjected Franco. Keenan gave him a savage glance.

"Franco mentioned a name: Kotinevitch."

Betezh nodded. "My controller."

"The politician?"

"Yes."

"What's her beef? Why the hell is she up to her tits in military stuff?"

Betezh shrugged. "She's a politician, General Activator for the Quad-Gal's Warfleet."

"She, also, knows of us?"

"Oh yes," said Betezh. "She took an active interest. In a past life, she even wanted you exterminated."

"Why?" snapped Keenan.

"After the Terminus5 catastrophe you almost caused… an incident. Let's just say your incompetence in the field nearly led to a massive Quad-Gal meltdown, never mind a mere reactor meltdown on the planet. You buried yourselves, Combat-K. You showed the military you were incompetent; a joke."

"Not so," snapped Pippa. "We were set up."

"That's right," said Keenan. "The whole gig was an arse-fuck. They knew we were coming. It was a charade. We were the central characters in a pantomime; we were the scapegoats, my friend."

"I know nothing of that." Betezh's dark eyes gleamed. Sweat glistened on his Frankenstein stitching.

"This has the sour stench of politicians," said Pippa bitterly.

Keenan nodded. "Yes, the work of people like Kotinevitch. I'd like to meet this judgemental bitch;

I'd like to find out exactly where her personal interest in our little outfit stems."

"You were merely an embarrassment," said Betezh.

"No, no," said Keenan. "That problem was sorted. This went further. This went deeper. There's another game being played here, and I don't like the smell."

"Whatever," said Betezh, quietly, "I was given orders to bring back Franco after his escape. That led to you. Kotinevitch knows of your re-formation; I believe it's called a GroupD Prohibition? You knew the consequences and still re-formed. How sad. How—ultimately—tragic. Every killer in the Quad-Gal will be after your skulls."

Pippa nodded. "He's right."

Keenan considered. Then he scratched his stubbled chin. He pointed at Betezh. "This conversation isn't finished. You hear me, little man? Little fucking internal affairs bureaucrat man? You're a long way from home. And we've got the fucking guns."

They left. Betezh deflated.

The Med Bay rolled into silence.

"You get that?" he whispered. Inside his head, a chip glowed.

"Every word," said the sibilant binary hiss of General Kotinevitch.

THE HORNET CRUISED, Ket turning majestically below. Sunlight glimmered from a distant horizon, skimming the planet, illuminating the vista. The Hornet banked, then dropped with a howling acceleration. Panels glowed and engines yammered with retro-thrust as Pippa skilfully took the attack vessel through the upper reaches of this idyllic and apparently peaceful world.

The air became thick: hotter, brighter. The Hornet started to vibrate, a resonation that hummed beyond hearing; Keenan glanced at Franco, who was gritting his teeth, hands clasped tight on the arms of his chair. Franco hated flying, especially planet entry without a SPIRAL dock.

"You OK, mate?"

"Yep." It was a clipped word; an ejaculation of fear.

"Relax," soothed Keenan. "Everything's cool, brother. It's not as if we're going to—"

They heard a distant *SLAM*. The Hornet shuddered. Franco stared hard at Keenan.

"What was that? What the hell was it? I thought you said we—"

The Hornet shuddered again, and they all felt it. The machine dropped violently, accelerating, engines howling in metal agony. Keenan could see Pippa fighting the controls.

"What's going on?" screamed Franco.

This time, the impact picked them up and sent them cart-wheeling through the atmosphere. Inside, Cam bounced from the cockpit windshield. Pippa, in her harness, was the only one to retain her seat as her face, tortured by G-force, fought with the unresponsive controls.

Keenan crawled across the wall—now the floor—and dragged himself to Pippa by brute strength. "What's—going—on," he forced through gritted teeth. Then, sirens screamed through the Hornet's interior. The fighter started to spin, flashing down through sunlight as the world swung and opened up below them, a panorama of lush wilderness and white water. Pippa was stabbing at controls.

"We're going to crash," she said quietly.

"What hit us?"

"I—"

More sirens screamed. There were a thousand *clicks* as crash-injectors flipped down from recesses. Keenan caught a glimpse outside; one of the Hornet's engines detached, flaming, and was snapped away; gone.

"Hold on!" shouted Pippa, and her voice was lost as the several thousand crash-injectors hissed and squirted, filling the Hornet's interior with Crash Foam.

Keenan turned, was hit by the foam, locked in place as it surrounded him and expanded in an instant; it filled his open mouth and nostrils and plugged his ears, and the world was hammered and descended into a cool green suspension as he was—effectively—divorced from reality. The Hornet's emergency systems took control. Keenan breathed the weird rubbery substance; infused with oxygen and a sub-prapethylene agent, it would sustain him in stasis for around thirty minutes... enough time to crash... and providing the Hornet didn't disintegrate in its entirety in the outside world, or, worse, explode.

The ship rocked, a quick succession of blows that hammered Keenan despite the life-saving Crash

Foam. He felt himself spinning, stop-motion rolling, turning like a fish in oil, and a distant noise like a subconscious roar of sea surf filled him and engulfed him. More and more blows devastated his being, and he was pounded into a state of tumbling unconsciousness... as an eerie muffled roar filled his drowning senses. He dived, falling and sinking and drowning under a great green ocean.

THE WORLD FELT wrong. Keenan choked, and it was as if he'd smoked a thousand cigars. He coughed, coughed and coughed and coughed, tears streaming down his face as his lungs disgorged Crash Foam, and he realised he was curled in a ball, retching, head pounding, pain needling his overstretched eyes. The world was a focus, a concentration of agony, a need to eject that which filled his mouth and throat and lungs.

He scooped thick acid goo from his mouth, plucked it from his nose.

Again, coughing fits wracked his body until he could... breathe.

Keenan sucked in precious air, and for a long time that was all that mattered. Bright red patterns dissolved from his brain and he opened his eyes. Damp sand met his confused stare and he lay for a while, watching the fine white that spread away from him, a perfectly horizontal platter laced with webs of splintered blue and pink shells.

He realised he was on a beach.

We crashed. Shit.

The heat hit him like a brick. It was terrible: hot and humid, unbearably so. So hot it was a fist in his throat, confusion in his skull, filling his lungs with liquid fire and making it almost impossible to focus.

He moved his head, and his neck and shoulder muscles howled in protest. With a groan, he slowly sat up and the world swayed. Keenan closed his eyes, put his head between his knees and concentrated on not throwing up. Losing the battle, he vomited, and heaved and heaved until his body groaned at him, muscles spasming. He crawled to the edge of the lapping sea and stared down at—

White. The sea was white.

Ket. I'm on *Ket*, he thought.

He cupped his hands, washed his face and cleaned out his mouth with milky brine. Then he scrambled to his knees, and the world smashed into arrangement. The Milk Sea stretched away, vast and calm. Waves rolled, breaking a half-klick out on an arc of blue coral, which half-reared like a bony arm from milky depths. Keenan turned right. The beach stretched away, a shimmering plane crusted with crushed shells, flat and packed where it met the sea. A few feet back a wall of solid, twenty-foot high jungle blocked his exploratory view. Thick hardwoods, creepers and ferns all fought for supremacy; the jungle was a solid mass, a wall, a fortress. Keenan licked sour lips. It frightened him for a moment. It was a real, dangerous, brutal intimidation.

The Milk Sea lapped. Something screeched in the jungle. Keenan's gaze turned slowly to his left, traced his own squirming marks in the sand, then came to rest on a figure. It was clinging to a rock as if seeking integration. It looked dead.

"Pippa!"

Keenan crawled, scrambling to his knees, then his feet. Weak, he struggled across the sand, sweat bathing his body as he tugged free some of his foam-splattered clothing in a feeble fight against the awesome, beating temperature. He reached her. She had been conscious at some point and had tugged free her heavier clothes. One boot trailed laces in the sea. She was draped spastically across what turned out to be a huge violet shell, rimed with a sand salt concoction. Keenan pulled feebly at her.

"Pippa? Pippa!"

She groaned, eyes fluttering. With a burst of effort Keenan stood, picked her lithe, muscular form from the curled shell, and struggled up the beach, leaving a wide, zig-zagging trail.

The heat smashed down.

The twin suns were copper pans nailed to the sky.

Keenan collapsed at the edge of the fearsome jungle, welcoming its shade like an old friend. It was cooler here, not much, but more bearable than the furnace of the sand and endless sky; the beach didn't scorch him. Keenan gently placed Pippa on her back and surveyed the creepers with a wary eye; pulling free a small knife he dragged free a long vine and sliced carefully into its flesh; water dribbled, thick and glutinous. Keenan touched it to his lips, then to his tongue, then allowed a little into his throat. He waited a few minutes to see if there were any sudden adverse effects, eyes scanning the white sea and the mirage of the horizon. There was no sign of the Hornet, or its wreckage.

Eventually, carefully, he guided the creeper to Pippa's mouth and allowed precious liquid into her bone-dry maw.

Pippa's eyes opened. She breathed laboriously. She ran a hand across her scorched brow and blinked rapidly, looking from Keenan to the beach to the white sea beyond.

"What happened?" she murmured.

"I was hoping you could tell me. The ship…"

"Of course, the ship. We were hit."

"Hit?"

"By ATA missiles. I didn't even know we were targeted; whatever took us out was very, very advanced. That Hornet was a modern fighter, had some serious hardware and advanced AI detection systems. Shit. It didn't even see the missiles coming!"

"Where is it?"

Pippa smiled. "The Hornet?" She gestured, a broad sweeping motion with her sun-scorched arm. "Out there, Keenan. Out there." She shook her head, then put it in her hands.

"You OK?"

"Mmm. Just like before, isn't it?"

Keenan didn't answer. Because he knew; knew exactly what she was referring to, Molkrush Fed: their abandonment; their survival, which in turn had led to their union; and the beginning of all their problems spiralling down and down and down, right to this very moment.

Keenan stood, moving away from the shade of the jungle. Behind, insects hummed. There was a crashing sound deep in the jungle, and a honking as of a great pig. He shaded his eyes and scanned the horizon. No sign of Franco, or Rebekka... or Betezh. No sign of the Hornet, their guns, their equipment, bombs, WarSuits, shit.

"Bastard." Keenan kicked sand into the air and turned. Pippa shrugged. She had pulled a large yellow fruit from a tree, and deftly skinned it with Keenan's knife. She cut a cube from the fruit, sniffed it warily, then swallowed.

"It's good."

Keenan accepted a piece and sat back down in the sand. "What a great start."

"Nobody said it was going to be easy," said Pippa.

"Great sentiment: optimistic. When the hell did you study for a philosophy degree?"

"Just stating the obvious. We should camp here, build a small fire, gather some fruit. I'll see if I can kill a pig—or whatever the hell was making that unholy racket—back in the jungle."

"I think we should look for Franco," said Keenan.

"What? And have both of us tear-arsing up and down the beach? No, we stay put, see if we can salvage gear from the Hornet. Franco will find us, if he is able. If we all set off wandering we'll end up moving away from one another. He should have the sense to find us."

"We have another problem."

"Which is?"

"If they—whoever they are—shot us from the sky, then they know we're here. Our enemies may know we survived; they will probably come looking for us."

"We should be discreet, then," said Pippa gently. She ate more fruit. "After all, we don't want to be forced to kill them... do we?" Her smile was sweet and deadly.

THE TWIN SUNS faded towards a muggy hot evening. Night was about to fall—for the entirety of one hour—and Pippa had gone a short way, exploring, while Keenan smashed his own route forcibly into the jungle and pulled free large Splay Ferns, which he arranged into a small makeshift shelter... but also as camouflage to disguise them from aircraft. Propped on canes Keenan had broken with a rock, the small shelter was sturdy and he lined the floor with more wide-leaved fronds. He made makeshift mugs from hollowed fruit skins, and filled them with drinking water found in a small pool deep in the jungle, balancing them on a small ledge of curved driftwood he found on the beach.

Pippa returned, walking warily along the edge of the jungle. She carried something in her arms.

"Well, well, quite the little homemaker, aren't we?" she said, voice heavy with sarcasm.

"Just keeping myself busy."

"Waiting for Rebekka to show?"

Keenan eyed Pippa levelly. "What's that supposed to mean?" Then he noticed the gun; it was an MPK crusted with jewels of sand. Pippa held it not quite pointing at him, cradled like a wounded babe in her arms.

"Well, you did have that cosy little thing going, didn't you?"

"What?"

"I saw you, in bed together, coupled like Siamese Twins. I thought I could smell the blossoming of true love; stank like rotting cabbage and old fish heads."

Keenan shrugged. "So what? Why would you care? You said you had no more feelings for me. So... why give a damn? Listen to Pippa, queen of the double standard. Hypocrisy's her middle name."

The MPK shifted. Keenan eyed the barrel warily.

They stood in silence for a while, both lost for words, caught up in emotions that tumbled back for a decade. Finally, Keenan noticed something flopping at the edge of the sea. His stomach lurched, a coldness flooding him like bad adrenaline. It was a body.

"Shit."

Pippa turned, following his gaze.

The body shifted with the surf, rolling, one arm flopping over. Pippa threw down her salvaged gun and they both moved uneasily across the sand, dreading, but knowing, deep down, what they might, or would, find.

The twin suns beat at them: relentless, uncompromising, merciless.

They slowed as they approached the corpse, apprehension filling both with toxins. Then Pippa barked a laugh, and Keenan glared at her. "What's so funny?"

"It's a WarSuit," she said. "Look."

"Jeez!" Keenan waded out, grabbing the high-tech integrated body armour and dragging the

WarSuit up onto the sand. He laughed too, tension flooding away.

"I was convinced it was Franco."

"Me too."

Pippa flopped down beside him. Her hair was tied up, and she removed the band, shaking free shoulder-length dark locks. They were matted with sand, but to Keenan she had never looked more beautiful. Her eyes glowed. Her face wore a simple radiance.

"I feel we got off to a bad start," she said. She smiled.

"Well." Keenan considered this. "You did say that if I got in your way you'd slit my fucking throat. And, I believe, you also mentioned gutting me like a fish. I think those were your exact words. Charming, I'm sure, but definitely not guaranteed to get you a date."

Pippa punched him on the arm. "You know that was only little old me."

"I kind of believed you. I seem to remember you saying that I broke your heart?"

"You did." Her tone was serious.

Keenan sighed. He breathed deeply. "When I thought Franco was dead, a whole shit-load of problems came into perspective. It's been... a long time... since I suffered like when... well, you know. It was hard, Pippa. It nearly destroyed me; nearly took me down. Months went by, where every morning and every night I found it hard to think of a reason to go on, a reason not to eat a bullet."

"So why didn't you?" Her voice was soft.

"My girls, Pippa: I kept seeing their faces. What would they have thought? Their daddy giving up, giving in, taking the easy way out, taking the easy option: the easy option was never my way, Pippa. You know that."

"So you're still alive because of stubbornness?"

"I'm still alive because I love my girls."

"And Freya?"

"You know I loved her. You know we drifted apart. You know... shit, Pippa. I loved you, I still love you. That's just the way the world works; it's the way people work. People change and shift and move on. Friendships morph and die, shift and alter. Relationships—something so passionate you would have killed for, would have died for—they become nothing more than a petty annoyance. Who left the cap off the toothpaste tube? Get your stinking muddy boots out of the hall! Why can't you flush the toilet when you've used it? I think, deep down, we're just solitary creatures who think we need permanent companionship, but we don't. Ideally, we need to be alone... more than anything."

"You're describing yourself, Keenan, not the whole of humanity."

Keenan shrugged. "Maybe. Shall we get back in the shade? I think the sun is making me jabber like a monkey."

"Hey. You're doing just fine." She placed her hand on his arm.

"So, we OK, then?" He looked at her. There was hope in his eyes.

"Let's walk first, yeah? Before we run."

"OK."

"After all, I've still got my gutting knife on stand-by, just in case."

"I wouldn't have it any other way," he grinned.

DURING THE COURSE of the evening they retrieved a large amount of kit, five MPK machine guns and a serious number of magazines. They managed to save three WarSuits, and quite a few HighJ bombs. Pippa made it her obsession to strip down all the weapons and clean them using Keenan's torn-up T-shirt. They stashed the kit in the leaf-lined shelter, and as night fell and a sudden total darkness blanketed the jungle, Pippa built a small fire and sat, staring into the flames.

Keenan, lying on his side, watched her face lit by a demon-glow.

"You're beautiful, you know that?"

"I know."

"So modest."

"Beauty is never enough."

"Yeah," sighed Keenan. "I know that. But you've got everything, Pippa: beauty, brains, the figure, the education. Why haven't you settled down? Why haven't you had children? What dragged you into this world of war?"

"I don't want to talk about it."

"It's something to do with scissors, isn't it?" His voice was soft, eyes fixed on her.

"I don't want to talk about it."

"OK. I hear you." He changed the subject. "I hope Francis is OK."

"Franco's a big boy. Well, five feet, anyway. He can look after himself."

"Yeah, I suppose he can. God, I wish I had a smoke."

"I didn't find your smokes, Keenan, but I did get you a present."

"What's that?"

She tossed something through the darkness. It landed heavily, thudding, and Keenan lifted the salt-encrusted Techrim.

He smiled. "Thanks."

"It was down by the sea. I'd give it a good clean first."

"Yes."

Pippa gazed into baby flames.

Keenan closed his eyes, cradling his gun. And, despite their predicament, sleep came far too easily.

WOW, THOUGHT FRANCO. That was some rush! What kind of drugs were they? They blew ma fackeeeen maaind! He blinked. His mouth tasted of sulphur, and was dry, very, very, very dry. He felt sweat trickling down his back and heat prickling his scalp. Hmm, he thought. So, some party hey? Wonder if I scored? Some sexy little blonde chick yeah I know the one, Kristel with her thick blonde hair and baby blue eyes sweet sweet sweet little Kristel, bet she goes like a slick whore on KY acid.

Salt. Sand.

Franco opened his eyes and stared at the white water before him.

A beach? Was it a beach party? Damn fine beach party if you ask me, sure there were lots of naked ladies and folks getting jiggy with it and giving it all the zigga zig ahhhh.

Franco rolled onto his back. He groaned, although hardly any sound escaped through cracked and swollen dry lips. That's some dehydration, he thought, must have drunk like a horse. If only I was as good looking as one ha ha ha!

A shadow loomed over him.

Ahh. This will be room service, thought Franco optimistically.

The figure leant close.

It was Dr. Betezh: Betezh, with a seriously stapled Frankenstein-reject face. Betezh, who looked as if he'd not only had a bad day, but a bad week, month, year and decade.

Franco's mouth opened in an inflatable doll O of surprise... as Betezh's still-bound sausage-finger hands came down with a double *thump* on Franco's skull.

"Ouch! You bastard! That hurt that did it really hurt!"

"Hurt!" seethed Betezh, "Hurt! I'll fucking show you pain my little ginger cockroach, have you seen what you did to my fucking face? I just spent a whole hour looking into a milky pool, trying to work out who's the most sexy, me, or a genetic experiment at the hands of the fucking Nazis!"

"You need to calm down," said Franco, as a flood of really bad memories tumbled into his skull: Mount Pleasant, escape, *Hardcore*, Pippa, PopBot, Right-hook, Guinness, Razor-droid, hotel,

Hornet, industrial staple gun, Crash, Betezh free...
ahhhhhhhhhh, Betezh free. Shit. "Calm down
lad," said Franco hopefully.

"Calm down, calm down, calm down!"
screeched Betezh. The look of a crazy man glinted
in dark eyes.

"Yes," said Rebekka. "Calm down." The chunk
of driftwood descended, *whammed* Betezh across
the back of the head, and knocked him out cold.
Rebekka leant forward. She smiled. "Better get you
out of that sun, Franco, before it sends you crazy."

"Hallelujah to that," he said.

Franco had been lying prostrate in a rocky scar of
pink rock, an inverted V formation reaching from
jungle to sea. Together with Rebekka, they dragged
Betezh's unconscious form up the rocky incline to the
shade offered by towering, hundred-foot hardwoods.

In the shade, they drank milk water from pools
in the jungle, and Franco felt his senses gradually
returning. He eyed Rebekka—now stripped to her
waist and wearing very little by way of clothing—
appreciatively.

"Don't get any ideas," she snapped.

"Just looking. Just looking."

"OK Franco. You're the military man; used to be
a member of a combat squad, and all that. Which
way now?"

Franco stood up, stretching his small barrel
frame. He glanced left, then right. He lifted his
nose, as if sniffing the wind. He puffed out his
chest. He wet his finger and lifted it, tilting his head
as if listening to some internal voice. Then, finally,
he shaded his eyes and scanned the horizon.

"Well?"

"No idea," he shrugged.

"Maybe this could help?" Rebekka held out a PAD and Franco beamed.

"Now that is perfect, my dear."

"Glad to be of service."

Franco primed the PAD, then rotated the inbuilt scanner. "Hmm," he muttered, "looks like we drifted. Point of impact was—shit, look at that."

"What is it?"

"Activity: men, armed, lots of men."

"You mean Ket-i?"

"Them's the fellas. Anyway, they've got guns and are... homing in on a location."

"Our location?"

"No, further up the beach."

"You think it could be Keenan?"

"I'd put money on it," growled Franco. "He attracts trouble like a primary school attracts paedophiles."

Rebekka tutted, frowning. "That's somewhat politically incorrect."

"Hey, I didn't say I *liked* paedophiles. After all, there was that mission where me and Keenan and Vodka set a trap, lured in twenty-three of the slimy good-for-nothing grease-ball maggoty pieces of shit and wasted them. It was like, cool man, and all off the record you understand. Then we buried their rotting corpses in an unmarked grave under Stavros's Scrap Cars Inc." He coughed, and fidgeted for a moment. "Anyway, we managed to fool the Crimes Against Humanity Committee. Although I don't know how the fuck they managed to class those slimy weasel-faced paedos as fucking human in the first place... always the same, innit? Some social governmental department protecting the slime of the earth: how can they? When the slime in question is a deviant misrepresentation of what we consider human?"

"Franco? Keenan? Big trouble? Armed Ket-i?"

"Yeah. Follow me."

"What about Betezh?"

"Hit him."

"What?"

"Hit him. Guaranteed to wake him up, after all, he gets a hard-on for violence."

"It's OK," muttered Betezh, "I'm awake. I've got another lump to add to the catalogue of abuse inflicted on my person, but I *am* awake. Wish I wasn't, though."

"Should have thought about that before coming after me! Ha!"

"Franco," said Betezh through squinting eyes, "you just don't see the bigger picture, do you? This isn't about you. This is about the whole squad: Combat-K, previously convicted of war crimes; General Kotinevitch; the whole damned War Fleet."

"Huh?"

"You live a simple little life, don't you, Franco?"

"Better that way. Keeps me more—" he twitched, "y'know, in focus. Now, come on! Get on up there ahead. Before I have to—y'know—prod you."

Betezh scrambled to his feet, and was poked ahead by a pointed stick Franco had found half buried in sand. It had curious notches and markings; if Franco had looked closely he would have realised it was not some simple tribal weapon, but made of the latest TitaniumIII MicroAlloy. The stuff they used to build starships and FTL craft: expensive.

"It's going to be dark soon," said Rebekka, voice soft.

Franco winked. "It's all right, love. *I'll* look after you."

"I know." She shivered. "That's what I'm afraid of."

KEENAN HAD SPENT his entire working life in the military. No: more. He had spent his entire working life in incredibly dangerous situations, and he had a nose for when something was wrong, an instinct that did not compute with normal, mortal man. This instinct made him good at his job: a sixth sense that kept him alive. And, as his eyes flickered open in the darkness, this otherness, this feeling deep inside his veins and his bones spoke to him, with words of warning, words of blood, words of violence. Silently, he moved to Pippa—asleep now beside the fire—and took one of the religiously cleaned MPKs. He slotted a magazine home with the tiniest of well-oiled *clicks*; the sound brought Pippa instantly awake.

"Trouble?"

"Yeah, I think."

Pippa took a weapon and they both moved to a crouch, the fire to their backs, the practically impenetrable mass of the jungle before them, a wall, a block, a tangle of living, breathing, squawking, screeching confusion.

"How many?"

"More than ten," said Keenan. "We're too open here; let's get into the foliage. That which hides them will also hide us."

"I hate jungle warfare," hissed Pippa, voice hardly more than an exhalation of warm air.

"Amen to that."

They moved forward with infinite ease. The jungle reared around them, above them, a towering mammoth stretch of creepers and ferns, bushes and trees. Trunks clamoured for freedom. Branches reached for life-giving sunlight.

In the jungle, everything seemed—suddenly—silent: a deep and oppressive silence; cloying, claustrophobic, like a hot pillow over your face, a pine-oiled gag stuffed down your throat.

Keenan halted, sinking to the ground.

Pippa followed, moving her back to him. They touched. She pressed a signal against his ribs and he responded. They manoeuvred weapons and waited.

They're coming.

I hear them.

They were like ghosts gliding through the jungle. They moved with care, footsteps picked singly, heavy weapons presented for action, eyes focused and alert. Was it just a coincidence they were approaching Combat-K's little campsite? Was it a coincidence that a few hours earlier they'd been shot out of the sky and crashed a Hornet attack fighter in the sea?

Keenan thought not.

He steadied his weapon.

Something screeched in the jungle, and suddenly everything was chaos, as a creature, large and bulky and squealing like a pig charged, bouncing from the trunks of trees. Three of the men opened fire, bullets screaming on trajectories of tracer through the darkness, thudding into trunks and slapping leaves and Keenan levelled his MPK and gave three three-round bursts. Bullets whined, kicking through foliage, and lifted one of the large Ket-i warriors from his feet, spinning him back to slap into a hardwood. His chest imploded. Blood spattered the trunk. Bullets turned on Keenan, and he powered his weapon, gunning down the huge tribal figures that loomed from the darkness; Keenan sprinted forward, to the right, circling the group of attackers. Their weapons yammered. Tracer spat orange confetti streamers through black. Keenan's gun picked another Ket-i soldier off his feet, ploughing him into the sodden blanket of jungle detritus. Pippa was gone in the mayhem. The squealing creature charged at the men, who gunned it down in a shower of blood and bacon. Smoke curled through the trees. Keenan picked off two more soldiers, watching stoically as they hit the ground, thudding dead. *Pippa,* he wanted to scream, but he clamped his mouth tight shut, tracked another dark-skinned warrior, and ducked as bullets whined overhead. Then it came, a cold caress in his mind and he half-turned but saw the Ket-i warrior too late. He saw the gun levelled and he couldn't do it, couldn't make it in time. The swing of his MPK would leave him dead and eating leaves—

Infinity fell. Smoke curled. Muzzles flashed.

The world dropped into a chamber of muffled slow-motion.

Keenan blinked a slow-time lazy blink and saw the finger pull the trigger; saw the sub-machine gun judder and buck, then steady, as bullets *wham wham whammed* from the cool-holed barrel on tiny flashes of fire and slapped a violent dance across the narrow clearing disintegrating petal fronds by his head—

He felt the cut of the bullet slicing his ear.

Stayed cool, and wished for a cigarette.

He reached—too late—for his gun.

CHAPTER 9
THE CHILDREN OF THE SEA

As BULLETS SPEWED around him, Keenan lifted his weapon, aimed, and fired a three-round burst. The Ket-i warrior slammed down, twisting and jerking to the ground, smacked hard to lie suddenly still and broken like some spastic marionette with severed strings. Keenan stared hard through the drifting smoke, allowed a single exaggerated breath to leave his body, then did an internal check: nothing punctured, nothing dead.

He glanced up, for a moment, as if in prayer.

Shit, he thought. So much in this world is luck.

He grinned.

By God, but that fucker was a bad shot.

Silence fell like rain. Footsteps charged the jungle scatter, and the rest of the attackers were gone: black ghosts, dissipated dreams. Then Pippa came gliding from the claustrophobic entanglement and knelt beside Keenan. Her eyes were alert, almost alien in the strange light. "You OK, boss?"

"Yeah. Fuck it. I'm great. Check the bodies. Get their weapons and ammo. God knows we're going to need it."

They checked the bodies, and it was as their earlier research confirmed. The warriors were big men, heavily muscled, covered in war scars and tattoos, and wearing bone jewellery taken—reportedly—from the bodies of warriors they had slain. This was a race whose name for stranger and enemy were the same thing. A race that lived for war, lived to *kill*, as their unprovoked attack had demonstrated.

Warily, Keenan led Pippa back to the beach. The sun was rising, tendrils of fire cutting the horizon into vertical streamers. Keenan moved down to the sea and washed the blood from his face and arms. He watched as a white mist drifted in over the knobbled angular coral and gradually obscured the horizon; it was thick and white, and smelt strangely cool. Returning to Pippa, he shook his head.

"This is a strange place."

"An alien planet?"

Keenan laughed. "Yeah, I suppose so."

They watched the mist, and heard rather than saw Franco's triumphant jog up the beach.

"Keenan!" he boomed. "You're alive!"

"Keep it down, Franco. We've already had one contact."

"Sorry mate."

The small group re-formed, smiling, and with Franco slapping everybody on the back, even

Betezh, who scowled through his bruises and dark, sullen mood.

"At least nobody is dead," beamed Franco, as Pippa handed him an MPK sub-machine gun. Despite his comedy, he handled the weapon expertly and checked its mechanisms, its mag, and its alignment. "We have to be thankful for small mercies."

"Is Cam with you?" asked Keenan.

"No. You mean... the little bugger might have been squashed?"

"I think he would have found us by now. He would have been able to scan for us. Shit."

"Yeah, but look at the positives," said Franco sombrely, and then broke into a grin. "He might have been squashed!"

Rebekka smiled, almost shyly, at Keenan. He looked away, back to Pippa, who was watching closely with a strange expression on her face. She turned to the sea and gazed distantly, away into a swirling, thickening mist.

"What now?" grinned Franco. He stood, hoisting his weapon. Milk mist crept up the beach and swirled around his boots, drifting off in skeins to infiltrate the jungle.

Pippa held up her hand. "Wait. Listen."

They all heard them: motors, low-level stealth engines purring close by. The sounds cruised and echoed eerily through the mist, one coming quite close. Franco, who had his battered PAD out on his knee, gestured to the team:

One boat, two occupants, heavily armed.

There's our transport, signalled Keenan. *Seems safer than going across land.*

Keenan held up his hand, fist clenched. *Wait here.*

He moved to the edge of the Milk Sea; white water lapped his boots, then he waded in to knee depth and glanced back. His companions were gone. The mist had grown much thicker, and was still developing and building. Keenan knew he had only minutes. For all he knew, the twin suns would burn the mist away into vapour and they would be exposed on the beach to yet more men with guns.

He focused on the *buzz* of the stealth engine. The boat was inside the enclosing embrace of angular coral, which they had spotted from the beach. Keenan moved further out into shallow waters, his MPK poised, eyes and ears alert.

The boat was coming closer. Keenan smiled a sick smile.

It suddenly appeared, gleaming and slick with white brine, the narrow hull and specialised markings designating it as a Raptor Boat, a special forces tool used across a thousand worlds. *What were you expecting?* he thought, *a bamboo canoe?*

There were two heavily armed Ket-i warriors onboard; their eyes widened as they spotted him, but too late, as Keenan's hand grasped the Raptor, and his MPK was in the pilot's face. The boat slowed. The engine *buzzed*. Keenan smiled a smile filled with promise.

"Do you understand me?"

"Yes, alien."

"Bring the boat in to shore, slowly, and I won't put a bullet in your pretty face."

The two huge warriors exchanged glances, and Keenan saw them tense, ready to attack. They were a warrior race. They were not taken prisoner; they fought to the death.

The Ket-i lunged for the MPK, and Keenan put a round in the warrior's shoulder; the bullet exited in a shower of shoulder-blade shards, hissing off into the mist. The soldier recoiled, face twisted in agony as he stumbled back into the Raptor Boat's interior, and Keenan levelled the MPK at the second Ket-i.

"You want some as well? This time I'll put you down."

The warrior shook his head, and Keenan climbed aboard the Raptor, rocking it savagely. The Ket-i steered the boat onto the shore, and Keenan gestured for the two to exit. The Ket-i warrior helped his wounded companion and they stood on the sand, looking a little sheepish.

"This isn't their way," said Pippa.

Keenan shrugged. "Live or die. They are choosing to live."

"Good choice," nodded Franco. He approached the huge warriors warily, and bound their hands behind their backs using raze-wire. Then, kicking the backs of their knees, he rolled them onto their faces and bound their ankles.

"Look how the heroes operate," sneered Betezh.

Keenan rounded on him. His face was a mask of controlled fury, and Betezh recoiled.

"Shut up," growled Keenan, "or I'll feed you to the sharks."

"Sharks?" muttered Franco.

"I thought you did your research?" laughed Pippa. "The Milk Sea is crawling with them. The water gives them powerful nutrients, and they hunt by scent anyway so the clouded waters don't impede navigation and feeding; they grow *real* big here."

"Don't like sharks," muttered Franco, and climbed onto the boat. He helped Rebekka to board, and the others climbed on, Betezh jabbed hard in the spine by Keenan's MPK.

Then, through the mist came a tiny buzzing sound, and Cam emerged, a little more battered, a little more dented, a little more aggravated. He floated graciously to Keenan's side, and the big man smiled at the machine.

"I knew you weren't dead, little buddy."

"I got caught up in a magnetic field from one of the engines; dragged me to the bottom of the sea."

"Thought you smelt a little fishy," guffawed Franco.

"Glad to see you haven't lost your sense of humour." Cam's voice was as cold as the tomb-world.

Franco pushed the boat out, then jumped in with a splash of spray. They bobbed for a few moments, and Cam analysed the boat's controls. "Pretty standard," he said, smugly. "Should be no problem for a team like this. After all, you're professional." He seemed to be staring hard at Franco, although they couldn't be sure. He had no eyes.

Franco made for the controls; Pippa halted him. "Where you going, midget?"

Franco frowned. "I will pilot."

"Oh no, that's my job."

"What, after you crashed the Hornet?"

Pippa reddened. "We were shot out of the damn sky!"

"You were still in charge. What about, y'know, anti-missile missiles? ATRAMS? Scorchers? And all that? I thought you were the best? Well, you did a damn shit job back there, lass."

Pippa shoved Franco hard. "I pilot. You keep an eye on your boyfriend, just in case he needs more stitches."

Now it was Franco's turn to redden.

Pippa revved the engine, then cruised out into the mist leaving the white-sand shore behind. She eased along the pink ridge of coral and, as they passed close, they could see creatures embedded, fossilised, in its angular flanks. All looked to be in agony: tiny mouths open, screaming.

"Hell, look," said Franco.

Pippa slowed the boat. There, embedded, was a Ket-i warrior, bent over almost double, mouth open in a terrible agony. He was frozen, fossilised in the pink coral, a bas-relief carving.

"Back off," snapped Keenan.

"What?"

"Get back! Now!" he hissed, voice tinged with panic.

Pippa slammed the engines into reverse and the Raptor spun, but even as they were moving, the coral also started to move... and with tiny *crackling* crunches its angular form jerked, sections piling out in staccato columns towards the boat and there, at the end, long pink razor-sharp teeth.

"Nooo!" howled Franco.

Keenan discharged twenty rounds into the crackling coral maw, which chipped and splintered, sparks flying, slivers of pink and white shearing free and tumbling into the Milk Sea. Pippa slammed the Raptor into power mode. The engines roared, suddenly unleashed from their stealth encumbrance, and the Raptor howled away back towards the beach.

She spun the boat around with a surge of water. They watched, horrified, and the coral crackled, and then returned to its angular rigid mould. In the blink of an eye it was static, a tableaux. Echoes of gunshots reverberated through the mist. Booms clattered distantly.

Mist drifted and swirled.

The sounds of other Raptor Boats increased.

"Get us out of here," growled Keenan, rubbing at his stubbled chin. Franco joined him, and they hung over the sides of the boat, MPKs tracking the mist as Pippa threw caution to the wind and slammed the throttle forward. Engines roared, the sounds reverberating and they hammered, bouncing across white waters, past the aggressive attack coral, or whatever the hell type of mutation it was, and out onto the open sea.

The mist was thicker and more enduring than they had thought. After ten minutes of flat out high speed, bouncing from one wave to the next, Pippa halted their progress and they sat, riding the gentle swell of milk waves as Franco stabbed at his PAD. They seemed to have lost the other boats.

"OK. Fortune gave us several points of reference in case of emergency. Using his navigation coordinates, I can take us to a disused military base, an old Gem Rig."

Keenan nodded. "Might be some supplies. God knows we need them, even the basics. Patch the coordinates through to the computer; Pippa, check he's doing it right."

"Hey!" snapped Franco.

"Hey yourself," said Keenan. "I don't want any more bullshit. This mission has been a farce from start to finish. From this point on, I want everything checking and double-checking. If you don't like it Franco, then you'd better swim back to that island, because that's the way it's going to be."

"What's a Gem Rig?" said Rebekka. She looked tired, weary from the heat and the tension of being hunted. Her hair was matted, face drawn, rings around her eyes.

"The Ket-i are renowned through the Quad-Gal for their extraction of jewels. Beneath the Milk Sea and areas of jungle there is a plethora of gems to be found: diamonds, rubies, emeralds, kankas, sapphires, yuyus, and all manner of even more esoteric gemstones. The Ket-i are experts in extraction, cutting and polishing. Their stones—at least before the war and accelerated unpopularity—were much sought. Gems made Ket a rich world; vast fortunes of which they spent on arms and hardware." Keenan smiled grimly. "A Gem Rig is just that: a floating platform out to sea used in the extraction of precious stones. This one is—according to Fortune—abandoned. It was a Gem Rig, then the fields were cleaned out and it was eventually used by the Ket-i military as an offshore storage depot. Now, it seems, it no longer has any intrinsic military value."

Rebekka nodded. "Yeah. Now I think about it, in The City such stones pass for great sums. They used to be smuggled in, back when we had customs. Those days are long gone." She smiled, rubbing at her eyes. "You look tired, Keenan."

"You too."

"I think we could all do with some sleep." She caught Pippa's stare and smiled sweetly. Pippa turned away. She worked with Franco on inputting PAD coordinates on an alien system; then she slammed the Raptor Boat forward through the Milk Sea on waves of pure white.

THE MIST WAS burned off within the hour, to be replaced by towering thunder clouds gathering quickly, silently, eerily overhead. The humidity was great, increasing by the minute, or so it felt; the air was filled with a charge of static, and the weather left most of the group in a state of undress as Pippa piloted the Raptor unchallenged across the apparently deserted waters of the Milk Sea.

"It's gonna tonk it down," said Franco, eventually, face beaming red with sunburn.

"Good," said Keenan, "I could do with a little coolant."

Pippa glanced at him, then at Rebekka. "I can see that," she said. Rebekka looked away.

They cruised through the day, hours dragging by in the heat as still clouds towered and the humidity increased. Rebekka and Betezh basked at the rear of the boat, Betezh's arms tied tight behind him, his eyes burning with an ever-increasing hatred. Pippa piloted, Keenan navigated, and Franco checked their weapons and played with the WarSuits, checking circuits and internal logic systems. Cam followed at a discreet pace, small black shell spinning, tiny yellow lights flickering against his battered shell.

Eventually, the rain came.

One minute the sea was calm, then a wind blew cool air in a welcome gasping relief. It grew dark. The heavens suddenly opened and a tropical storm smashed down.

Everyone on the boat turned faces to the sky and basked in the deluge of warm raindrops.

After an hour, something loomed ahead through the pounding rain. Made shapeless by the storm, it rose from the sea like a titan, an edifice, a cliff-side. Pippa halted, stealth engines back in play, the Raptor bobbing and rising on swells, then sweeping down into troughs.

"What do you think?"

"We have few options," said Keenan, hoisting his slick MPK. "We need food and water, better weapons and ammunition. I wish we knew what bastard blew us out of the sky; I'd like to give him some payback. A few bullets up the arse, for sure."

"The WarSuits are good to go," said Franco, glancing up. He held a small cross-head screwdriver. Keenan stared at it.

"What've you been doing with that?"

"Tweaking."

"Well, don't touch my fucking suit. I want it bespoke, not meddled with by a monkey on anti-depressants."

"Harsh, Keenan."

"Well, just keep your twin-thumb paws off."

"Plan?"

"Me and Franco will suit up, swim ahead, check out this Gem Rig. If it's clear, we'll call you in."

"And if its not?"

Keenan grinned with his teeth; and without humour. "I'll see what I can do."

KEENAN AND FRANCO, guns strapped to their backs, swam through the rain. The Gem Rig came gradually closer, towering above them for what seemed like a hundred storeys, but was probably closer to fifty. It shifted gently like a floatation sky-scraper, huge waist-thick mooring cables spanning from higher reaches and disappearing under the milk.

Keenan stopped, treading water. Rain smashed around him.

"We OK?" said Franco.

"You've got better eyesight, but I can see no lookouts."

"Me either, and the PAD is clear."

"I don't trust tek. It can be fooled."

"The PAD is advanced, Keenan."

"Stuff the PAD."

"You're in a fine mood."

"Well tek landed us in this crap. Why didn't the Hornet detect an attack? What a load of shit. I trust only my eyes and ears from now on... and my gun."

"A fine philosophy."

"Let's move."

They swam closer, under the shadow of the looming Gem Rig. Up close, it was truly, truly massive. A dark mass with decks rearing above them led to boxed-in quarters, then, further up, cranes and platforms, huge factories on stilts, then even further up the edifice more sections reminiscent of a hotel rather than a drilling and mining platform.

"It has no right to sit on the sea like that," said Franco. "It shouldn't be able to float."

Keenan grunted something incomprehensible.

They found a wide landing pad, once commonly used for boats but now rusted by the high salt and mineral content of the Milk Sea. Warily, they climbed free, each covering the other with MPK. Standing in the dark WarSuits—which had adapted organically to fit them like a second armoured skin—both men stared up at the monster above and around them.

"I've got a bad feeling about this," said Franco.

"Me too. Come on. Let's clear the place."

A metal staircase led up and they crept with guns primed. The next level was a loading bay with short, squat cranes and abandoned drilling gear. Huge wheels and machinery sat rusting silently. This platform must have been a hive of activity once; probably a quarter of a square kilometre, now it was cold and desolate. Even Franco shivered.

"How come the sun doesn't heat down here?"

"Mass, I think," said Keenan, voice low, almost reverent. "The whole structure acts like a huge heat sink. It would take twenty suns to heat this interior; the simple twins just don't have the firepower."

Franco checked his PAD. "Still nothing. I think you're being overcautious."

"Yeah, but who's the boss?"

"Lead the way then, boss."

Keenan moved through the ghostly interior. Rain pounded around the distant edges of H-section supported alloy, dripping from ledges in long white streamers. Shadows fell in strange patterns. Above, the whole world seemed to rest on vast metal shoulders. It was incredibly oppressive and claustrophobic, and Franco found he was ducking unnecessarily as he moved, as if frightened the whole bulk of the Gem Rig would come crushing down on his head.

They found another flight of stairs. Above, something clattered, distant and muffled.

Keenan shot Franco a glance. "Still think we're alone?"

Franco cocked his weapon and checked the mag. "Lead on, MacDuff."

The ramp was wide, trickling with intruding rainfall. Keenan walked slowly up, MPK tracking above him, finger on the hairline trigger. Franco followed close, covering arcs of fire.

A warehouse. Huge rusted crates stood abandoned. *Lots of hiding places,* thought Keenan. He moved warily, and came to a small flickering fire. Flames crackled within a ring of steel blocks, the edges of which glowed. Stools stood around the fire, again fashioned from metal and once set with precious gems, all of which had been prised free.

Now only rust and decay claimed these items; and the place as a whole.

"A ghost town," said Franco.

"Somebody was here."

Suddenly, Franco unleashed a hail of bullets at the ceiling. Metal screeched on metal. Sparks crackled, and Keenan half-ducked, eyes squinting and angry as he glared at Franco.

"What you doing, dumb arse?"

"Sorry! Sorry."

Distantly, they heard a scrabbling sound, and saw movement.

"It's kids," said Franco, voice low. He strode forward, and Keenan followed. Between two crates they came upon a group of six or seven children, it was hard to tell in the gloom. Not one was over the age of twelve years, and they stared back with wide eyes, stark against jet black skin. They cowered, as if expecting violence.

Franco lowered his gun and crouched down. "It's OK," he said, and held out his hand.

"They're not dogs, Franco."

Ignoring Keenan, Franco moved forward in a strange Quasimodo half-walk, half-crouch, and the children reached out, touching his hand as if it was a thing of wonder. Then Franco stood, suddenly, and the kids shrank back, fear etched on ebony faces.

"Come on," said Franco, "back to the fire. We mean you no harm. Can you understand me?"

One boy, the largest of the group, pushed to the front and nodded warily. His eyes were haunted. "I understand you," he said, his words coming thick and slow, slurred by the inevitability of different customs, different cultures, different worlds. In one hand he carried a slim bottle of water and he drank from it, nervously.

"We mean you no harm."

"I am Klik," said the boy. He held out his free hand, and solemnly Franco shook it.

"I'm Franco, Franco Haggis. What you doing here, lad?"

"We are from tribes on the mainland, near the capital city you know as Amrasar. When the tribes go to war and our fathers and mothers are killed, we are to die also. They slaughter us in our beds; they hang us from city walls by our necks. They cut off our arms and put out our eyes. They leave us impaled on spikes on the Crimson Walks leading up to The City of Bone."

"So you run away? Here?"

"Yes. This is Haven. This is our salvation."

"Why do they kill you?" asked Franco, voice soft, eyes burning. "You are but children?"

"We will grow into men: tough men, men with a good reason to kill and die, and seek revenge. Men like us would be a great danger in future years; so they slaughter us like cattle when our families are gone."

"How many are you?"

"Just this seven," said Klik. He smiled, narrowing his thin lips. "Yesterday we were ten; a week ago, twenty; but more will come, on boats, or swimming, or on rafts. Haven is an underground beacon. It calls to the children. More will come, and then we can fight the Dogs; maybe then we will find more food and we can eat like kings!"

They walked back to the fire and sat around the flames. Only then did Keenan and Franco realise that the fire was not a traditional, wood-burning fire, but a metta-melt furnace; a small one, but still metta-melt. They watched the spikes of metal melt and fold, then re-form to be burned again. The flames were tinged with purple and green. It was hypnotic; would have been romantic if their surroundings hadn't been so bleak.

"Why do so many die here?" asked Franco. His eyes locked on Keenan, and Keenan gave a single nod: patronage.

Klik put his head in his hands, for a moment. "This place is a maze. It used to be military base. Upstairs are the supplies stores, on Deck 15. This is the place we get our food; the place that allows us to survive."

"And the Dogs?"

"The Dogs guard the stores. We take it in turns, sneak in and steal what few tins we can. But sometimes the Dogs find us, sniff us out. When they do, they slaughter us."

"Are there many supplies here?" asked Keenan, and Klik looked at the large man for the first time.

He nodded. "Hundreds and hundreds of metal containers, boxes, drums; all stamped, some with clothing, some food, some weapons. But the Dogs are so dangerous; they are merciless. We have tried to kill them, but they are too powerful."

"We can take care of a few dogs!" beamed Franco, and hoisted his MPK. "Can't we Keenan? Time for a bit of muzzling, I think."

Ignoring Franco, Keenan stared at Klik. "What are these Dogs? Before my friend goes volunteering us for certain death."

"There are three of them," said Klik, carefully.

"Ha! Only three!" buzzed Franco. His eyes gleamed. He patted Klik on the shoulder. "We'll clear you a path to the food stores, lad. Don't you worry you none."

"'Don't you worry you none?' Franco, what the hell are you gibbering about?" Franco simply grinned and cocked his MPK. As if to say: "we mean business", which of course, they did.

"They are machines," said Klik, "with battle armour. Your guns will have no effect. We have tried; we got weapons from the stores, but their armour is too thick. They are indestructible!"

"Stay here," said Keenan, standing. "I'll go back for the others. Listen, are there other enemies on this Rig? Any men? Ket-i?"

Klik shook his head. "The Rig is deserted, except for the Dogs. But they are enough. They have killed... perhaps a hundred of us, over the past year. We let the sea claim bodies in a final ritual."

"A hundred?" said Keenan. His jaw hardened. "Well, it's about time we got you some payback."

THEY DRIED THEMSELVES in front of the metta-melt furnace. Franco tied Betezh to an array of thick pipes, and the shaven-headed man sat, battered head down, eyes hooded.

The children had hidden when the rest of the group arrived, but slowly emerged, wary and wide-eyed. Klik brought them food, meagre supplies of cheese and fish in tins. Pippa smiled, as Rebekka stood and moved among the black children, stroking their heads and patting shoulders. Her face had come alight, as if she had finally come home.

"I cannot believe it," said Rebekka after the tale had been re-told, "a hundred of you! Dead! By machines?" She stared hard at Keenan. "We must stop this. We must end this."

"And we must find weapons," said Keenan, voice gentle. He smiled. "OK, volunteers for Operation Dog Trap?"

"Me," said Franco. "I fancy me some road kill."

"You mean gun kill," said Pippa, glancing at him.

"Whatever."

"You been taking your tablets, Franco?"

"Funnily enough, after you got our Hornet blasted, flaming and honking from the skies, there doesn't seem to be a local pharmacy." He smiled. "But then, I've never felt better! Absolutely buzzing! Full of beans! Full of... life!" He grinned again.

"It won't last long," said Betezh, voice hardly more than a growl.

Attention focused on him, on his battered, dirt-smeared physique. His head rose slowly, eyes glowing dark by the light of the metta-melt furnace. He stared at the group with ill-disguised contempt.

"What's that supposed to mean?" said Pippa.

"The drugs," said Betezh, rubbing at his eyes. Raze-wire cut his wrists, opening old wounds.

Blood ran down his flesh, and dripped to the rusted metal between battered boots. "They were a very special concoction. Reactive, you could say."

"Reactive?"

"Tetra hydrochlorinate, fezta sulphide, pallium binoxroate: the drugs are ingested, bond to human DNA receptors, become part of the patient, until death. It's the latest breakthrough in medical science." He laughed, focusing on Franco. "Ideal for mental patients."

"Why's that?" said Franco, a deep crease furrowing his brow.

"Because if supply is withdrawn, the patient dies."

"Bullshit," said Pippa. "Don't believe him. He's bluffing."

"Am I?" said Betezh. "Why would I? It's not like I'm bartering. It's not like I really give a fuck. All I know is, if Franco doesn't get his fix—and soon—strange things will start happening to him, ending, obviously, in an instant but very painful collapse."

"What will happen?" Franco had gone ashen.

"Every molecule in your body will slowly implode. Takes about an hour. I've seen the results. Even the photos make you want to puke. Franco, I've never heard screams like it. I watched, from an Experiment Booth. I wasn't aware that human vocal chords were capable of such sounds, and for such a prolonged period." Betezh gave a fake shudder. "Gives me the heebie jeebies."

Franco levelled his gun.

"No," said Keenan. "No! Franco, get over there. Pippa, check him over. And for God's sake, take his gun off him… Betezh." Keenan put his own MPK in Betezh's battered face. "Keep your mouth shut, fucker, or I *will* drill you full of metal."

Betezh shrugged, but closed his mouth. His eyes returned to the floor.

"OK," said Keenan. "Me, Pippa, Franco, we'll go and sort these Dogs out. Rebekka," he handed her a gun, which she took, a little reluctantly, "you keep an eye on our resident shit-stirrer. If he blinks, shoot him."

"What, in front of the kids?"

"Yes, in front of the kids. Rebekka, they've seen a hundred of their friends ripped to shreds by mechanical creatures; I think one more atrocity won't tip them over the edge. And Cam?"

"Yes, Keenan?"

"Have you heard of these Dogs?"

"No, Keenan, sorry." The small PopBot spun. The metta-melt glittered from its dark case. "They sound a bit like Andalusian Mek-Backs, but those creatures are AIs. They'd never kill children. AIs are not like that. And anyway, they're very rare; were decommissioned centuries ago."

Pippa snorted.

"Well, we'll soon find out. Rebekka, you OK?"

She nodded.

"Franco, Pippa, let's go and see what all the fuss is about."

DECK 15.

The leading corridor was lit by a few stuttering lights. An enclosed area, the corridors were narrow and lined with pipes, silent and cold within the belly of the Rig... and as dead as the rest of the rotting shell. This was soon followed by an area of titanic proportions: the Gem Rig's storeroom.

It was dark, gloom-laden: a ceiling-high stacked hive of crates, metal cubes, alloy canisters, barrels, boxes, shelving, tubs, jars, tubes, and a myriad of alien storage units, several of which twisted into another dimension and created brain-ache at a glance.

Franco was sweating, and sweating hard. On his hands and knees, with distant red light giving weak illumination, he waited, listening, sweat beading his forehead, prickling between his shoulder blades, lathering his flanks.

"Volunteer," he muttered, a frown eating his brows. Then, affecting Keenan's voice, he said, "Ha! I need a volunteer. As the decoy! Ahhh Franco. So good of you to raise your hand!" And Franco, stood there, scratching his nose. "Wha'?"

Now he knelt, and jiggled like a pressure nozzle being gradually turned up. Franco had to admit it; his nerves were getting to him.

Somewhere in this warren, maze, labyrinth, hive, were three metal creatures the children referred to as Dogs, which had slaughtered their way through a hundred little people. It made Franco sick; it made him want to kill; but most of all, he knew how resourceful children could be, and so it made him a tad nervous of what he was actually up against. So far, Ket hadn't appeared too friendly.

Franco scampered forward on hands and knees. He checked his earpiece, linked back to the battered PAD and locked in to Cam's frequencies for relaying and bouncing signals.

"You still there, Franco?"

"Still here, boss."

"See anything?"

"Nada."

"There's nothing on the PAD, nothing at all: no movement, no life. The place is as dead as a very dead dodo."

Franco chewed his lip. He'd been in the game long enough to know that just because a scanner wasn't picking up danger, didn't mean it wasn't there. After all, a hundred dead kids were howling from beyond the grave. He had to push on; how could he let any more suffer when he had the hardware to do something about it? That would make him worse than any maggot.

"I'll keep on it."

"Good man."

Keenan and Pippa, some hundred metres behind Franco and tracking him carefully, wore their War-Suits with protection turned to full; their MPKs were primed and ready for an assault.

Franco halted. Red strobe-lights striped his face. His eyes gleamed like a demon's. He wiped sweat from his forehead and glanced around. Towering metal crates loomed over him, forming an unnatural tunnel. Red light gleamed from ersatz metal walls. Franco felt a glimmer of claustrophobia crawl into his mouth, down his throat, and squeeze his stomach in a fist of pressure.

"It's too quiet," said Franco. "It's unnatural."

"Keep moving. They'll be watching you."

"Cheers," said Franco sourly. "You make me feel a whole lot better."

He moved on in a crouch, eyes picking out shadows warily, head moving in steady turns as he tracked for danger. Something was out there; he could smell it, taste it. And it tasted bad.

Working his way through a maze of stacked metal cubic crates, each stamped with stencilled alien lettering, their frames a matt black, their walls polished chrome, Franco halted. He was painfully aware he was open from all angles. There was no wall to place his back against, no bulwark behind which he could seek cover. This was a place of openness, a place of... ambush.

Franco swallowed.

It had come up ahead of him, what appeared to be...

What appeared to be a swarm of glinting dust motes.

The tiny metal objects fluttered and swirled like a swarm of bees, interweaving and moving in almost modulated pulses. They flowed like liquid around the corner and formed into a broad, vaguely rectangular shape.

Franco blinked... and the fluttering, dust-like apparition hardened. It solidified. Went from dust to object; a bare, silver, plain rectangular block of what looked like metal.

Franco pointed his gun. He wasn't ashamed of the fact that the muzzle wavered.

"It's here."

"Yeah," crackled Keenan's voice through the far-from-technologically advanced temporary comms systems. "It's just shown up on the PAD. What is it?"

"It was dust," hissed Franco. Sweat was trickling under his WarSuit; heat prickled his scalp under his ginger shaved stubble. "Particles, all swirling. That's why the PAD couldn't get a fix."

"What do you mean, particles?"

"Like dust, like... shit," said Franco.

"I know what it is," said Cam's voice over the link. "It's an MMPS. Not an AI, but a system that runs to a set of algorithms. Therefore, it has non-life, non-human status. It feels no empathy, just carries out its job. It will be assigned to protect these stores; after all, you don't want any little mook wandering in and stealing military-grade RPGs or RPNs, do you?"

"What's an MMPS?" said Keenan.

"A Myriad Metal Particle System. Can take any shape the programmers decide; similar to a swarm of Nanobots, only much bigger, much less intelligent. At the forefront of military development about ten years ago, before NanoTek became involved and upped the stakes of nano-molecular technology. MMPS was the forerunner; the simple, and retarded, father."

"Is it dangerous?" asked Franco, eyeing the solid block with a squint of wariness.

"Oh yes," said Cam's voice, very soft now, little more than a digital whisper.

"What's it doing?" said Keenan.

"Nothing. Just... well, it's just there. A solid block, about the size of—wait, wait... it's growing."

The block seemed, for a moment, to become insubstantial, like a ghost. Then it flexed, and started to enlarge. Franco wanted desperately to back away, but decided not to move. What happened if it hunted on movement? Shit. *Shit*! He chewed his lip, glancing down at his MPK. It seemed, suddenly, pointless. He had no armour piercing rounds, no glow-shells, no liq-N bombs. How could he fight something that was, to all intents and purposes, a cloud of metal dust?

Franco heard the sound of tearing metal through his earpiece.

"We've found some weapons," said Keenan's voice. "We're going to tool up, come and meet you."

"Good," breathed Franco in relief.

Then he watched as the rectangular block of metal started to... morph.

"Keenan, it's doing something."

"Be there in a minute."

"Keenan, it's *changing*."

"Give us a minute, Franco. You're the decoy. You're there to let us get some better weapons. Use your brain. If it charges, run, lead it on a wild goose-chase... or something."

"Cheers Keenan!"

The block was changing, ghost-like, pulsing, legs extruding from the metal body, a head pushing forward with liquid smoothness. It morphed and transmogrified, until it became... a dog.

But it wasn't like any dog Franco had ever seen; this was monstrous, a kind of reptilian dog-shaped horror from the pit of a genetically mutated dog-hell.

He blinked. He frowned. He chewed his lip. He cursed. "Shit," he said, and he meant it, realising his hands were sweat-slippery against his matt weapon. The metal dog was moving, weaving its still elongating and pulsing head from side to side. Scales like armour rippled along its flanks, and huge disjointed teeth crunched from a maw without the ability to close. Pale blanks of dull silver—which served as eyes—turned on Franco and he felt chilled. The thrashing halted.

The Dog stood. It focused on Franco.

It growled.

"Great," snapped Franco, turned, and head down, he ran.

The Dog leapt after him, claws smashing sparks from metal panels on the floor. Its galloping thudded and boomed around the storehouse. Franco pumped his arms like pistons, jaw muscles rigid, MPK flapping uselessly against his chest.

He whirled around a corner, skidding along a stack of crates with the Dog's jaws snapping inches from his arse. Franco yelped, spun, and unleashed a hail of bullets that screamed from the MPK, clattering from armour plates, deflected like droplets of foam. The Dog slid, claws gouging the floor, losing ground. It turned and leapt again, closing on Franco, who pounded down another corridor of storage. Franco leapt, grasping the edge of a huge metal drum and hauling himself up. The Dog's jaws dug sparking grooves in the drum; then it bounced back, clattering to the ground. Franco hauled himself up, moaning and groaning, and stood, looking down at the Dog.

It growled again; a sound like spanners caught in cog wheels.

"Gods, you're one ugly little sucker," spat Franco.

The Dog snapped. Its blank eyes sent shivers down Franco's spine: no intelligence, no sentience, and yet a glimmer there, almost like headlights on a car. There was no life, but sometimes, just in the right light, it could almost look... *alive*.

Franco fired off more rounds. The Dog's metal hide deflected bullets easily. It ignored the irritant like fleas.

"Keenan?"

"We're in, Franco. Whoo-ee, holy shit, we have ourselves an arsenal!"

"Keenan, I've got a problem." Franco watched the Dog trotting away. No, he thought, it can't be that easy. And he was right. It wasn't. "Keenan, they're impervious to bullets. You're gonna need bombs. High J would be a good idea. We need to melt these little maggots."

The Dog was staring, not at Franco, but at the tall drum on which he stood. Franco glanced around. Crates teetered to either side, but were too far away for him to jump. He swallowed with a dry throat, and watched the Dog lower its head, and... charge.

"Bastard," he muttered as the metal thing pounded towards the drum. Franco tensed, and as the Dog connected so he leapt, screeching like a banshee, for the nearest stack of crates. His fingers, outstretched, shaved dust from the top crate, scraped lines of flesh down the wood, and lodged on the second crate down. Franco's legs slammed against the stack and he bounced, thudding, against the wood.

"I made it," he breathed.

The Dog's impact left a huge dent in the massive barrel, which slowly folded, the base appearing to melt inwards, and then crashed to the walkway. The Dog began to savage the metal, twisted jaws and fangs tearing stupidly at the barrel's rim, and pulling free long strips of alloy, curled spiralled shavings, which rattled on the ground.

Franco kicked, struggling to heave himself up to the top crate. His fingers, scorched by friction, scrabbled uselessly. Sweat dripped in his eyes. "Damn and bloody bollocks," he said, watching the Dog finish its impromptu meal of metal, and then turn slowly to stare up at him. It seemed to be grinning.

"Nice doggy," said Franco.

It growled, but the growl seemed suddenly to amplify, to take on a much deeper, resonant tone, a reverberation of metal animal noise that bounced around the corridor and filled Franco's head with a feeling of nausea right down to his belly. Franco altered his angle of viewing, and realised why.

Another two Dogs had appeared, and their growling seemed synchronous. Yet they looked different, one larger than the first, black metal with spikes sticking like spears along its arched ridged spine, and another smaller, sleeker, but with an infinitely more evil look on its long slim metal face. They all had the same blank platters of metal for eyes. Franco watched them pace around the base of the crates, watched the slim one peel off—almost like a fighter in a squadron—and pad away into strip-lit red gloom.

Where's it gone? Bugger. BUGGER!

"Keenan?"

"We're coming."

"You got bombs?"

"We got bombs."

"Thank God!"

"But we can't use them."

"Why the hell not?"

"Cam tells me this place is unstable."

"Unstable? *Unstable?* What the bollocks does he mean unstable? What's unstable about it? Keenan, I'm about to get bloody eaten by these horrible terrible ugly things!"

"Listen, the whole Gem Rig is a structure for drilling gems, not enduring a bout of grenade warfare. Because of its age, Cam thinks any heavy metal detonation might seriously weaken some of the supporting struts, due to resonation, or something."

"Great. Bastard. Just great."

"It's OK. I have 'A Plan'."

"It'd better be a good one!"

"Just hang in there!"

Franco stared at the ground. "I'm trying," he whimpered. He started trying to climb again, and made it halfway up the top crate. Then he caught sight of the slim Dog returning; with a high pitched whine it started to clatter down the corridor, gathering speed and then leaping, sailing through the air with jaws wide. Franco realised with fast-dawning horror that he was not high enough, that it could reach him, that, without its reduced size and weight, it could actually get to him.

He swayed, his whole body a pendulum as the Dog crashed into the wooden crate, crashed into and through the wooden wall of the crate to lodge, half in and half out of the destroyed cube. Franco swung back, his legs bouncing from the stack. The Dog started to kick, growling and whining in a sick parody of a real dog; its legs thrashed and tore at the wood as it tried to reverse. Franco felt a shudder run through the stack of crates, and remembered noticing earlier that the stack was— well—unstable. It had been unevenly stacked, listing dangerously to one side. That meant it could very easily and quite possibly... Fall.

Franco rode the crates like a rodeo cowboy, screaming all the way to the ground. The impact smashed the six crates into shards of exploding wood, and there, stranded in the middle like a turtle on its back was Franco. In the blink of an eye he was surrounded by... grenades.

"I don't bloody believe it!"

What a coincidence, screamed his mind!

What a stroke of incredible luck!

Franco's eyes went wide at the small, black, round alloy bombs—thousands of them—nestling like black eggs in their exploded polystyrene packaging. The Dog, which had been kicking frantically to free itself, rolled from splinters with grenades tumbling from its back like pebble dandruff. It found its feet, rotated to face Franco, and stared into a fist clasping a bomb.

Its mouth opened in a snarl.

Franco tossed the bomb inside, and stumbled back.

Falling and slipping as if on ice, Franco retreated. The Dog choked for a moment, a look of confusion passing across metal features. Then there was a distant, muffled *boom*. The Dog seemed to glow, and then blossom with radiation as its flanks and neck expanded outwards in a shimmering fireball, which, which…

Franco blinked.

A fireball, which was sucked back inside, and reformed into solid metal. The Dog turned. It grinned at him, and belched an acid detonation belch.

"What?" screamed Franco. "What? You little bugger. You should be dead!"

The Dog pounced, Franco slipping and sliding, rolling and tottering on the grenades that had turned suddenly from saviour to betrayer; he fell over onto his back, the Dog above him snarling a metal snarl as eyes narrowed and jaws slammed down.

With a whimper, Franco lifted his arm to protect his face. Teeth clamped his arm, clamped the arm covered in high-tech military WarSuit. There was a *whine*. The WarSuit held. Franco's face went through shades of red and purple. The Dog shook its captured arm like a terrier shakes a rat. Pulses of pain hammered through Franco's flesh and bones. The Dog grunted, exerting yet more pressure. Its jaws began to click and actually bend with the extreme force.

Franco, eye to eye with the beast, grinned.

"Not like eating little kids, is it?" he growled, face to snarl. The Dog shook him. He lifted his MPK, poked the barrel into the Dog's muzzle behind his trapped arm, and unleashed a volley of rounds which screamed into the machine. Smoke rolled from the Dog's nostrils. It started to make curious mechanical sounds, deep internal *whirrings*, but out of joint, out of synch, like an engine about to explode.

Franco kept firing. The MPK's barrel glowed red. More smoke poured free and the sound was terrifying, deafening, a din of metal, screeching metal, tearing metal, raping metal, and suddenly the Dog released Franco and staggered back, sections of it forming into metal particles, which flowed around the floating torso, which glowed, in turn, with a deep inner fusion.

The detonation was coming. Franco could feel it in his bones, in his soul.

Franco found his feet, and scrabbled for more grenades, stuffing them into his pockets. He turned to run, and came face to face with the other two Dogs. He smiled weakly. "Ah. Forgot about you two for a moment there," he said.

They growled, and leapt for his throat.

Franco staggered back drunkenly, and fell towards the juddering, near-fluid machine behind. It yammered. Its eyes rotated like marbles. It was quite obviously about to... detonate.

He heard the tiniest *click* of ignition.

Franco screamed, and covered his head.

CHAPTER 10
EELMARSH

FRANCO'S EYES REMAINED shut, chin between knees, arms folded disjointedly over his head in a parody of protection. He suddenly became aware that he was making a whimpering ululation that, in any other situation, might even have been funny.

And... nothing happened.

Silence fell, drifting like snow.

Franco opened his eyes and squinted through lead-lined lids into the red stroboscopic gloom; it came as a gradual wondering to understand why he wasn't being ripped to shreds by the Dogs... or torn asunder by fire, brimstone, hardcore detonation at the rear.

"You OK, Franco?" It was Pippa's voice, like honey. It melted his tension into a broiling pot of confusion.

Franco squinted harder, forcing himself to stop whimpering. He unfolded slowly, arms first, then his legs, then his cranked torso. He climbed warily to his feet and kicked his boots idly, like a naughty schoolchild scuffing toe-caps. Before him, about six inches from his nose, the two attacking Dogs appeared to be floating: front, war-spiked legs outstretched, jaws wide and glistening with machine oil, eyes blank and yet, in an alien way, intent on the kill, the fodder: Him.

Franco turned and looked at the slim Dog he had fed bullets; it was frozen in a state of swirling particle rearrangement. Inside its almost translucent metal shell a fireball raged in stop-motion. Tiny flames managed to escape and flicker at the edges of the Dog's shell, turning the joins of the glowing metal panels charcoal black.

"You took your time," sniffed Franco, somewhat haughtily.

Keenan strode forward. He held a small black box. He was grinning in victory. "Sorry about that. You nearly ended up as—ah—dog meat, yeah?"

"You look way too happy with yourself, Keenan. What goes down? I thought I was gonna get chewed! You made me wet myself! I even wanted one of my orange pills!"

Keenan waved the box. "Remote control," he said. "The damn things are remote machines; I can control them with this. All I did was freeze them. A pause button, you understand."

Franco rubbed his head. "Where'd you get it?"

"Cam discovered a signal and homed in on the transmitter. It was simply a case of pressing a button, just like on a Green Vision vid-player."

"Very pleased for you," sniffed Franco. He tapped the Dog on the snout, then stepped smartly to one side. "I want them destroyed, all three. I want them destroyed utterly."

"We can do that," said Pippa. She put a hand on Franco's shoulder, recognising how shook up he was. She smiled kindly. "There's a furnace. We can melt them down. Or drown them in the bottomless ocean."

"Amen to that."

Cam's voice came over their kube. "We've got a problem."

"What is it?" growled Keenan, rubbing at his temples. Gods, would it never end?

"It's Betezh," said Cam. "He's escaped."

COMBAT-K POUNDED through red-lit corridors, down ramps and stairs, and swung into the room with the glowing fire and huddled children. Rebekka was pointing the MPK at the entrance through which they emerged; she was shaking, badly.

The group came to a halt. The children were frightened, wide eyed. Even Klik looked shaken.

"What happened?" asked Keenan.

"He broke his bonds," said Rebekka, voice hoarse. "I don't know how. He had a knife, a large black bladed knife. Said he was going to skin us, gut us like fish. All the children..." She shook her head, licking at fear-dry lips. "All of them."

"Why didn't you shoot him?" said Keenan, voice gentle.

"I-I just couldn't."

"Where did he go?" snapped Pippa, trying hard to hide her annoyance, but failing. It came out in her expression, her stance, the whip-crack of her words.

Cam floated in, tiny green lights glowing. "I've just picked him up. He made the stores. Now his signal has just blipped and gone."

"Track blocker?" said Keenan.

"Yes," said Cam. "He knows what he's doing."

"Bastard," hissed Franco. "I knew we should have killed him back on the Hornet. You hear that, Keenan? I told you. I said we should kill him. I told you! Now he's got to the stores, tooled himself up! S'gonna come looking for me again." He twitched.

"Franco," said Keenan, "wait here. Guard the children. Me and Pippa will go after him."

Franco nodded.

"You ready, Pippa?"

"Sure thing."

"And Keenan?" Franco's face was deadly serious, eyes narrowed, face gaunt with exhaustion after his run in with the Dogs—and his narrow escape.

"Yeah?"

"Kill that son of a bitch for me."

"I'll do my best."

THE CHASE WAS a short one. Keenan and Pippa scoured the stores, realising they must have passed Betezh on their way back after disabling the Dogs. He had chosen not to engage them; he had helped himself to weapons, grenades, possibly even food, and fled.

They worked their way through the Gem Rig's stores, and as they approached the locked and frozen Dogs, Cam alerted them to movement down at the base of the Rig. Cursing, Keenan and Pippa screamed down ramps and stairs, just in time to see their Raptor Boat disappearing over the horizon.

A breeze snapped in at them from the Milk Sea. Keenan wiped sweat from his face and made a clicking sound of annoyance at the back of his throat. His eyes met Pippa's.

"What we going to do for transport?" she said.

"There are boats, in the stores: inflatables used by Special Forces. Transport isn't a problem, but that evil bastard on the loose is."

"We can chase him." Her voice was cool. Eyes hard. "Hunt him down."

"No. If he comes looking for us, I'll happily put a bullet in the back of his skull. We've wasted enough time as it is; first on The City, then, after the crash." Keenan sagged a little. Pools of shadow darkened his eyes. Exhaustion ghosted him. "We need some rest."

"The Ket-i might pick him up. They were sure happy to open fire on us. Looks like they don't make friends easily."

"Maybe. I'm still uneasy about leaving him behind, but we've no option. Rest, then push on. It'll take us two days to reach Amrasar; then we have to infiltrate and steal this Fractured Emerald."

"I hope Fortune's plans are accurate."

"So do I. Our lives depend upon it."

Pippa moved forward, close. Keenan's breath was a sharp intake. She smiled up at him, reached out and stroked his cheek. She said nothing.

"What's that for?" he asked gently.

Again, breeze snapped in from the sea. Water lapped at the landing ramp. Above them, the disused Gem Rig creaked, a titan sighing as it rested against great rusting legs.

"Does it have to be for anything?"

"Yes."

"Then, I'm worried about you. There, I've said it."

"Why?"

Pippa gave a half-shrug, turned her back on him, and strode up the ramp. Keenan stood for a while, staring at the space she had just vacated; then he turned, eyes narrowing at the distant spot that had consumed Betezh.

"I'd kill for a roll-up," he muttered, spat into the lazily slapping white, and followed Pippa into the belly of the beast.

THEY'D TAKEN IT in turns to sleep and keep guard. Klik had led a whooping, giggling raiding party into the Gem Rig's stores, where all the children had taken turns beating the disabled Dogs with metal poles—not so much for pleasure, but in a needful warlike retribution for so many of their dead friends.

Keenan, huddled in a thick sleeping bag in the corner, did not dream. He simply sank into an embrace of deep black, was swallowed by velvet and fur, sank down, down, down into warmth and softness, and then awoke, groggy and weary from his coma. He lay for a while, listening to the ambient sounds around him: the creaking of the Rig, the distant lapping of the Milk Sea. Children laughed occasionally and this brought lightness to his heart, lifting his dark mood. And he could hear Pippa and Franco arguing over what supplies they would take with them.

Pippa appeared, looming over him. She crouched, smiling. "I've brought you a present."

"Hmm?" Keenan rubbed sleep from his eyes, as Pippa handed him a tin of Widow Maker tobacco. He grinned like a schoolboy, face an illumination. "You'll tell me I'm dreaming in a minute, right?"

"No. The stores here are extensive. Military stores; have you ever met a squaddie who didn't smoke?"

"Not many," conceded Keenan. "What's the rest of the kit like?"

"Plenty of guns and ammo, Sig Sauers, Sphinx AT7000s, Steyr AUG Paras, Zastavas, Heckler & Koch Q90s, Barrett M2000s, even some esoteric alien machinery. There's also ammo for your Techrim; fifty-two round mags. Plenty of guns and bombs, but nothing incredibly high-tech; we've got bullet proof vests, but no additions to our War-Suits; there are a couple of boats, like you said, even some TT RPGs, and a single solitary RPN that Franco took a shine to."

"A Rocket Propelled Nuke?"

"Yeah."

"That's an insane weapon. Do not—I repeat, *do not*—let Franco bring it with him. That's all we need, a madman with a nuclear warhead strapped to his groin."

"I'll try my best. There's also about a million crates of tinned food. It's what the kids have been living on."

Keenan grinned. "So we've got supplies," he said, and finished rolling his first cigarette in what felt like a lifetime. He lit it with his trusty old Zippo, clouds of grey plumed and puffed from the cocoon of his sleeping bag. Keenan rested his head back and sighed, a deep sigh. "That feels good," he said. He closed his eyes.

"What's that smell?" he said eventually.

"Soup. Klik made a huge pan and the kids are all lounging around with full bellies for the first time in a year. Franco is dipping slices of cheese in his."

"Cheese? In soup?"

"Yeah, that rubbery tinned army cheese. It's quite disgusting to watch. I feel oddly ill."

Keenan laughed, then propped himself on one elbow. He watched Pippa carefully; she was radiant in the gloom.

"There's room in here for two," he said, voice level, low, edged with sudden nervousness.

He watched as Pippa's face changed. A mask slotted neatly behind her skin and her eyes went hard, cold. She stood, turned away, then turned back to him. She seemed about to say something, then chewed at her lip.

"I didn't mean sex," said Keenan. There was a gentleness about him. "I meant... just friendship, comfort, warmth."

She met his gaze.

Keenan smoked for a while.

"I'm not in the mood for your fucking games," she said finally, and stalked away. Keenan sighed, stubbed out his cigarette, and immediately lit another. Food could wait, but his fix had to be fulfilled.

"Damn it," he muttered, and snuggled further down into his sleeping bag.

* * *

TWO HOURS LATER, Keenan sat studying the TuffMAP™ of Ket. Cam floated beside him, strangely silent, a single white light blinking. Keenan had traced their route, and looked at the markings furnished by Fortune. They were heading to Amrasar, one of the five capital cities on the planet; it was huge, sprawling, heavily fortified, and according to Fortune, did not welcome strangers, at all.

"It will have to be a covert entry," said Cam.

Smoke streamed from the roll-up in Keenan's fingers. He nodded. "Yeah, I know. We could do with an insider, somebody who knows the place."

"What about the children?"

"No, I couldn't drag them back. They've had enough of a rough time as it is. It wouldn't be fair, especially when considering the nature of our mission—that of theft."

"Klik said he came from Amrasar. He will know the land."

"Maybe I'll talk to him," said Keenan, smoking.

"I would recommend it," said Cam. The small PopBot started to spin faster. Keenan nodded.

"It's been a hectic ride, hasn't it little pal?"

"You could say that, Keenan."

"So what's it like for a GradeA Security Mechanism with advanced SynthAI and an MIR of 3150 to actually *go* on an adventure? Is it everything you hoped for? Is it… shall we say, exciting enough to alleviate the boredom you felt back on Galhari?"

"Let's just say the ride has been far from dull."

"Have you forgiven Franco? For the right hook?"

"He told you about that, did he?"

"Yeah," grinned Keenan. "Look, you know it wasn't personal, don't you? I should have known nothing could stand between Franco, a pint of Guinness and a one-legged whore."

Cam seemed to sigh. He stopped spinning and just hung, immobile. "It's just," said the little machine, "it is a little degrading to be thumped and then volleyed like the main attraction at a penalty shootout. It's not something I anticipated; not something I appreciate."

"He has been locked up for a while, Cam. I can kind of appreciate his need."

"Listen Keenan, it is my opinion that Franco is a serious threat to this mission. He is unpredictable, unfeasibly cheerful, and quite obviously utterly mad."

"Ye-es, but he's a good bloke to have beside you in a fire-fight. He looks after his friends, and where it counts he's as good as ten men. He is also a demolitions expert, and I've got a feeling we're going to need that skill to get to the Fractured Emerald."

"It's in a vault?"

"Oh yes," said Keenan, "a mile beneath the surface of the city."

"That's a long way down. Also, while we're on the subject, I think Pippa is a serious threat to this mission."

"You're in a fine mood, aren't you little Cam?"

"I am your Security PopBot. My mission is to protect you. I cannot control you, but I can certainly advise you. Pippa is, in a different manner to Franco, unstable. I think deep down she truly does hate you. I think your little invitation to the sleeping bag was a bad move; you have set a timer ticking inside her head, ignited a bomb fuse. Before long, Keenan, she will explode."

"You heard that, did you?"

"I hear a lot of things," said the PopBot smugly.

"Yeah, I acknowledge it was probably a mistake. Maybe I'm just a little bit lonely. Maybe I thought... I don't know. Maybe I thought my charm would win through, pierce her armour; you know what I mean?"

"It would take more than armour-piercing bullets to pierce her armour," said Cam. "Like, maybe a tank shell?"

"Wouldn't that obliterate her from existence?"

"Exactly," said Cam. There was a smile in his voice. "Somebody's coming."

Pippa emerged, a frown creasing her forehead, her cold eyes locking on Cam.

"I'll go and check on the children," said Cam, and left.

Keenan glanced up from the TuffMAP™. "How's the loading going?"

"Fine, except all Franco wants to take is tinned PreCheese and bloody CubeSausage!"

"Why?"

"Says it's the best food a soldier can eat."

"What about dietary diversity?"

Pippa held up her hands. "Hey, you invited him, you can sort the little bastard out. All I know is, for the next month we're living off tinned cheese. Keenan, it's like chewing rubber. And the CubeSausage! Jesus, it's even worse, like swallowing a slab of pure gristle. Yum!"

"Tell Franco we need HighJ, and lots of it."

"We're doing some demolition work?"

Keenan nodded. "I think we might have to blow our way into the vault. This Fractured Emerald is still their prized possession, despite being unheard of across the Quad-Gal. They're not going to have it on display in the main hall, are they?"

"Klik wants to speak to you, and... Rebekka."

"OK."

Pippa's gaze lingered on his, and he felt uneasy, squirming a little in the tight-fitting WarSuit.

"Can I ask you something, Keenan?"

"Sure."

"And you'll be honest?"

"Have I ever lied to you?"

"All the time."

"Shit, yeah, well I promise you this time. I'll tell the truth."

"Did you sleep with her?"

"Who?"

"Rebekka, you dumb-ass."

Keenan considered this, eyes locked on hers. Then he gave a little shake of his head. "No, Pippa. I didn't. I swear it, on all that's holy."

"I was convinced—"

"I'm not saying she isn't attractive. And maybe, in a different time, a different world, who knows? We might have hit it off, but I believe the proxers are not able to make emotional attachments to humans, or other proxers for that matter. So it would have been purely sex, without any ties. That's not me, Pippa." He gave her a wry smile. "I'm an honourable man."

Klik arrived at that moment, with Rebekka floating in behind him. The black boy had changed since Keenan last set eyes on him. His face was more alive, there was hope in his eyes, not the dull disease of defeat. He sat down beside Keenan, placed a hand on his, and looked up into the man's eyes.

"Thank you," he said, simply.

"It was no big deal," said Keenan.

"But it was, Big Man. You saved us, saved all our lives. Now I am bound by Ket-i honour codes to give my life for you. I am yours to command. I am yours. I will kill for you, and I will die for you. You have saved my family. You have saved my soul."

Keenan squirmed uncomfortably as Pippa moved away, presumably to discipline Franco, who was getting carried away loading enough food to feed an army.

Rebekka sat down facing Keenan. She had a strange look on her face, illuminated internally by an almost ethereal light.

"I know this place," said Klik, staring at the map. "You aliens call it Amrasar; to us it is just The City of Bone."

"Interesting name," said Keenan. "Why do you call it that?"

"You will know when you see it! We call it The World Warrior. When he died, he settled into the Milk Sea and his flesh fell from his bones leaving them risen, like an island, exposed. On his back we built the city. When the Ket-i are threatened it is said he will rise again and grow a new coat of flesh. Then he will rain terror and molten fire on our enemies destroying them utterly."

"So the city is built on... bone?"

"The whole city," said Klik, settling down and making himself comfortable. "You seek to go there?"

"Yes."

"You need me."

"No."

"Yes, I owe you everything, Keenan. I will take you there. Without me you will never make it alive through the eelmarsh." Klik shivered. "Even with me we have only a slim chance. I have travelled it three times and survived. This is considered lucky."

"Can we take a boat through this eelmarsh?"

"No. The World Warrior's bones are too much in the way. Many thousands of little bones, they form the walkways through eelmarsh. The only safe traverse is by air, but we have no aircraft."

"No." Keenan's face darkened. "We were shot down."

"I can take you," beamed Klik. "It is my pleasure, my honour. The least I can do. And Rebekka will stay here and look after my friends." Klik patted Keenan's hand. "It is the way, my friend."

Keenan laughed, infused by the young boy's charm and enthusiasm. His eyes strayed to Rebekka. "You are staying?"

"Yes. I think where you're going is perhaps too dangerous. I used to run guns in The City, but I was surrounded by my family. Now they are dead. I think I will stay here a while; these children have touched me."

"I thought you proxers had no emotions?"

Anger flared in Rebekka's face. "No," she said, her voice ice, "that is a misconception coined by you humans during the First Prox War; you sought to dehumanise us, making it easier for your soldiers to kill us in our beds. We have emotions, but not as you understand them. We do feel love, and hate, and compassion, and empathy."

"I am sorry," said Keenan. "I did not mean to offend."

"Then do your research before offering insult. Your ignorance is awesome. But then, it is so with all humanity, even against your own species. I have read your history, Keenan. Never in the annals of any inter-galactic species have I experienced such fighting and despicable acts of atrocity committed against one's own kind. Your animosity, apparent self-loathing and acts of genocide are legendary throughout Quad-Gal." Her eyes were filled with tears. "Your Humanity—truly, it is something to be feared."

Keenan, feeling cold and dead inside, simply nodded.

"It is right I should stay here," said Rebekka. "These children need a mother."

"Your choice is honourable, then," said Keenan.

"Yes." Rebekka lightened. "I am sorry. I have been a victim of human prejudice before. It does not sit well with me; shall we say humanity's arrogance and abuse have hurt me deeply."

"Again, my apologies." Keenan stood, and with emotions raging inside him—including a burning shame at what his species had perpetrated in the name of war—he left the room.

She's right, he thought as he mounted the ramp. *Humanity is filled with decadence.*

Despondency fell over him like a shroud.

Darkness filled his soul.

And, sadly, filled him with a desire to kill.

FRANCO HUMMED A little tune from the hit musical *My Mamma's a Whore* as he loaded up the second WarMonger inflatable infiltration craft. He'd used an industrial inflation pump to get both boats full of air, then moored them at the jetty from which Betezh had stolen their Raptor. The first craft he'd loaded with weapons, and the second, larger craft, intended as a supply vehicle, he'd happily filled with crates of tinned PreCheese and CubeSausage. As a treat, he'd even loaded a single crate filled with jars of horseradish.

"What a feast!" he mumbled to himself, MPK slung over his back, open-toe sandals flapping across the rusting metal grilleworks. He hoisted the final crate onto the bobbing craft, jumped aboard, and manoeuvred it into position. "CubeSausage and horseradish! A meal fit for a prince!"

Happily, he surveyed the collection of stolen military food. Then he rubbed at his beard with a scratching sound of abrasive wire. *Hmm*, he thought, *I'm sure I've forgotten something.*

Pippa jogged down the ramp and stared with undisguised loathing at the collection of crates. "Franco, what about the Dogs? Remember? We're supposed to be dumping them in the sea? Unless you'd like to leave them on the Rig with the kids. After all, maybe they'll unfreeze."

"Hot goddam," said Franco, slapping his forehead. "You're right." Then he stared at the crates. "Shit," he said. "Something's going to have to go."

"Franco, how long do you actually think we're going to be on this planet? It's two days to Amrasar. Each crate contains a hundred and ninety tins. And you've loaded..." she counted, frowning, "ten crates. Mate, that's nearly two thousand fucking tins. Franco, you could feed a battalion."

"Wouldn't want us to go hungry," he mumbled, kicking his sandal against the hard rubberised surface of the boat. "Nothing worse than being hungry. I was hungry as a lad, you know."

"But Franco, this lot would keep us going for about five years."

"You should always plan ahead."

"And what's this? Horseradish? Fucking *horseradish*? That'll come in handy when we're starving to death! A hundred and ninety jars of horseradish, yum fucking yum."

"You're being unreasonable, Pippa!" His voice was almost a wail.

"And you're being a dick. You can take two crates. That's final. So get unloading, and get those damn Dogs down here where we can see them. You got that?"

"Yes Pippa," said Franco miserably.

Pippa stormed out. Franco stared at his stash. Then, with a long face, he began to unload the supplies.

* * *

FRANCO SAT IN the lead boat, ready to navigate, as Keenan stood on the platform facing Rebekka and a few of the Ket-i children who had come to say farewell. Pippa patted a few of the kids on the head, then jumped in beside Franco. The boat bobbed, and Franco fired twin engines. Water surged beneath the craft as the stealth engines settled into a quiet idle hiss.

Behind, linked by TitaniumIII cable, the larger of the two craft bobbed and tugged, and there, onboard, between two crates of tins, squatted the metal Dogs that had made the lives of the renegade children so miserable. Franco kept glancing back nervously, with his MPK not quite pointing at them and a grenade not quite unclipped from his belt.

"I'm glad we're getting out of here," said Pippa quietly.

Franco glanced at her, saw her... fear?

"You OK, Pippa?"

"Yeah, I'll be fine." She glanced at Rebekka. Franco noted the contact, but said nothing.

Klik appeared, face one huge smile and two guns strapped across his ebony back. He wore shorts and nothing else. His bare feet found purchase, and he landed lightly in the boat, moving to sit at the stern. He carried a bottle of drinking water, which he sipped at thoughtfully, surveying what he considered to be the aliens.

Keenan stood, finishing a cigarette and patting some of the kids on the head. They giggled, and several swung on his arms as he glanced up, into Rebekka's bright orange eyes.

"Seems like we've been through a lot together," said Keenan.

"We have," smiled Rebekka. "Listen, I'm sorry. About before..."

"Don't mention it. You were actually right. Don't apologise."

"That's extremely chivalrous of you."

Keenan shrugged. "I'm a regular hero," he said, voice sardonic, and he stamped out his home-rolled cigarette. "Listen... one day, one day soon, if I happen to be passing..."

"Call in," grinned Rebekka, "if I'm still here. If I've moved on I will leave word with Fortune; you'll be able to contact me that way. Although, I should be here for a length of time." She glanced down at the children, and Keenan detected love in her eyes: love mingled with sorrow, and a need to do something good, a need to do something selfless. He had seen that look a million times on the faces of a million aid workers in battlezones across the Helix War. He appreciated it, even envied it, but he did not truly understand. The problem was, Keenan was a killer. Deep down, when you stripped away civility, society, honour... when things got dirty and brutal, Keenan was just a killer. He recognised this in himself, and it shamed him.

"Good luck," said Keenan.

"I'll stay armed."

"Yeah, I'll make sure these Dogs never bother you again."

"Thank you."

She stepped a little closer. Keenan could smell her scent, her natural perfume: the aroma of woman, albeit an alien woman. He felt his senses go a little dizzy, and grinned.

"Goodbye kiss?" she said, raising her eyebrows.

"Never say no."

She leaned forward, her lips touching his. Their mouths opened, just a little, a symbiosis of breath, the most gentle touching of tongues. The kiss lasted not quite long enough to indicate love, but just a little too long for friendship.

Keenan turned, boots landing in the boat with a thud. "Let's go," he said.

Pippa glanced sideways. "Parting is such sweet sorrow."

"Fuck off."

"It was tender, Keenan, honest. I was quite moved; touched. Maybe you should stay with her? You could have a half-human half-prox family together."

"I'm not in the mood, Pippa."

"Are you ever in the mood?"

Keenan said nothing, but lit a cigarette as the convoy buzzed through the Milk Sea, under the protective embrace of the Gem Rig, and out onto open waters. Waves slapped the boats' hulls. Heat slammed them like a wall. He checked his maps, and nodded as Cam gave a tiny series of beeps; Cam was going on to scout ahead to try to work out just how dangerous the city of Amrasar was, and, more importantly, what kind of weapons they were stacking.

Cam disappeared, humming softly.

"Deeper into the lion's den," Keenan muttered, and watched the pink pastel horizon drift by.

* * *

PIPPA KILLED THE engines and they bobbed, riding gentle waves. There was nothing around them: no craft, no ships, no land mass. A soothing wind skimmed white waters. Franco, stripped to knife-hacked combat shorts and his sandals, clambered to the back of the craft, squeezed past Klik and a pile of RPGs, and tugged the two boats together. He stepped tentatively between the vehicles and looked back at Keenan. Keenan, as usual with bedraggled home-rolled between his lips, gave a single nod.

Franco moved to the first Dog, its twisted bestial face open in a frozen snarl of dripping mercury saliva. Franco grasped a plank of wood, levered it under the machine, and tipped it into the sea.

It made a *thunk* and a splash, and disappeared instantly. The waters rolled back in, surged. The Dog was gone. Franco tipped the second Dog into the Milk Sea, then moved to the third, a broiling frozen inferno. As he tipped the deadly, merciless machine into the white waters there was a sizzle. A cloud of super-heated steam shot up, and the Dog sank without trace.

"They're gone," said Pippa.

"Good riddance," said Keenan.

Franco watched the sea, and was joined by Klik who stared down. He thought the young black boy was going to dive in after them, for a moment. Instead, he raised his hand in a military salute.

"What you doing, boy?" Franco's voice was gentle.

"I am thinking of all those who died. It is right these Dogs were given a dishonourable death, not by blade or bullet, but by drowning."

"So on Ket, to drown is dishonourable?"

"Very much so," nodded Klik. He turned, and tears glistened in his deep green eyes. "You sink, you drown, you become a part of the sea. You are consumed by the World Warrior who condemns you to an eternity of pain and servitude."

"Will that happen to us if we drown here?" Franco tapped the inflated wall tentatively.

"Yes."

"Let's go," said Keenan.

Franco stared down at the opaque sea. He spat after the Dogs. "Rot in hell," he said.

THEIR TRIP WENT smoothly for the next two days, as they baked under the apparently endless Ket suns. Even Franco, a parallel to the most pasty of gothic game-playing indoor individuals, started to develop a tan, albeit the true lobster redneck tan of the ginger. Freckles rioted like measles across his shoulders, arms and forehead. The members of Combat-K took turns piloting the boat and its trailer in order to relieve the boredom.

Keenan and Pippa navigated, checking one another's directions and waypoints; Franco acted as cook, and everybody was heartily annoyed when they realised that his entire stock of food consisted of PreCheese and a whole damn crate of horseradish.

"I mean, horseradish," said Keenan as he tucked into his third consecutive meal of tinned rubbery cheese smeared with horseradish. "I don't even *like* horseradish."

"It adds a harsh and fiery epilogue to any meal," grunted Franco.

"One hundred and ninety fucking jars," said Pippa, "you mental, drugged-up moron!"

"Hey, you were the one who said I could only bring two crates!"

"So?"

"Technically, it's your fault."

"My fault?" shouted Pippa, spitting out a mouthful of horseradish. "Come here, I'll snap your damn neck."

Franco danced back, making the boat rock, and spilling a long stream of PreCheese cubes to bounce rubbery around the floor of the boat. Keenan grabbed Pippa's arm.

"Leave him be. We shouldn't have trusted a lunatic with the food supplies. It's all our fault. And, ultimately, it's my mission; if you want to blame somebody, blame me."

Pippa sighed, and softened. Her skin, now tanned a deep brown, glistened with sweat. She shook her head. "It's OK, Keenan. I'm just hot, tired, and not relishing fighting these bastards. Maybe I'm just getting old. I no longer look forward to the contact."

"You did real well back in The City."

"That was different. I had no choice."

"And we have a choice now?" Keenan's voice was sharp.

"We do, Keenan. We can walk away. Hire transport; get the hell out of here. We don't have to take on an entire bloody Ket city. God only knows what archaic alien weapons they've got; and that's the problem: they're aliens. We're not really sure what to expect, despite our research; not sure what we're going to find inside that city, inside the Metal Palace."

"Yeah, I noticed eye-witness reports were thin on the ground in the materials we got from the GalaxyWeb and Fortune."

"That's because the Ket don't understand the word prisoner. The Ket-i warriors do not build prisons; they do not have cells or handcuffs or even understand the concept of keeping an enemy alive. After all, they kill the children of their enemies, right? It was an ethos that went down badly during the days of The Helix War."

"I remember," said Keenan acidly.

They cruised in silence for a while, skimming waves, riding troughs. Klik sat in contemplative silence throughout the trip. Sometimes he would study Keenan's map; sometimes he merely closed his eyes as if in meditation.

"What you thinking about?" asked Franco at one point, just as the one hour night was falling.

"Death," said Klik quietly.

"That all?"

"And revenge."

"Revenge?"

"When I have repaid my debt to you people, I have a mission of my own."

"What's that?" asked Franco warily.

"I would kill the men who murdered my family. I will slaughter them in their beds. I will cut their throats as they have sex. I will shoot them between the eyes as they take a shit. I will find them, wait for the moment of greatest vulnerability, and then I will take them down."

"How many are responsible?"

"About thirty," said the young boy, his eyes dark and brooding. For the first time Franco shivered; this young child was no longer a child, but a machine designed for killing, an abomination created by the horrors of his violent childhood.

"Violence breeds violence," said Pippa, moving close. She looked at the sky as the most incredible sunset painted the world. Greens, yellow and purples radiated like a slowly revolving kaleidoscope across a tattered sky.

"I wish we could all love one another," said Franco. He leered at Pippa in the fast-falling gloom. "Actually," he began.

"No."

"But Pippa!"

"No!"

"We could have some of our own loving."

"We've been over this."

"Still got the hots for Keenan, have you?"

"*What?*"

"Well," Franco grinned, and gestured to himself, "how could you possibly pass this up?" He tutted and shook his head. "I know, deep down, that you're hot for me baby, crying for me baby, slick for me baby. But Keenan just gets in the way. What about if I tip him over?"

"Oy!" snapped Keenan. "I heard that."

"Sorry boss."

"Why don't we get some sleep?"

"I will keep watch," said Klik. "I am used to the short nights. I do not fear the dark."

"OK," nodded Keenan.

Wrapping K-blankets around their shoulders, tiny whines signified climate systems switching and aligning. They closed their eyes and within a few seconds Franco was snoring loudly and giving the occasional horseradish fart.

Pippa and Keenan shook their heads and snuggled down—not too close together—and certainly not touching, as Klik scanned the horizon through the purple blackness, and thought dark thoughts of revenge.

KEENAN OPENED HIS eyes in the black. Sleep fell from him like a cloak. Her arms were around him, holding him tight, holding him as if he were falling and she never, ever wanted to let go. Keenan shuffled down a little more into his blanket. A vast sky stretched overhead. Tiny stars glittered. Pippa snuggled closer against him, her face rubbing against his chest. He smelled her hair, and the perfume of her skin. She smelled good.

"Babe?" he whispered.

"Mmm." She nuzzled at him again and he was instantly hard, and instantly regretted it. Memories flashed into his mind: sex, hard sex, gentle sex, his tongue tracing trails on her sweat-streaked skin. And then... the gun, caressing his temple. "I should kill you," she growled. And all: crashing, like a black sea against black rocks and tumbling wild and brutal down into... the present.

He stroked her hair, gently, as if afraid that when she awoke she would stab him through the heart.

"Keenan," she mumbled, and her left hand moved across him and rested on his hip.

Keenan closed his eyes.

He tried to regain sleep, but it evaded him for a long, long time.

WHEN KEENAN AWOKE he was alone. They were moving and he sat up, groggy, and lit a cigarette. Pippa was hammering the boat across the waves.

"You OK?"

She flashed him a dangerous glance. "Yes."

"Franco, what you doing?"

"Making breakfast."

"Is it, by any chance, cheese and horseradish?"

Franco looked amazed. "How the hell did you guess that?"

Keenan chuckled.

An hour later a thin white mist sprung up from the Milk Sea. Much thinner than before, it still, however, slowed their charge across the still white waters. The waves were growing less and less in stature, the sea descending into a steady calm.

"We are getting close," said Klik.

Keenan nodded. "How long?"

"An hour, maybe a little more. The coast is often shrouded by Milk Mist, and for the eelmarsh it is a constant companion. We say it is the breath of the eels, emitted to entice non-warriors to their deaths. It is said the eels suck you down into the marsh and consume your flesh while you still live."

"Sounds a funky way to die," said Franco, looking up from his pan of melted PreCheese.

"Do not mock." Klik's voice contained not just awe, but something more, a sense of... reverence.

His young eyes seemed much older; his young boy's face a mask of wisdom.

They continued at a modified pace.

"Have you heard from Cam?" asked Pippa, as the mist thickened. It swirled around the two cruising boats; the reverberation of under-stressed stealth engines hissed, muffled as echoes bounced back from the mist.

"No." Keenan shook his head. He took the PAD and the relays; started to flick through channels. "Cam, frequency 557, come in. I repeat, Cam, frequency 557, this is Private Eye, come in, over."

Nothing.

"Try another frequency," said Pippa.

"This is our agreed frequency."

"Maybe he forgot?"

"No. Something's wrong."

"Like what?"

Keenan shrugged. "Maybe he went too far. Who's to say the Ket-i don't have advanced electronic systems of their own? In fact, I'm pretty positive of it. That's the only reason I brought Franco along!"

"Hey!" said Franco, holding up his wooden spoon. Melted cheese dripped like liquid rubber. "I heard that."

"Just cook your cheese," said Keenan. He tried again to contact Cam, and spent the next thirty minutes scanning frequencies and sending out PBs—PanicBursts—designed to get a response from the tiny machine. But Cam was silent, either silent... or dead.

Keenan sat, brooding, contemplating this new twist of events. Cam was—in all reality—going to guide them through the potentially hazardous minefield of electronic high-tech monitoring equipment that was rumoured to guard the Fractured Emerald; without him, success seemed improbable. Franco was good with machines, but more with weapons and bombs, not subtle surveillance mods. Keenan scratched his short blond hair and cursed.

What the hell's going on? he asked himself. First The City and the Syndicate; then Betezh, the Hornet crash, Betezh's escape, and now this!

"Shit," he said.

"You thinking the same as me?"

Keenan smiled at Pippa. "What, that we're on a cursed mission?"

"Sure feels that way."

"Don't worry," said Keenan with a smile. "We've got each other to rely on."

"Don't get too friendly," said Pippa, turning away. "You might end up regretting it."

THE MIST WAS gathering, swirling thicker and thicker, before thinning out into white and grey drifting pockets. The Milk Sea stilled: an eerie opaque platter that eventually levelled into something almost like glass.

As the boat's engines hummed, all talk ceased. And when somebody had to speak it came as a hushed whisper, as if this place, this still lagoon of severed sea, was a holy place, a place of sanctuary and worship, a place of dangerous reverence.

"There," said Klik, and Pippa slowed the boat. The following vessel bumped intimately against them, rubber walls mating.

Keenan, Franco and Pippa squinted through the swirling white. And suddenly, a wall of rugged white rock loomed above them, nearly a hundred feet tall. It was a sheer cliff-side, jagged and pock-marked, ridges undulating in radiating spans of bony protuberance, vast and vertical, and rising above them, leaping from the mist to surprise with height and suddenness and sheer bulk.

Pippa turned the boats, and for a while they cruised parallel to the mammoth cliff. They were close, close enough to touch. Keenan leaned over the side of the boat, running his fingers across the abrasive surface.

"Well?" said Pippa.

"It feels like... well, bone."

"I would say it's a physical impossibility."

Keenan glanced at Klik; the boy seemed more subdued, almost as if he were in a trance. Quietly, he said, "Yeah, well, you don't want to go disillusioning the local ethnic people, especially not about something integral to their faith."

"Keenan, here, we're the ones who are ethnic."

Keenan nodded. "I've spent too much time with damn humans," he said.

"Haven't we all," agreed Pippa.

They followed the wall of jagged rock—bone—and high above them the summit began to fall in a series of massive steps, almost mechanical cut-outs that dropped and fell, tumbling towards the sea, until finally the white rock lay at sea level and became a platform over which they could gaze.

"We are here," said Klik. "Just follow the platform for a hundred metres. There is a place to leave the boats."

The platform of white undulated gently, a bone desert, and here it was smooth, polished by the still water that occasionally lapped over the shining surface. Pippa turned the boats into a narrow channel and cut the engines. She stepped out warily, and, satisfied the surface was solid, helped the others to disembark.

They stood, staring off into swirling mist in all directions. The silence was eerie, broken by nothing more than an occasional *slap* of lapping sea. The temperature had dropped; was chilly after the recent heat and humidity to which the group had been exposed. Keenan closed his eyes, lifting his face to the blanketed sky.

"Smells like ice," he said.

"What do you mean?" asked Franco, loading his pack with ammo and tins of cheese.

"It smells fresh. You know, like after a fresh fall of snow. Or if you travel to an arctic region."

"There are no arctic regions on Ket," said Pippa.

Keenan nodded, and took the MPK and the grenade belt from Franco with a smile. "I know that. I'm just trying to figure out this insane climate; the weather has me foxed."

They packed their gear carefully, aware that although this mission was, officially, under way, and despite its apparent covert intentions, they could soon be heading into the heart of battle. Heavily armed, carrying locked and loaded MPK sub-machine guns, all with loaded twin Makarov pistols in shoulder holsters and grenades on their modified webbing, and dressed in their WarSuits— albeit without CrashHelmets—they shouldered packs and looked to Klik. With a nod, the young boy—his demeanour deadly serious—padded across the bone platform and into the mist.

Keenan glanced at his TuffMAP™, and patted his Techrim. "Here we go," he said.

"This is for Freya, and the girls." Pippa smiled.

Keenan gave a curt nod, and followed the boy.

THE BONE PLATFORM, slick with Milk Sea brine, glistened. Mist swirled, forming esoteric shapes, which twisted and entwined with integral ethereal strands, like the tentacles of some strange air-borne creature. The mist seemed alive, a constantly moving, shifting presence. The Milk Sea lapped with lazy strokes.

An engine hummed, then died, far out and muffled by mist. The prow of a long sleek craft emerged from the cotton white. It circumnavigated the two black boats abandoned by Combat-K and bumped gently against the bone shore.

The Ket-i warrior party disembarked with utmost care, weapons ready, eyes narrowed in concentration and fierce challenge. They were huge warriors, heavily muscled, scarred, tattooed, and with long slivers of bone piercing skin and muscle. They had Kevlar armour-pads woven into the skin of their faces, arms, torsos and legs, and huge jewelled Kukri blades—usually diamond, sometimes a deep flashing sapphire—bone-welded to their forearms. They carried automatic weapons, pistols, grenades and Laz-Spears, quite a primitive weapon technologically, but brutal and savage in close-quarters combat.

"The enemy are not far ahead."

"Yes, but they are a deadly enemy," said one mammoth, heavily-scarred warrior. He towered above the others, a monument of physical prowess. His eyelids were pierced with diamond shards. His lips were tattooed with military warscript from Helix. He showed teeth in what could have, with a lot of imagination, been a smile.

"JuJu, we will take them, rip out their spines and feast tonight under the Will of the Warrior."

"Yes," said the mighty JuJu. He breathed deeply, then moved to the moored boats so recently vacated by Combat-K and their guide, Klik. He leapt in, and the boats shifted allowing ripples to slap the bone shore. He crouched, motionless, body gleaming with sweat, then dipped his head and began to sniff the ground.

"Two men. One woman. And…"

His brow creased. The other warriors shifted uneasily. They wanted to be on the move; they wanted the hunt and they wanted the kill and the violence and rending and tearing and bloody ridged spine feast which would follow. Saliva hung like juicy umbilicals from several of the warrior's open maws… an ecstasy of anticipation.

"What is it, JuJu?"

"There was a Ket here. One of us."

"Improbable."

"No. I trace the aroma. I know this family. I know this clan. They were wiped out."

"Then…"

"It is a child. Escaped. A rogue." He glanced at the huge warriors; JuJu smiled widely. "Now we hunt *true* enemy, not just Ket-i impostors, alien renegades. We, the KellKet, the Supreme Ket-i, will have our kills tonight. We *will* feast, brothers."

He climbed from the boat, the scents of the enemy strong in his mind—like coloured patterns, each one individual, a sprinkling of bright shades fading into squares of colour.

The warriors arranged themselves into a tight unit on the bone-platform. Professional. Precise. JuJu sniffed the air; then turned, focused, eyes widening a little, nostrils flaring. Muscles tensed. And with a guttural harsh command more animal than human, led the eight-warrior hunting party after their blood-rich quarry.

The hunt had begun.

As THEY WALKED, Klik continually sipped from his bottle of water. Soon the platform became perforated, then broke into a series of narrow bridges and spans, which rose and fell, veered left and right at off-camber slants, making walking difficult. The bridges of bone twisted and turned, arched and bucked like smooth polished ribs, or like strung-out tendons, intertwining and criss-crossing. Tepid off-white water lay below the narrow walkways, brackish and stinking like death. Sometimes the pools were small, narrow little channels or rounded pools; sometimes they were lakes of almost sulphuric intensity, stretching off into the distance and spanned by narrow arches of bone.

After an hour, the group passed an incredibly tight traverse a hundred feet above a mammoth stinking lake of softly bubbling cream. Reeds and rotting grass emerged in clumps and occasional individual strands. They were truly in the marsh, the eelmarsh, a stew of rotting vegetation, a soup of putrefaction.

As the group descended the opposite side of the high arched bridge they came to a group of what looked like boulders moulded from the surrounding bone. They made a temporary camp amongst the rocky outcrop, and Franco got a pan of water boiling to make brews as he crouched by the side of the odorous lake. He peered over it, eyes focusing on the glass-still surface punctured in a million places by what Klik had called Spine Grass.

Then, something moved. It was oily, and glided for a moment, just breaking the surface; then it disappeared. Ripples cast across the platter, and Franco squawked.

"It moved! Bejasus, it moved!"

Keenan scowled at Franco. "Bejasus?"

Before Franco could answer, Klik was crouching beside him. He nodded, then pointed into the fetid lake. "This place, bad place. The eelmarsh filled with eels, many small and harmless, but some—some much larger ones—they eat flesh from your bones quicker than Tenka Clan strip flesh from body of an enemy."

"So we're not to put our feet in for a paddle?" frowned Franco.

"They would eat your feet," said Klik. He stood, and seemed to sway for a moment. He took a long drink from his water bottle and grinned at the group. "This is a place of high evil," he said.

Keenan stood and moved to him. Keenan took the water bottle from the boy, and took a small sip.

Klik stared at him defiantly.

"This is liquor," said Keenan, "like vodka, but not quite. Boy, have you been drinking all this time?"

"It makes a warrior strong!" snapped the youth.

"It makes a warrior pissed," said Franco.

"This is our way. We feast on the spirit of our enemies."

"What, you ferment their corpses?"

"Different cultures different customs," said Keenan. Then he turned back to Klik, who was swaying. "Where did you get this?" Keenan had to admit he was annoyed, but forced himself to remain calm. This boy was supposed to be their guide, confirming their route and double-checking maps. If he was drunk, or even worse, an alcoholic, then he would be more hindrance than use. Keenan should know; his mother had been an alcoholic, and as a child he had witnessed her gradual deterioration until she finally drank two bottles of whisky and threw herself down the stairs, cracking her head like a melon from the bottom of the balustrade.

Klik shrugged. "The stores back on the Gem Rig. Mr. Keenan, when you see so many of your friends die, you need a little something to keep you going. It brings great reserves of strength; it fortifies the blood; it makes a Ket-i warrior powerful."

With a hiss, Keenan tossed the bottle into the lake. It sank without trace.

Klik's eyes widened. "No!" he breathed, lips wet and glistening, face contorting in horror. "Mr. Keenan, what have you done?"

"Help you overcome your addiction, lad."

Klik ran to the edge of the poisonous soup and, for a terrible moment, Keenan thought the boy was going to leap in after the bottle. Instead he turned, his whole body shaking with... rage.

Despite the boy's youth, Keenan was suddenly glad of his MPK and Techrim pistol. He eyed the huge hunting knife at the boy's belt; its blade was serrated, black, more a machete than a knife. Klik had blessed the blade, said it was the weapon that would slay the enemies of his dead family.

Klik let out a howl, a screeching wail that cut through the mist, and then he was gone, stampeding through the group and disappearing into the swirling white. His footsteps, slapping on bone, quickly faded. A terrible silence seemed to close in, oppressive and claustrophobic.

"Shit," said Keenan.

"Well done," said Pippa, "ever the genius at child psychology."

"What would you have me do? Allow the kid to get slowly massacred, then lead us straight into an eel-lake?"

"No, but the lad's young and traumatised. He's seen so many of his friends killed. Is it any surprise he's turned to drink? After all, we're not so damned perfect; it's the first thing we do when we have a bad day at work, and we're supposed to be adults."

"Anybody for coffee?" said Franco, holding up the pan of boiling water.

The mist swirled around their hiatus in conversation.

Then a noise cut through the white. It was a howl, high-pitched, keen, reverberating. It held the high note for maybe a minute, wavering and fixed, then died into a lullaby of silence.

Combat-K stood frozen: statues, a tableaux.

"Was that Klik?" said Franco softly. The pan in his hand wavered.

Keenan gave a quick shake of his head, bringing his MPK round and making sure the weapon was ready to go. "Wrong direction." His words were clipped, economical.

"The mist can play games with sound," said Pippa, voice barely above a whisper.

Then they came: ghosts running in crouches, sprinting from the mist like a flood. One warrior, huge and frightening in visual ferocity, leapt at Keenan whose MPK screamed in hairline trigger-instinct, bullets raking the sky, the mist, as the alien crashed into him bearing him violently to the ground with one knee in Keenan's throat, the other in his chest. Keenan slammed against the hard bone-rock with a grunt of surprise, MPK gun useless and body shocked into a stunned incapability by the sheer blurred speed of the attack... and throat dry with instant fear. He fought back with a snarl hammering a right hook into the alien's jaw but the blow barely rocked the figure and a bone dagger rose above Keenan's eyes. Its tip was stained with enemy blood. The warrior's face loomed above him like a monster, contorted in a killing frenzy. Light sparkled from emerald shards woven in the warrior's eyelids making pools of green flood his face. Keenan scrabbled in desperation for his Techrim but he knew time was his enemy a brutal enemy. Pressure on chest and throat crushed him and he could not draw and fire before the dagger plunged into his eye and into his sweet soft brain beyond. He cursed his loose attitude and weakness and his unreadiness and it was gone and done in an instant as the dagger slammed towards his face and in reflex his eyes snapped shut...

CHAPTER 11
THE CITY OF BONE

KEENAN WAS A little boy again. He lived in a small house on a small street in a small town. The house had two bedrooms, no garden, and a sloping stone-paved back yard. His mother grew roses in pots, huge towering bushes with severe thorns and bright heavy-scented blooms of red and pink. In the summer bees came and buzzed around the flowers, and once Keenan—only eight-years-old—had been stung by a big fat bee. With tears leaving trails down his face he had run across the flags, sandals flapping, up the steep stone steps and into the kitchen. He skidded left, nostrils twitching on a strange, strange smell and then... stopped dead. His mother lay, at the bottom of the stairs, head to the ground and twisted to one side, legs still trailing up onto the lower stairs. One arm was caught beneath her, one arm tossed carelessly above her head. Her eyes were open and staring as Keenan moved close. "Mom," he said, his bee-sting forgotten, "Mom!" and the smell came to him from that black bottomless open stinking maw, the smell that always lingered on her breath and meant she would be bad to him because of the bad things he did, and more and more often the bad things had got worse, and her punishments were more violent as bruises blossomed like black and purple flowers up and down his legs, across his back and shoulders and backside. He crouched by her and looked into dead eyes. Something went *click* inside his soul as understanding flooded him, and he reached out and slowly prodded the corpse. Only then did he see the blood. A pool slowly expanded beneath her head on the wooden floor from a ten-inch crack in her skull. The blood was a deep rich crimson; a little like the full-scented blooms that grew in the back yard. Keenan dipped his finger into her blood and sniffed at it, then wiped it on his shorts.

THEY FOUND HIM two days later in a serious state of dehydration. The Urban Force kicked down the door after being alerted by neighbours, and a female officer called Ekaterina tenderly picked the little boy up, although he flinched at her touch as if she might strike him. She held him tight, her own pain melting in light of three miscarriages and a narrow walk across a tightrope, on one side of which lay the blade of a razor and oblivion; on the other, a vibrant beauty of new life.

It took three months to clear the arse-ache bureaucracy of adoption paperwork. And as summer drew to a close Keenan found himself sitting on a park bench with two strange fat women who smelled of sweat and kept shoving packets of boiled sweets under his nose. He pushed them away. Ekaterina came, like a dream, walking down the gravel path. She was dressed in civilian clothes, a short green flared skirt, a cream blouse, knee-high brown boots, and the sun shone against her radiant skin making her glow. She smiled when she saw him, crouched down and held out her arms. He tugged free of the restrictive fat women, symbols of a bureaucracy aimed not at simplifying the adoption process, but of turning it into a nightmare of paperwork and pointless obstacles. He ran to her; fell into her arms, pushed his face into her hair and smelled her femininity underlined by a distant essence of coconut. He cried and her hair absorbed his tears. "There, my little love," she was saying. "Everything's all right now, everything will be just fine. I'll look after you. You're mine now. Nobody will ever hurt you again."

KEENAN BLINKED AS the dagger slammed towards his face. His mouth opened as a tiny sound escaped an "O" of disappointment that his life should end like this and he blinked as the snarling teeth-bared face above imploded with a *crump* as the bullet ate into his head and exploded in a mushroom of bone shards and blood mist. Lumps of burnt flesh exploded outwards. Keenan twisted as the corpse began its sideways topple and Pippa, Makarov levelled, transferred her gaze as if in slow motion as the second figure crashed into her and she went hammering backwards and down. Keenan pushed the corpse from him, surging to his knees; the next warrior was on him. The bone dagger slashed at his face, but he took the blow against his arm, crashing his fist into the attacker's nose, a devastating blow that spread his attacker's flesh. Slivers of diamond embedded in Keenan's knuckles and he ducked a return slash, ramming a low punch into the warrior's groin and drawing his Techrim smoothly. The man stepped back, grinned a snarl, and Keenan shot him in the face. Features disintegrated with an implosion of gristle and exit of bone.

"Keenan!" Pippa's voice was panicked. Keenan leapt to avoid a burst of machine gun fire, his face dropping into a cool dark scowl of controlled anger and low-level hatred. He landed on his shoulder, rolled, came up firing. The Techrim barked in his hand, bullets past the boulders of bone and skimming a heavy-set warrior with yellow eyes. The Ket-i warrior's Laz-Spear came up and a burst of unseen energy crackled across the clearing. Keenan was already diving, hitting the hard bone ground with a grunt that stripped skin from the palms of his hands; from his prone position he aimed the Techrim. The first 11mm bullet entered the warrior's throat, destroying his voice box; the second smashed his clavicle and exited on a spray of shards like tiny raining teeth. The third found its mark between the Ket-i's eyes and he folded in half, deflating, as Pippa pushed him aside with a snarl and grabbed the Laz-Spear.

Keenan found his feet and whirled to see Franco engaged in a savage bout of fist-fighting. The Ket-i warrior was backing away as Franco delivered blistering combinations of left and right straights, left hooks and right uppercuts. The warrior's face was blistered, and Keenan realised Franco had used the pan of boiling water as a weapon. Keenan's Techrim tracked the alien Ket-i warrior, and slowly, with measured grace, he pulled the trigger. The bullet slammed the warrior's skull, and his legs folded neatly beneath him; with a grunt of vomiting blood he mated with the bone-rock ground. Franco frowned, then whirled to Keenan...

Who held up one finger, *wait*. He glanced back at Pippa. She was on her knees, her Makarov in both hands, head scanning from left to right. The mist swirled, thicker now. Silence flooded the clearing; a muffled silence after the sudden brutal onslaught.

Four down, thought Keenan. But... where had they come from? And more importantly, how many were left? He loaded a fresh mag in his Techrim, clicks echoing through mist like a crackle of discharge. Then another enemy, moving fast, Laz-Spear levelled and the *hiss* blasted heat across the clearing. It picked Pippa up, hurling her across the platform and against the rocks where she slammed like a rag-doll, limbs contorted and angular, and hit the ground hard, face down. Keenan's pistol was *cracking* as he tracked the warrior but he was there, a ghost from the mist, above Pippa's limp form holding a long black blade to her throat.

"I kill her."

The words were slurred but understandable, and Keenan froze, Techrim still locked on the warrior. I can take him, he thought. He flowed with the moment.

"No," said Franco, voice hushed.

Keenan lifted his gun, palms open: submission. "OK."

He turned to the right as the mist parted, and a mammoth titan of a man—alien, Keenan corrected himself—emerged. He was heavily muscled and garbed for war. He stopped before Keenan, a good two heads taller, a scowl on his terrifyingly pierced and scarred face.

"I am JuJu. You have invaded our world."

"We are not your enemy," said Keenan, eyes locked, Techrim a hot prick-tease in his hand.

"All are enemy. You must fight. You, and I, for supremacy here in this place; for your life."

Peripherally, Keenan saw Franco with two of the Ket-i; they held blades to his throat, and in deference to Pippa, to stop her having her throat slit, Franco had put up bloodied fists.

"Drop your weapons. Or we cut the woman's throat out."

Slowly, Keenan peeled free the MPK and it clattered on the bone platform. He tossed aside his Techrim and eyed the huge warrior warily. Hardly a fair fight, he thought, staring at the massive physical supremacy that greeted him. He grinned sourly. But then, who said life was going to be fair? Bitch.

Four left, then. This was the leader; the four dead had been the scout party, or "testers"? To see what Combat-K were capable of? Keenan growled. Well, he thought: fuck you; I'll show you what I can do.

JuJu was bristling, a powerhouse of meat. He stripped free his weapons and grinning down at Keenan, advanced. Keenan stepped forward, and JuJu attacked, faster than anyone so large had a right to move.

Fists lashed out, left and right and Keenan just managed to dodge. With growing horror he realised the Ket-i warrior was armed; JuJu had short blades bone-welded to his forearms, and tiny slivers of sharpened gems attached to each finger like glittering razor nails.

Keenan backed away, fists up. "Nice to see a fair fight," he snapped. "Pretty little jewellery."

"I will slice you open like fish," said JuJu. He no longer grinned. For the Ket, war was a serious business.

He leapt, and Keenan feinted left, then caught the warrior with a crashing right hook that powered the Ket-i down on one knee. Keenan slammed another right hook, then crashed his left knee to the warrior's jaw. Gem-blades flashed, and with tiny *cracks*, JuJu's forearm blades sprang forward past fists and slashed at Keenan's head.

Keenan laughed a short bitter bark. "So, fucker, no playing fair with you, is there?"

JuJu said nothing, swaying.

"Hurt you, didn't I, maggot?"

JuJu stood. Blood trickled from one corner of his mouth and his nose. He attacked again, a blur, blades slashing the air, Keenan stumbling back to avoid the onslaught. Reaching Franco's hissing burner, he scooped the small item up and launched

it but JuJu clattered the jet aside to rattle across the
bone ground and roll at Franco's feet, blue flames
jetting like tiny spears. Keenan ran at the Ket-i warrior, eyes focused and the blades flashed up to meet
him as Franco, eyes gleaming, tapped the burner
with his sandal. The hissing jet rolled into the
creamy pool and suddenly there was a *whoosh* as a
sheet of fire erupted across the gaseous marsh and
billowed out across the platform, scorching hair
and flesh as it screamed. JuJu, distracted, caught
the full force of a barrage of blows from Keenan
which ended with a double-booted hammer to the
face. The great Ket-i warrior hit the ground and
Keenan was on him, one boot beneath the warrior's arm, the other coming down with a *crack*
that snapped the bone-welded blade from JuJu's
forearm. The warrior screamed, a bloodcurdling
sound, as Keenan rammed another fist into his
face, breaking a tooth; then he stomped on the second bone-welded jewelled blade. This, too,
snapped with a geyser of blood from torn forearm
flesh which showered Keenan. Keenan snatched
one blade, head snapping right to where Pippa—in
the shockwave of erupting fire—had ducked and
rammed her elbow back into the Ket-i's throat with
the force of an assassin; which she was. The warrior staggered, and Keenan launched the severed
jewel blade across the clearing with a *hiss* of rushing air. It slammed the warrior's eye socket and
dropped him without a sound. Blood poured out
and turned the bone-rock red. Franco was struggling with his two warriors, and Keenan grabbed
the second severed forearm blade and pressed it

into JuJu's throat, hard. Blood welled against the razor tip.

"Call them off, fucker."

"Kazxai!" shouted JuJu. Instantly, the two warriors backed away from Franco, who deflated a little, his face and upper torso battered and covered in blood and bruising.

"Pippa, a gun."

Pippa handed Keenan his Techrim, and two cracks echoed across the bone platform. The Ket-i warriors reeled back, both with bullets in their skulls. One lay still, leg twitching, the other rolled and fell into the marsh where the flames had died to nothing more than an amber murmur. The body sank, and there was a sudden frenzy of activity as huge eels, their black glistening coils rising above the surface, fed. Bubbles rolled across the marsh waters. One arm lifted from the depths, stripped to the bone with only a few twitching tendons still attached to flexing fingers, but then the feeding was done and the arm sank, and the soup returned through ripples to a gentle stillness.

Keenan looked back, down at JuJu.

"You are a man of war," said the Ket-i around bubbles of blood. Keenan nodded, eyes hard.

"You prefer to die with gun or blade?" Keenan said.

"Blade," said JuJu, eyes fixed on Keenan's. "I expect no less."

Keenan nodded, and tensed. And realised JuJu was laughing.

"This a comedy moment for you, son?"

"I am just imagining, in this the moment of my death, your face when you reach the Fractured Emerald."

Keenan glanced at Pippa, then Franco. Franco shrugged, and dabbed at his battered lips.

"Tell me what you know?"

"They know your mission, those in the Metal Palace."

"And you are?"

"I am JuJu, one of the Princes of KellKet. I volunteered to hunt you down. Even men such as you will find it difficult to reach the Fractured Emerald. You will never penetrate the defences of the Metal Palace." His voice dropped, eyes glittering. "This is not your world, human. You must leave here. You must go home. Only death awaits you, death and something... more."

"I seek... information," said Keenan, "that is all. There is something I need to know; and the Fractured Emerald will find answers for me."

"Only if she chooses to Commune. She must give freely, Keenan. Did Prince Akeez not explain to you?"

"Prince..." Keenan grinned, relaxing back on his heels. He gestured to JuJu to stand, and in defeat the huge warrior climbed wearily to his feet. His shoulders sagged and he bore his betterment like a cloak. Blood pumped from his torn arms and pattered to the bone-rock. "Tell me what you know of Prince Akeez."

"Only that you are betrayed, Keenan. Akeez is an evil man. His dream is greater than you could ever imagine."

"Convenient. Maybe you're bluffing?"

JuJu shrugged.

Franco jogged over. "Are we killing him, Keenan? I'll be honest, this place gives me the creeps. And now it's filled with bodies, I'd like to move on; find somewhere to make a fresh pan of coffee."

"What with? Your burner went in the marsh."

"Damn and bloody bollocks."

Keenan glanced back at JuJu. "To answer you, Franco, no, we're not killing him. This son of a bitch is coming with us, back to the Metal Palace, back to the Fractured Emerald, back to his home."

"I am no guarantee of entry," said JuJu. Light glittered against the diamonds woven in his eyelids.

"A Prince of the KellKet?" said Keenan coolly. "Oh, I think you'll guarantee us entry, my friend."

JuJu LED THE way, arms bound tight behind his back. Pippa had applied hasty field-dressings to his wounded arms, and Keenan had hobbled him with raze-wire, a nasty and severe little trick he'd picked up during the Helix War. Wrapped tight around bare ankles, if JuJu tried to escape—to run too fast—he would damn near sever his feet. Blood already trickled from cut flesh and stained his toes. He left a trail of bloody footprints across the white polished bone of the walkways and sea-carved bridges.

They walked for an hour with their new guide, in silence.

Franco jogged to catch up with Keenan; he smiled. "You OK, boss?"

"Yeah, I was just wondering where Klik went."

"I've a feeling we'll meet him again."

"Me too."

They walked in comfortable silence for a while. Mist swirled, engulfing Combat-K and their prisoner. It wavered and twisted like eels in air, a strange and almost liquid quality to its presence.

"You did well back there, mate," said Franco, eventually.

"Cheers. You didn't do too bad yourself. Good idea, that, the thing with the burner."

"Just a thought. Saw it in a film once. Made me fucking jump when it actually worked! But I'll tell you something, Keenan, I'd forgotten how savage you could be."

Keenan gave a short laugh. "Which bit?"

"Shooting the last two."

Keenan shrugged. "They came looking for war. I gave them war."

"Still, you kinda shocked me."

"I have my mission to think about," said Keenan. "I have to find the murderer of my family. It is a... need."

"An obsession?"

"Yes."

"Freya wouldn't thank you."

"Maybe not, but my girls, Franco..." He drifted into silence, lost for a while in memories. "It's hard to explain, because you've never had children. Franco, when you hold your baby in your arms... Gods, it's so hard to explain! Before, I was a tough motherfucker: drinking, women, smoking, fighting. I did what the fuck I wanted, when I wanted, and all sanctioned by the military. I'd fight hard and play hard. But when I held my first little girl in my arms, huddled up in her white blanket, the beeps of the hospital machinery surrounding me... it screwed my mind into a ball and flushed my life down the toilet. For the first time, Franco, the first time ever I came to truly understand what love meant: not the love of a woman—or even a man if you're that way inclined—but the love of something that came from within you, was a part of you. For the first time ever, Franco, here was this tiny life, and it was something I would kill for, and something I would die for: no question, no exchange, no compromise."

He fell into a brooding silence.

"When I was at Mount Pleasant," said Franco, "when I wasn't fried on a cocktail of drugs and real bad cooking, I sometimes thought about you. And I'll be honest, Keenan, I was surprised by your contact; when you set up the rescue mission."

"Why?"

"I thought you would have been dead, killed by your own hand." Franco's eyes gleamed. "I remember your grief all too clearly. I remember your desolation."

"For years—every single fucking night—I played with the idea of eating a bullet. But all the time, at the back of my mind, I was waiting for the UF to come up with a lead. I was waiting for that call, just to say, 'Yeah Keenan, we know who the fucker is'. I had to see him executed. Only then could I die in peace. But as the years flowed by I came to understand the case was frozen, locked in stasis, lost in the vaults of the UF HQ, and I realised the son of a bitch would never be caught. It took a long time, Franco, a fucking eternity. And then?" He laughed. It was a bitter sound. "By then my anger at the world had kind of died. Colours lost their vibrancy. Music lost its serenity. The world became bleached in shades of grey. And so I turned to..."

"The bottle?"

"Yeah. I drank myself into oblivion."

"Hence your reaction to Klik?"

"To see somebody so young destroying himself? Franco, the whole thing stank of that loss of innocence which has always haunted me; yeah, something I carried in my soul from childhood, a state of perpetual high, a route down which I swore I would never travel. Yet, when it came, I opened my arms and embraced the evil like a long lost brother. Alcohol took me as a willing sacrifice and with a big wide evil grin. I was lost at sea, Franco, for a very long time."

Franco slapped him on the back.

"Well Keenan, you're back now mate, back with the old crew. And we'll find this murderer who thinks he's got away with it; we'll track down the killer of your kids."

"Yeah." He laughed. "Thanks, Franco."

"Don't mention it, brother."

THE BRIDGES AND narrow walkways rose and fell, sometimes searing far into the sky above the white mist, sometimes dropping beneath the marsh waters and reed grasses, where tiny slick eels slid over their boots and made Franco dance in his sandals. When above the mist, the world stretched out beneath them like a sea of cotton-wool, it was almost like flying above the clouds. Mountains glittered in the distance. Far to the right, a forest sprawled, hundred-foot hard-woods, a dense and compact mass of ochre green punctuated by rare, blue-leafed conifers called Kajaya.

"How far?" asked Keenan, prodding JuJu with his MPK barrel.

The large warrior turned; he had sunk into what seemed a depression. "Not far," he said, voice quiet, subdued. "Then you will witness the savagery of the KellKet."

Keenan nodded, not willing to debate.

The bone walkways grew narrower, and again soared above the mist, spreading out into a thousand strands, slivers of gleaming bone that stretched and spiralled, and entwined to form a honeycomb of white. After so many hours under the claustrophobic mist the heat from the twin suns was welcome, and as they climbed a high bridge, The City of Bone was suddenly spread out before them, gleaming like diamond.

"It's beautiful," said Pippa, simply.

"My Home," said JuJu. "My World. My Para-dise."

"Seen it all before," snorted Franco. "Are there any decent brothels?"

Pippa glared at him. "Franco, you're a heathen."

"And proud of it!"

"Have you no soul?"

"Burned in hell many moons ago."

They stood, panting after the climb, and surveyed The City of Bone. It sprawled as far as the eye could see; the nearest edges writhed with a thinning of mist, but there the invading white ended as eelmarsh gave way to the rising expanding city. All the buildings were a gleaming white, and mostly built from solid shells of bone-rock; there were a million different shapes, mostly carved with hard labour, and huddled in tight compounds between wide streets of paved jewels.

The roads glittered, catching the sun.

"You use precious stones to build your roads?" Franco's eyes gleamed. Here was wealth untold, lying, quite literally, under his sandals. Or it soon would be. He wondered how long it would take to fill a sack.

"These are non-precious," said JuJu quietly. "We have an advanced grading system; anything not meeting the required quality field is used to enhance The City of Bone. The KellKet build a fine city, yes?"

Keenan checked his map. "The Metal Palace lies at the centre, like a Hub... there." He pointed.

JuJu nodded. "Prince Akeez has sent you on a fool's errand."

"Really? Explain."

JuJu's face shut down. His jaw clamped tight. He would say no more.

"Let me cut him," said Franco.

JuJu shrugged. "Part of our initiation to manhood is torture. You would not believe the pain I am able to withstand."

"And you wouldn't believe the pain I can inflict."

"Calm yourself," snapped Keenan. His eyes gleamed. "Down there..." He left the sentence unfinished, but it was clear to Pippa and Franco what he meant. Down there lay answers.

"Thoughts on infil?" said Pippa.

"We go in tonight, under cover of darkness." He glanced sideways at JuJu. "You only have one hour, pretty much planet-wide, don't you, JuJu? That means you've got really bad night vision; a by-product of evolution, you might say."

JuJu said nothing.

"Trust me." said Keenan, "the Ket-i are as blind as a bat in the dark. They call it the Death Hour; they believe the darkness is a disease you breathe into your lungs, and from there it pollutes you from the inside out. It's a brave Ket-i who stays out after dark... and even then they claim they feel their bodies gradually decaying."

"What about the ones back by the beach? They seemed up for a good fight?"

"Yeah, and we slaughtered them. They were stumbling around like children; probably renegades, illegals, hunted by the rest of their race. Their attack on us was desperation."

Keenan sat, cross-legged, on the bone walkway. He laid his TuffMAP™ flat and flicked through several of the digital pages with a finger. It made a tiny clicking, whining sound.

"JuJu, we're going to study this together. And you are going to tell me the truth, or I *will* feed you to the eels."

JuJu nodded. "Your eventual death and the eating of your spine and brain will be my greatest pleasure." He stared hard at Keenan. "Your death is marked for me, human."

Keenan tapped the map. "OK. Show me the different routes to the Metal Palace; and show me the secret escape routes. Your people have a history of warfare and sieges; nothing like this is ever built without a secret back door, right?"

JuJu nodded.

Together, they waited for darkness.

"WE READY?"

"Sorted, Keenan."

The three members of Combat-K had studied the maps closely, listening to JuJu explain the workings of the Metal Palace. Basically a warren for the ruling elite of the KellKet Ket-i clan—the self-appointed royalty of this vicious warlike tribe—the Metal Palace was not something they had built, more something they had occupied. It was old, older than their history. The City of Bone had grown up around this apparent ancient alien artefact—alien even to the Ket—but at its core it was a relic that all dating methodology—Ket and Quad-Gal—had been unable to place. The path to the Metal Palace should harbour no great problems; after all, in their ruling arrogance the Ket did not suspect the hunting party led by JuJu to fail. Three humans? Easy meat for skilled Ket-i warriors, all the odds said so. However, forewarned was forearmed, and according to JuJu a veritable army of warriors stood between Keenan and his prize, the Fractured Emerald.

"How many guards?" asked Keenan softly.

JuJu shrugged. "A hundred, maybe two. It is our greatest artefact; you will not be allowed to take it."

"To be honest," said Keenan, "I'm not so much interested in theft, more in what the Fractured Emerald can tell me."

"But you have a contract."

"Yes, and you know of Prince Akeez; the whole situation stinks like a ten-day dog corpse. Prince Akeez can kiss my arse; his contract is forfeit. I am not doing this for Akeez, and if I am honest with you, I'll put a bullet in his skull as soon as look at him."

"He has betrayed you?"

"It would appear so," said Keenan.

"Then I respect your honour. Tell me, what would you have the Fractured Emerald predict?"

"Not a prediction, more a revelation." And Keenan explained to the hulking black warrior about his family, about their murders, about his own people's inability to solve the crime, about his fall from grace and the clutching at straws that led him here, to this place, now, with an outlawed brain-fried combat squad wanted throughout the Quad-Gal on a GroupD prohibition which equated to instant extermination when they were—ultimately, finally—caught.

"So your friends joined you? In your hour of need? Even though they would forfeit their futures... forfeit their lives when caught?"

"Yes. We are a clan unto ourselves, and like you, we have our own honour codes. JuJu, I do not mean to trick you, but this Prince Akeez, tell me what you know of him. It's too convenient that you know our plans; I have a sneaking suspicion that we are the decoys and he intends to instigate his own theft."

JuJu considered this. When he spoke, his voice was low, almost a rhythmical lullaby.

"We were approached by Akeez showing all correct protocols upon entry to Ket. He spoke of a renegade outfit commissioned to steal the Fractured Emerald; that they—*you*—would come with heavy weaponry and murder many of our people. He said it was, intrinsically, an act of war. Later he gave us coordinates of your entry point, only they became useless when your Hornet spacecraft was blown from the heavens. Akeez was very precise with his information and calculations."

Keenan nodded, eyes narrowed. Then he glanced at Franco and Pippa. "We've been set up, again. We're being played as pawns, my friends. We're being dicked with from high above."

"What you going to do?" said Pippa. Her voice was velvet.

"We're continuing with the plan."

"Even though it's a trap?"

"Is it a trap?" said Keenan, eyes bright on JuJu. The huge black man stared at him levelly, face unreadable, head held high in pride; with an utmost warlike bearing.

"I do not believe so," said JuJu.

"So you will take us forward?"

"I will, but if you do mean theft, I *will* kill you. We will not lose our sacred prize."

Keenan and JuJu moved away from Franco and Pippa, and spoke quietly for a couple of minutes; then Keenan smiled over at the two, nodding, rubbing his unshaved chin with a rasp of whiskers.

Keenan moved back, boots clumping on bone. He gestured to Franco. "Give JuJu a weapon."

"What?"

"Give him a weapon, Franco." Keenan spoke through gritted teeth.

Franco grinned and held up his hands. "Hey, do you know, for a crazy moment there I actually thought you suggested giving our captive prisoner, the one with raze-wire round his wrists and ankles, I thought you told me to give him a weapon. Ha ha."

"And take off the wire," snapped Keenan, turning and gazing out towards distant, staggered mountains, towering rugged peaks, flanks violated by forests of pink and grey trees; sheer violent walls reared, a parallel with the natural violence of the Ket-i people: uncompromising, unforgiving, brutal.

"Keenan..."

"We've got a deal," said Keenan. "And we're going in."

DARKNESS FELL.

JuJu led Combat-K down narrow calciferous pathways, which finally dropped and dropped until they reached a bridge of incredibly thin white, glowing almost fluorescently in the darkness. One by one they crossed, until it was Franco's turn and he eyed the few inches of bone rock warily, eyes narrowed, tongue licking desert lips.

"Not like," he muttered.

"Don't be such a big girl," snapped Pippa.

Franco stepped onto the bridge, damp from splashes of lapping white water; then, with a sudden squawk he danced a marionette jig and tumbled back into the small circular lake where he splashed wildly for a few moments, before surfacing with a splutter, realising it was only waist deep.

"Shit," he ejaculated.

Dark shapes moved beneath the surface; gliding dark bodies converged through the milk towards... Franco.

"Get me out!" he screeched.

Keenan grinned wryly. "You muppet."

"So much for the covert entrance." Pippa reached out, and Franco grabbed her hand, allowing her to haul his barrel-chested frame from the stagnant water. Franco wrinkled his nose, glancing back at the eels, which arced through the white, then disappeared once the promise of a sudden feed had vanished.

"Little buggers would have chomped my legs! I'm really not liking eels very much! Especially the promise of poisonous ones! And pooh! Now I stink a pretty stink! A stink of eel mush and rotting eel eye stink! I stink so bad. I stink I do." It was an acute observation.

"Elegant," smiled Pippa curtly.

"Come. We must hurry," said JuJu.

And trailing stagnant milk droplets, Franco followed the others, mumbling and moaning, into the encroaching darkness.

* * *

THEY WALKED DOWN narrow bone-sand streets. JuJu led the group with care, eyes alert, head flicking from left to right as he scanned for Combat-K's enemies. As they moved, Franco still pondered the warrior's odd motivations; the whole thing stank worse than a stagnant stinking fish supper to Franco's mind, and still he couldn't quite work out Keenan's angle. So, he thought, brow wrinkled, scratching at his shaved ginger head, and rubbing his bushy beard, if JuJu takes us to the Fractured Emerald, and the gem tells Keenan what he wants to know, then we leave it alone. JuJu will be happy, and Keenan will be happy. And, that way, we leave without a fight! But I thought they were a warlike people? Living for war and all that guff? Why would JuJu do that? Hmm?

He pondered as they moved down narrow streets. Something was not right.

Franco's attention diverted to the immediate; the immediate fact that he was soaked, and not just with any old water, but with something akin to milk shit from a cesspit creature. His clothing, sopping wet, rubbed at him in places he would rather not be rubbed, and a curious itching had transgressed up and down his spine in a most uncomfortable fashion. Reaching back, Franco scratched with the muzzle of his MPK; and realised in horror that the safety was off. A ND at himself would not be the best way to get this mission finalised.

Scratching again, Franco moved grumbling through the black bone-sand that stuck like mulch to his squelching sandals.

* * *

"HERE." JUJU HALTED, almost in reverence. A small, wide metal door stood in a massive blank metal wall before him. The edges were near perfect, nothing more than an unseen fracture. "This is an outlet for waste in times of plague; it was used to deposit bodies from the Metal Palace without having to open gates."

"A plague exit?" said Franco with a shudder. "You mean, like, diseased corpses?"

JuJu nodded. "There is nothing for you to worry about. It has not been used for many years; the plague virii do not live beyond months, our scientists have researched this. You are quite safe from the terrible and toxic effects of this killer disease."

"'Killer disease'," muttered Franco, voice a parody. "Just great."

"How do we open it?" said Keenan.

JuJu knelt in the fine sand and placed his hands on the metal portal. Then he bowed his head and touched it to the doorway; silently, it slid upwards. "Cerebral implants," said JuJu simply.

"Advanced," muttered Franco.

"We are not a backward race," said JuJu. "Just because we sport piercings, scars, tattoos, just because we wear war-paint and hunt to kill, it does not mean we are heathen pagan savages. We choose to express our technology in a different fashion."

Keenan peered into the steep, narrow chute.

"You leading the way?"

"I must leave you here," said JuJu.

"Oh no," snapped Franco. "I've heard that one before! 'You can trust me, I won't say a word guv'nor' then off you pop to the Chief Head High-man or whatever you call the dude and bring with you five thousand fucking guards carrying Laser Cannons and bearing a grudge. Oh no, no indeedy."

"I will stick to our bargain," said Keenan, eyes locked on JuJu. "Honour to your people."

"Honour to your people," replied JuJu, and melted into the night.

"Did I miss something?" snapped Franco, eyes wild. "What game you playing, Keenan? Letting our bloody ace wander off to make a cannibal stew?"

"Just get in the damned chute."

"But…"

"Franco! We're running out of darkness. In a few minutes the streets will be alive. Then we will be in the shit."

Grumbling, Franco followed Keenan into the narrow confines and started a long, sweating, grunting ascent. Pippa stood for a moment in the humid stillness of the night; she looked around, unhurriedly, as if seeking a sign. Whatever deal Keenan had done with JuJu she didn't like it; it gnawed in her guts; but then, Keenan was a tough and very determined son of a bastard. The deal—whatever it was—had to have been to his benefit. And yes, there would be risk involved, but hell, wasn't there always? That was the business they were in.

Pippa took a deep breath. The humid air smelt good. It smelt of life, and particularly potent, especially to somebody who wondered if it would be her last breath.

She rubbed eyes rimmed with exhaustion and clambered awkwardly into the narrow chute.

It smelled like death.

Silently, the metal wall closed behind Pippa.

And left Combat-K entombed inside the Metal Palace.

THE CLIMB WAS long and arduous. The chute was grease-slippery, steep, and with no obvious hand-holds. Keenan cursed as he pressed his shoulders against one solid metal wall and braced his boots against the opposite. Slowly, inch by jaw-tightened inch, he ascended; sweat ran in rivulets down his weary face, stung his eyes and dripped from his chin, tumbling into darkness and polluting Franco and Pippa below.

"How far up?" said Franco's voice after a while. The words eased between desperate pants for oxygen.

"I can see light," said Keenan. "Not far now."

"It stinks in here, Keenan."

"Yeah, like a year-old plague corpse."

"That puts my mind at rest. Thanks very much, buddy."

"Actually," grunted Keenan, "maybe it's just you, Franco. You did take a dip with your fish friends back in the swamp. Maybe they imbued you with some of their scent."

"They were eels, actually."

"Oh, eels, excuse me Franco old man. Eels, fish, hell mate, you don't half pick your moment to start larking about with the local marine life. Let's just hope you haven't been infected, eh?"

"Infected? What do you mean, infected?"

"I've read some bad stuff about this place, real bad shit about the insect wildlife."

"Like what?"

Keenan shook his head. "You remember back on The City? We were supposed to be doing background research for the upcoming mission? Remember that? But you bunked off, a swift right-hook to Cam and a hurried visit to the local hostelry to partake of warm beer and the company of itchy scratchy cheap-time dead-eyed hookers?"

"I remember."

"Well, you should have done your homework, Franco."

"Keenan!"

But Keenan had gone, pushing onwards and upwards towards the gleam of light above. Franco glanced down at Pippa, but her hard cold grey glare told him she held no sympathy. With a curse, he followed, shuffling upwards, ascending the narrow chute.

KEENAN REACHED THE summit of the near-vertical tunnel; hands grasped the sharp folded edge of the shaft and he shifted his weight, lifting and dropping lightly into a compact square chamber. He landed in a crouch, Techrim in his fist, eyes narrowed and roving. Underneath his boots the floor was metal, and gleamed with a coating of what appeared to be light oil. The walls were bare, dull, like old machined steel. Keenan glanced up to the blank steel ceiling, then around once again in case he had missed something. He had not. There was nothing to miss. The chamber was a lesson in stark simplicity.

Franco landed beside him, with a grunt. His wild eyes meandered, then focused on Keenan. Franco frowned, as Pippa's boots touched down and slid a little on the greasy sheen; she steadied herself with elegant, tapered fingers.

"What's this?" said Franco.

"It's like a prison cell," said Pippa with a shudder.

"This is how it works," said Keenan. "The Metal Palace—the entire construction—is a machine."

"A machine?" Franco's frown deepened. "I don't like the sound of that. It has a distinct echo of foreboding, reminds me of a meshing of gears, of a mincing machine... With me inside it."

"I have maps and timings," said Keenan. "Every fifteen minutes, certain parts of the machine shift and change; walls move, component parts retract: the whole of the interior is a giant maze and we have to work our way through in periodic steps. You with me so far?"

"Sounds... dangerous," said Pippa, rubbing at her mouth. She glanced around again. The air was perfectly still, as befitted the interior of a metal cube. It was warm; uncomfortably warm. She was already sweating beneath her tight combat clothing.

Keenan handed both Franco and Pippa a detached page from the TuffMAP™. "I've marked our route; the only problem lies in if we get separated. The interior works on an eight hour cycle. So, if we are separated, it would take another eight hours for the Metal Palace's internal schemata to rearrange itself for a reunion. And by that time, we'd probably be dead."

"Cheery fucking place you brought us to," said Franco.

Keenan slapped him on the back. "Hey, just call me Mr. Fun Time."

"So, do we go down?" said Pippa.

Franco grinned. "Baby, you can go down on me any time."

"When do you ever stop?"

Franco grimaced. "Actually, about now."

"Why?" She looked closely at him, staring past the mask of his bravado. "Franco... are you OK?"

"Well, I didn't want to say anything before..."

"What's the matter?" snapped Keenan.

Franco looked a little sheepish. "I think I need the toilet."

Keenan and Pippa stared long and hard at their Combat-K comrade. Finally, Keenan broke the stalemate silence. "So, you mean to tell me you waited until we got stuck in a four-foot square room together before announcing you needed a shit?"

"You dickhead," snapped Pippa. "You can't go to the toilet in here."

"But I need to go. It's damned urgent! I'm desperate!"

"Why the fuck didn't you go before we climbed into the chute? Outside? In the fresh air?"

"Because I didn't need the toilet then," snapped Franco. "Anyway, there's something else."

Pippa grimaced. "Yeah? You need to masturbate as well, do you? Pull off a quick one while we stand here watching? Class act, Franco, just pure fucking class."

Franco glared balefully at her. "Actually, I'm in a lot of actual pain, if you really want to actually know."

"What kind of pain?" said Keenan.

"Well, it's a little bit embarrassing."

"Franco, I rescued you from the metal grasp of a deranged and short-circuited robot whore. I had to help prise your flaccid encapsulated *dick* from a twitching metal vagina with organo-foam inserts. Believe me mate when I say it wasn't a fun adventure; some might suggest more embarrassing for me than for you."

"OK then. My problem." He took a deep breath. "It's my arse."

Again, Keenan and Pippa stared at him.

"Go on," said Keenan.

"My arse, it's sore."

"OK. Been doing anything you shouldn't? Sorry, only joking."

Franco, face sulky, lower lip protruding a little, said, "See, I knew you'd be like this, ganging up on me, taking the piss, mocking my terrible painful ailment."

"Taking the piss? Franco, you're giving it away."

"Well, it's like this." Franco folded his arms. "My arse hurts, it hurts a lot, and in real terms it's looking like my arse could jeopardise this entire mission. It isn't just normal pain, oh no, this is special real deep painful arse pain."

"Painful arse pain." Keenan looked unconvinced.

"Yeah, painful arse pain, right deep up there, like there's some mad little mongrel with a scalpel and he's crawled up my pipe to carve his fucking initials."

"You still taking your medication?"

Franco twitched. "I had a pink one."

"Is that good?"

"Dunno. I'm not a doctor."

Keenan tutted. "Pippa?"

"I'm on it."

Within seconds her med-kit was out. She gave Franco a shot in the neck. Euphoria slid slowly through his system like a snake through its own discarding skin. Franco's eyes rolled and for a few glorious moments he experienced life without pain... Then his frown increased—apparently into agony—and he yelped like a kicked puppy.

"Ow ow ow! It hurts! It hurts more! Even more now! What've you done to me, woman?"

Pippa glanced at Keenan. "It shouldn't have happened like that." Keenan nodded.

"What about a local?" gasped Franco. He leant against the wall, sweat beading on his brow.

"Local?"

"Anaesthetic!"

"Hey, I'm not going up there," said Pippa. "No fucking way. Some places are holier than holy."

"Please! It stings! It's like I'm being gang-fucked by fifteen well-endowed Highlanders! You've got to do something! You've got to sort out my arse pain right now! Come on, where's your sense of humanity?"

"Tell him Keenan. Just tell him. If he wants an injection up his arse, he'll have to do it himself."

"That's a little harsh, Pippa. You *are* our medic." Through his weariness, and tension, there was a trace of a smile on Keenan's lips.

"OK," she said, handing him the sting-bot. "You do it."

"Get to fuck."

Keenan passed the injection unit to Franco. "Sorry mate. A man's arse is his own affair, unless he's gay, of course. Even then, it'd take a brave and raving-mad homosexual lunatic to go anywhere near your hairy triple-cheeked monstrosity."

"You saying I got a funny arse?"

"Funny? It's like a comedy beachball."

"I resent that!"

"Just take your drugs and shut up. We've got the Fractured Emerald to find."

Pippa and Keenan covered their eyes as Franco gave himself a local anaesthetic, and he settled his clothing back into place with a series of grunts. With a sigh, he promised he could hold on for the toilet until a more sanitary location was located. However long that took.

TEN MINUTES LATER, and Pippa, who had an acute mathematical mind, was studying the map. Her head tilted slightly to one side, and she chewed her lip. "According to this, if I understand your script right, we should be ready for a move—"

There was a grinding sound, distant, as under a deep and fathomless ocean. Two of the walls slid upwards, turning the cube prison into a corridor.

"About now." She smiled. Her head tilted. "I see how it works."

Franco stared at the flowing data. "Well I bloody don't!"

Pippa patted his shoulder. "You just stick to blowing things up, dearest."

"This way." Keenan moved ahead, boots padding the metal walkway. The corridor stretched away, apparently into infinity. "Come on, we have a tight schedule to keep."

Pippa and Franco padded after him.

The corridor sloped downwards, and as they moved swiftly and silently through the Metal Palace's interior they could hear noises, sometimes distant, sometimes frighteningly close and deafening in their stark metallic suddenness. The noises were mainly sounds of mechanisation: the clang of metal on metal, the whirr of spinning discs, the occasional clanking of what could only be chains.

"It's exactly how I would imagine the inside of a machine to be," said Pippa.

"That's the whole point," said Keenan, stopping for a moment and checking his TuffMAP™. "The Ket-i did not build this place, they found it. It's an alien artefact, and scholars have come from distant universities, ancient planets, to study its intricacy and heritage. Admittedly, less so during the Helix War when the Ket-i were less, shall we say, friendly to visiting professors with nothing better on their minds than the next damned chapter of their thesis. I think the Ket-i shot some of the high-brow intelligentsia on sight, or, at least, hung them by the neck until dead. And, I acknowledge, many of them probably had it coming. However, all this concentration of study and hypothesis could only ascertain two facts about the palace in its entire-ty."

"Which were?"

"One, the greatest academic minds could not dis-cover why it had been built; and two, they couldn't actually work out what it *did*."

"Did?" muttered Franco. He looked to be in some minor discomfort and his brows had dark-ened to a foreboding V.

"Yeah. After all, every machine has a purpose, a function, right? This machine moves, breathes, is alive. It has a purpose. It's been ascertained it absorbs energy, from the sun, as one source, and from chemical underground deposits, as another. The machine sits in equilibrium with its natural environment, and yet despite absorbing energy, it produces nothing."

They moved on again. Keenan stopped at a junc-tion. Another, identical corridor, formed a T. "Down here." They moved again, across oil-slick burnished steel; only this time there were grooves at waist height in the walls. Pippa examined them, pushing her finger into their polished interiors.

"They look like rails."

"I hope not," said Keenan, "because that would suppose a vehicle, possibly moving at very high speed. Anyway, it doesn't matter, our exit chute isn't far."

"I see it!" said Franco.

Then they heard it: metal on metal, rhythmical, and getting louder.

"Up ahead," said Keenan with urgency, and they broke into a run. The thought was at the forefront of all their minds: the rails were polished, and thus regularly used. Something was approaching, fast. It didn't take a genius to understand the concept.

"Here?" said Pippa. The hole was small, rectangular, and at knee height. A cool breeze eased from the shaft. Keenan nodded.

"You should find a ladder. Climb down."

Pippa disappeared. Keenan gestured to Franco, who holstered his weapon, and with MPK grating against the metal wall, squeezed his barrelled belly into the cool descent.

Keenan dropped to a crouch and savoured the draught; then his head slammed up. The noise was loud now. Ahead, he saw it hurtling towards him, a block of metal mounted between the walls. It seemed to be spraying something before it as it howled down the corridor... something slick and clear.

Keenan squeezed into the aperture as the machine buzzed past inches from his fingers; thin oil coated his hands and the back of his head. Keenan shivered.

"Nice place," he muttered, "efficient."

"Every action of worth requires effort," floated Franco's disembodied philosophical meanderings from below. Franco sounded just a little bit too smug. Keenan scowled down into the gloom.

"You don't say." Grasping slick metal rungs, he eyed strange narrow slots behind each rung, almost like grooves, but deeper. He shrugged, and began his descent.

* * *

"DEAD END."

They'd been climbing down for nearly an hour. It seemed a very, very long way. Pippa had stopped, and shortly Franco and Keenan stood beside her. Her torch played about the dark walls; rust smeared in large patches, and the whole essence of the place seemed less cared for, more neglected.

"Where now?" said Franco.

"We have to wait," said Keenan. He checked his weapons, and kneeling, tapped the floor. A hollow, reverberating sound echoed from the butt of his Techrim. Then, they heard… no, almost sensed— beyond the edge of hearing—a whine of subtle gears.

Pippa raised her eyebrows.

"Something's not…" began Keenan, and the floor dropped away, unfolding swiftly in a series of triangular steel petals. They lunged for the ladder.

Keenan slammed the wall, hands closing on a metal rung, legs smashing against the rungs below and sending pain lancing up him. Franco bounced with his shoulder, turned, started to fall and with a mad grappling of blurred limbs managed to entwine one arm and one leg around the ladder. Pippa, however, hit the wall. She reached for the ladder, but it was beyond her grasp. She slid down the wall, down into darkness, teeth grinding as her hands frantically grasped at slick steel. Below, there was a thrashing sound: metal on metal, spinning, grinding, increasing from a standstill with the acceleration of a charging turbine. Pippa felt a scream well in her throat. Her hands, outstretched against the metal, encountered a flaw: a lip, a protuberance she couldn't see in the gloom. Her fingers flexed, dug in and locked. Her legs banged the wall, hard. Her knees sent shockwaves of pain to her skull. Pippa released a long breath and looked up at the distant silhouettes of Keenan and Franco, and then down at what appeared to be spinning discs of metal. She blinked, and reappraised her position. They weren't discs; they were blades.

"Holy Mother," she whispered, and glared across at the ladder. It was too far to jump.

"Pippa!" bellowed Keenan, voice bouncing metallically. "You OK?"

"Just about," she said, voice unnaturally quiet.

"What's the sound?"

"Cutting blades," shouted Pippa. "I recommend you don't make a jump for it, or you'll end up juiced."

Clatters and bangs echoed down the chute as Keenan and Franco descended. Keenan stopped across from Pippa, looked over into her grey eyes and smiled. He reached out. "Come on, jump."

She glanced down.

"If you miss me, Kee, I'm sushi."

"I won't miss," he said.

"You'd better not. Or I'll kill you!"

He grinned at her, face boyish. "Darling, if I let you drop then I'll dive right in after you."

Pippa leapt, hands grasping frantically for Keenan; he caught her, took her weight, and swung her up to him where she took a firm hold on the rungs. Face to face, chest to chest, with nowhere to move, they breathed one another's sweetness.

"Have to stop meeting like this," smiled Keenan.

"You're messing with my head," said Pippa.

Keenan nodded. He agreed. His life, his whole existence, felt like a tumbling confusion, but now, here, only one thing was for sure. He gazed into her eyes and saw the glint of light from wet lips, felt her taut coiled body pressed tight against his. And he wanted her, for a fleeting moment, more than life itself.

"This feels suspiciously like a trap," said Franco. His voice echoed off into distant metal. "You say that fucker JuJu gave you directions? And timings for this huge arse-fuck of an internal puzzle? This rat maze? This hamster slaughter-house? Well, the big dumb Ket-i bastard stitched us up."

"Maybe," said Keenan.

Below, the discs—with tiny serrated contusions on their whining upper surfaces—spun faster and faster and faster, whirling in a blur that was still accelerating on a platter of noise; the piercing metallic shrieks increased, the *thrum* of the blades vibrating the very walls.

Above, high above, there was a *clunk*. Keenan saw Pippa's eyes narrow. Franco, above him, glanced up. There was another, solid, *clunk*.

"What is it, Franco?" snapped Keenan.

Franco strained his neck, squinting, mouth a tight line. There was another *clunk*, then another and another. They started to get faster, and Franco's drug-fried brain suddenly made sense of the image moving towards him.

"Keenan!" he shrieked. "It's the ladder, it's folding in on itself!"

The ladder, in small sections, was folding down and retreating into the narrow slots behind each rung. Viewed from below, it seemed as if the ladder was racing towards them... leaving nothing in its wake: no handholds, no handy ledge to hang from, just narrow slots too thin to get a human finger inside.

Keenan glanced down. Then up.

They were trapped, between sea and shore, hammer and anvil, between a rock and a hard place.

Anger boiled through his veins: a slow injection, a terrible rising of hot blood.

The metal discs spun faster and faster. They shrieked. And in that sound of discordant metal music, harsh and unreal, it seemed to Keenan they laughed at him.

He snarled something incomprehensible...

And stared down into shimmering blades, which mocked him with an impending slaughter.

CHAPTER 12
VAULT

POLKA YUX WAS a rocky, barren, desolate moon, which squatted, a forgotten bastard child on the lesser-known fringes of the Sinax Cluster. Lifeless, with nothing worth mining, no breathable atmosphere, no discernable purpose, and located away from all viable trade routes, umbilicals or SPIRAL docks, Polka Yux was—in the main, and quite rightly—ignored as the actuality of pointlessness it was.

Kotinevitch stood on an Ion Platform two klicks from the moon's bleak surface and floated on a stream of synthetic radiation uplift. She gazed around the vast oval level, at its gently glowing green edges where sparks streamed from Friction Buffers in glowing trails all the way down to the moon's surface. She strode to the edge, her FRAG Bulk Fighter silhouetted behind her. A vast blackness lay above and a vast darkness beneath her, her vision moving and tracking and drawn by the streams—a curtain, in fact—of tiny green fireflies, which tumbled and danced and fell into infinity, blending and merging on trajectories to become a blurred haze-like semi-transparent mist of fire.

Kotinevitch watched the phenomenon for a while, entranced by the simple raw beauty, and enamoured by an almost romantic inclination at her position. Standing, like a God above a planet, it was as if she stood on a platform floating in space, surrounded by eternity, master of all she surveyed.

Eventually, aware she had to dock the advancing machines, but unwilling to pull her gaze from the majesty of—rawness—surrounding her, Kotinevitch wheeled, boots squeaking against the slightly corrugated surface of the platform; she moved to the central tower.

The Tower was a machine, a hub, and the majority of its intelligence was a concentration of navigation data built with one specific function: to gather the War Fleet.

In readiness, for... The Time: a Time, which hopefully, would never come.

Because, if this Fleet was needed... then it was already too late.

Kotinevitch eyed the machine warily as she approached; like a white needle it rose from Platform Central, piercing the infinite black with radiant brightness. A beacon, a guidance module, a totem, it seemed to Kotinevitch this pinnacle of modern technology was almost... alive... sentient, and, if not alive, then certainly divine.

She exhaled, breath escaping as white smoke. The platform was cold, colder than ice.

She climbed into the Tower's feeder hatch and felt a moment of disorientation as it elevated her to the summit several thousand feet above. She stepped out onto the Controller Ridge and knew awe.

Kotinevitch gasped.

She felt like a Star Strider; a Builder of Worlds.

Is this what they felt like? she thought, remembering the old stories, the ancient tales of heroic pioneering Terraformers who, with the aid of World Builders—mammoth tank-like machines used in the terraforming of planets—had left Earth on decade-long journeys to find new places for the creation of colonies, in order to extend the longevity of the parasite mankind. They had travelled the years, searching out, creating, terraforming, and, ultimately, aiding with the final transfer before Earth had spun into decline and frozen to become a static dead world, a raped shell. *Is this how they felt? Surveying an infinity from the bridges of their great and terrible, and powerful machines? And knowing they held in their hands the infinite power to create and destroy... knowing they had, to some extent, become a reality of apotheosis?*

During the thousand years of the Helix War the World Builders—fifteen working models—had been utterly destroyed. However, these machines were not created by mankind; they had been discovered; and despite the billions of man hours spent in an attempt to duplicate, to replicate, to understand, to remanufacture, Man—in his arrogance and actual ignorance of technology—had failed. The World Builders used materials humanity had never before seen; they used Creation Minds that humanity could not understand. And so, listed (by many Professors) as one of the greatest crimes of the Helix War, the annihilation of the World Builders had been a tragic loss, an obsolescence of the art of creating new worlds.

Still, maybe it was for the best, thought Kotinevitch. *The loss of the machines meant we had to spread our wings, had to wander and search and diversify, had to seek out other life forms and amalgamate, accept them, integrate with different cultures and customs and religions.* Kotinevitch smiled. She had a feeling that, after Mankind fled the diseased and dying Earth, if the World Builders had continued to exist—if Halo and Tetrol missiles hadn't vaporised them into component atoms—then maybe Mankind would have remained the secular, insular beast He had always been.

Now, she thought, Man had been forced to integrate, to become part of a quad-galactic mixture of alien races, ethnic species and genetic experiments, all living together in one big happy boiling pot of politics and religion, and of culture and understanding. *We're a cosmopolitan species, now,* she thought. *Ha!*

Kotinevitch reached out and, fingers a blur, allowed the computers to transmit coordinates; then her head lifted and her eyes narrowed and, with one hand on the hilt of her yukana sword, she waited.

Sophisticated, multi-species, integrated: there's no such thing as a fucking alien any more.

Vitch smiled a very grim smile.

Well, not for long, she thought as the first massive BULK Attack Craft slammed into view, space around it distorting and wobbling, and battering Kotinevitch's stance with a terrible pressure.

The first BULK craft fired bright purple jets and shifted, banking, and filling her vision with sheer volume. It filled not just Vitch's vision, but also her head. It was huge. It was a world killer.

Now three BULK Freighters arrived, followed by D5 Transport Craft and a swarm of Piranha Fighters; the vision before Kotinevitch, as her fingers coordinated data on the computer, swam like nothing she had ever before witnessed. More and more ships arrived, hundreds of craft decelerating from Dead Space and distorting reality for just a moment; again and again space rippled with an Empty Displacement Effect as wave after wave of ships, shuttles, fighters, transport craft, freighters, mobile weapon units, energy organisers, mechs, and mobile brain units, all flowed into and around Polka Yux turning the desolate area of space into a hive of insane activity; turning it into a mass of devastating weaponry ten times greater than anything ever witnessed during the Helix War.

Kotinevitch looked out over her fleet.

Kotinevitch smiled grimly at her armada.

And yet, despite the apparent simplicity of her mission, she hoped she would never need this Might.

Inside, inside her breast, inside her heart, inside her soul, something finally relaxed as the fruits of her labour and pain, and anguish for the last decade ranged before her in all its magnificence, all its brutal military glory. Everything she had worked for, everything she had fought for, everything she had risked: it glistened like a dark jewel, a dark God, beckoned her to step forward to the precipice and use that which she had created for its final terrible ultimate purpose.

Kotinevitch licked her lips.

She fought herself.

And fear tumbled through her brain.

She descended the white ethereal tower, back out onto the oval platform; everywhere, in every micrometre of space surrounding the desolate moon, appeared the bulk of military craft, of Kotinevitch's gathered War Machine: so many vehicles the eye could not count. Enough to fill the most feared enemy in Quad-Gal with absolute and unshakeable terror. Kotinevitch had amassed the greatest military fleet ever gathered. She was in control of a New Age.

And yet...

It is a deterrent, she thought.

But if we must go to war, then we will go to war.

If there must be bloodshed, then it will be terrible.

Keenan, you have a lot to answer for. Your ignorance is colossal. And you will destroy everything we have fought to preserve; you will bring Him back from the Eternity Well.

I will make sure you die for your sins.

Vitch smiled the smile of a woman ready to sacrifice everything: a woman ready to kill, to murder not just on a planetary scale, but on a canvas that spanned four galaxies.

She watched the War Machine.

It glittered dark.

"KEENAN! SHIT! AHH! What do we do?" Franco was flapping; in fact, more than flapping... he was practically plucking his own feathers in his eagerness to escape the blades.

Keenan nodded, as if taking counsel from an internal dialogue. "Drop a bomb," he said in a lazy, almost emotionless, drawl. Franco glared into lizard eyes.

"*What?*"

"Wait there."

Keenan struggled to climb up past Pippa, and squeezed onto the ladder next to Franco. He unclasped Franco's pack, delved inside, and by experience of touch pulled free a funnel grenade, or what those in the profession liked to call a Funnel Fuck. Keenan pulled the digital pin, heard the *click* of DNA recognition, and held the bomb in his fist as Franco craned his head trying to meet Keenan's eyes.

"You might blow us up!"

"Either that, or we get minced."

"Shit," said Franco.

"Exactly."

Keenan nodded, leant back, and dropped the bomb into the mesh of spinning discs.

Franco and Pippa cowered against their treacherous, slippery rock. There was a hiatus in time, an apparently endless pause filled with nothing but honeyed silence as the bomb fell, a spiralling trajectory, and above them with thundering great crashes the ladder folded over and over and over, down into itself leaving a slippery oil wall in its wake.

The funnel grenade connected with the blades.

They heard screams of shearing metal, the *shrring* of tortured circular saw steel, then a devastating *crack*. The world seemed to topple. Metal exploded outwards, two of the huge discs jigging and disconnecting from their framework; one went down, spinning and bouncing into dark nothingness, the other spun up, a huge distorted wheel with razor edges whirring end over end as it chased its own metal tail and reached the soles of Pippa's boots.

She screamed.

The disc, losing momentum, hung for a moment just beneath Pippa, threatening to cut her in two. Then it fell away, tumbling silently into darkness. A stink of chemical explosive filled the shaft. Above, the shock of the explosion had upset some deep internal machinery; the self-folding ladder halted, one rung half in and half out of its aperture. It made tiny groaning noises, and moved half-heartedly in a fractured cycle. Then, with a final click, it stopped.

The three members of Combat-K shivered.

Their world plunged suddenly into silence, and complete darkness.

"Are we all OK?" said Keenan.

"Yeah, said Pippa.

"Yeah boss," sighed Franco.

"Let's move, then."

The smoke cleared a little, allowing light to shine up from far below. They descended the shaky, brittle ladder, past the battered smashed machinery of circular blades, now a scorched and broken mess with huge black streaks smearing the walls, and onwards, downwards, into the bowels beneath the Metal Palace.

They reached the real floor of the shaft, littered with debris and with a huge battered saw blade propped bent and broken against the wall. The chamber was a central hub, with six narrow corridors leading away. Each was a squeeze, especially for Franco's girth of belly, and as they squatted down and Keenan waited for the pulse that would tell him the right direction through the web of metal arteries, so Franco moaned.

"There has to be an easier way than this."

"There is," said Keenan. "But the path to the Fractured Emerald is—unfortunately—littered with hundreds of Ket-i soldiers. This is what you'd call a back door."

"Nice of them to fit one."

"This place isn't a vault, Franco. It's a machine. The Ket-i may have turned it to their own uses, but they have made few alterations. They don't want to stop the machine working... cannot afford to upset the equilibrium. After all, they don't know what it does."

"Maybe it makes their oxygen?" joked Pippa.

"Now there's a horrible thought," said Keenan.

The jolt of machinery jerked through the Metal Palace; around their little hub, corridors and passages whirred and shifted, some folded into metal cubes, some opened like the petals of rare flowers. The whole circumference of the shaft base altered and flowed, like liquid. Pippa found she had her hand on Keenan's arm. She withdrew it quickly.

"Not far now," he said, watching her.

Pippa nodded. Her voice was husky when she said, "Let's go."

In a gloom of thin smoke and oil residue, Combat-K moved further into the machine.

THEY CRAWLED DOWN a series of narrow, claustrophobic corridors. It stank of old oil and grease. Sometimes, rancid steam or oil smoke came floating past, making them gag. Keenan stopped at one point, wiping sweat from his brow and checking his map. He felt a great weight, a great mass above and around him, as if he were deep underground, trapped almost in a confined coffin. Yeah, he thought, a tomb: a tomb with my name stone-chiselled on the door.

"You OK, Keenan?"

"Never better," he muttered, and pushed on.

Franco, in comparison, had become pretty chirpy and cheerful after his drugs. His recent anal anaesthetic had pepped him up no end, and he'd managed to stop moaning about needing the toilet. At one point he had winked at Pippa and said something about internal compression and the power of mind over bowel. Pippa hadn't looked impressed.

They stopped at a junction, and Keenan stared at his watch.

"Here it comes," he said.

"What?" scowled Franco.

Suddenly, gears whirred and the narrow corridors started to jig and move; they spun and rotated, and Combat-K felt as if they were inside a giant simulator on some crazy ride. And then... the floor was gone. With yells they fell, twisting, through a large bright chamber, and landed lightly, coiled, weapons at the ready... and facing three large, near-naked but heavily armed Ket-i warriors.

Teeth bared, they levelled Laz-Spears. "Ket hei?" hissed one, and fired his weapon.

Combat-K rolled apart as unseen energy crackled across the metal chamber and sent petals of molten metal running down the wall. Keenan's Techrim was out, firing as the two guards leapt at Combat-K. There was another crackling burst, and the Techrim was torn from Keenan's fingers with several strips of skin. He watched as his bullets, caught in the Laz-Spear's stream, flowed into spinning molten trajectories leading to the floor. His Techrim followed, creating a black shining puddle. Franco leapt at one Ket-i warrior dodging under a sweep of the spear's savagely barbed point and hammering a right hook to his jaw. Pippa attacked the third guard, her own weapon firing. A bullet entered his eye and removed the back of his head. Blood sprayed and he stumbled back into his colleague, limbs flailing, bone cubes scattering like dice across the floor. Another Laz-Spear burst sent Keenan rolling, and he charged and leapt. The warrior lifted his spear too late, and Keenan's boot struck his face. He stumbled back. Another high kick caught the Ket-i under the chin and he dropped his weapon; as he fell Keenan was on him, a small black blade in his hand. He cut the warrior's throat swiftly, head snapped left to where Franco was fighting a losing battle. As he watched, Franco was slammed to the ground by the butt of the Laz-Spear. The weapon levelled ready to remove Franco's head. Keenan hurled his blade, which entered the huge warrior's ear and sliced into brain. The Ket-i warrior stumbled, then righted himself. He turned and, amazingly, glared with narrow dark eyes at Keenan.

Keenan, rigid and poised for attack, watched in disbelief as the warrior altered his stance and lifted his Laz-Spear in Keenan's direction. Keenan grabbed the fallen Laz-Spear beside the still pumping corpse on which he knelt. Arm coming back, he hurled the weapon and the barbed point punched the warrior's chest, to the left, just beneath the shoulder.

The Ket-i warrior took a step back, but even then remained standing. Combat-K uncoiled, and Franco jumped to his feet clutching his throat. The Ket-i warrior gave a savage grin, and in a sudden movement fired his Laz-Spear... which picked Pippa up and hurled her across the chamber like an accelerated rag-doll. She smashed the wall and hit the ground in a crumpled heap as Keenan's MPK came round from his back and he held the trigger hard. Bullets screamed across the short space, riddling the Ket-i guard. The gun juddered under Keenan's hands and the guard's body danced, chest caving in under metal onslaught showing yellow fat and jagged crushed ribs. Keenan released the trigger. Silence slammed them. Smoke curled through the bright chamber. Keenan turned and ran to Pippa, screaming, "Check the corridors!"

Franco, his own sub-machine gun free, ran to check for more Ket-i guards. Keenan reached Pippa and gently uncurled her.

Her eyes were closed.

For a horrible teetering moment he thought she was dead.

Then her eyes opened and she smiled painfully at him. She coughed, and tried to sit up. With a spark and a crackle, lights scattered through her WarSuit.

"Shit," she said. "That fucking hurt."

"Your suit took the blast," sighed Keenan, breathing deeply.

"It fucking killed it. I can feel it getting hotter and hotter!"

Keenan turned. "We clear?"

"Clear, Keenan," bellowed Franco, gun covering the corridor.

"I thought you were dead," said Keenan.

"Take more than a molten Laz-Blast of 50,000psi to kill this woman!"

"Without the suit, you'd have no body left."

"I'm painfully aware of that." She coughed again, and managed to get to her knees. "Shit. It feels like I've been hit by a tank." She struggled out of the damaged WarSuit. Lines of horizontal light spat and hissed through the damaged fabric, and tiny wisps of smoke appeared at collar and cuffs. Pippa stood, shivering momentarily, in her thin cotton under-suit.

"I feel naked without the WarSuit."

Franco, who had just returned, ogled her. "You might as well be," he said. "Don't you wear a bra under that thing? It traces all your curves perfectly." His eyes dropped lower. "Phew!" he said, shaking his head in appreciation. "You're a fine specimen of a woman, Pippa, I'll give you that."

Pippa scowled. "You shouldn't be looking!"

"How can I not? Talk about peepshow!"

Her hand slammed his face, a stinging slap that left an imprint against scorched skin.

"That's fair," smiled Franco.

"Right, come on," snapped Keenan, checking his TuffMAP™. "Franco, I'll scout. You take the rear. Pippa must stay in the middle; she's more vulnerable without her armour."

"But there's at least one added benefit to Pippa losing her WarSuit," said Franco. "A silver lining, you might say."

"Oh yeah?" Pippa's voice was dangerous, cool, and filled with snake poison.

"I can watch the sway of your arse," he beamed.

THEY WORKED THEIR way down narrow tunnels for another hour, one flooded with oil, which left them all slick and greasy, and Franco complaining of pains in his eyes. Down they moved, ever downwards, through corridors and shafts, tunnels and vents. They finally reached a small room at the end of another corridor, which forced them to crawl on bone-mashed knees. Standing, stretching, Keenan smiled.

"We're here."

"Where?"

"Above the Inner Sanctum."

"The Inner Whatchum?"

"The place where they keep the Fractured Emerald."

"Ahhhhhh," said Franco. He thought about it and scratched his chin. "Ahhhhhh," he said, again.

"Now it's down to you."

"Me?"

"I need you to blow a hole in the floor."

"Won't people, like, hear?"

Keenan shrugged. "According to JuJu the majority of guards lie on the way to the Fractured Emerald; the Inner Sanctum is a Holy Place, revered and sacred, not a place for guns and RPGs. Can you do it?"

"Hey!" said Franco, throwing his arms wide, "When it comes to bombs, I can do anything!"

"How long?" Keenan checked their back-trail.

"With calculations, PAD scans... give me fifteen minutes, if you want a proper job."

"Yeah Franco, a proper job."

But Franco wasn't listening; he'd removed his Combat Head and had replaced it with his *Demolition Head*. He was already scratching his bearded chin and muttering under his breath. His eyes held a distant look. Keenan retreated, left Franco to it.

Keenan slumped in the corridor next to Pippa, accepting a canteen of water from her. He drank deep, handed it back, and stared at the wall. He closed his eyes, rubbed at pounding temples. Exhaustion taunted him.

"You OK?"

"Yes," he said, voice quiet.

"Tension getting to you?"

"No." Keenan glanced at Pippa. Franco had been right. Without her WarSuit—her armour—she was indeed voluptuous. He swallowed, hard, and breathed deeply through his mouth. No, he thought, no time. Not now. Mission: mission, to find the killer of my family. Must focus...

Pippa drank her water, then rested her head on his shoulder. She felt him tense, then relax. Something went *click* inside her head and she wondered just what the hell she was doing. *Why push him away? Because he fucked you over. Betrayed you. Left you. Yeah, but then, didn't he have the right? You always knew it was a temporary measure... always knew he worshipped his little girls and put giving them a good home, a good upbringing before anything else. How could you ever compete with that? You couldn't. Face reality, a reality you knew and understood, deep down inside when you started this thing. Indignation. When I fucking started it? Yeah, when you started it. When you ran half-naked across that beach on Molkrush Fed. What did you expect? You expect him not to fall in love with you? But I never wanted a lover... never wanted a man... I hate men, have always hated them, and I always fucking will.* And she could see them, in her hands: the scissors. Scissors, spotted just a little with droplets of blood.

"Son of a bitch!" Pippa sat bolt upright, shivering. And realised, suddenly, she had fallen for Keenan; again. For a few minutes only... but it had been enough. Vitality rushed her veins like narcotics. She looked at him; saw him staring at her with a strange expression.

"Bad dream?"

"No."

"You said... something."

"What?"

"You spoke, in your sleep, about scissors. Then you jumped; you woke."

"It's nothing."

"You can talk to me; if you like?"

"Maybe once, Keenan, not now."

"Am I so different?"

Their eyes connected for a long moment, a moment that stretched into perhaps a minute, which was infinite. She shook her head. "No Keenan, you haven't changed. You're still the man I..."

She chewed her lip. Her grey eyes sparkled; changed from the emotionless gaze of a killer, melted, mellowed, showed a little of the girl deep inside.

Keenan put a finger to her lips. "Shh."

She shook him away. "No, I'll say it. You're still the man I loved: the man I fell in love with, the only man I ever wanted, physically, emotionally: my lodestone, my rock, my anchor. But it can never be like that again; and I see it in you, in the way you look at me, the way you watch me, feel it in the way you touch me. But no, Keenan, no, it can't happen. It must not happen again."

"I betrayed you," he said. "But things are different now."

"Yeah, damn fucking right," she snapped, immediately contrite. "Sorry. Sorry. See? Let me try to explain: it's not you that's stopping me falling into your arms, welcoming you back into my heart, into my head, into my bed. It's not you that's the damn problem. It's me."

"Why?"

"Because of what I've become, because of the things I've done. You haven't changed, Keenan, but I have. When we were together it was a wonderful thing; a time of happiness. I was locked deep in a shell, and you gradually coaxed me out into the sunshine. But, then you smashed the shell, and with nowhere left to hide I became the worst and most brutal of all creatures, the harshest of all predators. I think I lost the woman inside; I think hatred won. I became less than human. And I did things, Keenan, I did so many terrible things... things you would not believe."

"I'm hardly an angel."

"Let's just say," whispered Pippa, breaking their visual umbilical and placing her head back on his shoulder, "that before I can forgive you, I have to learn to forgive myself. And I don't think I can do that."

Keenan lifted his hand, tentatively and stroked her oil and grime-smeared hair. Still it felt beautiful under his touch; he closed his eyes and he had his Pippa back, for just a second of perfect total reality; he had her back and she was his.

"What unforgivable crimes?" he whispered.

"I killed..."

"Done it, guys!" boomed Franco, sticking his head in the tunnel. "It was hard, I have to admit it... no, it was damned near impossible, but as usual the wonderful and talented Franco worked out depth and elements, process and conversion; I realised the alloy was an extract—or amalgamation to be more precise—of Tiberium IV-2 and the PAD measured to within a few microns of eighteen inches. Using a relay connected to a funnel device and coupled with acid strips, I narrowed and concentrated the potential blast to..." He stopped, staring at them. "What?" he said. He held out his hands. "*What?*"

"We were having a private moment," said Pippa. Her eyes were full of tears. She had felt it, in herself. She had... nearly told him everything: her father... and, deep down within... the scissors... what they represented. She took a deep breath, and banished the images. They could wait... for an eternity.

"Well, of all the damned cheek, you bloody well ask for my competence and skilled—no, *expert*—cooperation and I work like a grease monkey to get the job done; and here you two sit canoodling in the tunnel while I'm left to do all the graft."

"Franco, get the fuck out."

Franco looked into Keenan's eyes and saw a terrible but controlled fury there. He chewed his lip.

"OK, boss."

Franco disappeared.

Keenan turned back to Pippa.

He opened his mouth—

"Hey boss?"

"What is it, Franco?" snarled Keenan.

"Just thought I'd mention it: it's nothing really, an inconsequence, but I've set the charge sequence; in just—" he checked his watch, "forty seconds, if you decide not to move your precious arse, then we'll all be blown to whichever particular hell you don't believe in."

THEY WAITED AT the end of the tunnel, Franco focusing on his watch. His sandal slapped the metal impatiently. There was a *crack*, and smoke stinking of metal and hot oil pumped down the corridor. They all coughed, and Franco crawled back to the point of detonation to find a jagged melted hole, two feet in diameter. He waved his hand, waved away the smoke, and peered down into what appeared to be solid blackness.

"You sure this is the right spot, Keenan?"

"Yes." Keenan also peered into the gloom, then unpacked his Line and drilled into the metal of the floor. He tapped the edges of the hole, waiting for them to cool; then glanced at Pippa. "You OK?"

"Yes."

"Right guys, we'll drop slow, with MPKs charged. I don't know what's down there, if there really are guards or if JuJu was sucking my dick. What I do know is that the Fractured Emerald is directly beneath us. So... any questions?"

"If there are hostiles?" said Franco.

"Shoot to kill. No games. This is the mission climax; I don't want any fuck-ups."

KEENAN DESCENDED INTO the black of the Inner Sanctum. It was terribly cold after the corridors of metal, and a breeze eddied, giving the impression of a vast underground space. There was a green glow in the distance.

The Fractured Emerald!

Keenan felt his pulse quicken, but was overcome by a sudden flood of doubt. Would he be able to use it? To interact? Would it look into his past? Would it give him the name he required? For death. For vengeance. For justice.

Combat-K dropped lower and lower in the chasm.

The darkness swallowed them.

THEY HUNG, SUSPENDED. Everything was perfectly quiet, perfectly still. The darkness was a shroud. Keenan swung, MPK moving uneasily. Pippa, eyes trained on her PAD, shook her head.

"There's nothing here: no activity, no life-signs. According to the PAD, this is a vast natural chamber a kilometre deep and three kilometres square."

"What's the light? The green glow?"

"The PAD can't get a lock."

"You ever known a PAD to fail?"

"It's rare," conceded Pippa.

Again they dropped in formation, Lines hissing softly between gloved fingers. As Keenan's boots touched down he folded into a crouch. Pippa and Franco joined him. They unclipped their individual Lines and waited for the tiny machines to self-reclaim.

"It's too obvious," said Franco, staring at the distant green glow. "It's a come-on."

"Yeah, I know," whispered Keenan, "but we haven't got any other options. Have we? I'll lead; you two stay a hundred metres behind. Cover my back, OK?"

"Keenan, the PAD's picking something up."

"What is it?"

"It's analysing. It's... oh, it's the floor of the chamber. It's made from... it seems to be made from human bone."

"Human bone?"

"Yeah, it's quite specific."

Keenan removed his glove and ran his hand across the polished smooth surface. It was indeed bone, slick with the passing of millennia. He shook his head. Unease clasped his spine and shook him. "That's way too fucking creepy."

"I say we get out of here," said Franco.

"What, and not claim our prize?" Keenan's eyes gleamed. "We've come this far. Wait here if you want, I'm going on."

"I'm with you," said Franco, voice soft, fear a glint in his eyes. He shook his head in annoyance. *This place*, he thought. *This unholy place! It's getting to me, eating my balls. God, I wish I had my pills, the pink ones used to make me feel so mellow...* and he realised with a sudden rush that, bizarrely, sometimes, he actually missed Mount Pleasant. Yes, Betezh had been a bastard, and yes, sometimes his testicles underwent the odd electrocution. But, in his little cell with his little shelf and his few possessions, life had been so uncomplicated. It was like being a child again: controlled, without fear, somebody else doing the thinking.

Keenan walked across the bone floor towards the glow. His senses started to scream at him; not just the concept that this whole thing, this mission, this theft, was a set-up, a trap, but also the possibility that maybe the Fractured Emerald didn't do what it said on the tin. His MPK traced arcs through the darkness. His boots trod softly and his eyes were narrowed, scanning, looking for trouble.

The glow started to enlarge, went from distant firefly to ethereal globe. As Keenan's eyes adjusted to the Inner Sanctum, he realised there was a black column, intricately carved, certainly archaic, and—according to the PAD—also made of bone. There was a niche in the column and there, on a small square of black velvet, sat the most fabulous gem Keenan had ever seen. It emitted the green glow. It almost pulsed with a rhythm of its own. It was flawless and beautiful, and drew the eye of the watcher, sucked at any who glanced into its deep and fathomless depths. Its purity was unquestionable. Its power was real, like smoke in the air, insubstantial, drifting, but with an awesome, random energy that oozed an ability to kill.

Keenan stopped and stared hard at the Fractured Emerald.

"It's beautiful," said Pippa, voice honey.

"It must be worth a fortune!" boomed Franco boorishly. "Just think of... think of the whores!"

Keenan stared, entranced, but at the same time wary. Something prickled his scalp. He shivered. He glanced left, then right, and blinked, seeing for the first time the black throne carved of black bone. A woman sat on the throne, petite and delicate, almost painfully thin, her skin a deep and vibrant ebony, her beauty in her slim nakedness stunning. Her skin was oiled, and her black hair tumbled and fell in deep rich ringlets. The glow of the Fractured Emerald shone reflected in her narrowed green eyes, and the surreal witch-light made her veins stand out green against her black skin.

"Who is she?" gawped Franco, staring hard. It was not often he saw a woman in the nude, especially not in the middle of a dangerous mission, and especially not during the theft of a priceless and magical artefact. Franco's priapism knew no bounds.

The woman, eyes glowing almost regally, surveyed Combat-K. She smiled with full wet lips; parted them a little, a sensual and almost sexual movement.

Keenan looked back to the emerald; its pulse seemed to quicken, seemed to match his heartbeat. He turned, face on, to the woman, lowered his head a little and stared at her, hard.

"Come on," growled Pippa.

"Yeah," snapped Franco, "let's grab the gem and do one."

"Something's wrong." Keenan's voice was hushed, husky. He remained, gaze fixed on the woman.

"This ain't the time for an erection, compadre," said Franco with irony.

The woman stood, elegantly, and swayed before the black throne. Keenan was transfixed, like a snake before a charmer. She took a step towards him, then another, and a third. Her hands came up and rested lightly on his shoulders.

"Keenan," said Pippa, with almost a wail in her voice.

"This is her," said Keenan.

"Who?"

"The Fractured Emerald. It isn't the gem; is it?" He stared down into her eyes. His face was serene, a totality of relaxation, of understanding, of calm. "It's a misconception, the automatic reaction of a greedy bunch of nomads and thieves. The Fractured Emerald isn't a gem of incredible worth, it's a woman, a woman of power."

She nodded. When she spoke, it was as if angels sang. "My name is Emerald," she said, voice husky and deeply, deeply feminine. She moved closer to Keenan, pressing up tight against him. Again, his head lowered until their lips were only an inch apart.

"Look at her veins," said Pippa, voice hushed in awe.

Keenan stared down past her face; every vein in her body pulsed green, pulsed as if linked to the gem; or the gem linked to the power of this unorthodox individual.

"Kiss me," she said.

"Excuse me?"

"Kiss me," said Emerald, "and I will know you, understand you. I will delve your deepest desires and fears and needs. I will flow with your saliva and blood and semen. I will be a part of you and you of me, fluid, joined, together for eternity."

Keenan kissed her.

He could not help himself.

THE KISS LASTED for an eternity. He flowed through her veins and knew her and understood her. She was not of Ket; she was a prisoner in this place, used for her powers of prophecy, her ability to see into the future, and into the past. To use her was to become a part of her; and she of you. That way she gained immortality.

Keenan felt himself staring out from a dying world: a black desert world, staring out into the fathomless voids of space; out into a bleak infinity filled with nothing. And he understood, truly understood what it meant to be alone. A scream welled through him as he felt himself slip, slip and tumble into that bleak everything of emptiness, but then she was there, guiding him, holding him, sharing him, and that kiss, that simple kiss was more intimate than any conversation or sharing or holding or loving, more deep and integral than any simple act of copulation; they were one. They were together. Keenan opened his eyes, pulled away from her sweetness, gasped and dropped suddenly to his knees.

"Keenan!" Pippa was there, beside him, holding him, and he gasped and choked as if his entire insides had been sucked free. He rolled over, onto his side as Pippa coolly stood and levelled her MPK in Emerald's face. "What have you done to him, fucker?"

Emerald ignored the gun, turned, and moved back to the throne. She sat, drew her legs up beneath her, and then looked beyond Combat-K, staring off into the blackness of the vast and empty chamber.

"Keenan!" snapped Pippa again, kneeling, confused, torn, but he patted her arm and managed to crawl back to his knees. He forced himself to stand, to breathe deeply; he met the gaze of the Fractured Emerald and gritted his teeth in pain.

"You are trapped here."

"Yes."

"A prisoner of the Ket-i?"

"Yes."

"They use you to predict enemy movements; they use you as a tool of war?"

"Yes."

"You want us to free you?"

"I do as I am told." She looked back at Keenan, meeting his gaze. "I am a machine, a magician, a prophet, a soothsayer, a tool; I am a thing of the ground, an element from deep beneath The Mountain, to be used and," she laughed softly and her voice held the resonance of dying worlds, "abused."

"What do you want from me?" breathed Keenan.

"From you?" She smiled. "I want nothing. But you require information from me. You need me to trace the stems back to reality; to focus on those threads which are Connect Integral and for me to tell you the name, the identity, the code-call of the person who took away those whom you loved and still love."

"Yes!" breathed Keenan, lips wet.

"I can see Eternity," said Emerald. Her eyes glowed. "I can see beyond Time. I can see the pulse of The Galaxy Soul."

"You do want something," snapped Keenan in a moment of primitive intuition. He stood. He approached the black bone throne. He knelt before

Emerald, reached out, and touched her oil-slick skin. His fingers seemed to melt into her, and he rubbed idly at her thighs without cognition.

"Yes. You are perceptive." She smiled. It was a smile on an alien face, a smile formed by an imitator using second-hand muscles.

"What do you want?"

"You must take me to Teller's World."

"That's a Forbidden Place, a place of a Dead GodRace. It is death to go there."

"And so. Yes."

"Nobody has left that place alive, not in a million years of recorded Quad-Galactic history."

"This is my price for information. You accept?"

Keenan glanced back at Franco and Pippa, who stood with their useless wasted weapons, eyes wide, stunned by what was happening, by this interaction between man and...

What is she? thought Pippa, mind a maelstrom. Pippa glanced at Franco, then focused on Keenan. She gave a little shake of her head. "Kee," she said, "to do that is to welcome death."

"What do you want there?" said Keenan, ignoring Pippa's plea, the simple desperation in her voice. They knew; they all knew. A million people had visited Teller's World. Not a single one—not one—had returned. It was a place of fabled treasure, of infinite danger, of the promise, the immortal promise, of revealing a fabled Leader... and for some brave and fearless treasure-seeker, supplying the answers to Eternity: Eternal Life, Immortal Power, To... become a God...

"I want to regain my former position, to become what I once was, to grow strong again! To grow proud again! And then—when I have tasted the Galaxy Soul once more—then I can die," said Emerald. She blinked, slowly and lazily.

"I will take you there," said Keenan, giving a single nod. He turned back to Franco and Pippa; they understood. He intended to take her alone, and to die, if necessary, in the process.

"No problem," growled Franco, mask a frown. "We'll fly in there, drop you off, get the intel, fight whatever dark unholy creature has killed a million people and eaten Battle Cruisers whole, and then pop back for a spot of lunch: piece of piss. No problem for a solid MPK and a heart of pumping stupidity." He scowled at Keenan. "Dickhead."

"First you must free me," said Emerald, and touched her breast. Keenan saw a tiny black square against her flesh, the size of his thumbnail. It reminded him of a computer chip. Emerald smiled again, only this time her eyes were hard, hard and brittle, and unforgiving. "This is my controller."

"Yes!" boomed a voice, and bright light flooded the vault.

Keenan, Pippa and Franco started. They were surrounded: surrounded by a thousand Ket-i warriors, carrying Laz-Spears and a small arsenal of heavy weaponry. The army moved forward in a line, a wall, a circle, closing in swiftly on Combat-K... and the Fractured Emerald.

"Told you it was a set-up," muttered Franco from the corner of his mouth.

As the circle closed, and halted with a booming of Laz-Spears striking the bone floor, one Ket-i warrior came closer and stopped. He was adorned with a hundred gold trinkets and chains, head held high, a mantle of emerald spikes bone-welded to his skull and spine. His forearm blades had been repaired after his savage wounding, and his eyes glowed with power and...

Insanity, thought Pippa.

"First you must free her," said JuJu, head turning, surveying the group. "And the only way to do that is to destroy her, for she is a creature you cannot understand, cannot comprehend. She may never leave this place. She must never leave this place. That is why she is Controlled."

Keenan strode towards JuJu and stared up at the huge warrior, up into his eyes. "I thought we had a deal," he said.

JuJu shook his head. "I understand you, Keenan. I sympathise with you, but I cannot allow you to take the Fractured Emerald and break the promise of a million years. She is a danger to all life in the Quad-Gal. You cannot understand this concept; it is from before a time of Humanity. She is my Ward, my Prisoner, my Nemesis."

"She is your victim," snarled Keenan.

JuJu shrugged and smiled. "Yes, imprisoned. Her want and need is of little consequence. What matters is that she remains here, trapped and powerless. Ket is a harsh place, Keenan, a harsh place to live and a harsh place to die. You could never understand; you are not Ket-i. You know not our history, nor our lore, nor our legends."

Keenan nodded.

"What happens now?" His voice was low, dangerous. His stance a hairline trigger. "I fight you and if I win, then everything's OK? That seems to be your way; the way of Ket."

"No, Keenan. You fight the Fractured Emerald; if she wins, you die."

"And if I win?"

"You will not win."

JuJu carried something in his hand: a small alloy device strapped to his wrist, which he turned. He glanced past Keenan, to the dark carved throne where Emerald sat, legs drawn beneath her, face touched by the fear of the enslaved. Her eyes narrowed and she stared from behind her mortal mask with a pure and undisguised hatred.

"No," she crooned, voice suddenly inhuman and filled with tiny *clicks*.

"Keenan!" hissed Pippa. "JuJu is..." but her words were cut off by a tremendous *cracking* of bone and tendon. Emerald rolled forward from the throne, and as she hit the ground she suddenly distorted. Her limbs twisted and bent backwards, all four moving and striking the ground together and thrusting her body into a central taut stance, so she resembled a four-legged spider, back-broken, legs formed from human limbs. She screamed; her howl rent the cold air. The green gem in the column pulsed faster, and liquid emerald flowed hot through the alien's veins.

The surrounding warriors smashed their spears once again into the ground with a crashing boom. They began to chant, the words primitive, simple, primeval. The chanting increased in pace as Emerald bucked and twisted, gyrated at angles impossible to the human form. She scuttled backward and forward between throne and column as her hands and feet elongated into black, armoured points. Her body shed a thin film of black skin, leaving the gleam of oiled insect carapace. With further cracking sounds, bones rearranged themselves, her head dropped, neck twisting with a series of bone-jarring crunches, black armour spreading like cancer across her inverted face in panels, until only the green glowing eyes remained, staring out from an insectile form so far removed from a human shell as to be something ejaculated from nightmare.

Keenan had taken several steps back, realising that the Ket warriors had formed not just into a circle, but into an... arena.

The creature that had been Emerald stopped its pain-filled gyrations and turned, focusing on Keenan. A low sibilant hissing emerged and armoured mandibles clicked, rubbing together. Long strings of saliva fell from the distorted face; a pulped, almost human face; the eyes were fixed on Keenan, locked to him with a focus of steel.

"Shit." He laughed in horror. He glanced at Pippa and Franco, who had also backed away as far as the wall of Laz-Spears would allow. Pippa gave a little shrug and eased into the relaxed stance of combat that Keenan had witnessed a thousand times past. Franco dragged round his pack and started rummaging for a bomb.

"JuJu, you are disgracing your tribe," hissed Keenan. His MPK was solid and real in his hands, but he was loath to use it; how could he? If he killed Emerald then he would kill the knowledge he so craved. How could he destroy that which would be his ultimate saviour?

"Prince Akeez thought a simple group of mercenaries could release That Which Was Enslaved." JuJu shook his head, high spikes glinting with shearing light. "You are all fools: master and servants alike."

Keenan tensed for battle; his mind flowed cold and brittle. All thoughts of knowledge and information, and reading backwards into the seeds of time were dispelled as Emerald, rotating with a clatter of iron claws on bone, leapt with a sudden flashing blur of speed which had Keenan stumbling back in panic, MPK firing a line of howling bullets on instinct. Rounds rattled up Emerald's armoured belly and she landed, lightly, one claw lashing out to slice the MPK clean in half. The dead submachine gun spun across the bone ground. Keenan leapt away, narrowly avoiding being severed at the waist.

He landed in a crouch.

Emerald attacked with the savagery of a lightning strike.

An armoured point ripped a tear through Keenan's WarSuit and opened the flesh of his chest. Keenan gasped as pain slammed him, and he staggered back, feeling a warm flush of blood beneath the suit, feeling the armour's shrill cry of damage, and watching numbly as Emerald circled him and he clutched his own cut flesh. Skin and muscle parted beneath questing fingers, a sick gaping mouth.

It sliced a *WarSuit*, screamed his mind.

It does not remember what it was.

In horror Keenan realised he could not fight this creature, could not kill this creature. With an insight that cursed his brain he suddenly understood: this thing was old, older than humanity, older than the Ket-i; what had JuJu said? She was a danger to all life in the Quad-Gal? From a time before Humanity?

Emerald looked at him. A black maw grinned treacle saliva.

And it nodded towards him, swaying.

It gave him Insight... sprinkled his mind with confused understanding.

Bright lights glittered.

Emerald was Old Life.

Emerald was a Servant of a long extinct GodRace.

Emerald was a Servant of Leviathan.

PART 4

REDEMPTION SONG

CHAPTER 13
CEREBRAL FRACTURE

BETEZH SQUATTED IN the jungle, smeared with grime, exhausted, eyelids drooping, but an edge of fear kept him clinging to consciousness, and wondering just what the hell his next move could be.

After escaping the Gem Rig and paddling off across the Milk Sea like some diseased and grotty Gollum, Betezh had soon realised that the engines on the Raptor Boat had been disabled, immobilised. Oh, how he had smiled nastily at that: Franco's last laugh? You bet.

And so, Betezh floated for long endless hours, dragged this way and that by tides more powerful than anything he could have dreamed, more forceful than anything against which he could simply paddle. Ket was a savage planet and the Milk Sea was no different. Occasionally, he'd paddle furiously in the hope he could achieve some distance, but, alone, a single oar against the wilds of Ket Nature, it was a useless thankless task.

The bastard known as Franco, eternal thorn in Betezh's side, had efficiently disabled Betezh's escape, crippled him. Betezh was a soldier, a murderer, could even pull off a reasonable impression of a doctor specialising in mental breakdown, but a mechanic he was not. Yes, he could hack away at a simple engine, but the beasts that lurked in this craft were beyond his admittedly simple engineering skills.

He floated for eternity, his shaved head reddening alarmingly under the beating suns. He cursed, double-cursed and triple-cursed Franco Haggis; it had seemed such a simple mission. Contain the maggot at Mount Pleasant. No problem, a walk in the park, easy peasy. But through a series of unfortunate escalations, Betezh found himself up shit creek... yes, with a paddle, but a paddle that was useless in the face of an aggressive tidal system hell-bent on his demise.

Betezh floated, bobbed, rode waves, sank troughs.

He muttered, a lot, cursing Franco, cursing the Gods, and, ultimately, cursing his boss Vitch the Bitch. "What a bitch," he would grumble to himself, before splashing around uselessly with his paddle for a while, then giving up—always giving up—and lying back, baking in the boat, tortured skin nagging him with a pain he tried—unsuccessfully—to push away.

Night fell.

With it came a relief from the agonies of torturing sunlight. Without water—an important oversight—Betezh wheezed and panted, moaned and groaned; a twig tongue probed bark lips.

He tried to sleep. Sleep would not come.

He tried to think of happier times, but, strangely, there didn't really appear to be any.

What did I do with my life? he thought sourly. He'd only wanted to be a soldier, a squaddie, an infantryman. He'd loved the sound, the work, the ethos. He'd signed up aged seventeen; threw himself into Boot Camp, worked his knickers off to make a good soldier. Impressing his COs, he'd been drafted into Special Ops, a long slippery slope of gradual mental and ethical degradation, which had led, eventually, over many decades, to him working as a Spook for a politician slick bitch like General Kotinevitch. And, yes, for a while he had revelled in his role; he had been important, made serious decisions, been up, up, up, launched flying to the top of the ziggurat, and if not directly in charge, then at least seriously influential. However, the toes that you step on while you're on your way up, may be the same ones that you kiss going down. And now? Irony, now he was a piece of burnt toast in a boat, and, more importantly, a piece of blackened toast... about to die.

No children, he realised suddenly.

Always been too busy; never met the right woman.

He had always wanted children. He nodded to himself.

Shit.

There was a gentle bump.

Betezh lay for a while, trying to ease a droplet of non-existent water from some porous orifice within the desert cavern of his mouth. Then he frowned. His harsh features compressed, aided by severe dehydration. A bump?

Betezh had crawled across the alloy floor of the boat, and sunburnt hands like cooked lobster grasped the rim, hauling his bulk to the edge; land! Land! "It's land," he croaked, hauled himself onto the rim, and rolled off amongst the rock pools. He struggled, splashed about, made it onto hands and knees, and then crawled sideways like a crab up the beach towards the protection of the jungle.

He halted a few feet away, staring suspiciously at the massive black expanse; it was even more forbidding under nightfall. He shrugged. What did he have to lose?

Betezh had crawled into solid blackness...

And around him, the jungle creaked.

FRUIT!

He'd found fruit!

Betezh gorged like an animal on the ripe soft Ket melon. Chewing a head-sized hole in the rind with gnawing sounds, he plunged his face into the soft flesh, slurping juice, allowing the coolness to soothe his baked skin as he drank his fill, ate his fill, then tossed the huge empty husk aside and belched. He lay on his back, staring up at wavering creepers in the near-absolute blackness, and listening to the *chirrup* of insects and the far-off lumbering of some prehistoric monstrosity; Betezh sighed.

I'm not going to die after all! he thought.
I'm not going to die! Not going to die!
I will father children! I will meet the right girl!
I will...

"Get up!" The voice was harsh, guttural, and did not inspire confidence. Betezh opened his eyes and looked up into the glowing tip of a Laz-Spear. He scowled. Oh how the Gods mocked him!

Dawn was breaking. Streamers of fire from two directions divided the sky with jagged oil blades. Steam rose from much of the jungle undergrowth. Heat and humidity were already increasing, and Betezh, sweat stinging his sunburn, climbed warily to his feet.

There were twelve Ket-i warriors, huge powerful males wearing bones of the slaughtered with pride. Several were armed with sub-machine guns, most with Laz-Spears and shoulder-holstered plastic pistols.

"I am a stranger in your land," began Betezh, and the Laz-Spear cracked against his skull and he hit the ground, hard. Betezh growled something incomprehensible and touched his head. Blood came away on his fingers. He glanced up, lips baring teeth like a rabid mutt, but the warrior wasn't watching him. He was gazing off into the jungle, eyes narrowed, nostrils twitching.

Betezh slowly followed this line of vision, but could see nothing.

There was crashing through the undergrowth, as of a panicked sprinter; a warrior burst into view, slammed to a halt, and gestured wildly behind him.

"Alien," he managed between gasps for oxygen.

The warriors spread out, Betezh forgotten and left prostrate near the centre of their sudden battle formation. Betezh made as if to scramble for cover, but a glance and wave of a Laz-Spear made him stay put. "Between the devil and the deep blue sea," he muttered, and spat into the woven jungle matting.

"Not the devil," said a soft, fluid voice. The man stepped forward, boots creaking the jungle carpet as he walked. He stopped, looked around at the twitchy Ket-i warriors, now numbering thirteen and brandishing weapons at this new intruder. "Just me."

Betezh gawped like a child without a lollipop.

The man was small, slim and wiry, head bald, torso naked and gleaming under virgin sunlight. He wore simple baggy trousers and tight boots. He was powerfully muscled despite his size, and his flesh was heavily scarred. He carried nothing more than a long knife, black and serrated, dull and held nonchalantly. He was smiling a disarming smile. No man should have been smiling when facing thirteen Ket-i warriors.

Betezh swallowed, despite dehydration.

It was Mr. Max.

"Betezh? What are you doing down there? I've come to take you back." Mr. Max leant against a tree and surveyed the group idly. He stared hard at Betezh with those black fish eyes. "General Vitch is most displeased. You have shown a distinct lack of progress."

Betezh nodded; with one hand, he toyed with the staples in his face.

The Ket-i, hardened by millennia of war, attacked with unity. They moved fast, hard, Laz-Spears and sub-machine guns combining to form the perfect integration of violent assault.

Betezh watched as if in a dream.

Mr. Max moved between the Ket-i, his simple blade cutting and slicing. He ducked, disembowelled a warrior, swayed right as a Laz-Spear flashed by his ear, severed the outstretched arm, and as blood pumped over him, the Laz-Spear detonating charges in its fall to the ground, he whirled, ducking low, blade stabbing into a belly, slashing through a windpipe. It was neat, economical. Bullets whined past his face and he swayed back, turning the dance into a roll. He cut another throat, stabbed a warrior through the eye, left elbow ramming back into a face, knife coming round on an arc of blood droplets to slam into the forehead of the huge leader. Mr. Max rode the man to the ground, knees on the Ket-i warrior's chest, then wrenched free the blade and cleaned it thoughtfully.

Betezh gasped. "You killed them all," he blurted.

"You expect me to stop and play chess, perhaps?"

"You moved... so fast."

Mr. Max, who had been checking the butchered corpses, stopped. His head turned and the black eyes fixed on Betezh, who shivered. *He's a fucking machine,* thought Betezh... and then something came to him, information he'd read years previous, a concept he had once overheard, from Kotinevitch. Only now did the puzzle slot neatly into place.

The concept had been that of *Seed Hunter.*

Betezh shivered again. Previously, Mr. Max's reputation had been just that, a reputation. And yes, he had completed his missions, but then, so did a hundred other mercenaries under Kotinevitch's command. She was a General; that's what she did, had people killed for the greater good. But Betezh had watched Mr. Max work, and work was the correct word; there had been no emotion there, no empathy, not even detachment, just a brutal and methodical economy.

"You're a Seed Hunter, aren't you?" said Betezh.

Mr. Max was there, beside him, his speed a blur, and the knife pressing Betezh's throat. He stared into those black eyes—like glass—and knew he was dead: an emotionless dispatch.

"You keep your thoughts to yourself, Betezh. Or I might forget Vitch's instructions to bring you back alive. You and I both know, Seed Hunters are illegal, killed on sight, burned." He relaxed a little, settling back cross-legged, his knife before him like a totem. He idly pushed a severed arm out of the way, and fixed Betezh with a smile. "You do not understand my kind."

Betezh licked dry lips. He gave a single nod.

"Seed Hunters are not like you read in the text books."

"I thought you were supposed to have metal skin?"

"It is an alloy, woven into our flesh; makes us hard to kill."

"And you have a machine brain?"

"Don't we all?" said Mr. Max.

"I thought you would be... bigger. You are presented as robots... machines, like the AIs."

"That would be... incorrect," said Mr. Max. He gave a smile that had nothing to do with humour.

"General Kotinevitch knows, doesn't she?" said Betezh with a sudden flash of intuition.

"Yes."

"And yet she still uses you?"

"Our kind are efficient."

"To the point of genocide?"

Mr. Max rose smoothly. He looked back through the jungle. Sounds of engines echoed, revving and screaming; somewhere distant, machine guns yammered.

"We all die," said Mr. Max. He turned and strode away.

KLIK HATED THE darkness, despised the cold. Having spent most of his childhood in the jungles and The Bone City, amongst fallen heat-dried trees, windblown sand and bone houses, and mostly outside in the daylight, the place in which he found himself was a horror he could not fully absorb, could not truly comprehend. During Klik's formative years he had spent the short night hours of Ket indoors by the fire, watching the flames and revelling in their dance, enjoying the heat, talking with the demons therein and allowing the dancers to soothe him. Now, in this underground vault, the coldness had quickly penetrated through his scant clothing, and he felt as if it was eating his bones, eating his soul.

The infiltration had been surprisingly easy; a few local charms stolen from small children, and Klik soon reinvented himself as a member of the tribe that had once spat him free and banished him to a future filled with no hope, only a promise of oblivion. Klik, however, had insider knowledge on how tribes operated: customs and styles, subtle speech patterns and hand gestures, and so was prepared— physically and mentally—for the challenge ahead.

However, the further he progressed with his plan—the more he was successful, victorious!—so the more his confidence wavered, the more his surety was eroded by the acid stench of fear... not fear of death, but a desolate horror at the possibility he would not accomplish his task before death embraced him.

The cold, the darkness, the feeling of being entombed beneath the ground was also affecting him mentally. He continually shivered, shudders flowing like a wayward tide through his flesh and left him drained, weak, deeply sick to his stomach. But still he forced himself on, deeper and deeper, and finally into a vast dark cavern, the black arena he had overheard from slack-jawed guards on patrol as he hung like a monkey from overhead pipe-work. Something big and dangerous was going down, and instinctively Klik knew it involved JuJu.

Ahhh, JuJu, the warrior who had killed his father. Klik had been only seven at the time, watching in fascinated horror as JuJu descended with his Royal Honour Guard, exchanged a few short words and slammed his Laz-Spear through his father's unprotected chest. Klik's father had fallen to his knees, and JuJu had remained, casual, holding the dying, twitching man rigid on the end of the weapon, and, amazingly, still speaking as if discussing the weather, or a recent gem crop. JuJu's eyes had been wide and unfocused, spiritually empty on the hallucinogenic root of Gatella Cheop.

JuJu finally kicked the dead body from his spear with contempt, ducked and entered the family home, a modest—some would say poor—bone house, and stood with hands on hips staring at Klik's mother. Klik had whimpered, withdrawing to the corner of the room as his mother was ordered to disrobe; in fear, she had removed her silks and bone trinkets, as Klik's older brother emerged from a side room, screamed, attacked, and was batted easily to the ground like a useless insect. JuJu rammed his spear through Klik's brother's head. Klik remembered quite clearly watching for a while as brains and blood seeped from a fractured skull where the Laz-Spear connected him to the floor. The rape had been short and brutal, the knife across Klik's mother's throat silencing her fake moans of ecstasy and then…

Then JuJu turned his attentions to Klik, silent in the corner.

The huge warrior, angry now for some reason—maybe at the lack of sport from this weak and socially deprived family—retrieved his Laz-Spear by standing on Klik's brother's head and wrenching the weapon free with a *crunch*. He advanced on the youngest member of the family, who intuitively hunched down, frozen in terror, mouth agape like some injured fish… ultimately, waiting to die.

JuJu stood before Klik, Laz-Spear in his fist, eyes filled with a furious anger.

Klik's mother, throat slit so that she gaped with two mouths, lunged across the floor, driving her dagger through JuJu's foot; Klik heard quite clearly the grating of serrated blade slicing flesh, muscle, bone, heard the rainfall pattering of ejecting blood droplets, but did not wait to see JuJu slam his Laz-Spear through the brave woman's breast, piercing her heart. Instead, he turned, clambered out of the window, and ran with all his might towards eel-marsh... and the sea beyond.

There had been no pursuit.

KLIK BLINKED.

The memories were still brutal, sorrowful; they filled his eyes with tears and his throat with dry pain. It had been a time of great learning, of achieving manhood. The possibility of survival had been remote, but Klik had survived. And now he was back.

He pulled free a fresh bottle of clear liquor—stolen hours earlier—and drank deeply. Alcohol rimed his veins and he welcomed the easy release; yet he knew, deep inside, that he was cheating himself. He lifted the bottle and stared at the clear but potently powerful liquor. He frowned. No, not now, he thought. The drink was wrong. It would deprive him of victory, remove his senses when he needed them most.

He stowed away the bottle, his need, his release, and moved on through the darkness. Sharp eyes finally discerned the circle of Ket's finest warriors, and Klik approached.

He halted behind the throng of armed guards. They were locked, eyes and minds entranced on the events unfurling ahead. With brittle cracks, their War Prophet, the Fractured Emerald, was transmogrifying into something more alien than alien. Klik took little note. All that concerned him was the one large regal Ket-i warrior central to the action: the one who had murdered his family, the one who had stolen his life. Honour dictated Klik's actions; honour and pride gave him the energy and bravery he desired.

Only death could end this mission... one way or another.

The ranks of warriors, despite appearances, were a poorly structured unit. The Ket-i, whilst none could overlook or dismiss their bravery and ferocity in battle, did not adhere to any form of battle order or rank unity. Their formation was a scattering, and between each man was simply enough room to wield a Laz-Spear. Klik moved through these arteries with care, not wishing to arouse suspicion. Despite his youth, he was tall, and his disguise fitted neatly with the culture. He passed more and more warriors until, up ahead, he heard the skittering of sharp-bladed claws on the bone ground, and at last was close enough to see—

Keenan, backing away to Pippa and Franco who had been seized by guards, their weapons taken. Keenan's eyes were wide and filled, if not with fear, then a terrible apprehension.

Emerald attacked.

Klik blinked, the movements were so fast. The creature left Keenan reeling, blood on his hands as he tried to hold himself together. Klik licked dry lips; Keenan was not his problem. Klik turned. He saw JuJu. JuJu was entranced by this dance of violence. Klik smiled. *Violence breeds violence,* he thought. He knelt, withdrawing a blade from a Helk-leather sheath against his calf; then, again moving slowly, with easy confidence, he approached JuJu, whose large body was tensed, bathed in sweat.

Klik leapt, arms circling JuJu, and with all his strength he jammed the knife into the man's throat, feeling the keen-edged metal bite into skin, through windpipe, pushing deeper and deeper with warm blood flowing, flushing over his hands, and it was all a dream a beautiful dream. JuJu thrashed beneath him, but his blades were as nothing, useless and pointless. Klik dragged on the knife with a slight sawing motion, felt tendons pop beneath the blade, felt more blood gush in pumping great waves as he pressed and pulled and sawed, and was finally thrown free by the huge gurgling thrashing warrior.

Klik hit the ground, rolled, came up on his elbows. His knife had fallen into infinity. He stared up as JuJu staggered back, the surrounding Ket-i guards opening like a doorway to give him room. Then JuJu dropped to one knee, eyes fixed on the boy, Klik, hands pressed against the huge flap in his throat, as blood poured from the smiling wound and formed a perfectly round puddle on the bone floor. JuJu tried to stand, staggered again, and this time slipped on his own gore and fell to both knees. He stared at Klik for what seemed like an age; then he slowly reclined back, chest heaving, hands clutching his opened throat.

Klik stared at the guards around him; they looked down, back at JuJu, then back to the boy. They did nothing.

Klik climbed to his feet, found his dagger, and approached JuJu. Nobody stopped him; nobody tried to halt, or intervene, in any way. It was a matter of battle. Klik knelt by JuJu's speechless and fast dying shell.

"You killed my father, my mother, my brother." Klik's tears fell, fell into the open wound at JuJu's throat, but no amount of tears would wash the blood free. "Now you will be their Eternity Slave. I swear this, with my blood, with my honour, and seal it... with death."

Klik leant forward and continued to work at cutting JuJu's throat, at the muscles and tendons of his neck. JuJu struggled weakly to push the boy away, but Klik slapped at the hands, knocking the warrior's blood-slippery grip away from the task that consumed him. He struggled when he came to the spinal column, but his knife was both sharp and serrated, a saw, and he worked methodically, leaned all his body-weight into the task and finally there was a *crack*, and Klik tugged the head from the corpse and staggered to his feet. He lifted JuJu's head into the air, streaming blood and torn tendons, and flaps of skin. He simply stood there, snarling his defiance at the people, the tribe, who had made him outcast.

Klik waited for the killing blow.

It did not come.

He waited, anger fading gradually like a storm-bleached sunset dying. He dropped JuJu's head, and the spikes bone-welded to the dead leader's skull clattered hollowly. He turned, and saw Keenan lying on his back, arms above his head... but Emerald had frozen, one pointed spike lifted as if to smash Keenan's face from existence. He heard a voice, shouting, "Get the controller, it's on his wrist, Klik... get the controller!" Then he was falling as if into a soft pastel ocean and the surf roared in his ears, in his mind, and his vision turned to foam. He dived beneath the surface and sank into blue-green depths.

KEENAN AWOKE IN agony, chest searing hot laser fire. Before he opened his eyes his hand moved to the wound, and he heard a shushing, soothing noise as one might make to an injured child. He opened his eyes and grinned.

"Thought that had to be you," he said.

Pippa smiled down, face shadowed by the single bulb hanging in the stark cell.

Cell? Shit.

Keenan, groaning, sat up and glanced around. The cell was indeed a cell, hollowed from what appeared to be a single bone. The walls, floor, ceiling, all had a curious hand-scraped look, as if laboriously chiselled by blunt tools. Franco sat in the corner, knees under his chin, snoring. Pippa offered Keenan a bone cup, and he drank milky water, choking and dribbling it down his chin; then he accepted a longer draught with greedy necessity.

"They catch us, then?"

"Yeah," said Pippa. "You are one lucky son of a bitch."

"What happened?"

"Klik killed JuJu; slit his throat. Cut his damned head off, in fact."

"Can't say I'll miss him; stitched us up like a kipper. What happened next?"

"Emerald froze. JuJu had her controller hot wired to his own system; when he died, she no longer received his controlling impulses. So she turned back into... well, into her human form." Pippa shuddered. "It was horrible. What is she, Keenan?"

"A creature drifting a long way from home."

Franco woke with a snort. His face carried excessive bruising, and he grimaced, a movement Keenan realised was a grin. "You OK there Big Man?" he said. "Thought that Emerald lass was going to whup your ass."

"Me too," nodded Keenan. He stretched, and groaned as pain lashed his system. He stood up, paced around the cell. It was small, had thick bars of bone, and no obvious weakness to exploit.

"You told him yet?" said Franco, casting a sly glance at Pippa.

"Told me what?"

"So I see she hasn't. OK, buddy, it goes like this. Basically, they've arrested us for attempting to steal their greatest living artefact; they've invited Quad-Gal media—and I mean the Big Boys—over for a feast of high-profile front-page prime-time coverage. Keenan, we'll be going out on all two million channels. I can just imagine it, 'Combat-K, Wanted in over Five Thousand Systems! Enlivened, Exciting Execution on the 'morrow!'" Franco beamed proudly at his expansive use of jargon media-speak and alliteration.

"Executed?" said Keenan.

"By Laz-Noose," said Pippa. Her smile was a weak one, "Laser noose, to a layman. The Captain of the Guard was explaining it to us with much relish before you awoke; apparently he fears we have defecated on their religion, attempted a mockery on the Ket-i people's system of social and political stability. He thought that, if we had been successful, then Ket-i would have entered a state of civil war."

"The whole damn planet's been in a state of war for the past ten million fucking years," snarled Keenan. "The only benefit the Fractured Emerald offers is that of insider information. JuJu's tribe were waging a war by utilising illegal information on future tactical movements! Jesus! The Ket can stick their fucking execution. We're going to get out of here."

Pippa shrugged. "What happens is this: We'll be given brain-stim injections and then executed by Laz-Noose, all in front of a baying, bloodthirsty, Quad-Gal media-savvy crowd. Apparently, we drop through a trapdoor on a specially built platform, we strangle; then the Laz-Noose initiates to cut off our heads. But, because of the injected brain-stim, the decapitated head then stays alive for another 72 hours, allowing successive and extensive torture to continue. Headless, a victim is subjected to a whole host of face and brain mangling. It's a wonderfully inventive system. Wouldn't you agree?"

"Just ace," said Keenan, slumping back to the floor. "We'll have to act before the brain-stim, is that what you're saying?"

Pippa nodded. "When they give us that, it's game over. We're puppets."

Keenan thought for a moment. "We're puppets anyway. What happened to Klik?"

"After killing JuJu, he passed out. They carried him away, then overpowered our little band. Franco put up a fight, as you can see, although he looks like he took more than he gave."

"Hey, there were fifteen of them, all big buggers, and they jumped me from behind," said Franco.

"That's the way you always tell it," laughed Pippa.

"Hey, but that's what happens to little guys like me."

"No chance, Franco; I've seen you drunk, and you cause a hundred damn fights! You always come off worse, and in the morning regale any poor bastard who'll listen with the tale of how you were jumped by an unfeasibly large group of blokes, from behind, naturally, but you put up a stunning display of bravado before they wore you down and the final, swaying pugilist knocks you out with his dying breath; or something."

"Get stuffed," said Franco.

"Aww, don't sulk liccle Franco. I'm sure you'll get plenty of opportunity to play at being the martial arts hero real soon. After all..." She peered between the door bars, "they'll be coming to kill us in a few hours."

"Will you two be quiet," snapped Keenan. "I'm trying to think."

"Better be quick," said Pippa. "They're coming now."

Keenan and Franco leapt to their feet. Stripped of weapons and armour, they felt naked. Keenan's chest, which had been stapled together without anaesthetic, filled him with a raw burning fire. It added a necessary urgency to his predicament, a reminder that he wasn't immortal and could die as easily as the next man.

A door hissed open.

Footsteps padded quietly.

Emerald appeared, slim and black-skinned, her veins still standing out as green against ebony flesh, only dull now, as if an inner light had been turned down. She stopped, ringlets tumbling around her naked body, feet scraping a little on the bone floor. Her toes were dusted with pulverised bone. Her fingers took hold of the bars. She looked in at Combat-K with glowing green eyes.

"Nice of you to attend the peepshow," growled Franco.

Keenan kicked him.

"Ow! What you do that for?"

Keenan gave a short bow. "I'm sorry. I didn't manage to get the controller. I failed right at the start in this simplest of challenges; I apologise."

"There is no need for apology."

Emerald opened her hand; there against her skin nestled a chip, which was the twin to the one implanted above her heart—or where her heart would have been, had she been human.

"You are free?" asked Keenan.

Emerald nodded. "Thanks to you and your team. You led Klik to JuJu. You instigated this whole situation, if not directly by removing the controller from JuJu's dead grasp."

"So you are free?" repeated Keenan.

"Not yet. It's taking them a while to work out how JuJu controlled me; it is, apparently, a secret passed from clan to clan, from father to son, down the ages. When I shifted back..." she paused for a moment, and Keenan thought he caught a haunted look in those deep green eyes, "I regained a degree of control. In the confusion, and while Franco battered many of the Ket-i guards, I crawled to JuJu and regained what was rightfully mine."

"Hey, don't mention it," said Franco, beaming. "So you going to break us out of here or what? They're going to stimmy our brains and laser slice our heads, y'know?"

"I know," smiled Emerald.

"Do you have the codes for the door?" said Pippa.

"They are not necessary."

Emerald reached forward, took hold of the bars, and there was a slow warming of the air. The bars glowed, and Emerald made several cuts with the edge of her hand; she lifted free superheated bar segments to reveal a large gap.

"Follow me; I have transport waiting."

Pippa stepped free and Emerald, moving less like a human with every passing moment, and more like a... Pippa searched her memory. Yes, she decided, more like a feline, with lazy grace: a tightly reined but incredible power, not easily recognisable without combat to bring the obvious lethality to the fore.

Pippa followed Emerald closely, and, stopping at the end of the corridor, Emerald ripped a steel door from a locker and showed them their weapons and packs. Eager hands took guns, and Franco turned, eyeing a gun-rack bearing Kekra quad-barrel machine pistols. "Hey, Emmy, can you..." he gestured. "Y'know?"

Emerald snapped the lock as if it were plastic.

Franco hoisted the bulky weapons and checked their payload.

He grinned at Keenan.

"Smashing," he said.

SMOKE FILLED THE corridor. Machine guns screamed. Franco, hoisting his guns and crouching behind the steel bulkhead, loosed off a volley of rounds that picked the last of the guards up, sending him cart-wheeling backwards, trailing arcs of blood, and deposited him in a bloody, rag-doll heap. A puddle spread from beneath his peppered corpse. Franco stood up gingerly and stared down at the hot Kekras with something akin to reverence. "Shee-at," he said.

Emerald stepped over the six bodies and led the way down the corridor within the summit of the Metal Palace. Here, bone-carvings were melded in a curious half-organic smearing of steel, alloy and bone, as if The Bone City was attempting to repair itself—or update itself—with more modern materials.

"That's the last of the guards," she said. "It would seem JuJu's Honour Platoon is loyal to the end."

Keenan nodded, following Franco closely, their guns covering arcs as they stepped through an arched bone doorway and onto an open-air roof-top platform. Heat slammed them. Sweat coursed their bodies instantly. Emerald, however, appeared perfectly cool with no indication of discomfort, no evidence of sweat or overheating. Pippa brought up the rear, her MPK set to fully automatic. She'd been surprised twice by rearward attack parties, and a Laz-Spear had stripped the skin from one shoulder, leaving a long nasty blister. Her face was grim and focused for battle. She hated this damn place. *In fact*, she thought, *damned is the right word; a curse on the planet of Ket.*

There, gleaming on the platform, sat an Ion Gun-ship.

Down one side, in neat lettering, it displayed its name: *Reason in Madness.*

Pippa whistled.

"Looks nice," said Franco, "efficient. And I like the name; reminds me of home, kind of."

"What the hell is that doing here?" said Keenan.

"That machine is bordering on military kit," said Pippa, with a frown.

"It was JuJu's personal transport, although he rarely used it. The Ket are superstitious about flying, and it's bad for morale." Emerald shrugged, dark ringlets bouncing against bare shoulders. She halted beside the craft. "It would appear JuJu had powerful connections to afford such technically advanced military transport."

"Something stinks," said Keenan. "The ship doesn't fit this place; and yes, you're right, we're talking real powerful connections. We're talking big money, and bigger friends."

"Who knows what political connections JuJu made during the Helix War," said Emerald.

"But Ket withdrew from all aspects of Helix," said Pippa.

Emerald smiled; it was a little patronising. "Don't believe everything you read in the media," she said. "I helped War Control down here; after all, they wanted me to predict the future, yes? Ket wasn't a simple withdrawal. It was more... political. But for now, we need to leave this planet. The Ket-i are tired of your little invasion force; they are mustering weaponry to take you down. There was an unexpected hiatus with JuJu's death; now he has been replaced. They have fresh leadership."

"What of Klik?" asked Pippa, suddenly.

"He has escaped," said Emerald. Her eyes were glazed. She tilted her head and smiled. "He has slipped past guards, and is heading for the Milk Sea, and a place beyond, a Gem Rig he calls home. I believe he has a lot of friends there; a place that offers him security, sanctuary."

"Will he be safe?"

"As safe as anyone can ever be," said Emerald, and her voice seemed a little cold.

Pippa hit the door release. A ramp descended on a cold hiss of hydrogen. Climate Control rolled out to meet her and she smiled, smiled at the civility of decent air-con.

"Can you predict our future? Right now?" said Franco, intrigued.

"I need no special powers for that," said Emerald. She stared at Franco, at his leer, which took in her unclothed breasts and vagina, goggle-eyed. "I predict that if in thirty seconds you are not aboard this craft we'll be leaving you behind. And you will get shot."

Franco saluted. "Aye aye, Ma'am."

Emerald ascended the ramp, Pippa close behind. Keenan glanced at Franco. "Aye aye Ma'am?"

"Saw it on a film. Come on, last one to the cockpit's a cheesy codpiece."

"Franco, you're unbelievable."

"Better believe it."

Franco ran up the ramp... and with a whimper of need, headed for the toilet.

SUNLIGHT GLEAMED ACROSS the *Reason in Madness*. Green jets fired with a roar, and Pippa lifted the Gunship smoothly, high into a bright blue sky. Below, the world unrolled as on canvas: mountains and jungle, The Bone City, the Milk Sea, the eel-marsh, and distant islands and coral streaming off into infinity. The Ion Gunship banked, sunshine leaving tracer down the stubby wings, climbed yet higher and accelerated powerfully away, Sinax Tapes loaded for an illegal and, according to Emerald, unregistered SPIRAL dock. Emerald was correct with her information; within minutes they docked at the portal, which, technically, and according to Quad-Gal law and history, should not exist. Motors whirred, and they were fired up the

SPIRAL and through the EYE, leaving at a velocity of LS 0.6 and still accelerating. Ket disappeared into dark velvet folds of space.

BEHIND, AN INTERCEPTOR uncloaked and locked the Ion Gunship to its Beacon. Inside, Mr. Max smiled a cold insect smile: metallic, without humour, anodyne; and with an imperceptible nod at some complex internal dialogue, the Seed Hunter followed.

CHAPTER 14
BAD OLD DAYS

EMERALD SAT IN the cockpit of the Ion Gunship in silence. Occasionally Keenan or Pippa would ask a question; Emerald simply waved a long-fingered ebony hand, eyes closed, lost to the world in some deep state of meditation. Beyond the gleaming new (and frighteningly thin, oh how technology advances!) alloy walls, the *Reason in Madness* cruised through the darker corridors of space. Pippa plotted a complex course, attempting to avoid the busier, more populous arms of Quad-Gal; and, thankfully, the ship seemed to be operating well. Pippa had checked out all systems thoroughly; the Gunship had only a few hundred thousand klicks on the clock, and that always made Pippa nervous. To her, this machine was an untested plaything. And, they were heading into battle: into war. They needed more than the real deal.

As Pippa worked on Sinax Tapes and trajectories, and checked the ship's idents, inventories and digital charts, Keenan and Franco moved through the stores. Leaving in rather a hurry, they possessed only what the ship stocked; thankfully, it was stocked well.

"We've got two InfinityChefs, clothes, weapons, bombs, shit man, we'll want for nothing! We're going to have a ball! We're going to have a party! A gig, my man!"

"Yes, but there's a high possibility we may die at the end of it," reminded Keenan.

"Hey, yeah, shit happens. But what a ride it'll be in the process!"

Keenan laughed, buoyed by Franco's persistent and, some would say, insane optimism. They moved back to the cockpit to give Pippa the good news, and found her, at last, in conversation with Emerald.

Emerald smiled apologetically. "Please, be seated."

They sat; Franco produced a long greasy sausage, which he'd sneaked through the InfinityChef, from some hidden pocket. "Just to check it's working." He bit the ubër-gristle and chewed oily slick meat thoughtfully.

"As you know," said Emerald, voice low, eyes studying the floor, "I wish to regain my former power so that I may, ultimately, die. To do that, I need to travel back to my Homeworld, the planet of Teller. You all understand Teller is a Forbidden Place, and has claimed the lives of millions. Not one person has ever, ever returned.

To you, the living organisms of Quad-Gal, this is fact."

"Hmm, that sort of shit was playing on my mind a bit," said Franco through a mouthful of sausage. "After all, y'know, this impending death lark could soon put a dampener on any highfalutin party-time we'd like to work into our travel. You dig?"

Emerald smiled. "You, Franco, have a long and fruitful life ahead of you," she said.

Franco grinned. "Go Emerald baby go!" he beamed.

"As long as you agree to be put down at the next available SPIRAL dock. This is not a mission for the faint of heart, nor for those who fear for their lives and the journey beyond."

"Shit." Franco chewed, subdued.

"You think of me as a Prophet, a being that can read the future. But it is not so clear cut." She smiled. "Nothing ever is. I can read certain pathways, but these Skeins don't always come to fruition, don't always blossom into flowers. It is not a science, more an art form. However, once, a million years ago, when I had my seat in The Factory, I was more powerful."

"What's The Factory?" said Pippa.

"A place where all documents are real, where the spellbook comes true. The Factory holds the source, the essence, a physical manifestation of the things that bind all life together through the cold voids of Space. It is a place of truth, of justice and of reasoning. It holds my power, my soul, and I am organically bound to it; it is what creates my

Prophet. Inside The Factory, with my power returned, with the Leviathan Song bright in my mind, I could read your future for all eternity, and I could, without fail, give Keenan the answers he so desperately seeks."

Keenan frowned. "You're telling me you can't see into the past?"

"I can search," said Emerald, with a gentle smile, "but it is harder than you could ever imagine. What you have to realise is that for it to become factual, to extend beyond Art, I must become what I was. I must elevate to my former position; I must retake my Mantle, my Crown, my Seat of Dominion."

"What are you?" said Keenan.

"I am Kahirrim," said Emerald, eyes glowing bright, "a name you would not know. I am part of the Family related to what you consider the Dead GodRaces. However, I never was, or ever could be, as powerful as they." Her eyes grew distant. "They were... awesome to behold, striding the stars, creating the planets and moons." She sighed.

"You have fallen from grace?" said Pippa.

"Yes. And, I'm a long way from home. There was once a great war. I was party to the losing side. I was stripped of rank, of powers, of dignity; I was cast into an eternity of oblivion; into the Pit."

"So you seek to regain your power?"

"Yes," said Emerald, "but for one purpose only: so that I may die, know peace. I am tired, humans, I am so tired. However, I would fulfil my part of this bargain. I need to reach The Factory... and there, by fire and dark energy, you will have your answers, Keenan. You will have the name you seek. Take me to face my enemy, my haunted past. Allow me salvation, redemption. Allow me the ability to die. Help me to leave this place." She bowed her head.

"What do I need to do?" Keenan's voice was little more than a whisper.

"You will have to kill my greatest enemy, the One who stripped me of rank and life, and dignity and power; the one who banished me from Teller's World. His name is Raze."

"Is he powerful?"

"He is my brother."

FRANCO SAT ON the injecto-toilet, face contorted in pain. He grimaced and chomped, chewed and ground his teeth. He grunted, coughed, sighed. Shit, he thought. And that was just the problem, his shit.

Why me? he thought.

Why the hell is it always me?

Since his tumble into eelmarsh, to put it bluntly, his arse had been far from OK. Pain had become a constant companion; that, and an unwilling and unnecessary need to defecate, which seemed to strike him every fifteen minutes or so, and forced him to grind and gromp, chimp and churn, hump and squawk.

It'll be OK, he thought.

He smiled through the pain.

Damn that alien planet!

Damn that alien arse-virus!

He pulled a small bottle from his pocket, removed the cap and tapped free a tiny blue pill. He smiled; it was a knowing smile, but his eyes echoed with un-spilled tears.

Franco ate the pill, closed his eyes, and waited for sanity to kick in.

KEENAN SAT IN the darkness of the cockpit, while the others slept, brooding. His chin rested on the heel of his hand, his thumbnail between his teeth as he chewed thoughtfully. He shook his head. Shit. It was impossible. How could it be possible to kill a creature like Emerald? With guns and bombs? Missiles and fire? You think Raze had never seen such weapons? He was older than the stars, and apparently in charge of a dead black planet, a featureless ball of nothing that consumed humans like a plague.

Keenan remembered seeing the ProbeScouts: a series of a hundred unmanned ships sent to Teller's World on exploratory missions, and carrying the most sophisticated in penetrative surveillance and survival equipment. The ships used PlatinumPropulsion, had voluntary AI, and shields that could withstand SunFloating on a photosphere of eight thousand degrees. They were advanced, and built in order to unravel the mysteries of planets such as Teller's World. Keenan had watched with a billion others as live relays fed back video of the ProbeScouts swooping down through a harsh toxic atmosphere. Below, a panorama of flat black nothingness opened under an onslaught of storm and then...

Bam, nothing: instant obliteration.

Every single ProbeScout destroyed.

No warning, no missiles, just instant... disintegration?

Debates had raged for weeks between various academic facilities, each striving to provide an answer, but one thing was for certain: no global economy rushed with further financial funding in order to explore the unexplorable. Teller's World was hostile, and the first planet discovered that was so insanely dangerous as to be dubbed DeadWorld. Since that moment, another six planets were investigated and labelled Forbidden Zones, but none were as alluring as this.

Teller's World: the First.

"How are you feeling?"

Keenan glanced up, watching Emerald ease into the cockpit and sit at the controls. Still naked, her ringlets tied back, she turned ancient eyes on him. He felt himself squirm under that gaze.

"I make you nervous."

"No!"

"It is fine, Keenan. No need to be shy. Which elements of my construction sit unholy in your mind?"

"You have a way with words," grinned Keenan, relaxing a little.

"I have had time to practise."

"It's that thing you turned into, no offence meant. I just wonder if it could happen again. Without your, ah, knowledge? You said you were a slave to JuJu, and he had a controller unit."

"The controller has been imbibed. The change cannot happen again without my control. I have removed the slave circuitry, the organic mechanisms. I have regained some of my lost dignity."

Keenan scratched his stubbled face. "Something's really bothering me about that. How did someone like JuJu and his people—admittedly fearsome warriors, but in terms of Sinax technology not the most advanced example of a species across the Cluster—how did they manage to imprison you? If you are what you say you are."

"They were given a mechanism, and instructions. It was passed down through the ages, from a very, very long time ago: from the beginning, when the Kahirrim were a slave race to Leviathan."

"So," Keenan frowned, "somebody brought this controller back from Teller's World?"

Emerald nodded.

"I thought none had ever left?"

"I never said that. That is part of your social misinterpretation, not mine."

"So people, humans, aliens, have visited Teller and come home?"

"I believe so."

"So it is possible?"

"Yes, but highly improbable."

"Tell me what we are facing." Keenan's eyes were bright. "I need to know details. I need to plan strategy. If we are to take you to this Factory, so you can regain your power, I need to know exactly what I'm up against, and how to kill it."

"All in good time," said Emerald. "First, I need to explore your memories." She saw Keenan withdraw a little, curl into his shell. "You will feel no pain, but I want—need—to get a... how can I explain? Get a smell for the Threads."

"What would you seek?"

"What makes you, what created you, what drives you, how you came to be a part of Combat-K; your dreams, desires, gifts, hatreds, impurities... Keenan, do not be frightened. I will not change my mind. We are locked together in an embrace of fate. We must trust one another. Only then can we both discover peace."

"OK."

"I will need to search Franco and Pippa as well, for together you are a Unit. You are, whether you like it or not, whether you acknowledge it or not, integral cogs in a single working machine. You are Combat-K. You are Warrior Class. You carry a Dark Flame, a Dark Seed within you."

Franco appeared, rubbing sleep from his eyes.

"I heard voices."

Keenan glanced at Franco, smiling. "Emerald wants a chat."

"What sort of chat?" Immediately suspicious.

"An intimate one."

Franco perked up. "Really?"

"She wants to read your soul: your innermost desires, you darkest demons."

"Will it hurt?" said Franco.

"Trust me." Emerald took his hard-skinned hands.

Franco stared at her breasts—he just could not help himself—and felt himself being dragged suddenly down, down into the freezing depths of icy annihilation.

How DID I get like this?

How do any of us get like this?

Take a normal, hard-working, OK kinda guy, sprinkle liberally with bullshit and unnecessary bureaucracy and BAM! Instant psycho. Or so it could seem when nobody understands what bubbles beneath the surface. After all, nobody truly understands what goes on inside somebody else's head, in the private places, in the nightmare zones.

FRANCO WORKED THE quarries, had done for a long time after being kicked out of university for fighting and putting his Geography lecturer in hospital with a well placed essay. Good honest work from now on, he told himself; none of your academic masking, none of your hiding behind language. I thought language was supposed to simplify meaning, not increase the basis of misunderstanding?

Franco's day was a nice tight unit. Get up, brush teeth, full hearty breakfast of sausage and bacon, walk to work through town—usually just before the sun was rising—clock in at Reinhart & Seckberg Quarries Ltd, put his jacket and lunchbox in his locker, then head for his Section, of which he was Sec Leader. Such was the privilege of time. Put in the hours, earn that promotion. And Franco had put in the time: a huge block of his life, driving diggers, working the belts, operating sorters, but more often than not he was in charge of demolitions. Franco choreographed the perfect explosion: no mistakes, never any mistakes. His perfection and dedication had been commented on many times by superiors, and he'd even won an award for his destruction in *Blast! Monthly!* Franco's blasts were always an equilibrium: the perfect amount of explosives, the perfect choice of explosives, accurate timing and with, guess what, perfect end results. Whatever was asked of Franco, he delivered: a half mile desecration of mountain range? No problem. Call Franco. The collapse of three miles of abandoned quarry tunnel? Give Franco an hour with a head-torch and a notebook, and you'd get that perfect detonation, no worries.

Franco was proud of his job, proud of his work, and, dammit, he enjoyed his work, in there with the stone and the dust, the chemical smell of HighJ or OptionX, cloying at his nostrils, and his experienced eye tracing fractures and contours in the rock. He'd instruct a bore hole for a sample just there, or pick up and rub fine particles of stone between his calloused fingers, grinning because he knew one mistake, just one mistake, and he could well be a dead man: dog meat. What a buzz!

If the truth be known, Franco had no idea where his innate talent originated. It had been a latent skill, untapped. And, without training or specific education, it had been a miracle Franco had stumbled into this: his perfect career.

For eight years, Franco worked the White Tooth Range, part of the Southern Sector's permitted

Blasting Area; and in that whole eight years Franco had never, ever had a single day off. And not just that, he had asked for nothing, and was therefore indebted to no man. It was just the way Franco's brain worked, and just the way he liked it. He came in, did his job, and fucked off home.

Franco lived at home with his mom, a fact many found comical, but something of which Franco was decidedly proud. His father had died when he was fifteen years of age; a savage blow which had, for a few years at least, sent him careering violently off the rails of socially acceptable behaviour. Slowly, his mother had reeled him back in, and nurtured him, and now he was glad to play at Master of the House. And anyway, reasoned Franco, who had had limited success with women (before his bare-knuckle fighting days, at least), his mom cooked for him, washed and ironed his quarry uniforms, made interesting chit-chat when they were watching TV, and generally—and this was the clincher—did not nag the living shit out of him. Franco watched many friends bemusedly as they slowly drifted and whined in shadow-lives of servitude, of new settees and beige carpets, of forced candlelit meals and missing the football. And gradually, one by one, his friends became encompassed in their little nests: like tree trunks with all their branches excised, so friendship umbilicals were gradually severed by their loving (m)other halves.

Franco chose the good hard solid honesty of whores, instead, and, when he won a fight, the charity of those who wished to bask in his glory. Of which he turned away none.

The fighting started when Franco had been working the mines for a year. He had heard rumours of underground bare-knuckle matches where huge sums of money could be won. Franco, however, did not consider himself a fighting man; he knew that he was stocky, powerful and fast, but he had never trained, never worked at pugilism, never really had a fight, except for one or two incidents in his teenage years when he had decimated his challengers. No, Franco kept his head down, his eyes on his pint, and resolutely out of trouble. This was because a) Franco believed that there were reasons to fight, and reasons not to fight. If somebody threatened his mom, then smack, down they would go, but a spilled beer? Here mate, let me get you another pint. But there was also b) and b) frightened Franco a lot more than a) ever could. It was something inside his head: a knowledge, an understanding, a self-confessed fear that once he started... he would not—could not—stop. If fury took him in its fists he was capable of so much more than knocking a man to the ground. And this latent power frightened a young Franco worse than any simple name-calling in the playground or pub. When Franco went out, he went all the way.

One day Franco was working the quarry when he accidentally drove a digger over Korda's stranded lunchbox. Now, Korda was a giant of a man, a man-mountain, a titan with a reputation for heavy-handedness, a powerful right-hook and a love of beating women. Franco did not like Korda, but Korda had never noticed Franco. Franco did not enter Korda's sphere of proposed violence; to

Korda, Franco was simply a ginger midget with a comedy beard.

With the digger's engine still running, Franco jumped down from the cab and stood looking at the crushed blue plastic lunchbox, which had once borne the faded picture of a Nuke Train. Franco looked up, looked around to see if he'd been spotted, and turned into a right straight that sent him staggering backwards with a split lip to sit down in the dust. Within seconds, a crowd of men had sprinted to the scene and formed a circle with Franco and Korda at the hub. Franco had blinked away his shock and tested his nose, which he realised was broken. Anger radiated through him. However, powerfully, he calmed the savage beast.

"You crushed my box!" bellowed Korda, his brutal flat face filled with naked aggression and a look that said he would willingly kill any man for even touching his shitty little lunchbox, never mind crushing it into a platter of plastic shards.

Slowly, Franco climbed to his feet.

Korda rolled up his sleeves.

"You shouldn't have left it there," said Franco, retaining his calm.

"My lunchbox!" screamed Korda.

"I'm not disputing ownership," said Franco gently, "I'm just saying it was a mighty dumb place to leave it. This is where all the diggers pass through. To leave it on the floor here was... well, dumb."

"So you calling me dumb?" intoned Korda, who was not the brightest bulb in the pack.

"We-eeell, yes," said Franco, still tenderly dabbing at his battered nose.

"Bastard whore piss pot!" screamed Korda, and charged.

Franco swiftly side-stepped, and Korda lunged, missing. He whirled, boots kicking up dust.

"Put fists up and fight!"

"I really don't think this is the place to fight," said Franco, glancing nervously about. "After all, we're at work, right? And if the bosses see us…" But then he noticed the bosses were present, even the rotund and short-haired CB, normally so reserved and severe, but now with a coloured flush to her cheeks which spoke of something they all thought impossible in the sterile stern old goat: excitement.

Korda slammed a right hook; it took Franco in the side of the head and sent him hard to ground. He lay there for a while, coughing on the dust, and smiled to himself. OK, he thought. It's going to be like that, is it? Going to fight dirty, are you? But again, he calmed the flutter of savage rage in his chest and lay there, allowing Korda to have his moment of glory.

Let it go, he thought.

Let it be.

The steel-capped boot connected with Franco's ribs and lifted him from the ground, rolling him over in the dust with stars flashing pain through his ribcage. He'd felt two crack. The pain was incredible.

He opened his eyes to see Korda looming over him. The giant of a man hefted a titanic black rock above his head. He was grinning, a light of insanity flashing motes in his eyes… a triumph that spoke the pitiful language of the bully, not just of beating a man, but the worst trait of all true cowards: kicking a man when he's down.

Inside Franco, for the first time in his life, something went *click*. A tiny door opened. Black light flooded his soul. And, as death stared down at him from a stupid flat face with the lop-side of the inbreed, Franco allowed everything—everything—to flood away. He reached out with a rangy powerful hand and slammed a devastating blow to Korda's kneecap. There was a *crack*. Korda howled, and dropped his rock, which landed on his other foot. Korda reeled back staggering on two injured limbs, as Franco reverently climbed to his feet, dusted himself down, and strode towards the big hopping man.

Korda saw the approach, and put up his fists. He attacked, throwing several jabs, a powerful straight then an uppercut. Franco dodged them all, ribs grinding, and slammed such a powerful blow to Korda's face that the man's cheekbone cracked, splintered and disintegrated within the skin sack of his head. Korda went down on one knee. Blood rolled from his nose and left ear. Franco smashed another punch to his head, and Korda rocked; a third hammer-blow sent Korda to the dust... and to his coffin.

Nobody messed with Franco after that. Of course, word went around, and other men of fighting calibre would come to challenge Franco: reigning champions of the Reinhart and Seckberg site. Huge sums of money ran on these fights, usually conducted underground in abandoned mines or deep quarry chambers, in blast holes or beside underground lakes. Franco won every fight. No quarter was given. Whatever thread had snapped inside his soul during that first bout... well, it unleashed a demon.

IT WAS ON the 31st October—Halloween—that Franco's mother first fell ill. The diagnosis was swift, the medical prognosis brutal: cancer of the stomach. She had six months—at best—to live.

Franco stood on the hilltop by Rannok Tower under the dark and acid sleet, a bottle of vodka in one hand, a cylinder of OptionX in the other. It had been his intention to kill himself that night: to scream at the world, to defy the world, and God, and everything; to vent his misery and fury in the only way he could see and understand, with violence and death and annihilation. But a small voice spoke to him; it said *you're being a retard, Franco Haggis, and yes your mother is going to die and we all die and what the hell are you doing drinking and revelling in self-pity? Do you think it will help your mother to bury her only son, to go to her grave knowing that you did something so fucking foolish? Not to benefit her, oh no, but to benefit your own selfish little bout of pitiful squirming self-pity? Put down the explosive. Go home. And look after your mother as best you can... make her final days peaceful and filled with love. Be a good son. You'll only get this one chance. You have a gift. Seize it. Give love.*

Nodding to himself, Franco stumbled from Rannok Tower, down the stone pathway and through pools of mud. He returned home and started as he meant to go on, with an out-pouring of love and caring.

The next day, Franco followed his usual routine. Get up, brush teeth, full hearty breakfast of sausage and bacon, walk to work through the town just before dawn, and clock in at Reinhart & Seckberg Quarries Ltd. He placed his jacket delicately in his locker and then put his lunchbox on the shelf. However, instead of heading for his Section—as he had every day for the past eight years—he headed for the Office, and more precisely, for CB's Office. CB controlled all operations at Reinhart and Seckberg Quarries Ltd. It was to CB he needed to speak.

He knocked. There was a long pause that CB used intentionally to make people feel uncomfortable. "Come in." Her voice was gravel: lips on cock, throat filled with raze-wire.

She did not look up. Meekly, Franco seated himself in a rigid plastic chair before her desk, which was overflowing with important looking paperwork and digital dockets. CB continued to tap into her computer, then scrolled using a 3D Airmouse, which glittered like a tiny sun about a foot above her desk. Finally, her cold blue eyes turned on Franco, and he took in the full open horror of this... woman.

"Yes?" The voice was a cold snap of wind on a winter's morn.

Franco smiled. "Hello. I've worked here for eight years..." he began.

"Yes. I know how long you've worked here Mr. Haggis. Get to the point."

Franco felt a little tug at the corner of his eye. His smile fell from his face like a virgin's dress on her wedding night.

"I have worked here for eight years. Not once have I asked for anything, but recently I had some bad news regarding my mother. She's been diagnosed as having stomach cancer, and I was wondering if I could possibly reduce my workload? Just a little? Cut some of my hours?"

CB had been looking down at paperwork on her desk as Franco spoke. But now she glanced up swiftly, her lips a line of poisoned coke, bloodless and white.

"I empathise with your predicament, Mr. Haggis," she said, without managing to show it, "but as you know it is company policy to allow no reduction in hours. I believe it would be bad for Workflow. Bad for the Department, you understand."

"But I..." said Franco, tilting his head. CB held up a finger, as if to chastise a naughty schoolchild.

"The situation is this. Reinhart and Seckberg has a huge series of orders coming in over the next four months. I cannot, cannot, allow any of the workforce the slightest reduction in hours. After all, if I gave you one day a week, how could I possibly replace one day a week? Who would want to work one day a week?"

"But it's my mother," said Franco, "she's dying."

"I appreciate that must be very difficult for you," said CB. She stared at him with glass eyes. She was a machine, a replicant, a deviant. Franco felt a winter ice-storm flow over his soul, and he shivered, despite the ersatz warmth in CB's Office. "However, the answer is still no."

"So that's it. No, just like that?"

"Is there anything else Mr. Haggis? Of course, if you don't like my decision you could always resign." She smiled a frosty smile. "Although you'll find your contract binds you to a six month resignation clause. In breach, this is punishable by imprisonment as per local by-laws." She smiled again. "Was there anything else? No? Well close the door on your way out, there's a good lad." She returned to her keyboard. He had been dismissed.

Franco bristled. Anger bubbled inside him. It was a carefully controlled furnace. He tried once more.

"If you could just see it in your heart to allow me even a few hours a week? If you want, once my mother has—passed away—I can make up any hours you might kindly allow. I will work them back tenfold; I swear it. I just need this time for my family, but I need it now."

"Goodbye, Mr. Haggis," was the cold verbal ejaculation. CB did not even look up.

Dejected, destroyed, decimated, Franco climbed wearily to his feet and shuffled from the office. He went to his work and spent the day in a morbid mental chasm; darkness settled over him like rat plague.

For the next three weeks, Franco plodded methodically to work, carried out his job, returned home, and cared for his mother. Her love and gratitude were bright cheerful things: candle flames; but it was hard work, and many nights Franco got only three hours sleep. Exhaustion became his best friend, despair his lover.

Then, returning home from work on a Wednesday evening, he found his mother dead. Her body was shrivelled and cold, skeletal in the hold of the cancer, which had so viciously swept through her like a black gnawing tidal wave.

Franco sat all night and cried, holding her rigid hand.

Then he realised: he had not only been cheated of those last moments of life with the one he loved the most, but his own lack of strength had perpetuated her misery. She had died alone. And nobody should have to die alone.

Franco finally stood, stretching his powerful frame.

Outside, dawn light filtered through the window, and he realised he was late for work, for the first time in his life. The kube buzzed and Franco's head snapped left.

"Yes?" he said into the mouthpiece.

"This is CB at Reinhart and Seckberg Quarries Ltd. It would appear you are late for work, Mr. Haggis."

"My mother has just died," said Franco, a black hole collapsing his heart. "Give me an hour."

"If you are more than an hour I am sorry to say you will be an ex-employee, Mr. Haggis. And we all know how many people are out of work in this town. With regard to your wages: they will, of course, be docked."

"Of course, CB," said Franco.

The kube buzzed again and died.

Franco looked up. His eyes were full of tears, but he did not allow them to fall. A terrible rage slammed through him like an axe blade. He licked his lips slowly, stooped and closed his mother's eyes, kissed her cold dead lips, and then strode to the door. He took his jacket. He looked back at the room—the house—which seemed suddenly so small; it had shrunk with the passing of She who filled it with warmth, with life.

Franco remembered happy times: playing with friends, joyous meals around the small timber-plank table; slumped, watching TV or playing games on his Smash System.

All gone, he realised, cold and dead, and gone.

You want me to come back to work? he thought savagely.

OK, I'll fucking come back to work.

The door slammed, and Franco strode out into the cold.

THE FOLLOWING NIGHT was as clear as black liquor and filled to the brim with glittering stars. Ice crackled across streams and lakes, layered roads with a crust of sugar, and sent frosty crystals sparkling into a starlit sky.

The night was cut by the harsh drone of a truck. Headlights the size of dinner plates segregated the darkness as a mammoth vehicle laboured up a steep incline and paused for a moment, gears crunching, before lurching onwards with a flurry of slippery ice-rimed tyres.

This was no ordinary truck. This was a Fuk-Truk, military spec, and able to carry a tank across the moon. It was currently being abused beyond the call of duty. Oil dripped from a desecrated engine, leaving a tiny trail from inception to completion.

The gates were locked. Metal security dogs—Jawz—patrolled inside, diamond eyes glittering as the FukTruk rolled to a halt with a crunch outside the razewire laser-fence; lights illuminated a sign which read, on a bent and rusted platter: REINHART & SECKBERG QUARRIES LTD. Occasionally, the sign would fizzle and flutter, something wrong with the electronics.

Franco jumped down and smiled grimly. Only a lunatic would make a highly technological sign appear so rusted and beaten, as if preserving a heritage.

"Ha."

Franco stomped up to the gates; beyond, the six metal beasts padded over to him, curious. They were each as high as Franco's shoulder, their jaws easily able to bite—and squash—a man's head. They were bullet proof, bomb proof, hell, probably even nuke proof, thought Franco as he fiddled with the door locks, which were digital, effective, good. Franco nodded, attached something to the lock, and took a step back.

"Go on, shoo."

One of the metal Jawz growled at Franco. He tutted, reached through the fence and patted its head. "What, you don't remember little happy Franco? You don't remember me rubbing your belly in the kennel and giving you bowls of used engine oil to lap when you were a liccle off-duty puppy?"

The beast whined. Franco nodded, smiling in understanding. There was a connection.

"Good boy. Now go on, get out of the way."

He jogged back to the FukTruk, climbed into the cab and initiated the cold charge. There was a *whump*, and the lock on the gates blew. Franco revved the engine and ploughed forward, smashing through the barriers and growling up the sweeping road towards...

The Stores, and—more importantly—their contents.

IT TOOK HIM an hour to load the FukTruk, and a further hour in the dark cramped tunnels beyond the Stores. Then, grinding gears, he left the quarry behind, and rattled and bumped his way through this small town in the middle of nowhere, the arse-end of beyond, only recognised on a map of the area because of the damned quarry and its precious cargo. Franco grinned grimly. Well, he'd show them a precious cargo all right.

The town lay decadent in semi-darkness, scattered with a witch-light of the small hours. Franco passed a parked-up police car, but the officers inside were too busy snoring through sugar-peppered beards to notice the wagon full of explosives cruising the dark mean town streets.

Franco followed little used roads, emerging from the town like a bullet from a gun. Darkness swept down over him. The FukTruk's headlights cut swathes from the night pie. Grumbling up narrow roads, twisting and winding between gulleys and huge formations of rock, Franco finally emerged, the engine smoking and honking, onto a plateau that overlooked the town. CB's white-walled mansion stood before him; huge steel towers reared into the night, and a light rain began to fall, making fine white stone glisten.

"Honey, I'm home."

Franco grinned, and put down his foot. The gates parted like butter beneath the grille of the Fuk-Truk, and ploughing up the gravel drive, he saw activity within. Lights flickered; several came on, tiny yellow squares in the mammoth façade of white and steel bleakness.

Franco jumped down and lit a cigarette while he waited. Not normally a smoker, he coughed heavily, but inhaled the alien jaja tobacco, and felt his head spin and colours start to reverse. It also stopped his hands from shaking, and took away his desire to kill. Very important that. He didn't want to go losing his temper too early, oh no.

CB appeared at the door. She was frowning. Behind her stood... a priest? He was dressed in old-Earth garb, white collar, magenta silk shirt. Over this, he wore CB's silk effluvia-stained dressing gown, which kind of ruined the effect of believable Holy Man.

She came down three of the sweeping steps that led to her mansion and squinted, blinded by the FukTruk's lights. She shielded her eyes. "Who's there? Show yourself! I have already called the police." Her night-dress was frighteningly short, riding up to allow glimpses of her straggly grey pubic hair.

"Nice house," said Franco, stepping forward and taking another blast on his cigarette. Smoke plumed around his head, accentuated by the Fuk-Truk's beams.

"What do you want?" She showed teeth in an ugly smile.

Franco opened his long coat and pulled free a sawn-off shotgun. The metal gleamed, evil and dull. Franco held the weapon nonchalantly, pointing at the ground, but implying his threat. He smiled at CB.

"I want you to watch something."

"The police will be here any moment!"

"Yes, but unfortunately, not quickly enough."

"Do you want a pay rise?"

Franco snorted a laugh. "What? *What?* You see me here, with a gun, and a FukTruk loaded with enough HighJ and OptionX, not just to blow up your mansion, but to remove the fucking hillside; and you ask if I want a pay rise? Lady, you've got your head screwed on inside-out."

"What d-do you want?" CB was sweating. It glistened on her moustache.

"Follow me."

"Where we going?"

"Over here."

The rain increased, and CB's slippers crunched on gravel. Her priest lover bravely stood his ground in the arched doorway of the mansion; Franco ignored him with unspoken contempt.

"Wh-what do you want with me?"

Franco led a soaked CB to the edge of the hill. The town spread out below like a map. Beyond, glittering, they could make out the weave of lights like a distant runway, scattering and flowing, and eventually leading to the quarry, and the circle of floodlights cut into the wall of the mountain.

"You see the quarry?"

"Yes."

"You see a disease, burrowing into the mountain, taking from the mountain, eating away at the land like a parasite. You feed, people like you, feed from the little people. Well, I'm a little person. Nothing wrong with that, I like being a little person, never right interested in politicking or running the country or such-forth. I've got no interest in education or law. I've got my happy little life, my family, and that's what matters to me. I am a cog, in the machine, and happy to be a cog. That's all I ever wanted."

"What are you gibbering about, man?" snapped CB, her natural hateful arrogance returning in force.

Franco pushed the shotgun under her chin. The rough hacksaw-edged twin barrels forced her head to lift and she met his gaze. Then she realised she was staring into the eyes of a maniac.

"All I needed was some free time to spend with my mother," said Franco.

"But I—"

"All I needed was time with her before she died."

"Please don't—"

"And you couldn't even give me that."

Franco removed the gun, spat on the ground and stared out at the quarry. Then he produced a small grey box from his pocket. CB's eyes fixed on the box. It was a standard Grade F detonation control. She glanced back at the FukTruk, gleaming under its slick shroud of rain and sleet.

"You're going to kill us all!" she wailed.

"Be serious," growled Franco…

And threw the switch.

Distantly, fire blossomed, huge orange and purple petals unfolding against the distant mountainside. A rumbling concussion slammed through the ground, and even at this distance they felt the *crack crack crack* beneath their feet. The ground shook. Flames rolled up into a mushroom cloud, filled with a dense grey of pulped stone and dust, which eventually expanded and blocked out the fire. A terrible darkness filled the night sky, rolling up into the rain-filled heavens and spreading out, covering the town, blocking out all lights.

Franco held up his hand. He laughed.

Dust fell from the sky like ash, and settled in their hair.

"What have you done?" hissed CB.

"I've blown the quarry. All your access tunnels have gone: all your carefully cut research tunnels, your detonation tracks, everything. I've returned the mountain to itself. I've closed you down for good, fucker."

CB paled beneath the mountain fallout. Realisation hit her like a sledgehammer, and she swooned. Franco had blown all her excavations, her jewel extraction mines, her structural survey tunnels. That meant the mountain had become nothing more than a mountain. To continue quarrying and mining, she would have to…

Begin again.

Sirens wailed, coming up the hillside road.

Franco put his shotgun under CB's chin again.

"You've destroyed me," she whispered.

"It's funny that," said Franco.

"What?"

"The way, you know, you help destroy my life, and then I return the favour, and you have this fucking hangdog look on your face, like, how could I be so cruel? Well, I always believe you should treat people how you would have them treat you. You, CB, have proved your worth, and you've been found wanting. Now it's time to die."

CB pissed herself. Urine ran down her legs and tickled the toes of Franco's boots. It dripped yellow from her unruly mass of deviant pubes.

"Drop the weapon, motherfucker!" screamed a policeman, squatting unceremoniously behind his squad car, gun over the bonnet, fat face contorted in the rage of the moment.

Franco looked over at him. He lifted the shotgun and threw it to the ground. "Whatever you say, Big Man."

"Get down on the ground"

Franco lay on the ground. It stank of piss.

More cars arrived, tyres crunching gravel, brakes squealing. Stroboscopic lights lit an eerie blue scene through rain and falling dust.

Franco was cuffed, beaten, and bundled into a car.

They drove him away, back down to the town and the cells.

On the hill, CB was earnestly, and with many self-pitying tears, explaining to the twelve attending officers just how brutally she had been treated. Sirens wailed through the darkness. She pointed to her filthy piss-slippers. Her lips flapped about shotguns. Four officers wrote in notebooks, continually brushing at falling dust, which smeared as it mingled with sleet.

"A disgrace," CB was expounding. "And as for you useless fuckers, arriving so late and giving this, this, this filth the opportunity to destroy my quarry and mining concerns, well I shall be complaining to the Commissioner over your comedy lack of response times."

"Excuse me, ma'am?"

"Yes?"

"How did this…" he checked his notebook, "this Franco Haggis arrive on your private premises?"

"In that." A quivering finger isolated the offending FukTruk.

"Hey Bob, check the back of the wagon."

Bob checked the back of the wagon.

"It's full of explosives," he shouted back, peering under the damp tarpaulin.

"What kind of explosives?"

"How the hell should I know? I'm not an explosives expert."

"Why the hell would he come in a truck full of explosives?"

Realisation dawned like a new sun rising.

They heard the tiniest of ignition *clicks*.

And night turned to day.

* * *

"I'M NOT PROUD of it," whispered Franco, staring into Emerald's eyes and wishing like hell he had one of his rare purple pills. The one that, y'know, kept him sane.

"I am not here to judge you."

"What then?"

"Just to understand."

"And you understand me?"

"Yes."

"Shit. Well, can you explain it to me then?"

Smiling, Emerald turned and looked down at Pippa. Pippa seemed to shrink away, retreating into her deep leather seat. "It won't hurt," Emerald said, with an honest, open, pleasant smile, a smile on an alien face.

"Nothing hurts any more," said Pippa bleakly, yet she still reached out, and their hands touched. Pippa's eyes narrowed, and she felt Emerald invade her, enter her veins and flow slowly with the beat of her soul. For long minutes Pippa fought her, fought without wanting to fight, fought because... well, that's just the way Pippa was.

And in a world of darkness, of infinite loneliness, she was a lost little girl who had no choice.

PIPPA SWAYED; SHE danced without moving, floated without floating, cried without tears... then laughed as she glanced at the scanner's image and the representation of reality scattered across a pale plasma screen. The nurse moved the hand-held scanner across her abdomen, wriggling the machine across thick glistening jelly. Sonic images transferred from womb to screen before Pippa's wide hopeful eyes. Her heart leapt. Joy swept her. Love filled her from a bottomless pit and tears invaded her eyes because there, there! She could see the foetus. She could make out the representation of the baby, could distinguish the child, her child, curled neatly within a wonderful protective life-giving sack, and an incredible uplifting surge of indescribable life filled her with a love, and violence for love she could never have believed possible. It was the most awesome feeling she had experienced, rushing like drugs through her veins: greater than love or hate, more intense than anything she had ever felt, and rendering all past life experiences as pale imitation. This moment, this instant diluted the past world in which Pippa had lived. It gave her intensity, energy, and a need to go on.

A single silver tear ran down her cheek. A beaming smile hijacked her face by force of arms.

This was her child, her baby, her little boy... an amalgamation of love, of joining, of everything her life had ever meant: the whole point of a human organism's existence, a concentration of her totality.

And...

She glanced up into the midwife's face, an innocent and almost subliminal movement, a mere arching of her neck a tilt of her head, and... a slab of stone slammed her face, iron pliers crushed her heart, a cold wind blew mourning through her soul, desecrating the grave of her memories and pissing on her joy.

A terrible darkness embraced her world and existence, and crushed it with a gauntleted fist of spiked steel, scattered with black rose petals, smeared in her blood.

Something was wrong.

Something was terribly, terribly wrong.

She stared at the midwife, face ashen. She suddenly understood, she understood perfectly, but a fist slammed the centre of her brain as she fought with the unexpected implications, the reality. "What's wrong?" she managed to say through parched lips. Her eyes lifted, glanced up and met the strong, courageous gaze of the midwife, who took a deep breath through a haze of her own tears.

"I'm sorry, the baby stopped growing weeks ago."

"I don't understand." But she quite obviously did. She just didn't want to admit it. She needed it pointing out to her, the hard way, the painful way, the mocking way, in an infinite, endless torture, a perpetuation of piercing pain.

"The shadow you can see, it's the sack. The sack has continued to grow, but the baby is far too small; there is no foetal heartbeat, Pippa. I'm very, very sorry."

The world swayed. The room tipped and she was falling, falling into a dark grave, a stone tomb world of unexpected endless sorrow. She could not understand, it had been perfect, it had been right, it had been good, and now...

Now it was fucking bad.

Pippa was allowed to clean up with dry paper towels, then led from the room into another anonymous suite where she had to wait to see the specialist. The waiting room outside the scan room was filled with expectant mothers, happy fathers: joyful parents. Her gaze swept across them like the after-effects of a nuclear winter, and she touched the Makarov in her belt. Her hatred welled in her breast with an unquenchable fire, and she suddenly urgently wanted, needed to kill and kill, and kill, and kill... and then she stumbled across the gaze of a middle-aged woman, holding the hand of a little girl. The girl's eyes were wide and bright; she was staring up at Pippa from beneath a mane of dark curls. She smiled. There was love in the girl's eyes, and in that smile, an unconditional love that burned Pippa's hatred into a stump and cauterised it with drifting echoes of a long lost emptiness.

Pippa closed her eyes, felt the world crush her, felt Nature smash her to the earth to lie in broken glass pieces, shattered, pulped and fucked by the very same God-fist which had wantonly and without mercy or undue forethought Given.

The door opened. A woman entered; Pippa was unsure of her status, but she wanted to kill, to take life, to punish. God could, would and had punished her without justification, indiscriminately, so why the fuck couldn't she? But even as her unreasonable anger smashed through her spinning mind, so she severed the brittle thought, snapped the thread of spun insanity.

"Mrs. Tasker will be with you shortly," the woman said. There was pity in her eyes, and in her voice. Tears pooled her gaze, nestling like streams of un-spilled mercury.

Then, all Pippa felt was—nothing.

Emptiness: a vast, rolling bleakness spreading into desert...

Desolation.

Pippa swayed; she danced without moving, floated without floating, cried without tears... then screamed without pain... The whole universe swayed with her: the mint-green walls; the bed on which she perched, scuffed boots resting lightly against polished sterile tiles; the cheap reproduction artwork hanging limp against wires. She turned. A white china sink squatted against the wall, chrome taps glinting under strip-lighting. An old PC stuttered in the corner, incarcerated by the ball and chain of an ancient red-screen monitor.

Once again, she was alone.

Pippa swallowed. A bitter taste invaded her mouth.

The taste of...

Death.

She turned, stared at the sink and felt sick, terribly, terribly sick.

Once again, the door opened as the world swayed like a staggering drunk.

The Consultant entered.

If she says a wrong word I will kill her, thought Pippa bitterly. The Makarov dug in her back, a threatening friend, a dark comrade, a Sister in Death and Despair: Widow Maker, Soul Taker, Life Fucker. Pippa smiled and it was a fucking nasty smile.

In contrast, Mrs. Tasker smiled in kindness, her eyes understood. Her sympathy was real, not contrived and plastic, but genuine: a gorgeously scented rose blossom in a desolation of black cloying weeds. Her assistant gave Pippa a simple sterile leaflet, and she glanced at the square-stencilled lettering: *Understanding Miscarriage*. Pippa shivered; it was as if the black letters on the neat white sheet made it all real, made it official: your dead baby, stamped with a genuine one hundred percent guaranteed seal of approval; and scrawled with the omniscient authority signature of an evil and unforgiving God.

The following conversation was a dream—a hazy, half-realised dream—an unreality through which Pippa gyrated. Pippa spoke without breathing, understood without truly understanding, and made the final decision. She would have to take a tablet, which would force the foetus to detach and pass naturally from her body. Pippa did not want to go to theatre, to endure the slice of the knife; but there could still be a chance the tablet would not work and she would have to endure a D&C.

Eventually, after a billion years of torment, she left the hospital, stepped out into the cold miserable world, and stood dumbstruck on the pavement for long minutes, unable to focus on direction.

Pippa was crying, and she wiped her eyes on the back of her neat black leather gloves. The wind howled from the west, smashing across the hospital shuttle park, and Pippa stared into the middle distance and spat poison into the wind.

How cruel the world could be. How fucking cruel, how fucking uncompassionate, how fucking bleak.

She floated like a restless spirit across the dark concrete and climbed into her shuttle. Jets glowed, and she roared into the sky and headed for home.

IT WAS NOT real. It could not be real. How could something so terrible be real? Pippa wanted to inflict hurt; once again, she wanted to maim and kill and punish. But there was nobody to punish. There was nobody to blame. For once in her life, there was no external enemy. Frustration, instead, was her Mistress.

The baby had ceased to grow; one pregnancy in three suffered a miscarriage sang the stoic song of statistics. Didn't make it any easier, though; didn't sweeten this bitterest of bitter acid pills.

As she lay in the darkness, remembering the joy of pregnancy—the wonder at carrying another life within her—just to have it cruelly snuffed from existence—tears rolled down her cheeks and soaked like crystal honey into her pillows.

And she knew, deep down, she knew she would never be the same again.

INVASION OF BODY, and spirit, and mind.

Pippa fought the intrusion, and looked up suddenly into glowing emerald eyes. There was a pair of shining, silver scissors in her hands. "Get the fuck out of here," she snarled, lifting the scissors.

"What happened next?" soothed Emerald.

"You are not entitled to know!" screamed Pippa, swirling, dazed in the depths of mental slurry. She lifted the scissors to her eyes and saw her face reflected there.

She remembered the hospital; wanted to vomit.

"Let me back," said Emerald.

"Get out!" she screamed. "Get the fuck out of my head."

PIPPA WOKE WITH a start, breaking contact with Emerald.

"Do not be afraid," said Emerald.

Pippa glared at her. "Don't ever go inside my head again. You hear me? Or I will fucking kill you."

"Why are you so frightened? Is it the scissors? What do they represent? Is it something to do with your father?"

"None of your fucking business, bitch."

Pippa grabbed a bottle and drank deeply, then poured water across her face. She rubbed at her eyes, then her temples, and sank deep into her seat. She scowled around at the other members of Combat-K.

Franco, wide-eyed, stared at a fixed point between Keenan and Pippa. He said nothing. Pippa's reaction had been... unexpected. He gazed at Keenan, a sideways glance, and Keenan knew what he was thinking; that glance meant "and you went to bed with that psychopathic woman?"

Pippa continued to breathe deeply, and her fury gradually abated. Her head swivelled, fixed on Keenan, and she gave a single nod. "OK, your turn, Keenan. Let's see how you like being mind-fucked."

"Was it that bad?"

"Bad memories," she grunted, then grinned a savage grin. "I hope you enjoy the ride. You've got stuff locked away in there as well, bad stuff. The bad gigs that *I* know all about, anyway."

Keenan glanced over at Emerald, at those elegant, tapered fingers, which only a few short hours ago had tried to smash his face to a pulp. He grinned. *How bad can it be?*

"Do it," said Keenan.

Emerald stretched forward languorously and took his hands. He gazed into the perfection of her face; then he remembered the changed thing she had become. He shivered as a feeling of cold swept him, and then he was falling backwards, falling downwards into a well of memories, and he remembered all too clearly the Bad Old Days.

KEENAN SAT ON the hillside, his back to a sprawling gnarled oak, and looked down over the city of Burylesh-Ka. The city squatted, a smash of concrete and high-rise buildings filling the horizon like some crazed aerial photograph. Above the chaos, clouds of rusted iron hung in a sky the shade of lead. Raw tracers of dying fading sunlight tried valiantly to break through. Keenan watched their hazy fingers spotlighting areas of the city, but gradually the clouds bunched together into one huge centralised mass of foreboding. They pushed away the sunlight, pushed away the warmth and happiness and brightness.

Fitting, thought the young Keenan.

How fucking apt.

Keenan stood, groaned, and stretched his back. He had been sitting a long time and his bones ached with cold. His uniform—police uniform—was crumpled and stained; it had been a long evening shift sifting the streets for killers, pimps, whores, skinners and shells. They had been successful, Keenan and Volt. They didn't pull their punches; they used the old rough justice and took no shit. Still, it had got to Keenan, tonight: bitten him. Injected his veins like the shite skinners used; filled his arteries with toxic slurry; drained him of emotions and feeling, and warmth and love, and understanding.

So the clouds wanted to drown the city?

He laughed bitterly.

Fuck it. Let them, he thought. Let them all drown.

He took a few steps forward, emerging from under a looming ridgeline of trees. Below him lay Lakanek Prison, a massive spread of concrete, Worm Wire and Lazy Towers. Keenan watched it carefully, aware of their internal slack ways, understaffing, rule by idiot bureaucracy. Maggots, he thought, just another poisoned wheel in the whole degraded machine.

Was it always like this? Always so bad?

No. He shook his head. Three years ago—Gods, only three years?—he had signed up, fresh-faced and twenty-two years old. The Helix War, decelerating from atrocity, seemed like distant news: an old man's war fought by bitter old soldiers. Here, now, Keenan could make a difference. He would cleanse the streets of Burylesh-Ka, make them safe for good honest people, make them a haven free of filth and corruption. He laughed, mocked his innocence, his naivety. How had he been so stupid? So blind? So downright fucking green?

Keenan watched the changing of guards in the prison below. The storm swept swiftly over him, blanketing the sky, clouds blocking out any remaining evening light. Rain smashed him, dripping from the brim of his black steel police helmet. Night fell. Behind him, the dead tox forest became an army of angular skeletal limbs. Below, water ran in rivers down gutters clogged with detritus.

It was the girl that finally did it.

The eight year-old girl, what was her name?

He couldn't remember. Only picture her face: round, white-skinned, chalk white, oval grey eyes, full pouting lips. She had been pretty, beautiful. One day she would have made somebody proud, been a fine wife and mother. But not in this place, in this world, on this day, because some fuck had raped her and killed her, and dumped her gutted corpse in a skip. A woman walking her dog found the body. Keenan and Volt stood, staring down into the slag of burnt rubber on top of which the young girl lay, her belly spilling bowel, her throat opened wide like a second crimson grin. "Look what they did to me Mr. Policeman", that opened throat seemed to say. "Look how they murdered me." Her knickers were still twisted around her ankles, both legs broken and bent at impossible angles. Whoever had dumped her hadn't even bothered to cover the young corpse. Such was the depravity in Burylesh-Ka; such was the arrogance and filth.

Volt steadied himself against the rust-smeared mass of the crumbling skip. Keenan glanced around, aware that everything was strangely fuzzy, unreal, even the corrugated wall of iron behind him, a platter of graffiti sporting illiterate hatred of race and sex, and religion. How did the world come to this? Was I blind? Or just protected? Yeah, protected by a rich step-mother and fat step-father with good jobs out of the city; and Mr. Policeman had come to play his sad little game helping the poor and the weak and the socially depraved. But look at you, just look at it: a fucking farce, a set-up, and Mr. Policeman, Mr. Richboy, Mr. Do-gooder just couldn't do the righteous good in time and sweet little—Emily, that was her name— sweet innocent Emily became the plaything of some depraved fuck with a taste for little girls and a handy sharp razor.

Keenan reached forward; lifted the dead girl from the skip.

"What are you doing!" screamed Volt, grabbing Keenan's arm. "Forensics need to tab her!"

Keenan shrugged off Volt's grip with a snarl, laid Emily out on the pavement and rearranged her torn skirt. He smoothed back her hair, took a handkerchief from his pocket—fittingly, black—and tied it around her gaping throat.

"You'll be in the shit, Keenan."

"So I'll be in the shit," he said. "She deserves some dignity. I'm not leaving her like that."

An hour later Keenan and Volt were pacing the floor outside Logistics; they had several matches on local scumbags, paedophiles with previous

out on the loose in this good holy fair city of
ours. One came up bright: DNA match,
Jonathan Bird. The fucker hadn't even tried to
disguise his actions. Keenan's square jaw set in a
tight hard line as Volt followed him down to the
Squad Shuttle.

"Let me drive," said Volt.

"Fuck you."

Volt didn't argue; he'd never seen Keenan this
way. He trailed behind, a limp puppy, aware that
actions were running away with themselves but
unable—maybe even unwilling—to halt the rollercoaster. Keenan would do what he had to do; his
naivety had finally been burned to a fetid stump.

They sped through the rain-filled sky, mixed it
with low clouds and smog-bursts. Keenan drove
recklessly, and Volt placed his hand on his friend's
arm for the second time that night.

"I'm calm."

Keenan met Volt's gaze, and Volt saw a raging
inferno in those eyes, like nothing he had ever seen.
They landed in a quiet alley, checked weapons,
headed for the apartment. A TV crackled lazily.
Jolly Joker the Jolly Jokeman was playing one of
his usual Prime-Time Tricks. Keenan led the way,
kicked down the door, found the suspect lying mas-
turbating on his bed.

"Hey, get the fuck out of here, I know my fucking rights!" he screamed as Keenan strode in, no
warrant, no rights—as the scumbag pointed out—
and put a bullet in the man's abdomen. He
thrashed around a lot, and there was a lot of blood.
The Pazza Medics said he'd never use his cock

again. Keenan had smiled at that, just before they cuffed him with Lazer Right and drove him to the SickCells.

"We'll look after you, son," said the Desk Sergeant. "You're one of our own."

Keenan nodded sombrely. And, he was only moved to solitary confinement after he'd cracked the third skull of some scumbag in on night-drill and out for police-kill.

Keenan was released, the Police Council saw to that; and the dirtbox rapist paedophile Bird went on trial, fully televised with constant updates from Jolly Joker the Jolly Jokeman. The trial lasted a week. For the entire proceedings, Keenan divided his animosity and open hostility between Birdy and his Barrister, a narrow man who walked with his arms pinned at his sides. Keenan could not believe how the Law protected such people: how the Law provided representation for such maggots, and how intelligent, educated, should have known better Lawmen stooped to defend the "rights" of such blatantly open sewer-rat shit.

Birdy was found guilty.

Keenan cried with relief; his brutal methods had nearly cost the Police Council the trial, but, thankfully, and for once in favour of the police, his actions had been put down to excessive emotional stress. He was allowed to walk free.

Not so Jonathan Bird.

He was sentenced to two years in Lakanek Prison: parole in ten months.

The press got some great pictures of his grinning face as he was led from court.

Keenan sat in the bar, sipping *Jataxa*; twenty-five year eyes stared back from rich honey depths in the back-bar mirror. He could hear the other Mr. Policemen around him.

"Bastard should have got at least six years, he was as guilty as fucking sin."

"Yeah, but the Keenan lad didn't do us any favours shooting the man's dick from his body."

[Laughter]

"Ain't that right Keenan old boy?"

[Keenan snarled something incomprehensible]

"But still, out on parole after only ten months! Jesus wept! After what he did to that little Emily? What the hell is the world coming to?"

Those words still echoed and rattled in Keenan's skull as he stood on the hillside, later that evening, and watched the grey van deliver Birdy into the prison's depths. Three guards met the convicted paedophile—Keenan used military NVGs to confirm arrival—and then he checked his map. Getting into the prison would be easy. He was Skull Chipped, so the Lazy Towers would ignore his presence; he had clearance there. He also knew some of the guards, so he could probably even bluff gate entry. Keenan scowled. He would cross that bridge when he came to it. And, he smiled a nasty smile, there was always force. A bluff, of course, against his own kind, but he knew how to put on a good violent realistic show all the same. Poker had taught him that. And, still remembering the feel of Emily's dead stiff body in his arms, it gave him the fuel and determination he needed to see the job through.

Keenan returned to the tree-line and stepped into bleak undergrowth. Rain pattered from sculpted branches. Keenan knelt, lifted the tank, and strapped it to his back. He checked the hose, zip-tied it down his arm, then pulled a heavy rain-cape over himself. He knew from standing in front of his bathroom mirror several hours earlier that the cape disguised the slim tank on his back; square and matt black, it was a piece of decommissioned military kit, obtained illegally. But hell, in Keenan's eyes, the whole fucking city was illegal: a haven for criminals. The only people who ever suffered were the good, the pure, the righteous. Keenan was sick to his stomach with it all.

He moved out into the rain, and it rattled on his plastic cape. He picked his way carefully down the hillside, aware of the highly dangerous and volatile container he carried. Above, several Squad Shuttles swept by in close formation, and their ident.sweeps picked up his Skull Chip and they left him alone. At last! One privilege of power, he thought with a cruel sense of irony. And, here, now, was something Mr. Policeman could finally do: something that wasn't the result of bribed police, corrupt lawyers, or judges with unrealistic fat heads up fat brandyport arses. This was something real, something right, something that Emily, ultimately, deserved... from beyond the desecrated grave.

Lightning split the sky. Thunder growled. Keenan stepped from the grassy slope, boots slick with mud, and stood on wet tarmac staring down the road. Darkness closed in. The rain increased, drumming his surroundings. He walked with long powerful strides, determination etched on the stubbled features shaded by his dripping hood. As he approached the guards—alert enough despite the late hour—they levelled weapons and scanned him; green registers flickered, and Keenan threw back his hood and gave them an easygoing smile.

"Hi guys."

"You're not on the list, Keenan," said Graves, scanning the plastic document.

"I've got some questions for the one they've brought in: Bird, just committed; it's nothing official, just something the family of the murdered girl asked me to do."

"Yeah," nodded Graves, "we watched the trial. Bad luck, that scumbag getting a piss trickle of time. Don't worry, Keenan, we'll give him hell in here."

What, spit in his food?

Take away his books?

Bend over for the soap, fat boy?

Keenan smiled. That just wasn't good enough, but he appreciated the sentiment.

"This way, mate." Graves nodded to the other guard and led Keenan down a narrow poorly lit hall. Keenan dripped water, which ran into long polished drainage gulleys. "I'll have to frisk you."

"No problem, pal."

They turned a corner, towards a large holding cell. It was deserted. "Bird in High Sec?" asked Keenan idly.

"Yeah," laughed Graves, "to protect him from himself, know what I mean?" He turned to wink, only didn't get that far. Instead, he stared into the stubby barrel of a Kekra 8mm Compact.

"Sorry, Graves."

"What the hell you doing, Keenan? You'll lose your job! Shit, they'll lock you away for this!"

Keenan shrugged, and cuffed Graves to a nearby bar. "Honest, I like you Graves, so don't raise hell. I'm only here to do the dirty work some anally retentive judge didn't have the balls to finish. So…" He let the words hang, shoving the Kekra tight under Graves chin. "Be a good boy. It's been a damned long night and I'm a little twitchy."

He gagged Graves, took the guard's keys, and moved back into the corridor. Lakanek Prison was running Graveyard Shift with Graveyard Staff; it wasn't just quiet, it was deserted. A reasonably high-tech prison, it had a hundred sophisticated gadgets to stop prison breaks—or the interloping of foreign bodies—but, thanks to his Skull Chip implant, Keenan bypassed the nested High-bore machine guns, the laser wires and garrottes; he even sauntered past the Anti-ankle Mines, nasty little charges designed to remove a prisoner's—or unauthorised entrant's—feet.

He made it as far as the High Sec internal gate; the man there, Roberts, knew Keenan well—they'd even been out drinking on occasion—so it hurt Keenan to do it, but he did it anyway. With Roberts bound and gagged, and another bunch of digital keys in his hand, Keenan strode the dark halls of Lakanek Prison like some depraved Grendel seeking retribution. He used Roberts's PDA to find the exact location of Bird's cell; it was on the ASM

Wing—the Area for Sexual Misconduct. Yeah, he thought, brain dark and nasty, like it's some kind of fucking minor misdemeanour; not really their fault, right? Just something naughty we really need to *learn* to *understand*. That's it! Understanding's the key! Rape and murder a child, sure, all we've got to do is discover what social complexities have made this poor, poor criminal what he is: a victim of upbringing, circumstance, poverty. Poor bastard just couldn't help himself. In fact, why not label the fucking child the criminal? That way, the Justice System can dispense with petty imprisonments altogether and blame the victim for the crime. Keenan smiled. Keenan's mood could easily be described as *unstable*.

His boots left a trail of dried mud pointing to Jonathan Bird's cell. He accessed the door, and it slid neatly back on alloy rails. It was dark inside. "Lights," said Keenan, and not just the cell—but the whole wing—was illuminated. He heard other, high-level sex offenders, stirring in other cells.

"Yeah?" said an arrogant snarl. "You've only just turned the fucking lights off, fucker!"

"I'm here about a different justice," said Keenan gently. He stepped to the doorway, his frame a dark silhouette. He threw back his still-slick rain-cape; an awkward and confused silence descended on the scene. He pulled free the long matt-black nozzle from where it was zipped to his forearm, and he held it like a hose.

Bird squinted, sitting up on his narrow pallet bed. He rubbed his eyes, and stared at Keenan without soul. "So it's you," he said, and then tried to peer past Keenan, looking for the rest of the guards. "More fucking questions you'd like me to answer, eh?" He cackled. "You can shove your questions up your arse. I don't have to cooperate no more."

Keenan's head tilted. "No, actually, no questions this time."

"Tell the guards to shut the door on your way out. Some of us need our beauty sleep."

"Funny that." Keenan took another step forward. His face became serene, relaxed, almost... at peace. "There aren't any guards with me. It's just me. Me and you; ain't that nice, Birdy?"

Suddenly, the strangeness of the situation struck Bird. He came fully awake. Fear flared his nostrils. He scrambled back in his bed, his grey flannel prisoner's smock riding up his legs to expose bare feet and shins.

"Let's start there, shall we."

Keenan discharged the Phos-Thrower, and watched with detachment as bright white sprayed over Bird's shins and feet and immediately began to burn. Bird screamed, rubbing at his feet, and then staring down at his fingers as the white phosphor reacted with his hands.

"What are you doing?" he shrieked.

Keenan spoke slowly, calmly, as he watched Bird burn. "I have a full Can-Chamber of white phosphor, commonly held to be one of the most savage incendiary chemical weapons used in infantry warfare. In fact, there's still debate as to classification. Some think it should be made illegal. Inhumane, you understand."

Bird was screaming and thrashing on the bed. He jumped down, collapsed, and dragged himself to the sink. With fingers dripping flesh, he smacked the tap down, and a gush of water started to fill the basin. Bird grabbed handfuls of water, splashing them onto his legs, where the glow of the white phos flared.

"Funny thing about it," said Keenan, still detached in his manner, "is that it reacts with oxygen." He smiled, as if remembering a favourite family outing. "Your natural reaction is to cool a burn, so you throw water on it. And the phos reacts even more violently."

Bird turned tortured eyes on Keenan.

"Make it stop," he croaked, slumping to the ground. His feet and fingers continued to burn. The cell filled with the stench of cooked chemical flesh. He reached out and pleaded to Keenan for sympathy, and empathy, and compassion.

"I'm sure that's what Emily said when you raped her."

"Please, make it stop."

"And then slit her belly, and her throat."

Anger rose in Keenan; an anger so pure and hot and violent it totally consumed him. It raged through his veins as nuclear fire. It scorched heart chambers with acid. It bleached his brain as molten rock. The fury burned him to eternity.

Keenan discharged a flurry of white phos over the man, and then stepped from the cell. There was no joy in watching—even the evil—suffer.

Coolly, he cast his gaze around the nameless face-less doorways, each protecting a ripe flesh prize of human degradation. Inside, thought Keenan, are this city's worst sex offenders: the paedophiles and child rapists, baby killers and the abusers of pregnant women. He smiled a very, very dark smile. His eyes were holes falling through the universe and shining into an evil place. He was no longer Keenan. He had been pushed backwards, into a corner, and felt his humanity stripped away like flesh under a sharp, sharp knife.

Understanding filled him. They were not human. Something had happened to these deviants, turned them into what they were: some alien virus, some genetic malfunction. They had no sorrow, no empathy for their victims. They were focused, entirely, on their own petty sexual desires, enthralled within a cocoon of spiralling depravity.

Keenan walked slowly around the ASM Wing, opening each and every door. "Come out!" he bellowed. "All prisoners onto the Wing, now!" His voice roared with authority, power: a primeval command from some deep place of primitive intuition.

Slowly, like zombies, the prisoners emerged; they gathered in a ragged huddle at the centre of the hallway, numbering perhaps forty. Keenan cast his gaze over the collection of deviants.

"Not human," he whispered.

"No! Wait!"

The voice was Volt's. Keenan could sense a heavy armed presence. He checked his watch. "Pretty poor response time, if you ask me." He did not, could not, turn. His finger rested on a slick layer of sweat, the only thing between him and the trigger.

"Don't do it, Keenan." Voice a lullaby. "You burned the one that mattered. You avenged that little girl."

"But they are all like that," said Keenan. Understanding flooded him. "The only ones punished are the victims. This isn't murder, Volt. When a rabid dog kills a child, you destroy it. It's no longer a dog. This is the same. Can't you see that?"

"If you do it, they'll shoot you."

Keenan heard the rustling of Kevlar. He nodded. "So be it."

He pulled the trigger, pulled it hard and watched a spray of white phos spurt over the collection of prisoners. Screams rent the air, high-pitched, like burning pigs.

A shot sounded, then another. His Kevlar absorbed the intrusion. A bullet smashed into the back of his shoulder and he stumbled forward, but still agent poured from the fizzing nozzle in his hands, and the throng of squirming scorched prisoners writhed on the ground like something unreal. A blood red veil washed over Keenan's eyes, and the trigger was finally wrenched from spastic-taut hands. He smiled, a cold smile, thinking how ironic it was; in burning, these sexual heteroclites were parodying the one act they had enforced on innocents.

Behind him, Volt turned and was briefly sick. The rest of the armed police stood by, grim-faced and uneasy... and watched the helpless writhe.

EMERALD RELEASED KEENAN's grip. He was sweating heavily. He looked up into her eyes.

"I realise I was wrong. I should not have killed those men."

"I am not here to judge you."

"I was sentenced to life imprisonment. I served two years, and then Combat-K came for me. General K. Steinhauer held out a hand of friendship, a lifeline, a way for me to turn my abilities to some good, a way for me to seek... forgiveness? Aye, that, or some bastard form of the same emotion." He laughed, and rubbed tired eyes.

Emerald's gaze swept all three members of Combat-K.

"You were running away," she said, her voice incredibly soft. Her eyes were lit with understanding, empathy. "You all needed a place to hide, to think, to compose yourselves. And Combat-K gave you a Home, a Family, a Unity. Yes, you were instructed to kill for the military, but the ultimate aim was a good one: to end the Helix War. That was a noble objective. I believe you have atoned for your pasts."

"Steinhauer recruited the psychos," said Pippa savagely, "and there was only one reason for that; we were fucking expendable." She laughed a bitter laugh. "You talk of nobility and atonement; that's a crock of shit, Em. Personally, there can never be atonement for the things I did. I made my choices, and I don't need no alien speaking on my behalf. I know what I did, and I live with it. I'll live with it until I die. I don't need your fucking permission, and I don't need to be patronised." She stood, burning with fury, and left the cockpit.

"Don't mind her," said Franco, settling back into his seat. "She's always hot-headed. She'll calm down. You'll see. She'll be cooking us a fine beef pie in the next half hour, and right tasty it'll be. Yummy in my tummy."

Emerald nodded. "One thing is for sure," she said. Her eyes glittered like jewels.

"What's that?" asked Keenan. His face was haunted by images of a distant past; events he had forced himself—until now—to forget. He had not just taken the key; he had purposefully dropped it down a bottomless well.

Keenan took a deep breath.

Emerald smiled with sincerity.

"You're the right people to make sure I die," she said.

CHAPTER 15
BLACK PLANET

IT WAS CRAMPED and unbearably hot inside Mr. Max's Interceptor. The ship slammed up from Ket and, as one sun gleamed through the port window, Betezh turned and watched an idle sparkling array of fire dance across his vision. Greens, blues, oranges, yellows, all merged and coalesced, fanning out, before fading from view as Mr. Max accelerated at a phenomenal rate.

"Where are we going?"

"Classified."

"When will we get there?"

"Classified."

"What kind of ship is this?"

"Classified."

"This is going to be a real long journey, Max, if all you can say is 'classified'."

Mr. Max turned and smiled a smile full of teeth. "I didn't pick you up for your companionship, Betezh.

I picked you up because General Kotinevitch thinks you are valuable to the War Effort. I, however, have serious reservations." He looked Betezh up and down, as one would a particularly mangy cat.

"You're quite an un-likeable fellow, really," said Betezh.

"I'm not here to be liked. I'm here to get the job done."

"Still, there are certain protocols regarding manners that allow a person to act as a simple human being."

"Who said I was interested in being a human being?"

Betezh shrugged and settled back. He was red and sweating, and could feel trickles running down inside his clothing, which aggravated his sunburn. This did not put him in a mood for bantering with—in his opinion—a retard, or at least, retarded in the sense of one who could not control his actions, or tongue.

The Interceptor *hummed*. It cruised fast at illegal speeds and proximities. Mr. Max did not care. His middle name was "illegal". To Mr. Max, rules were for somebody else to obey.

"This is an Interceptor, right?" said Betezh eventually.

Mr. Max gave him a foul look. "Your point is?"

"They're military, classified, as you said earlier."

"Your point?"

Betezh sighed. "Ahh, mate, I'd always heard rumours about you; I'd heard you were a skull-fucking, arse-sucking, mind-bending, anti-human, shit-filled son of a bitch."

Betezh stared down the barrel of a gun. He had not seen Mr. Max move. However, the weapon was there, a 9mm bore directed straight at his brain. Betezh swallowed. He laughed woodenly, without humour.

"Of course, they were views I never subscribed to myself. Just stuff I heard, y'know? In the canteen, by other people." He gritted his teeth in a non-smile, "Other people who were, you know, ignorant to your finer salient points and obvious sensitive nature."

Mr. Max removed the gun smoothly.

"Keep your mouth shut. Or I'll knock out your teeth."

"Fine, fine."

"And don't think I'm being unreasonable," said Mr. Max. "I saw the torture you put Franco Haggis through at the Mount Pleasant Institute. You had your moments of sadism, Betezh. Now keep it shut while I navigate this worm-field; I don't want to find the ship covered in fucking SPAWS. Or we'll both end up dead. And, I don't want to end up dead, because I am Mr. Max."

"GENERAL KOTINEVITCH."

"Mr. Max." Her voice was cool, controlled, in command. "Did you manage to locate Betezh?"

"I found him. He's here. Unfortunately, he survived."

"Very droll. Are things going to plan?"

"With a sweet precision," said Mr. Max, "although I have altered a few timings."

"Why?"

"There were some random factors introduced to my timeline. The Fractured Emerald reacted as we predicted, unfortunately, and has helped Combat-K to escape from Ket. I could not get there in time to halt integration."

"So you have not yet killed Combat-K?"

"No."

"But you will do so." It was not a question.

"Yes, when we land on Teller's World."

"Isn't that cutting it close to the bone?"

Mr. Max shrugged. He enjoyed listening to Vitch's voice; it gave him some glimmer of sexual arousal; although he had to admit, of late, even that basic desire was fading. Age was encroaching; it was a feeling he did not relish.

"The job will not be difficult. Even should I fail, I have a little helper who will get the job done."

The camera tilted to Vitch, and zoomed in on a small, black metal casing. It had several panels removed, showing a massively intricate interior. Lights flickered across the shell, mostly red.

"Is that his PopBot?"

"Yes, a basic security device. It calls itself Cam." Mr. Max laughed. "Seems to think it's alive."

"You will booby-trap it?"

"Of course."

"What with?"

"StrangleTox."

"Nasty."

"When I want them dead, I want them dead."

"Will Emerald intervene? After all, she will be growing in power as she closes on to The Factory."

Mr. Max's eyes gleamed. "No, Emerald will be a good little girl."

"Betezh, are you there?"

"Yes, lady."

"Don't do anything foolish, and do not—I repeat—do not aggravate Mr. Max. I need you alive, at least for now. Accompany him to Teller's World; do anything he asks."

"Teller's World?" Betezh's voice quavered and he hated himself for it. He did not want to die. "Nobody ever leaves," he hissed. "It is a Forbidden Place."

"You fool. The picture is bigger than the living sphere can ever imagine. Do what you are told. I will rendezvous on Teller with both of you, and we will see what song Emerald sings."

"You are coming to Teller's World?" Betezh sounded incredulous.

"Of course," said Vitch. "I want to see Combat-K die with my own eyes."

"YOU KNOW, THE further we travel in deep space, and the longer the actual journey, the darker it always seems. You know what I mean? It's like we've entered a tunnel and we're cruising further and further into the emptiness of the void. Stars seem less bright; suns dim." He shivered. "It's like being buried alive."

"Sounds like a childhood fear to me," said Pippa, sipping her coffee.

Franco shook his head. "No, no, this is something weirder, deeper, like an affliction, a disease or something."

"I thought you liked that feeling?" said Keenan, turning from the controls. "I thought it gave you a buzz?"

Franco frowned. "What the hell are you talking about? I never said that! I've never, ever said that. You know I like cities. I like the brothels and bars, the slack women and mugs of beer. Where the heck do you find a woman ready to sit on your face in space?"

"I meant the tunnel metaphor," said Keenan.

"What metaphor?"

"You know? Long tunnel... equals vagina."

"I never said that!"

"But you meant it," said Pippa.

Keenan grinned. Franco put down his bowl of cereal, and milk hung in droplets on his ginger beard. "Franco, my man, I love you to bits, but you never, ever shut up about sex. You're depraved. You're a maniac. You're a down and out fucking deviant. But hey, we've got used to your little foibles; we even like you, sometimes, well, occasionally, when your depraved ranting doesn't get in the way of a mission."

Franco pouted. "Listen, how can I help it if I'm priapic? How can I help it if my testosterone levels are so damn high I could take a different woman to bed every single night of my life and still have room for more? I'm the man who put sex into sexual, the gas into orgasm. Guys, I put the cunt into cuntry." He beamed.

"The sex into sexual?" queried Pippa. "Yeah, right."

"Don't mock!"

"Yeah, don't mock," said Keenan. "Little Franco here is just the product of a warped, hedonistic and sexist society. Ain't that right mate? A woman's for life, not just for Christmas. Or maybe it's the other way round."

Pippa yawned. "Look guys, I'm turning in. Much as it's fun to sit here bandying words with a sexist moron, that foray on Ket really took it out of me; the damned heat!" She stood and made for the cockpit archway. She yawned again. "Have you seen Emerald?"

"She's staying in the Hold, says she needs space to think, finds the ship claustrophobic."

Pippa nodded. "OK. Goodnight, guys."

Franco stood. "You want some company?"

Pippa stared at him. "That question is below contempt."

"Still." He winked. "If you need somebody to warm your cockles during the long flight through space towards an impossible mission and the certainty of an untimely demise, you know where to find me."

"Yeah Franco, I know where to find you."

She disappeared.

Franco winked at Keenan, and rubbed at his beard. "I think I'm gradually wearing her down."

"You think so, do you?"

"Yeah." He missed the sarcasm in Keenan's tone, or ignored it. "How long we got on this crate? Three weeks you said, right? OK. OK, three weeks... yeah, I think I can crack this particular honey-filled coconut."

"Hmm," said Keenan, and watched Franco disappear with the sort of macho stride reserved for wooden heroes in action movies.

Keenan stared out from the cockpit. Black filled his vision. Occasionally, something distant would glitter, just the hint of, well, if not exactly life then at least existence: the concept that they weren't simply floating through a vast and fathomless nothing, an eternity of darkness, an Infinity Void.

Some people get space crazy, he realised idly as he pulled out a tiny battered tape-wrapped Skooby—a metallic storage unit—and clicked it into the console. He turned a dial to the smaller, right hand screen and sat back, face locked into something more than rigidity. Images flickered rhythmically across the screen: images from Keenan's past, and he closed his eyes and thought back over the long cold years; thought back to a past life, and a different time and a different world. Slowly, tears trickled down his cheeks. The Gunship's engines hummed.

And, remembering his children, sleep gradually claimed him.

PIPPA EMERGED FOR a glass of water. Dressed in black cotton pyjamas, she padded through the silent halls and corridors of the Gunship. The alloy walkways were cold, hard, uncomfortable beneath her toes, and as she passed the cockpit, she glanced at Keenan, asleep, could hear his gentle snores. She stopped for a moment, paused uncertainly; then she peered in, and caught sight of his screen. Images scrolled on the console screensaver, scenes from Keenan's previous life: a life with a wife, and two young daughters. There: Keenan lay on his back, on a red and white striped rug with Rachel and Ally, both girls attacking him with the vigour of youth, mouths wide in laughter, eyes sparkling as they beat up daddy. Keenan was looking back over his shoulder towards the camera; his eyes shone, were alive, pleading for rest from the torture. There: Keenan walking towards the camera along a metal road. His head was lowered, eyes hidden from the shot, each arm extended, twin umbilicals at the end of which grew and swung his daughters. Rachel had hold of him with both hands, was in the act of trying to wrench his arm off. Ally was more demure, more laid back. She walked alongside daddy, glancing off to her left, and the deep drop that tumbled down grey rocks to a gleaming blue lagoon ringed by yellow trees. There: Keenan asleep on a brown leather settee, looking cramped and uncomfortable, both girls encircled in his powerful arms, and all three snoring with looks of comfortable innocence tattooed on faces. They were conjoined in serenity.

Pippa stepped back into the corridor, bare feet scuffing the alloy, but just as she retreated, the images changed again, and she caught a glimpse of a pretty face, a young woman, laughing with hair tossed back. She was white skinned, smooth and pale, with cream roses woven in her hair. It was Freya, Keenan's dead wife, on the day of their wedding.

Pippa stood for a long time in the corridor, head lowered, eyes masked by the gloom. Finally, she seemed to wake, to breathe again, and she padded to the mess, to the InfinityChef, and ordered a glass of water. She sipped the sterile liquid, and carried it back to her SleepCell.

PIPPA PULLED HER pyjama top over her head, hair lifting in disarray, breasts riding high as she tugged free the black cotton slip and dropped it at her pretty feet. She reached behind her back, undid her bra, and released her full breasts to the cool air of the ChillCell. Franco gazed longingly, but did not move, did not breathe for fear that this moment would die if he acknowledged its existence. Pippa stepped forward, smiling, lips wet, and kissed him. She tasted sweet oh so sweet and his tongue probed savouring the contact the moment the meeting of physicality of flesh of this the most intimate of intimate connections: the simple and perfect kiss. Her hands ran down his powerful body. He felt her squeezing him, appreciating his solidity, his rigid muscles, his *power*. Her hands moved between his legs towards his hardness then danced away tantalisingly: prick-tease. He opened his eyes then, grinned, and revelled in the taste of liquor on her lips, and on his. His hands slid down her smooth powerful taut flanks. They reached her rounded muscular buttocks and tugged down her pyjamas with her underwear; he dropped to a kneeling position, pulled Pippa's pants down to the floor and glanced up, face to cunt, revelling in this holy vision. Franco licked his lips, leant forward a little, and nuzzled her sweetness. Her hands took his shaved head and gripped hard, and he heard an animal groan a million miles away and in a different century. "Yes, Franco," she said, hands rubbing his head in eagerness, desire, need, lust, want. He pushed her back and felt her fold willingly over the couch and her legs parted so easily so readily. He pushed his face deep into her, tasted her, tasted her drug honey and inhaled the heady thick aroma of the moment. Her flesh was firm and young and sweet. He toyed with her, using teeth and tongue to bring squeals of delight and then his tongue traced a spiral through her warm slick nectar flesh, up her belly and across her right breast, lingering for long moments on her aroused nipple and aureole. Then he was on top her, his erection iron and hurting so hard to be inside he thought he would die. He kissed her again, enjoying the moment of sex honey on both tongues then he reached down, parted her athletic willing legs, found the soft hot eager place and sank inside her and fell fell fell tumbled down and down, and down the never-ending spiral into an indescribable euphoria which took him and closed claws around him and brought him almost immediately to a point of climax and held him there, toying, teasing him, as Pippa's perfect muscle control locked him tight at the brink of orgasm and they were One.

PIPPA LOOKED UP from the novel, allowing plastic pages to whish back to the contents. "Yeah?"

Keenan grinned, a somewhat depraved grin. "He's in there again."

"You sure?"

"Oh yeah," said Keenan. Then added, "And... no, I can't, I just can't. I can't bring myself to tell you."

"Tell me," she growled.

"I heard him utter your name."

"So I was fucking right!" she snapped. She sprang from the bed, and Keenan back-pedalled hurriedly to get out of her way. In her black pyjamas—and wearing white socks against the hard sterility of the alloy walkways—Pippa hurtled down the corridor.

Keenan grimaced, winced, sighed, and almost reluctantly went back to the cockpit... and lost memories.

"YES, YES, YES!" roared Franco, fucking her hard fucking her right slamming her crying and screaming into another place another realm another world of ecstasy and swaying writhing bucking fucking pleasure.

"Fuck me Franco, fuck me harder! Yes, yes, yes! Fuck me like I want to be fucked!"

Franco obliged, sweat stinging his eyes, lost inside the animal, lost to the world, lost to all of Creation.

"Well *fuck me*," said Pippa.

Franco stared down into her eyes, only half-noting the subtle shift in her tone. Slowly, his humping decelerated, and he blinked, blinked again, and the words: **USER INTERRUPTION** flicked like a V sign across his vision. Franco cursed. Then he realised the vulnerability of his position. He disengaged from the Immersion Console, and back in the real world, back in cold stark reality and existence, he stared down at his naked—and somewhat erect—form, half-submerged in the gooey

Immersion Bath. Yellow slime slopped around his nakedness, and his erection stood like a priapic periscope in a sea of toxic custard.

Very slowly, Franco turned his head.

Pippa stood, hands on her hips; and despite her pyjamas—in fact, maybe *because* of the pyjamas—she looked truly fearsome.

Franco found himself torn between arousal and fear.

"Ahh, Pippa," he said, admittedly, and even to his own ears, with rather a large dollop of lameness: like a puppy next to a pile of poo, like a pale-faced kid next to broken crystal.

"Don't fucking 'ahh Pippa me' you fucking little pervert," she snapped. "You loaded me up, didn't you? Used a DNA strand? What was it? My hair? My toenail clipping?"

"What? Oh no no, come on Pippa, I'd never do that, how warped and desperate do you think I am—no offence meant—I mean, is there no trust in this contemporary world we inhabit?"

"Computer?"

"Yes, mistress?"

"Replay the last five minutes, on the screen, from Immersion Console 6."

"I really don't think…" muttered Franco with a worried glance.

An image of Pippa appeared on the screen, legs apart, vulva exposed for all to admire, a technically perfect simulacrum, because the experience was based on her own DNA. On screen, Franco danced a little jig and got ready to get jiggy on the job.

Pippa turned on Franco, a whirl of madness. "You are one disgusting pervert fucker."

"Yes, well, I mean…"

"How could you, Franco? A no is a fucking no!"

"Yes, but, you see, technically…"

"I feel dirty," she snapped. She turned and stalked from the narrow chamber. Franco relaxed back into the bath, and was just considering whether he dare risk putting the machine back on, when Pippa stormed back in.

Franco raised his eyebrows.

"I forgot something," she said.

"What's that?"

"It's in my hand."

Franco peered close. Pippa leant forward.

"What is it?"

"This."

She slammed her fist into his nose. Franco yelped, went under the custard immersion fluid, spluttered and choked and appeared, greased and lathered, to find that Pippa had gone.

He touched his nose, which was pounding at him with flares of pain; then he grinned.

"Feisty tough bugger," he nodded, in appreciation, and wiped thick slime from his eyes. "Must add that to the immersion scripting directives for the next load… only, only after I've had a suck on one of my lusty red pills."

IT WAS A week before Pippa would even look at—never mind speak to—Franco Haggis. He took it rather well, and with an air of nose-in-the-air respect and dignity that did nothing to sedate Pippa's fury, he continued his massacre of German sausages and the quaffing of multitudinous alcoholic beverages.

During these tense days, Keenan had his work cut out pacifying Pippa, who was never stable at the best of times. On several occasions, Keenan heard her muttering phrases like, "I'll show him" and "I'll cut out the little ginger fucker's spleen" and "son of a bitch deserves castration". This distinct negativity, coupled with her long forages down in the Weapon Stores had Keenan on edge, and continually trying to ram warnings deep into Franco's apparently impenetrable skull.

"You are checking under the bed, aren't you?" said Keenan over coffee one morning.

"What for?"

"Bombs? Guns? Some form of impaling device?"

"Don't be a dick, Keenan."

"Moi? A dick? I'm not the one provoking the most psychotic member of our little squad into violent action over a form of mental and sexual abuse she has every right to be pissed about."

"Yeah, but you did provoke her."

"Meaning?"

"She thinks you betrayed her."

Keenan stared into his coffee, and realised that Franco was right. He sat, senses compressed. He felt as if he had a corpse in his mouth. Slowly, reality bled back into Keenan's mind like a living rainbow, and he looked up at Franco, still happily eating his foot-long Bratwurst and chattering on aimlessly and gormlessly.

"...and I smiled at her and said, 'Nothing feels as good as tits,' and we all laughed, we did, because it's so true." He stopped, and stared at Keenan. "You OK, brother? You look a little peaky? I think maybe you need a holiday."

"Not much chance of that."

"After the mission then?"

"Unlikely, as there seems to be a ninety-five percent chance of death."

"Nah, what a load of shite. We'll be OK. We'll pull through. We've been through worse shit." He laughed, chewing sausage, his feral eyes glowing in the cockpit lights.

"Does nothing ever worry you, Franco?"

"Hmm? No, not really. When you've been locked away for as long as I have, you always look on the bright side of life. Either that," he grinned, "or you go mad."

An orange light glowed on the console.

Franco nodded towards it. "We getting close?"

"A day away."

Franco stared distantly. "We're out on the edge of explored space, aren't we?"

"Yes."

"And nobody knows we're here?"

"Hopefully."

"It's a bit spooky."

"A bit spooky?"

Franco shivered. "Yeah, wouldn't like to be out here alone." Suddenly, he lurched across the cabin and gave Keenan a big hug, the slimy bratwurst pressing against Keenan's cheek.

"I hope that's still your sausage in your hand," mumbled Keenan from beneath the cumbersome mass of Franco's bulk.

Pippa entered. She stood. She stared, long and hard.

Franco emerged from the embrace with his sausage in his hand like a greased child's lollipop.

"Hi Pippa," he said.

"So you'll be cutting and pasting Keenan's face into your porno machine next, will you? Give him a good humping? Stick your uninvited todge in his well-lubed orifices?"

Franco chortled, and bit his sausage. "Ha ha. Good joke, that is. You've got a wicked sense of humour Pippa. Glad to see you've got over our unfortunate misunderstanding. Ha ha."

"What misunderstanding? There was no damn misunderstanding about it, that's for sure. You abused my digital representation using my DNA for accuracy. You took pleasure from an avatar you knew would piss me right off."

"Ahh, but only if you found out," winked Franco.

"Well, I found out. And I'm not happy."

"Anyway, I resent the word abused," sulked Franco.

"Look, look, guys," said Keenan. "Listen, we've got a long way to go, and a lot of things still to do. If I can't trust you not to squabble like kids in the playground then I'll be hitting the surface of Teller's World alone. You get that?"

"Yes boss," said Franco.

Pippa scowled.

"Pippa?"

"I suppose so. I suppose, in some ways, I should be flattered."

"That's the way to look at it! Atta girl!" beamed Franco.

"Not with your digital mauling, fuckwit, with accompanying Keenan on the last leg of his mission. I know he would rather we weren't here; you'd rather not be putting our lives in danger, hey, Kee?"

"That's true," he said, "but a selfish part of my soul is glad you're here, all the same, both of you."

"I can feel a three-way hug situation coming on," smiled Franco optimistically.

"Not now," said Keenan.

"I think it's time we packed our gear. I've had a good rummage through the stores. I reckon that bastard JuJu was stocked up to invade the whole of Sinax. He's got everything from 9mm ammo to Gas RPGs. We could supply an army with what's in the hold, never mind the ship's armoury."

Keenan stood up and stretched.

"Let's tool up," he said.

IT WAS THE last night.

Packs were packed, weapons stashed, guns cleaned, ammo checked, food sorted, maps plotted, PADs charged, and DNA-locked, primed and initiated. After a brief meeting in the Comms Room, checking what sparse map data they could gather, mainly from scattered dead satellite photographs and synapse translations/predictions of geography and geology, Emerald had turned in for sleep. Keenan, Franco and Pippa sat round the table, staring at one another with an air of expectation.

Oval plates with steaming piles of chicken jal-frezi, cooked the Franco way, sat in front of them. He beamed expectantly. "Go on, tuck in; looks good to me!" His smile widened.

"What I don't understand," said Keenan, slowly, warily, lifting his fork and poking at dubious items squalling in the steaming mush, "is why you didn't just order it from the InfinityChef?"

"Is not the same."

"Why not?"

"Just isn't."

Pippa lifted a forkful. She stared at its quivering contents and then glanced at the expectant look on Franco's face. "So," she said, "you ordered all the ingredients separately, from the InfinityChef, and then peeled them and poked them and put them all together in what you call... cooking?"

"Is right."

"And you heated it all up? Into this mush?"

"Aye. Try it. You'll like it."

"It smells... funny."

"Just taste it!" exploded a frantic Franco.

Pippa tasted it, savoured it, and glanced at Keenan.

"You going to die on me, girl, or what?"

"Actually, it's really good."

"Is it?"

"Yes."

"Well I didn't expect that." Keenan took a mouthful. His taste buds exploded like firecrackers in his head. He took another, and another, until his plate was empty.

"Is good yes?" barked Franco.

"Excellent," smiled Keenan. He patted Franco. "Good boy."

"Yeah, good doggy," smiled Pippa. "Your culinary skills almost make up for you being a psycho pervert."

"A little harsh, I think you'll find," said Franco.

"Not in my world."

Suddenly, Franco produced a bottle from under the table and popped the cork. He filled three glasses and lifted his into the air, which shimmered from the heat off the jalfrezi. Green wine sparkled, and Franco said, "I thought we should have a toast!"

"What's the occasion?" said Pippa, "Our impending deaths?"

"No! Combat-K re-formed! We've made it this far, haven't we?"

"Yeah, only by a miracle," snorted Pippa.

"You're wrong," said Franco, deadly serious. "We've got back that old magic, the magic that saw us through a thousand blood-drenched missions. We're here, we're back; we're rocking the magic party, baby!"

Keenan clinked his glass against Franco's. "I've got to say, it's been a pleasure working with you two. Yes, as a team we're eccentric; but what the hell, there're no other people alive I'd rather team up with: salt of the earth."

Glasses clinked again, and the atmosphere filled with warmth. The gentle lull of alcohol was cosy and filled with unity and a sense of good spirit. They drank more. Franco refilled glasses. They drank again in a comfortable silence.

Franco yawned; he'd been hard at work for most of the day, servicing the engines and checking onboard systems on the Armoured Drop Buggy. As he pointed out (repeatedly), one didn't want to get stranded with no engine oil. To which everybody constantly replied, "Yes, Franco".

"I'm turning in." He glanced expectantly at Pippa.

"Don't even ask."

"This could be our last night alive."

Pippa nodded. "Exactly, and I don't want my dying memories to be of your hairy arse."

"I could shave it."

"Franco!"

"All right. Goodnight. Sleep tight." He disappeared, with a pint glass of green sparkly as a winter warmer.

Keenan and Pippa glanced at one another over the remaining liquor. Pippa stood, moved to the console, and the lights dimmed. Keenan raised an eyebrow, but said nothing.

They sat in comfortable silence for a while.

"He was right, you know," said Pippa at last, voice low and husky.

"What's that?"

"This could be our last night alive."

"It's not like you to be a pessimist."

"Yeah, but we've never had a mission quite like this before."

Keenan simply nodded.

Pippa shuffled closer, and placed her hand over his.

"I'm... sorry."

"For what?"

"Being so… unpredictable. I know I come across psychotic."

"What? Sweet little you?" Keenan was grinning. Pippa punched him on the arm.

"Don't get too cocky."

"I forgive you," said Keenan magnanimously.

"There's so much else I want to say to you." Pippa stood, leant over Keenan, and kissed him. He savoured the moment, head spinning, reeling back to old times and better times. Her lips were sweet, warm, slick, her tongue powerful and yet gentle at the same time. There was a lot of emotion in that kiss, and a lot of love. Keenan's hand moved and rested against her hip. She groaned, and the sound was an animal one.

Keenan pulled away. "I can't…" he said.

Pippa put her finger against his lips. She tugged him to his feet, took his hand, and barefoot, led him down the corridor to her SleepCell. She guided him to the bed, and then turned and closed the door.

She undressed him in darkness, kissing him all the while. Her tongue traced circles across his neck, his throat, his chest; she tugged free his shirt, popping buttons with an almost childish giggle, then pulled free Keenan's black combats and stood, gazing at his nakedness in the gloom.

"You coming over all dominatrix on me?"

"You wish."

"Actually, now you mention it…" said Keenan.

She undressed, and it was a slow dance that held Keenan hypnotised; he was a snake under a charmer's spell; a planet in the pull of a black hole. Finally, she stood naked and proud before him, and he drank in the sight of her, revelled in her beauty, her taut flesh, her readiness.

"It's been a long time," said Keenan.

She moved towards him, pushed him back on the bed, and straddled him roughly. "And look what you've been missing," she growled. Her hands rubbed up over his chest, her body dipping towards his erect cock, touching him, then moving away. Keenan groaned. Pippa kissed him.

"Have you missed me, lover?" she whispered in his ear, warm words tickling him, taunting him, teasing him.

"I missed you," he said.

"Do you want me?"

"I want you," he said.

"What do you want to do to me?" She nibbled his ear, his throat, her hands stroking his forehead, his chest, his belly, his thighs. Keenan groaned this time.

"I want to fuck you," he snapped.

"Gentle or hard?"

"Hard," he said, and grasped her hips. She lowered herself onto him, and he fell into her warmth, into her honey, was taken by her and held tight. He buried his face between her breasts and she started to fuck him, her body taut, rigid, yet soft and pliant at the same time. Her mouth and hands were everywhere, her scent filling Keenan's senses like a rich aroma not just of woman, of sex, but of something more, something deeper. He was infused not just with sex and lust, but with a deeper love.

"I wanted you for so long," she breathed in his ear.

Keenan kissed her throat, her breasts.

"I wanted you so bad."

Her tempo increased, and Keenan realised he was perspiring, sweat stinging his eyes, his breath coming in ragged gasps as this beautiful rampant wild psychotic woman thrashed above him, worked him fucked him used him abused him. He did not care and he took what she had to offer and rode with her fell with her and they spiralled at breakneck speed into an oblivion where nothing mattered, not life nor death, just the intimacy and the violence of the moment.

Pippa screamed as she came, rigid above him, body arched back and locked to him; her whole frame was a clamp holding him tight and only a bullet through the head would have stopped her. Keenan came a second later, rushing into her, emptying himself into a bottomless vessel and the world and Pippa's smell was around and everywhere. He may have screamed. They fell to the bed, joined, exhausted, slippery in one another's sweat.

As they cooled, Pippa chewed his ear.

"I missed that."

"You should have come back sooner."

"Absence makes the heart grow fonder."

"You were wild."

"Yeah." She smiled in the darkness. "A regular wild child."

Keenan ran his hands through her hair, and together they pulled silk covers over their languorously chilling bodies; she snuggled against his chest, one leg over his thigh, her hand idly rubbing his taut muscled abdomen.

"Do you love me, Kee?"

"Until I die," he said.

"That may be tomorrow," she pointed out.

"Maybe," agreed Keenan.

THE ION GUNSHIP *Reason in Madness* cruised the darker edges of the Sinax Cluster. Teller's World was a world apart, lit only distantly by four suns which, between them, managed to heat the ball of rock to a temperature just about habitable by the human species. Except, the planet was forbidden, and—reportedly—uninhabited: a forced emptiness, enforced by unseen execution.

The Gunship cruised, engines howling, and gradually began deceleration, as the grand barren vista of Teller's World spread out in all its wonderful desolation. The ship gained the upper edges of the atmosphere. As requested, Pippa slowed the *Reason in Madness* to a crawl, and Combat-K and Emerald stared out over a distant arena of barren black. Far away, jagged rock rose in a violent staccato range of volcanoes. Fire glowed briefly. A storm raged, and molten rock seared the land.

"Looks like there's no life down there to me," snorted Franco.

"It's a Forbidden World," said Keenan. "What did you expect, a carnival?"

"I just thought, you know, a few trees or plants or something, maybe a beautiful mountain or two, a few lakes, a town, a brothel: Not... *that*." He glanced at the terrain scanners. "I am right, aren't

I? It's just a black flat desert and some volcanoes. No seas, no forests, no mountains, just no god-damn nothing for a man to get his teeth properly into."

Keenan stared at him. "Are we ready for the descent?"

Emerald approached, and looked out into the drifting desolation. She smiled, and Combat-K sensed her mood lift.

"I am home," she said.

"And what a god-awful shit-hole it is," snapped Franco.

Pippa kicked him.

"Ow! What you do that for? It's true, isn't it? Just take a look! It's a wilderness of desert and rock that sucks the bloody life out of people, bejesus! It's a shit-hole, guaranteed. I wish I was back in The City."

"Shall we tell him about the mines?" said Pippa.

"Mines?" twitched Franco, as Pippa strapped herself into the pilot's seat.

"Yeah, mines," said Keenan. "The place is rid-dled with them. First we have to navigate what Emerald calls the Starfield; the whole atmosphere is alive with billions of tiny Pin Mines."

"I've heard of them," said Franco, eyes wide. "They're bad."

Keenan strapped himself into his seat. "They're so small, a ship can't detect them, yet they cause just enough damage to stop you going home. If you're really unlucky they start detonating one another: you get a domino effect, a chain reaction that takes in a square kilometre of Pin Mines, and of course, you're stuck in the middle of a molten soup, and dead as dog meat."

"How do we get through?" breathed Franco.

"Emerald will guide us." Keenan pulled the locking straps tight.

Franco turned to Emerald, who had also strapped herself in. She smiled brightly at Franco. "Don't worry, I travelled this path many times, in the Old Days."

"I thought you'd been imprisoned for thousands and thousands of years?"

"Yes."

"So… you haven't travelled it recently then?"

"Not for centuries," agreed Emerald.

"So… things might have changed?"

"Possibly."

"What happens if they have?"

"We are dead," said Emerald without any hint of a smile.

"Why did nobody tell me?" wailed Franco.

Pippa placed a hand on his arm. "We didn't want to worry you. I suggest you strap yourself in. We might be in for a bumpy ride. Try not to think about the mines covering the planet at ground level, as well."

"On the surface?"

"Yeah."

"Is this why nobody ever returned from Teller's World?"

"One of about a hundred reasons," nodded Pippa.

"Why wasn't I in on this very important discussion?" Franco sounded prim and wounded.

"Because," said Pippa through gritted teeth, "you were otherwise engaged with plastic friends in your little console game. Now, this is going to take a lot of concentration on my part; I suggest you shut up before I ask Keenan to kill you."

Franco closed his mouth, and his eyes, and started to pray.

ENGINES SCREAMED.

The Ion Gunship smashed from the heavens, jets fighting the massive gravitational pull, and Pippa focused totally on the emergence before her.

Emerald had told her of a pathway, an invisible road weaving through the Pin Mines. And, while Emerald watched the altitude meters, she guided Pippa with a precision that could afford no error.

The *Reason in Madness* flowed through the atmosphere, veering left then right in a gentle sine wave, towards a flat and barren black desert below. The ship's occupants held collected breaths for long minutes, waiting for the initial explosion that would tear their craft from the sky, and send them reeling like a smoking corpse carcass to the wasteland far below. It never came.

The Ion Gunship shuddered and screeched, wailed in torture, and fought Pippa's commands, but within twenty minutes of entering the upper atmosphere, landing struts ejected from flaps, and the Gunship touched down on an endless black plain in the middle of a roaring, raging sand storm.

Engines died, crackling.

Franco looked up through sweating fingers. "Are we alive?"

"For now," said Emerald.

"Can I unstrap?"

"Be my guest. Just don't go outside."

"Why not?"

"The sandstorm would rip the skin from your face. You'd survive for about three minutes."

"Charming. Nice homeworld you have here," said Franco.

"It's like this for a reason," said Emerald.

"We've got company," said Pippa.

Keenan's head slammed left. "On the planet?"

"No. Some crazy bastard has just tracked us. I was so busy controlling this heap of junk, I never thought to look for a tail; he must have been cloaked near our entry zone."

"Who'd want to follow us down here?" said Franco.

"None of the possible answers fill me with hope," said Keenan.

"He's just touched down."

"What kind of ship is it?"

"Scanning now; we have no visual 'cos of the storm... Wait... got it. It's an Interceptor."

"Like the one we thought we saw back on Ket?" Franco was frowning.

"Yeah, that's it," said Pippa.

"Just before we got blown out of the sky?" said Keenan. "I wouldn't mind a chat with that bastard. I think we might have a score to settle. Pippa, lock out the shields, and let's tool up. I think there's a guy who would like a chat."

"You'll get your chance in about ten minutes," said Pippa. "The Geo Relays say the storm is about to subside."

Keenan hoisted his MPK. He smiled a lop-sided smile and lit a home-rolled Widow Maker ciga-rette. "Let's go say hello, then," he growled.

THE RAMP LOWERED into the tail-end of the storm. Black sand whipped into the loading bay, and the wind howled, wailed, cried, and ululated with a saddening forlornness. Keenan crouched, staring out into the bleak wilderness. The ramp thumped the sand, and Keenan strode down, MPK hoisted, cigarette dangling between his lips.

"Fuck it. I've had enough of being somebody else's pawn."

He turned, staring at the sleek, illegal Intercep-tor; there was no activity inside, and as sand curled around Keenan's boots and knees, a swirling dervish of activity accompanied by a song of the land, Keenan pointed his weapon at the ship and unleashed a violent volley of bullets. Sparks chased one another up the cockpit, and Keenan jumped, boots sinking as he waved his MPK at the occu-pants.

"Come on out. I'd like a word."

Smoke plumed again, and warily Pippa and Fran-co followed Keenan down the ramp, both heavily armed: Pippa with a battered MPK sub-machine gun nestled against her breast, Franco with his favourite Kekra quad-barrel machine pistols, stocky in outspread fists.

"Take it easy, boss."

"Just want a chat, that's all," said Keenan. He moved forward, challenging, glaring up through the drifting dancing sand. There was a *clunk*, and slowly the Interceptor's ramp descended to reveal two figures, blurred by the storm.

Keenan heard Franco gasp; he half-turned.

"It's you, you maggot!" Franco stalked forward. "I thought we left you for dead on Ket!"

Betezh held out his arms, his expression curious. "What can I say, Franco? You know how I feel about my patients. I'd follow you ten times across the galaxy just to get you under my loving care once again. That's just the sort of guy I am."

Franco hoisted his weapons. "Well, it's time I ripped off your stupid fat face and pissed down your neck!" he snarled.

"Whoa." Keenan held up a hand. His eyes were fixed on the second figure, and he half recognised the small, unimposing man, wiry, taut, with rough features under heavy black eyebrows. Keenan took in the short beard, the black emotionless eyes. He shivered. He knew the man, but for the life of him, could not place him in his catalogue of memories. Keenan held a deep suspicion that it was to do with something very, very nasty.

"Mr. Keenan," said the small man, pushing past Betezh on the ramp and jumping lightly to the sand. As he approached, Keenan took in the multitude of scars criss-crossing his torso, arms, shoulders, and even his throat. Something rang a distant alarm bell.

"I know you?"

"Yes. Although the drugs we administered to make you forget may have left trace residues in the brain. You may suffer an after-image—as if you remember me from somewhere—yes? In the same way you get an uneasy itch whenever the name Kotinevitch is mentioned."

"What game is being played here?"

"No game, Keenan." Mr. Max smiled. "Forgive me. Let me introduce myself. I am Mr. Max, paid by General Kotinevitch to, shall we say, make sure certain events never occur. Your job is done, Mr. Keenan. You have brought Emerald home. You gained her trust with your pitiful sob stories, and now you have discovered her, removed her, and delivered her like a lamb to slaughter."

Keenan turned. Emerald was standing at the top of the ramp, her body limp, her stance defeated. Keenan frowned, understanding of the situation slipping away like some complex technical problem in seven dimensions twisting in on itself.

"What is happening here?"

Mr. Max replied for her. "The Fractured Emerald is to come with me. The execution will be swift. There will be no pain."

"No! I will not go with you!" Her voice was startling in its hatred.

"I think you will," said Mr. Max. "We know your plan."

Keenan took a step forward, threatening. "She came here with me, not you. I don't know you, fucker. All I do know is that you'd better get back on your fancy little fighter and get the hell out of my way, before I give you something you won't forget."

"Careful, Keenan," said Franco. His voice was low; Keenan logged the tone. Franco knew something, something bad about Mr. Max, and his voice held an embedded warning.

Where do I know him from? came Keenan's unbidden internal voice.

Where? *Where?*

"He's a Seed Hunter," said Emerald, her voice a lullaby of fear.

Keenan glanced at her, at her defeat. He felt suddenly sick.

"You cannot kill him." She smiled. "It," she corrected.

"And he wants you?"

"Yes, they want me dead. They want my power."

"A lie," said Mr. Max. "She seeks to bring back Leviathan."

"Leviathan is gone," said Emerald.

"For now." Mr. Max stalked forward, hands stretched into claws, face undulating, rippling as if something beneath the flesh wanted to get out. Subliminally, Keenan saw Betezh sag on the ramp, surprised, horrified even by what he was witnessing.

So, this fight was with Mr. Max— alone.

Keenan leapt forward, braced MPK tracking Max's head and intersecting his journey to Emerald. Mr. Max halted and blinked, as if seeing Keenan for the first time. Then he smiled a far from human smile. The emotion looked wrong on his face, more pain than humour; far less than organic.

"Get out of my way."

"Fuck you."

Keenan opened fire, bullets howling, fire blazing from the MPK's stocky barrel. Suddenly the world went crazy, filled not just with the remnants of the dying whipping sandstorm but also the harsh scream of bullets, Franco running for cover with his guns yammering, Pippa hitting the ground, her MPK tracking, and Keenan dropping to one knee... to blink, as he felt the MPK smashed from his gloved hands. He watched as if in a dream, fascinated by the still-spinning bullets that squirmed under Mr. Max's skin, under his face, inside his head. They wriggled like live creatures, and popped free of entry-holes in his blasted skull. Flesh ran liquid and knitted together, wounds healing instantly. Mr. Max bent Keenan's MPK in half and there was a *crack* as alloy broke. Bullets scattered to the ground from a torn magazine like pebbles and were swallowed by the black desert. Keenan looked into a face of inhuman fury; he smiled, and smashed a right straight to Mr. Max's groin; he whirled low, leg striking out to sweep Max's feet from beneath him... Max toppled, but did not hit the ground, instead, he turned shifting and bending and flowing as he fell, reversing the fall into a thrusting uprising attack. The blow caught Keenan under the chin and threw him a good twenty feet across the sand, where he rolled and tumbled, coming to a ragged halt. He spat blood, and a tooth, and then pushed himself painfully to his hands and knees.

Mr. Max, scowling, turned, and felt the cold touch of metal against his temple. He began to twist, a blur moving fast, but Franco pulled all four triggers on the quad-barrel Kekra, and four bullets sang on angel wings of fire, caving Mr. Max's head in and punching him in a flurry of whirling limbs across the sand... to lie still.

The quad gunshot echoed like feedback across the barren desert, reverberating with a metal *crack*.

"Suck on that," said Franco, and blew down the hot barrels with a hollow whistle, grinning a grin filled with big teeth.

Keenan stood up, swaying, and moved back across the sand towards the *Reason in Madness* where Pippa knelt, shocked, by the ramp, but even as he moved he immediately saw that something was wrong and Mr. Max was still flopping about, his body a skin-bag of pulp that went suddenly rigid. He sat up. Mr. Max stared down at his hands and fought to regain control... over death. There was a *crunch,* followed by the crack of bones realigning, and woodenly he climbed to his feet, flesh falling and rolling into place across the terrible quad gunshot wound to his head, which closed in a concave seal. He looked up, face contorted as flesh flowed into place. Then he breathed, a deep exhalation, and smiled a cold smile, colder than the void, as black eyes glittered and he surveyed the two men holding guns... and beyond, Pippa, head down, face unreadable.

"Unexpected," he said, and strode swiftly towards Franco.

Franco's guns came up and he fired but Mr. Max moved fast, leaping, sprinting, evading many of the shots and absorbing others with flesh *slaps* as he accelerated into a blur. Franco screamed as a heavy blow hammered his face and dropped him without a sound. He hit the ground, blood pouring from his caved-in nose; he rolled over several times, then lay still.

Keenan fired his weapon, his Makarov thumping his fist as he charged Mr. Max who met the charge head-on and they clashed, bouncing from one another in a flurry of blows and bullets. Keenan was knocked away, but rolled, finding his feet, his gun lost, and attacked with all his power and might. His attack was filled with the frustration of a mission, a halted journey, an abated revenge unquenched. His arms were pistons and his fists piledrivers as he smashed blow after bloody blow against Max's pulverising skull knocking the Seed Hunter back and back and back. Keenan launched himself, boots spreading Mr. Max's lips across his face, splintering teeth. As Max hit the ground Keenan was atop him, a small blade between his knuckles. He was snarling, an animal face filled with rage hot fury in his eyes and all humanity sympathy and empathy gone in a violent red blinding surge of something he could not comprehend. He punched out Max's eyes with the dagger and watched milky fluid pop and spurt across the Seed Hunter's face. But Max did not scream, did not cry out, and behind those eyes, those fake eyes, Keenan looked down fell down into a million minute glittering globes. He realised, deep inside his soul, that Mr. Max was so far from human as to be beyond understanding, and his punch dagger slammed Max's throat cutting deep and sideways, severing the main artery in a gout of warm human blood. It was fake, all fake and false and inside Keenan could sense this charade this petty ersatz production and a sense of imminent danger went *click,* a detonation trigger, inside his head.

He did not see the blow. It sent him squirming across the sand, rolling, coughing on dust.

He glanced up... into Max's boot.

Again Keenan spluttered, choking, blood pouring from his nose, a forehead cut feeding his eyes and face with a sheen of slick crimson, blinding him. He rolled, over and over, as if trying to get away, a deep groan emanating from his stomach to his lips.

He pushed himself to hands and knees...

Tried so hard to breathe.

The next blow broke three ribs and left him ten feet away on his back.

Mr. Max loomed into vision, his eyes all gone, and deep recessed clusters filling Keenan with a visual madness and an urgent need to laugh like a maniac. He cannot see! screamed Keenan's brain. But of course, he could. Mr. Max was not human.

"I am sick of this shit," snarled Max. He kicked Keenan again, sending him rolling across the desert like a limp sack of pulped bones. Keenan gazed weakly towards the tail-end of their Gunship. Colours swirled in his head. Pain receded, and he was filled with a curious light-headedness. He wondered if he would die there, lying in the sand, so close to discovering the truth...

His girls, his dead girls.

So close.

Keenan coughed, then blinked. It seemed to take a long time. His eyelids weren't working properly. Max appeared, and behind him the Gunship was a blur of dark circular exhaust ports, ribbed with bands of TitaniumII alloy. Keenan tried to roll away, pushed himself onto one elbow, and levered himself up. He could see Emerald beyond; her hand was over her mouth, body deflated with horror, and she was doing nothing, doing nothing to help... fear etched acid on her alien face.

This is it, thought Keenan.

This... is... it.

He slumped back. Mr. Max was staring down at him. He bared his teeth, long black slivers nestling behind the false smashed stumps from Keenan's blows. He stooped, drawing a long serrated black knife from his boot, the knife that had killed so many Ket warriors... and a million others down through distant centuries.

Max clenched the blade tight, like a lover.

He stepped over Keenan's wounded, battered body, and straddled him.

"I'm going to cut your throat. I'm going to watch you drown in your own blood. It may take a little while."

Keenan said nothing. He was filled with pain that pounded him from a hundred sources, a raging surf, and he was incapable of speech. Max filled his vision: a terrible frightening immortal deity looming above him like a dark shivering ghost, and Keenan felt so weak, so lost, so pitiful, so small. Self-loathing and disgust flooded through him, because strength had fled him betrayed him deserted him and he was going to die on a sand-whipped desert floor, begging silently for a life he didn't deserve.

And he realised.

There were some things you could not fight.

Some creatures just too powerful...

Keenan laughed a cold laugh, bubbling blood...

And watched the slow blade descend.

CHAPTER 16

STRANGE BROTHERHOOD

MR. MAX HAD killed thousands of people during his life. He had murdered women, children, and animals. He had cut the hearts, spines and souls from a thousand species of alien. He had destroyed families, cities, worlds. Empathy and remorse were not words in his lexicon. Mr. Max was a Seed Hunter... only the Seed mattered... the essence of every living organism on which he fed.

The blade gleamed dull in his fist.

He bent towards Keenan; all else was gone, a blur, dust.

There came a *click*. Mr. Max's head snapped left, and inside the holes where his eyes had been clusters of vision globes shrank as a billion neural pathways opened to his brain and...

Understanding rocked him.

The *Reason in Madness* fired its ignition, engines whined and a sheet of purple flame fifty feet long blasted from exhaust ports. The fire hit Mr. Max from the waist up, instantly vaporising his skin and human flesh and forcing a terrible high *shriek* that was cut off almost instantly as the jets reached thousands of degrees.

Keenan, on the ground, felt a searing scorch of heat and started to roll away through sheer instinct: pain flooded him and he needed to get away, away from the heat, the fire, the roaring agony. He nudged past Max's useless legs and rolled and rolled; then Emerald was there, her hands on his smoking WarSuit, which clicked and buzzed in rapid malfunction. Keenan opened his eyes, gazing up into Emerald's green orbs. He touched her cool hands with their green veins on ebony skin, and something in her eyes made him shiver. It was triumph, a glare of success.

Keenan looked left, where Max—or what remained of him—seemed to dance. The boosters on the Gunship were firing hot, bright white and hard to see, as Pippa, inside the cockpit, increased the fuel throughput, and the whole Gunship vibrated and shook, held in place by stabilising jets, its boosters eating away what was left of Max's upper body.

Then the fire was gone.

Exhaust ports glowed white-hot; they crackled like breaking ice.

Silence descended; a veil of ash.

Mr. Max was still there, his human legs almost intact below the knees, the rest of his surviving flesh charred. From the waist up he was nothing more than what appeared slick oil bones, not a human skeleton, but narrow lines, a stick-man of greased steel. The spinal column was a single piece, brown, oiled, the skull a tiny sphere. Arms were splinters with serrated points for hands.

Mr. Max sat down, a slow folding, and then slumped sideways to the black desert.

Emerald helped Keenan to his feet; her hands were strong, guiding him up, and he could see Franco across the space occupied by Max's strange corpse. Franco was playing with his battered nose.

Pippa ran down the ramp.

"Keenan!"

She was in his arms, and he yelped.

"Thank God you're alive!"

"Well," he coughed, "I didn't want to point out what a huge risk you'd just taken, But seeing as you've volunteered the guilt—"

"Shut up!" She punched his chest. He wheezed.

Franco arrived, kicking up sand, a Kekra against the head of Betezh. Betezh was staring forlornly at the ground, eyes wide, flesh sickly and pale. He looked terribly shaken.

Franco prodded him.

"Shall I kill him now?"

"No," said Keenan, leaning heavily on Pippa. Pain shuddered through him. "What was it, Betezh?"

"I... don't know." He glanced at the oily brown stick-corpse. "I... I heard he was a Seed Hunter, but does anyone here know what that is? Look at it! It ain't fucking human, that's all I can say."

"I think we should kill Betezh right now!" urged Franco.

"No!" snapped Keenan. "There's been enough death."

"But Keenan..."

Ignoring his friend, Keenan moved towards Betezh, and their eyes locked. "You were with him." His voice was soft; inherent threat tangible. The words did not need to be said. You are both enemies. Mr. Max is gone and dead. Is it your turn?

Betezh shook his head. "This is all wrong, Keenan. I've been used, just like you!"

"What?"

"Kill him," whispered Emerald. She was standing to one side, staring at the sky. Her eyes glowed. She seemed suddenly infused with power, with an energy that bubbled along green veins. Her head dropped. She fixed Keenan with a decisive stare. "Kill Betezh. I have seen it. He will slaughter Combat-K in their sleep."

"No!" snapped Betezh. He made to take a step back, but Franco prodded him with his heavy Kekra. "Listen, Keenan!" There was desperation in his voice. "Don't trust her! You mustn't trust her!"

"Why? She's not the one trying to kill us!" snarled Franco.

"Mr. Max; he wanted her dead, for good reason." Betezh pointed at Emerald. She smiled a sickly smile. He turned on Keenan. "You've got to believe me, man."

"What a crock of stinking bullshit," laughed Franco.

"I heard Max talking about her. He was mad, muttering to himself. He may have been a Seed Hunter; he may have been one of the greatest killers in recent history, and I know a streak of insanity when I see it. But Max and Emerald, they go back a long way. Max was trying to protect what we know, trying to maintain our equilibrium."

"And you're an innocent party in all of this?" said Keenan.

"No, Keenan. I work for Vitch. But things have got out of hand; we're not talking about a few people dying here. We're not just talking about Sinax politics, we're talking about a bigger game. Something's going down and none of us understand it. None of us..." he pointed at Emerald, "Except her."

"Ridiculous," snapped Emerald. "You came to me," she said, staring at Keenan. "You rescued me! You sought my help! And then this little man sees his one avenue of escape and tries to turn you against me." She laughed bitterly. "Kill him, now. Do as I say."

Franco's finger tightened on the trigger.

"Wait!"

The voice was familiar, and Keenan's head came up. A small black PopBot hurtled from the depths of the Interceptor, spinning wildly and with a myriad of glowing colours scattering across its surface. It raced towards the group and slewed in a wide arc.

"Keenan! Keenan! It's me, Cam!"

Keenan grinned a sly grin. "I wondered what had happened to you, you little bugger."

There was a metallic sigh. "I was abducted! Kidnapped! Tortured!"

"Damn lucky you," muttered Franco.

"Don't be like that," said Cam, dropping and rising into the air again. His spin seemed agitated.

"It's been booby-trapped," said Betezh, meeting Keenan's steady gaze. "Max filled the little bot full of explosives, and that biowire shit that sneaks up on you when you're asleep: StrangleTox."

Keenan nodded, and glanced at Cam. "You dangerous, buddy?"

"I have disabled it internally," Cam said smugly. "After all, I am a GradeA Security Mechanism with advanced SynthAI and a Machine Intelligence Rating (MIR) of 3150."

"I remember," said Keenan. He winced in pain. "How could I ever forget! You sure you disabled that toxic AI shit? I don't want a nasty surprise in my bed."

"Yes. Trust me, Keenan!"

"OK then."

"Come on," said Pippa. "We need to get you to the Medical Hold."

"You want me to kill him, then?" repeated Franco, like a dog with a bone. He prodded Betezh hard in the head and produced an *ouch*.

"No. Not yet. Bring him inside."

Franco leaned close to Betezh's ear. "Just like the old times," he murmured. "We really should stop meeting like this. But let me tell you one thing, you're not safe, not even if Keenan wants you to be. Understand, maggot? Me and you, Betezh, well, we've got bad history. I'll never forget your..." he ran his tongue over Betezh's ear, "little intimations. So let's just say from now on, my friend, we're entwined, like lovers. And, like lovers, I'm looking forward to the day when I give you a good hard fucking."

Great, mused Betezh sourly as he was prodded up the ramp of the *Reason in Madness*. *Just what I need, a leap from the bosom of one madman to the crotch of another. Out of the frying pan? Shit. What did I do to deserve this?*

"So what's the score?" beamed Franco, bounding into the cockpit. His face was smeared with chocolate and... something crumbly and white.

"What is that?" said Pippa.

"Blue stilton," said Franco smugly.

"What the hell have you been doing to him?"

Franco looked suddenly sly. "Nuffink."

Emerald spoke, words gentle. They listened, for the members of Combat-K knew their lives might depend upon it. "This place, Teller's World, is not a normal world as you would understand it. It has... I suppose a word in your language, in your understanding, would be layers. You have to enter a meditative state, you have to take your mind somewhere else. Only then can you Shift, only then can you experience the wonder of Teller's World, of the homeland of Leviathan."

"What do you mean, Shift?" asked Keenan.

"I cannot explain it in words, only in images. I will do so when we reach the Altar."

"I'm assuming we can fly there?"

"No. The world—this place—this layer—is dominated by mines; not just those you encountered on our entry, but across the entire surface—billions, buried under the sand and littering the skies. Believe me when I say they are the most effective anti-aircraft measures you will ever encounter, designed with only one concept: the bringing of death."

"I assume you know a path," said Keenan.

"Of sorts, although some areas shift, and the patterns change. But I can sense them; each mine is organic, an extension of Leviathan's legacy. Some once said he was protecting his world for a time when he could awake. Impossible, I am sure."

"Sounds dangerous," said Franco grimly.

"That's why you're here," smiled Emerald. "Get me to the Altar, get me to The Factory; there I will regain my lost powers, my abilities, and each of you will be magnificently rewarded. I have not forgotten our bargain, Keenan. I have not forgotten our pact. I will find the information you seek, the name of the killer."

"You make it sound too easy," said Pippa; she seemed agitated, on edge. "If it was just a case of navigation through minefields, why would you need us? There's something else, isn't there?"

"Yes."

"Go on," grunted Franco, wiping stilton from his beard.

"We can fly for maybe three, four hundred kilometres. Then we reach a crack in the crust of the planet, beneath lie the Three Lakes: the Lake of Diamonds, the Lake of Protons, and the Lake of Desecration. We must cross all three. We cannot take a ship there, but the Buggy should manage the journey. After the Lakes come the Woods of

Mekkra, and a Shrine—the Altar—where we can perform the Shift. Once in the altered state, we can finally enter The Factory."

"A factory?" said Keenan. "I thought this was a forbidden zone; I thought there was no life."

"There is life, Keenan; maybe not as you would understand it, and not the kind of life easily identified by Sinax probes. It is a life based on metal, a life based on machines. The Factory is a bad place; it is not an environment for humans."

"Are there robots there?" asked Cam, inquisitive.

"Not as such. Not as you would understand the concept. You will see—and understand—soon enough."

"And all these places, these obstacles, they will offer resistance?"

"Bring guns," said Emerald, eyes dark. "lots of guns."

EMERALD BRIEFED COMBAT-K for an hour, and then, with packs packed, guns oiled, explosives primed, they were ready. Betezh— handcuffed—was invited to the cockpit, and, all crammed in together, Pippa fired the ignition.

Rockets roared, engines whined, and the *Reason in Madness* lifted from the desert surface. Pippa pointed up through the glittering cockpit ceiling. "Look."

"Stars!" beamed Franco, ever the star gazer.

"Pin Mines," corrected Emerald. "That's what we came through; that's what I guided us between."

"It's like a star-field," said Franco in awe.

"Nothing so glamorous: it's a weapon, pure and simple, designed to wipe out organic life, designed to protect this planet from the races of the Quad-Gal, maybe for a time, as Emerald said, when Leviathan returns." Pippa scowled.

"So… is this old goat planning on making an appearance, or what?" Franco grinned. "He's supposed to be one of the Five Great Creators, a creature of wisdom, honour, love, learning. Not that I believe in contemporary mytholology."

Pippa slapped his leg. "I'm sure if—when—he does appear, you'll be first in line for a pat on the back, my dear. After all, it's not every day a newly awakened God finds himself—itself?—referred to as an 'old goat'. Trust Franco to worship at the altar of bad insults."

"Hey, I just tell it as I find it," said Franco.

Pippa accelerated the Gunship—gently—and beneath them rolled the undulating dunes of the black planet. Occasionally sand rose, crested low hills, then tumbled in sweeping wind-swept curves. Volcanoes glowed in the distance. To Keenan, locked in a mental depression and brooding on his family, it was entirely a vision of hell, or its nearest approximation.

Franco crept close. "Looks bad, don't it?"

"Yeah," agreed Keenan, "real bad."

"You think we'll get to fight some monsters down there?"

"Have you been drinking, Franco?"

"Just a tipple or two," he said, sheepish, "to warm my winter cockles."

"Franco, we're about to enter a combat situation. The last thing I need is a ginger Hobbit putting ten fucking rounds in the back of my head. Lay off the vodka, OK?"

"OK." Sulky.

"Look, Kee." Pippa was pointing.

The black scenery outside was distantly blurred, and as they swept towards the vision, towards the towering dark clouds, Keenan frowned and muttered, "A storm?"

"Snow," said Emerald.

"Black snow?" said Franco.

"Yeah, freaky, right?"

They watched, fascinated, as they approached the wall of apparently solid darkness, and swept inside. A curious silence enveloped them; swirling velvet swamped the Gunship and they seemed suddenly...

"Buried," said Pippa. "It's like being buried."

"Entombed," agreed Franco, eyes wide.

They cruised, a few feet above the ground, Pippa flying blind and using bio-scanners for navigation and proximity. Her hands lay spread wide across controls, brow locked in fevered concentration. Emerald was also concentrating; occasionally she would close her eyes, lift her face to the ceiling of the cockpit as if in silent communion, and breathe deeply, veins pulsing with alien blood.

Cam floated in. "You OK, Keenan?"

"Yeah."

"You seem..."

"Distraught?" He laughed. "I need a cigarette."

"I've been trying to reach Fortune; no signals are leaving Teller's World. We are trapped in the black hole of a communication deadzone."

"Are you even remotely surprised?"

Cam spun a little. "I surmise this situation to be instigated by the effective blanketing effects of a number of Pin Mines; their secondary function, it would seem, is to block signals, either that or it is intrinsic to their nature. They have, effectively, isolated us."

"Wouldn't be the first time," grunted Franco. "We've got a history of weevils sending us on missions and then severing all ties. Remember the Terminus5 reactor?"

"How could I ever forget," said Keenan, harnessing a shiver.

They cruised through the silent dark snowstorm for more than an hour, Pippa keeping their speed down and scanning for what Emerald described as localised bouncing mines: metallic spheres that would surge up out of the desert and leap to connect with anything metallic in proximity. She advised they could blow a mile-wide hole in a starship; their detonation load was incredible, like nothing before experienced throughout Quad-Gal.

"Wouldn't mind getting my hands on one of those beauties," said Franco, listening intently.

"Why?" asked Pippa.

"Just because," said Franco.

"What kind of answer is that?"

"Come on Pippa," said Keenan, "you know Franco has a hard-on for explosives. He's like a kid with a new toy; this must be the equivalent of a candyfloss dip for our resident detonation psycho."

"Actually," said Franco, "I am profoundly interested in all proximity technology."

"Balls," said Pippa. "You just like things that go bang!"

Franco winked. "You include yourself in that line-up, baby?"

"Don't start again."

"Well you certainly started last night, baby."

"What?" Her voice was ice.

"All those noises you were making in your Sleep-Cell. Most distraught I was, lying there alone, listening to your wailing and moaning, groaning and thumping; anybody would think you had a man with you."

He leered at her knowingly.

"I couldn't possibly understand what bumping and moaning you're referring to," said Pippa primly. "Nothing like that happened in *my* SleepCell last night."

"Or… maybe you had a woman in there?" Franco glanced at Emerald, lost in her private meditation.

"You wish," snapped Pippa.

"Now you come to mention it, I've compiled a list of possible candidates for a fantasy of hardcore lesbian coupling."

"God," said Betezh quietly. Franco stared at him.

"What, slack boy?"

"You're like children," said Betezh. "I'm honestly quite stunned that you ever came back from a single mission alive. It's like listening to a bunch of acne-riddled teen-angst muppets squabbling in the playground."

Franco shook his head. "No no no, you see, the way it works is this."

"Enlighten me."

"We're facing certain death, on regular occasions, right? So the best preventative tonic is to banter, lighten the mood, chill baby, so when you are required to blow some motherfucker's head clean off," he cocked his Kekra and placed four barrels against Betezh's lips, "then it comes just that little bit easier, you can sleep at night, and not be haunted by the horror of your actions; comprendé?"

Betezh nodded behind squashed lips.

"Franco, leave him alone," said Keenan. "Look, something's coming up. We're on. Put the gun away and get Betezh a pack; if he's coming with us, he can carry the fucking ammunition."

"Me?" said Betezh.

"You don't think I'm leaving you here alone with our only damn transport off this barren rock world, do you?"

"I... well, I..."

"Although, yeah, you might be right, you may turn into a burden. I can do without having to check over my damn shoulder every ten seconds." He smiled a sly smile. "I'll let Franco deal with you, shall I?"

"No, no. Carrying ammunition is just fine, great, dandy, in fact. Just show old Betezh where the heavy donkey-load is; Betezh the name, humping the game."

Franco slapped Betezh on the back, making him wheeze. Franco grinned a deaths-head grin. "That's the spirit lad! You'll fit in just fine mate!" He turned and, bristling with guns, headed for the ramp.

KEENAN, WINCING DESPITE a heavy load of painkillers, stood with dark sand staining his boots, and watched Franco bounce the Buggy from the ship's hold. The Buggy was a little battered, its balloon tyres chunky with tread and grinding through sand as Franco revved the powerful 1000bhp engine. The machine flew down the ramp with a roar, spun, sending showers of desert cascading into a dune, and slammed to a halt inches from Keenan's knees. Keenan smiled coldly.

"Good to see I've still got it," grinned Franco.

Pippa looked serious. "Move over, I'm driving."

"What? No! But!..."

"Yeah, move over," said Keenan, brushing sand from his combats. "Pippa is definitely driving."

Keenan sat in the front with Pippa; Emerald, Betezh and Franco sat in the back, and Cam attached himself with a metallic *clang* to the Buggy's hull. Without a backward glance, they set off across the featureless landscape, Pippa racing the engine and hammering along at a ferocious speed.

Overhead, clouds the colour of lead bunched and fought. Lightning flickered in the distance. Wind howled a mournful song over rolling desert. Ancient sand churned beneath the Buggy's wheels.

"There are few mines in this vicinity," explained Emerald. She seemed weak and drawn, her skin stretched back over her face, eyes narrowed as if in pain. "It became too treacherous for our people; we call it The Runway."

"Are you OK?" asked Pippa, glancing back.

Emerald nodded. "My weakness is increasing. I think... something strange is happening to me, organically, biochemically, physiologically. I feel as if my homeland is drawing out my energy, my life. Maybe I'm not wanted." She laughed.

"We need to get you to The Factory," said Keenan, and turned back, eyes scanning the desert. Clouds raced above him, and more black snow began to fall, thick, cloying, huge flakes tumbling idly through the air. The wind had died; apart from the Buggy's roaring engine—even now subdued—a curious blanketing silence settled like a shroud across the land, across the world.

"I don't like it here," said Franco.

"You don't like it anywhere," said Pippa.

"I like The City!"

"Only because you're a whore."

"Nothing wrong with that."

The more snow fell, the more subdued Keenan felt. His depression grew. It was as if a huge cloud was sinking, enveloping his existence. Dark snowflakes settled on his shoulders and hair, and he shivered, not just from skin-chill but from a deep wound inside his heart. He ground his teeth, ignoring the dull pain from the vicious battle with Mr. Max; he had to push on, had to see this thing through. The memories, and honour and justice for his dead family, depended on it.

Pippa slowed the Buggy. "Something's coming up," she said, dropping another gear. The Buggy shook and rumbled, restrained with engine-braking, then slowed to a halt. A narrow tear appeared across the ground in the rocky substrate, perhaps only a couple of feet across; it dropped, a crevasse, into darkness below.

"Follow the crack," said Emerald, rubbing at her weary face. "There is an entrance."

Pippa cruised, the Buggy's suspension pounded by the desert and rocky ground. Suddenly, a low black archway loomed out of the thick falling snow; Pippa stopped the Buggy with a *crunch*, and Keenan climbed out.

He strode forward, MPK ready, eyes alert. He reached out, then snatched back his hand, leaving a layer of his glove on the archway's surface. "Gods, that's cold," he hissed. His head lifted, following the archway, reading the deeply carved inscription there.

"What does it say?"

Emerald gave a weak smile. "Only those with the Dark Flame may pass."

"Meaning?"

"Something in your heart," said Emerald, and Keenan met her gaze. They stood there, locked, and Keenan felt suddenly foolish; suddenly, deeply unsure of himself, his motivations, his direction in life. He gave a cold bark that masqueraded as a laugh.

What the hell am I doing here? he thought.

Is revenge so damned important?

Am I just another pointless fool?

He rubbed at his head, closing his eyes, breathing deeply. This whole place, Teller's World, was beginning to get to him, to eat into his heart and soul like a maggot in an apple, compressing him, destroying him from the inside out.

Despite reports to the contrary—that of no life on Teller's World—he could feel something there: a presence, something mystical or magical, not a lifeform as Quad-Gal understood such things, but a dark entity, an oppressive existence, a… dark God…

Leviathan.

It came as a whisper from the darker reaches of his imagination, from the factory that churns out nightmares. Looking at Pippa, and Franco, he saw they were experiencing a similar feeling. He forced a smile through gritted chipped teeth and hoisted his MPK. Sweat glistened on his brow, despite cool whispering air and chilled snow.

"What now, boss?" said Franco: a gentle exhalation.

Keenan glanced at the arched gateway. Beyond, the slope led very, very steeply down. A foul air exhaust blew up, howling just at the edge of hearing. He looked again at Emerald, but her bright green eyes were closed; her breathing was ragged.

"We're going in," he said, "and I'm driving."

He climbed into the Buggy, slipped the clutch, and spun the vehicle round, leaving ruts in the desert sand. Then, with a final glance at the open spacious world about him and above him, he accelerated hard, hammered through the archway and bubble tyres left the ground—were airborne—

before touching down on the slope and slamming Combat-K in a near vertical descent into blackness and cold, cold oblivion.

THE SLOPE WAS an umbilical, a rollercoaster road leading ever down. Gloom flooded in the absence of light, and the Buggy's headlights cut bright white swathes from the charcoal. The path cut steeply through rock, twisting and turning, sometimes cutting back on itself, hairpin following hairpin, and in grim silence Keenan unleashed the Buggy, dropped with alarming and insane speed into the nightmare of descent and horror he knew had to come... had to be overcome. And yet he could not help himself, could not hold back speed for fear of pain or death and with gritted teeth as wind and rock flashed by at incredible velocity and he heard Franco gasp, then scream, Keenan focused and rushed headlong into the abyss...

The Buggy growled, tyres and suspension thumping. Rocks thudded from the chassis. Several flicked up, bouncing from the vehicle's plastic windshield, and flew over their heads. Franco, knuckles white, hung on for dear life, and when he glanced across at Betezh, he found the shaven-headed ageing ex-doctor grinning inanely at him.

"What are you laughing at?" screamed Franco.

"If I'm going to die, at least you die with me!"

Franco was about to scream a retort when the narrow road soared upwards, leaving the rocky walls behind, and they were suddenly suspended on a high bridge in the midst of an enormous cavern. Engine growling, Keenan reined in the power, and the Buggy finally slowed, coming to a halt with a judder on a treacherously high narrow walkway. Franco peered over the side, but couldn't leave the confines of the vehicle, only a severe drop greeted him. Keenan eased the Buggy forward again, more sedately, and the bridge dropped and turned, spiralling into a corkscrew that dropped down and down, down to the broad flat rocky floor. Keenan killed the engine, feeling sick, and it died with a burble of unspent fuel.

He climbed out, scratched at his chin, and breathed the stale, metallic air.

"Emerald?"

"Yes?" Her voice was frighteningly gentle, like silk smothering a candle flame.

"Something's coming."

"I know. Be calm. You must remain calm."

Distantly, something moved. The rock seemed to waver like a desert mirage, and then it shifted, advanced, and a wave of bright metal flowed forwards, hugging the ground as it skittered towards them. The carpet shimmered in the eldritch light of the cavern, rippling, undulating with insect union, and a sound came drifting like storm-sand. Keenan squinted hard, trying to add clarity to his blurred vision.

Franco took a step back. He drew and cocked his Kekra. Pippa, mouth dry, also cocked her MPK sub-machine gun, and started tracking this imminent and vast new threat.

"No!" snapped Keenan, holding up a fist. "No shots."

"But Keenan..." breathed Franco.

"Wait. Don't do anything. Trust her."

"I trust nobody," grated Franco, but he hefted his weapons and stood his ground. The sheet of metal sped towards them, a flood of fist-sized metal objects which, as they neared, turned from a buzzing humming vibrating blur into—

"Machines!" blurted Franco.

"They're robots," said Pippa.

"Whatever you do, don't fire your weapons," growled Keenan. His eyes were narrowed, and he recognised an unstoppable threat when it approached. Each machine was the size of a child's fist, and comprised a tiny cylinder with spinning, cutting blades. There were hundreds of the machines, thousands: a swarm, like a metal disease, glittering bright and oiled, and humming as they jostled and merged, and sped towards the group. The wave hit them like a cold metallic wind, invading their senses, and they could smell oil and grease, and taste metallic flakes in the air. The tiny machines bumped them, rising up, surrounding them, engulfing them, and all the group could see was a shimmering metal field.

And yet—

Despite Franco opening his mouth to scream, there was no pain.

"Keep calm." Emerald's voice cut through the billions of tiny vibrations surrounding Combat-K. Even Betezh was silent, mouth and eyes tight shut, praying to a God he didn't believe in for a miracle that wouldn't happen.

And then... then they were gone, flooding back across the rocky cavern floor, a jostling, bumping, humming buzzing. Keenan stared, steel-eyed, watching the flood change into a metal waterfall that flowed into a kilometre wide slot in the ground. He released a pent-up breath, wiped sweat from his brow, and allowed himself the luxury of oxygen.

"What happened?"

"They tried to eat us!" squawked Franco.

"If they'd tried to eat us," growled Keenan, "then we'd already be dead." He glanced at Emerald.

"They are autonomous drones; they respond to aggression. If you attack, they simply pulp you into an organic mist. I, of course, was immune because of my Kahirrim blood; you would not have been so fortunate."

"Were they sent by your brother? Raze?"

"No. He has no control on these upper levels. Despite his prowess, his might, he is trapped by the same mechanism that held me on Ket for so long. However, he guards The Factory, and will kill me before allowing me a full return to power. These machines are part of Leviathan's internal protection system, part of the natural defence of Teller's World. One of the reasons nobody leaves this place alive."

Keenan nodded. "Let's move."

"I think I've soiled my pants," grunted Franco.

"What, again?" snapped Pippa.

"You're so damned understanding."

Pippa lifted her MPK, grey eyes bleak. "Understanding? That's not a word in my vocabulary," she hissed, and stalked ahead, MPK sweeping the surrounding area. She turned, calming her breathing. "This is a bad place, Keenan. I think I might just regret following you."

"I never said it would be easy," said Keenan.

Pippa returned to him. "That's right." She touched his arm, returned to a state of calm. "Don't worry; I'll follow you through the gates of Hell, and beyond, into Eternity."

"Me too!" said Franco.

Keenan laughed. "It's good to be among… friends. Come on, back in the Buggy. I get the impression we've a long way to go, and Emerald is starting to look… odd. I think this place is draining her, draining what energy or power she has. I'm worried that if we don't get her to this Factory…"

"She might die on you?"

Keenan nodded.

"And you need your answers, right?" Pippa's eyes gleamed with silver tears.

"I need revenge, Pippa. I need to make them pay."

"I'm sure you will," she whispered.

THEY CLIMBED BACK into the Buggy, and Keenan drove fast and straight, following Emerald's directions. The huge tyres thudded over the slots that had disgorged the swarm of drones. Then they were slamming along to a high-pitched engine scream.

Keenan felt Cam, spinning by his ear. He glanced at the tiny PopBot. "You OK?"

"We've travelled a long way together, Keenan."

"Yeah." Keenan fumbled out a home-rolled cigarette, lit the weed and took a deep toke. Cam made an annoyed buzzing sound, but didn't comment. He'd been trying to get Keenan to quit since their time back on Galhari. "And you've been a good little PopBot." He stared hard at the machine. "You did disarm that internal bomb, didn't you?"

"Of course, Keenan. It was primitive. Mr. Max should have stuck to sneaking up behind innocent old ladies and murdering them with a garrotte. Explosives, alas, were not his forte."

"Good. I mean, I'm glad you're not going to explode."

"So am I. What I want to say, Keenan, is that since arriving on Teller's World I've been experiencing a few tiny malfunctions."

"Oh yeah?"

"I've run systematic and repeated internal diagnostics on all systems and sub-systems; there are no hardware or hardwired errors. That means I am being subtly altered by an external power source."

"What power source?"

"The point is, my casing is Special H graded, which means I am built to a set of military standards, and that means that practically nothing can infiltrate my shell. After all, I wouldn't want to be marooned on a distant world and have me develop a fault—unable, for example, to open a can of beans."

"Very amusing. You've waited to slip that one in, haven't you?"

"The point is, there is an awesome power source, here."

"Where?"

"According to my covert and tentative explorations it's... everywhere. But it's confusing me, Keenan; the whole damn planet of Teller's World is just downright odd. It's not something you can see from the outside... but from the inside..."

"What?" Keenan glanced at Cam.

"There's something not right."

"What do you mean?"

"I'm not sure. It's difficult to quantify." If Cam had possessed shoulders he would have wriggled uncomfortably. "The place doesn't work right. I've analysed mass, velocity, spin, diameter, and gravity: the whole package doesn't add up."

"What are you trying to say, Cam?"

"This isn't a planet."

Pippa, who had been listening from the passenger seat, snorted a laugh. "What the hell are we driving across? A custard pie?"

"No." Once more Cam adopted a prim pose. As the Buggy rode chasms and ruts, dipping and riding rock waves, so Cam remained perfectly level between Keenan and Pippa. His flight control was phenomenal, accurate to an nth degree.

"A jelly donut, perhaps?"

"This is not a planet." His voice went hard. "It's a machine. And it's hiding something at its core: something big, something with the sort of energy output to create worlds."

"Or destroy them," said Keenan.

"And that's why nobody has been allowed to explore this planet; that's why it protects itself so violently, why millions have died... to protect the Big Secret!"

"What are you thinking, Kee?" Pippa's eyes were bright. She placed a hand on his knee, and he touched her gloved fingers; a small sign of affection in a dark cruel place.

"I'm thinking that what started as a simple quest for knowledge has turned into insanity, a maze of complexity: GodRaces, Forbidden Planets, awesome power sources at the core of machine worlds... All I wanted was a simple life. All I want is to commit a bloody act of retribution; then I'll die a happy man. But it's as if God is laughing at me; he keeps throwing random variables into the damn mixing bowl and expecting me to cope. I've pretty much had enough of this shit. I never thought I'd say it, but I'm ready to go home."

"Settle down?" asked Pippa.

"That's right."

"You still want me by your side?" Her voice was a lullaby.

"If you'll have me," said Keenan.

"I think we'd make the perfect couple."

"What, you with your psychosis, me with my smoking habit?" He laughed. "We'd make a fine couple of lunatics."

"If that's what it takes."

"Maybe in another life," said Keenan, turning his eyes back to the road.

Pippa said nothing.

KEENAN HALTED THE Buggy with a grinding of stones on a high ridge. Before them, the world fell away, a vast scoop carved from the rocky internal plateau on which they travelled... and in the distance, something sparkled with a bright, jewelled clarity.

Emerald climbed from the Buggy, and stood on the lip of the drop beside Keenan and Pippa. A breeze caressed her dark ringlets. Franco joined them, but Betezh remained in the Buggy, his face a thunderstorm of raging unhappiness.

"The Lake of Diamonds," said Emerald, reverently.

"We could be rich!" grinned Franco.

"They are not for the taking," said Emerald, "on pain of death."

"Not even a handful?"

"No."

"What about a few? Just a few sparkling diamantes? Just to bring a smile to old Franco's face? Eh? Eh? What about it?"

"No."

"One?"

"No."

"A half?"

"Franco, how can you steal half a diamond?" said Pippa quizzically.

"Cut it, with a Vibro Saw. I've seen it done. Worked right well, it did."

"Let's get moving," said Keenan, holding his ribs in pain. "The sooner we get this thing done, the sooner we can go home."

"You really believe that?" said Pippa.

"No, but I'll die trying."

"That's why I love you," said Pippa.

Keenan's eyes met hers, and he saw the shining light that had haunted him through so many years.

Their relationship had never been stable, but he saw hope there. Something hardened inside him; after all, in a few minutes they might all be dead.

"Let's move out."

They climbed into the Buggy, and Franco nudged Betezh, his eyes gleaming, his lips slick. He rubbed at his ginger beard with rustling sounds. "We could be rich," he muttered, face displaying wily cunning.

"You still taking your pills? After all the ones we gave you back at Mount Pleasant?" said Betezh.

"No! I don't need no pills!" But Betezh caught it, the lie.

"Good," said Betezh, settling back into the bucket seat and fixing his gaze on the back of Keenan's head. "Well, let's see what finale this adventure can bring, especially when you don't take your medicine. You sure you feel OK?"

"Why?"

Betezh smiled. "Oh. No reason."

"Bugger off."

"Tsch. Tetchy."

"Bugger off!"

Betezh shrugged.

The Buggy surged ahead, tipping over the lip of the near-vertical descent and ploughing down with a sudden screaming acceleration. Suspension crashed, tyres squealed and squirmed, and the Buggy's occupants held on for life as the vehicle clattered and smashed its way to the distant rocky floor... where it levelled out, and Emerald called a halt.

"You must follow my directions with care," she said.

"What's wrong?"

"The ground is created from a cold liquid rock. I will guide you through."

Keenan followed Emerald's instructions, and as they cruised down invisible pathways they glanced nervously over the sides of the Buggy. The rock, very slowly, and very subtly... flowed. It looked solid enough until closely scrutinised, but it was a liquid, viscous, moving, and deadly as quicksand.

"Nasty," said Keenan after a while.

"A trap for the unwary," said Emerald, voice sombre. She threw a glance at Franco, "And the greedy."

As they came close to the Lake of Diamonds, a glittering white light gradually filled the horizon, spreading out, making the cavern grow with brightness and clarity; the light grew, dazzling Combat-K with sparkling shafts of iridescence.

"It's beautiful," said Pippa.

"Diamonds are a girl's best friend," chuckled Franco.

"Meaning?"

"If we weren't facing certain death I'd ask you to marry me."

Pippa turned. "You serious?"

"Deadly."

"I think I'd have to turn you down."

Franco sighed. "It's the beard, right? I need to lose the beard."

"Um. Yeah, it's the beard, and your perverted indoor deviant habits."

"Ahh, but a good woman would cure me of those!"

"And you think I'm a good woman?"

"I think you're a... a... a woman."

"Well, thank you *very much*."

"Look at that," whistled Keenan, as the sparkling from the spreading Lake of Diamonds grew in clarity, filling not just their horizon but their world. And there, in the midst, sat a bridge, a narrow umbilical, which reared and stretched away, high above streaming diamond fingers of dancing iridescent light.

"The Bridge of Bone," said Emerald.

"Looks like a spine to me," snorted Franco.

Everybody looked at him.

"What?" he snorted. "What?"

"You don't exactly cheer the situation," said Pippa, finally.

"Just adding input." Franco scratched his beard. "Is it dangerous?"

"Very," said Emerald. "Take care, Keenan, the road is as slippery as ice, and the Bridge of Bone moves, it ripples, undulates, shifts as if alive. Move slowly, but never stop."

Keenan gunned the engine, slammed the Buggy forward and mounted the Bridge of Bone; they soared out over the Lake of Diamonds, high into the air above the shimmering lake, which spread out around them, became the ground, became the glittering air: became the entire world.

They were stunned by the vision, the vista, the panorama. Never had Combat-K witnessed such breathtaking spectacle, and just as their awe was reaching a peak, the Bridge suddenly bucked, wrenching sideways and dropping towards the surface of the lake. Franco screamed, clinging on with white knuckles as hairs stood on end, and his body tried forcibly to rise from its seat. Grim faced, Keenan, half-blinded by the sparkling sea of jewels, powered the Buggy down, around, wheels spinning and losing traction, the vehicle lurching as it fought and squealed to stay on the undulating bridge, which slammed right, then reared into the air like a live thing: a snake, a dark bone eel. The intensity of the Lake of Diamonds was too much; Keenan felt himself blinded stunned hammered against an anvil of diamond with all the breath ripped from his guts and life smashed from his frame. The Buggy screamed, and went into a sideways skid with engine yammering howling spitting dark oil blood. Franco was screaming, Pippa crying in fear as adrenaline kicked her skull but all turned to liquid turned to light turned to brittle intensity as the world folded over and over, down on itself. Nothing mattered, nothing could fill Keenan's head like the brightness and the nausea that swamped him, and flooded him, and took him in its fist and crushed him.

CHAPTER 17
SILVER

KEENAN OPENED HIS eyes. The sky was the colour of copper shot through with rusted iron. A vicious wind blew, cutting across him, chilling him instantly to the bone. He was lying on his back. He pushed himself up onto his elbows, wincing as they dug the sharp rock floor, and realised he was on a mountain summit. A cairn of rounded black stones squatted to his left; ahead, the world dropped away to an apparently infinite chasm spreading out to endless mountains, distant, snow-capped, jagged, violent and unwelcoming. Keenan glanced right, and his breath caught in his throat.

"Rachel... Ally..." he murmured, aware this was a dream, had to be a dream, because the two girls were dead, throats cut and cold in a grave on a distant planet, in a lonely universe. The girls, sitting on flat round rocks, looked up; Rachel squealed, and both scrambled up, and ran to him, buffeted by the violent snapping wind. They were in his arms, engulfing him, and tears coursed hot streaks down his cheeks, falling like mercury snowdrops into their hair, and he held his girls to him, held them tight and smelled their hair and felt their warmth and life, and he wept. He wept for a past that was gone, wept for a crime that should never have happened... wept for a criminally unjust loss of innocence.

"Daddy!"

Keenan pulled away a little, staring down into both girls' tear-filled eyes. They hugged him again, hugs so tight he knew they would never let go. He kissed their heads, their hair, their eyes. And he knew, then, realised with a certainty he had never believed possible...

He wanted to die.

He wanted to be with them.

Revenge meant nothing; revenge was a fable, an empty promise, an unfulfilled dream. It would solve nothing; not now. It could do no good. All Keenan wanted was to spend eternity with his children.

"Listen, Daddy." It was Rachel, her face set, stern despite its youth, serious.

"I love you two so much," he smiled, tears still falling.

"You're in great danger, Daddy."

"What do you mean?"

"You must trust nobody, not even those close to you. They will get you killed."

"Rachel?"

Then Keenan felt the tug, felt himself being dragged away from the girl by snaps of wind, and pushed, cracked, heaved towards the edge of the mountain. The girls were straining to hold on to him, straining to touch him, to never let go... they could never let go, and the mountain lurched, tipped violently as if upended by a roaring giant, and the copper sky flashed before him, crashed before his eyes, and nausea swamped him.

"Keenan! You OK, Keenan?"

He opened his eyes. Pippa was staring down at him.

"I saw them," he whispered, as he became aware of the rumbling engine of the Buggy.

"Saw who?"

Keenan frowned, then clamped his jaw shut. The warning came back to him, but he shook his head, clouded, confused; just a dream, the product of a fried mind in a near-death situation. He closed his eyes, and could still smell his children's hair.

Keenan heaved himself up, and stared bitterly down into a diamond infinity.

"What happened?"

"You lost... control?" said Pippa, eyes concerned. "You were out of it, but somehow—by some miracle—you stopped the Buggy before we went over the edge. Otherwise, we'd have been dog meat. Keenan, you'd better let me drive from now on."

Keenan nodded, did not argue, could not argue. Below, the Lake of Diamonds shimmered, and seemed to beckon him with a beautiful decadence. However, it just seemed sour now, fake, a cheap imitation of something rank and pointless. What could replace love? Want? Need? Nothing, nothing material mattered.

He swapped seats with Pippa, and she expertly eased the Buggy back from the precipice. She drove the vehicle away, slowly, getting a feel for the Buggy, and watching for random movements in the spine of the bridge. Gradually, she increased the speed, and Keenan slumped back in his seat, chin to chest, hooded eyes staring darkly out over the Buggy's battered bonnet.

Franco touched his shoulder. "You OK, Big Yin?"

"Yeah," he grinned, glancing back. "Sorry. Seems I'm not as reliable as I think I am."

"Hey, we all suffer shit, man. I would have seen us killed years ago. You and Pippa are the only reason I'm still breathing good clean air. Don't worry about it, bro'. We're here as a team."

Betezh snorted.

Franco pushed his Kekra under Betezh's chin. "You got something to add, motherfucker?"

"No, no, nothing to add."

"I still haven't forgotten the bad drugs, or the fucking testicular electrocution."

"I'm glad I made a lasting impression."

"I'll make a lasting impression in your fucking skull."

"Franco," warned Keenan.

The Buggy rode the twisting bucking bridge, and Pippa with her innate skill and confidence-inspiring pilot's eye brought them safely down to the opposite bank. The Lake of Diamonds receded behind them, changing from a sea of stars to a glittering wall, to a line, to nothing more than a twinkling firefly. Darkness flooded back into the underground chamber, which seemed to go on beneath the crust of Teller's World for ever.

"What's coming up?" said Pippa, warily, slowing the Buggy at the approaching wall of black. She turned, glancing at Emerald, who was slumped back, eyes closed, breathing ragged. Pippa shot Keenan a look, as if to say, "she's deteriorating", and Keenan gave a single nod. His lips were a tight compress. If Emerald died he would not get his name, but then, did it matter? Did any of it matter?

Emerald sighed and opened her eyes, and for a moment they were pools of oil before rotating, becoming the bright green Combat-K knew.

"Emerald?" Pippa's voice was soft.

"Yes." She grunted, shifting her weight. The Buggy creaked on battered suspension. Despite her size, Emerald was a lot heavier than she looked. "You are looking at the Lake of Protons, although the description is inaccurate. As we approach, you must avert your eyes; the protons are twisted matter, the deviant material found on the other side of Black Holes."

"I thought that was fable?"

Emerald shook her head. "Twisted Protons are real." She coughed, a cough heavy with phlegm. Her smile was diluted. "With the right equipment, it can be mined."

"What is its purpose?" asked Betezh.

Emerald turned to him, eyes bright. "Why, little man, it is the stuff of War Machines."

Betezh licked dry lips. "There is something wrong here. Something doesn't fit the puzzle."

"It's dead easy to understand," said Franco. "You keep your mouth shut, and we get the job done, or I blow your head off. You understand that equation, dickhead?"

Betezh gave a nod.

The Buggy continued.

The wall of black came closer, only it wasn't a wall of black; there was something on the other side. It was like looking at a billion reflected images, mirror upon mirror upon mirror, all reflecting the same colour but with angular disjoints through every conceivable atom. As Pippa looked she felt her gaze being drawn, wrenched out of her head, and immediately—even from a distance—she got the most incredible pounding migraine. She cried out, one hand snapping to cover her eyes.

"How will you drive over the bridge?" asked Franco.

"There is no bridge," said Emerald. "We must wade the Lake, but everybody has to keep their eyes tight shut, or this place will lever your skull out through your ears."

They halted, and Keenan tore a pair of black combats into strips using his knife. Each member of Combat-K—and Betezh—covered their eyes with the makeshift blindfolds. Once ready, Pippa cruised the Buggy, and hydraulics ejected floaters. Slowly, the Buggy descended a slope and was soon half submerged in the Lake of Protons. A curious euphoria flooded the group. A gradual ecstasy flowed through sluggish veins, and Pippa, power-ing the vehicle, felt an orgasm building within her so powerful and intense she could not stop herself; her hand dropped to her groin, felt the flowing wetness between her legs... but instead of the orgasm building into pleasure, it built into—

What did she feel?

It was wrong, a basic wrong, like orgasm in rape, being fucked by a father, molesting a child.

"Get us through this shit!" growled Keenan, panic in his voice, his body shivering violently. "It's fake, a second-hand false experience. Pippa, put your boot to the floor and don't you fucking stop."

They heard Betezh throwing up over the side of the Buggy, and then scrabbling with his blindfold. He grasped the cloth, pulled it free with a cry, opened his eyes, and stared into the surrounding twisted envelopment, into the mesh, a matrix, of the Twisted Proton world.

Betezh screamed, drool ejecting like vomit from between frozen lips. His eyes grew wide, danger-ously wide, and he saw things—bad things—that no human should ever see.

Franco's right hook connected, and dropped Betezh into a well of instant unconsciousness. Franco massaged bruised knuckles as Betezh slipped down to lie, half in, half out of the Buggy's foot-well.

"Good thinking," said Keenan, voice sober.

"I've been waiting ages to do that," said Franco.

Pippa powered the Buggy through the... it felt like treacle, and offered serious resistance to the vehicle. But, with a howling engine and a slipping clutch, she slewed through the matter. After what seemed like hours, but was probably only a few minutes, tyres found purchase on a slippery black slope, and the Buggy lurched free of its elastic prison, wheel-spun up the gradient at 17,000 revs. It leapt like a bird from a cage, soaring through brittle cold air and landing, suspension *clanging* as it bottomed out, and then screaming for a while until Pippa eased free of the accelerator and finally came to a juddering, shuddering halt. She stalled the Buggy with a cough. It clicked violently.

Keenan removed his blindfold, and glanced back at Betezh. The man was slumped, limbs useless, mouth open, eyes open, blood oozing from tear ducts.

"Is he dead?"

Franco checked for a pulse. "No, more's the pity. The maggot has a pulse like a tom-tom played by a fitting epileptic after injecting a cocktail of speedballs and acid."

"Nice simile, Franco." Pippa gave him a full-teeth smile.

Franco beamed. "Thanks."

"It wasn't a compliment, you arse."

"I know that, you pussy."

"Let's get on," said Keenan, rubbing at his thundering temples. Despite not looking at the Twisted Protons, a pounding had come upon him, needles driving into his brain. Even from the edges of peripheral vision, the warped and deviant visual array was affecting him—torturing him—with a visual toxicity.

"What we going to do with him?" Franco pushed Betezh with the tip of his boot.

"Well he's your doctor, you can carry him."

"I'll be bloody buggered if I do!" snorted Franco.

"That can be arranged," said Pippa, with a touch of nastiness to her voice.

"Anyway, what's this third lake called?" asked Franco. "I'm getting sick of this place. I want it done and over, and out of the way so we can get back to the ship and enjoy some sausage."

"The Lake of Desecration," said Emerald.

"How does that work?" said Pippa. "I didn't think there was—or could be—a physical embodiment of... desecration?"

"In this place, anything is possible," said Emerald. Again, her voice was gentle. Her eyes were closed. Her chest heaved with the effort of speech. "This is a place where the evil go to die."

"Like a graveyard?" asked Franco, face illuminating fear.

"More a spiritual resting place," said Emerald, "for those you would consider evil, those who have desecrated life, those who have forfeited the right to an eternal peace."

"So, a bit like Hell, then?" said Franco.

"A lot like Hell," agreed Emerald.

"So," he considered this, rubbing at his hairy chin, "not much money to be made here, then?"

"Only the currency of misery," said Emerald.

Franco grimaced. "I take your point."

THEY CONTINUED ACROSS the rocky, uneven floor, the Buggy thundering, wheels pounding, and slowly the walls started to close in, narrowing from a massive expanse and converging on a point far ahead: a huge, underground inverted V of rock.

"I feel like the walls are closing in," muttered Franco.

"They are."

"I know they are, but I feel like they are as well, up here, in my head." He tapped his skull.

"That's the only thing going on up there," said Pippa caustically.

Franco shrugged, and started rummaging through his pack, sorting out his bombs, his explosives, his timers, his detonation charges. Subtly, he was getting ready for war.

As the walls closed, so too did the light. Darkness fell, closing in on the group and their little Buggy; ahead, an ethereal glow filled the world, and all guessed it was the Lake of Desecration. Pippa slowed their advance, tyres pounding rock, suspension creaking, and finally drew the Buggy to a halt. With the engine rumbling, she climbed out and stood, hands on hips, staring out over the Lake.

They had halted at the tip of the Lake, which stretched off before them, long and narrow. The water was silver, with a hint of a sheen, as if reflecting moonlight. It was perfectly still, glass, a platter of molten metal. Pippa licked her lips.

"There's no way round, or over."

Emerald roused herself, wearily climbed from the Buggy, and stood beside Pippa, staring out over the serenity of the Lake. "No. We must travel by foot from this point."

Franco and Keenan joined them, and Cam came buzzing over to float beside Emerald.

"That's not water," said the little PopBot.

"No," agreed Emerald.

"What is it?" asked Franco.

Emerald gave a small shrug, then swept the group with her bright green eyes. She smiled then, a warm smile, a smile of… not just friendship, but sad friendship.

"You do not have to continue," she said, suddenly, and her eyes closed, fingers coming up to her temples. Something writhed under her skin, like a maggot trying to break free of a black cocoon. She went down on one knee, her whole body tensed like coiled steel, and then it was gone. She released a deep breath, and climbed to her feet.

"I feel weaker than I could believe possible," she said. "It is this place; it saps the soul, draws the spirit. Can you not feel the evil? The evil of the trapped, condemned souls?"

Keenan stepped forward, and glanced down. There was no reflection from the silver surface. He frowned. "I don't feel evil," he said, breath smoking a little. He shivered at the sudden chill. "Come on. How do we cross?"

"The ledges," said Emerald and gestured. Around both sides of the Lake of Desecration narrow channels had been hewn from the rock; they were inches wide, and quite obviously treacherous.

"What happens if we fall in?" said Franco. His voice was wary, brow creased into a frown. He knew shit when he saw it, and he was seeing it right now. He flexed his fingers and licked dry lips.

"You are accepted," said Emerald.

"Meaning?"

"You won't resurface. You will be... consumed."

"Great," snapped Franco. "I suggest we rope ourselves together."

"A brilliant idea," said Pippa, "if only we had some rope."

"You mean you didn't bring any rope?"

"You'll be asking me for a jetpack next."

"You mean you didn't bring the damn jetpack?" Franco slapped Pippa on the back, making her pitch forward and nearly stagger head-first into the Lake. "Only joking, love." He chuckled, and Pippa scowled at him, hand on her sword-hilt.

"Come on," said Keenan. "Let's get it done."

"What about him?" Franco gestured back at Betezh. The man's eyes were open, his breathing ragged.

Keenan shrugged. "There's nothing much we can do for him. Leave him there. We'll pick him up on the way back... if we survive, and if he hasn't died. We certainly can't carry him where we're about to go." Keenan's eyes tracked along the narrow ridge. It was a treacherous traversal alone, never mind attempting to manoeuvre an unconscious and heavy-set man like Betezh.

"Things might come out and... eat him," said Franco, eyes wide.

"And you care?" said Pippa.

Franco shrugged. "I'd kinda hoped I'd be the one to put the finishing touches to him. After all, the fucker kept me drugged up at Mount Pleasant for years. I owe him a little suffering."

"Do it," said Pippa.

"What?"

Pippa drew her Makarov, cocked the weapon, and reached out, offering the gun to Franco. "Shoot him, between the eyes, right now. Here, take my gun. Finish him."

Franco hopped from one sandal to the other. "What? Here?"

"Yeah, Franco, here."

"What, now?"

"Yes!" barked Pippa. "Go on. You said it yourself, you hoped you'd be the one to finish him. Well, I for one don't want him creeping around on my back trail. So shoot him, between the eyes. Bam! Dead."

"But... he's unconscious."

"Your point is?"

"It's hardly sportsmanlike."

"*What?*" Pippa's eyes were gleaming.

"It's just... look at him... laid out like that... I just can't do it. I can't kill a man when he's down. It's just not fair."

"Life's not fair," said Pippa, turning and aiming. Franco cannoned into her, and the gun *cracked*, a bullet whining off to strike sparks from the roof. Pippa gave Franco a cold smile.

"Not like that," said Franco, voice hard. "Leave him. It's not the way to die."

"You're weak," said Pippa.

"I'm human," said Franco. "I ain't no fucking executioner."

"Well then," said Pippa, slipping her Makarov back into its shoulder-holster with a whisper of steel on oiled-leather, "that's where we differ, isn't it, little man?"

EMERALD LED THE way to the lake's edge, her movements still lethargic, but her eyes brighter, as if she sensed an upturn in energy not far ahead. The track started off low and wide, and they stepped onto the rough-hewn path warily, each member of Combat-K reaching out to touch the rough wall and casting eyes down at the flat silver liquid perhaps twenty feet below them.

From its narrow headland, the lake quickly widened, stretching off into a long, almost solid expanse of shimmering opaque rigidity. The group eased along the ledge, which soon narrowed to just a few inches, forcing them to turn flat against the rock wall, hands and bodies pressing tight against the rugged, sandy texture, nostrils smelling damp cold rock, unable to look down for a sudden fear of falling.

"This is fun," moaned Franco, as they edged along. He tried to peer ahead, past Pippa's pack, but could only make out a glitter of silver in his peripheral vision.

"It's not supposed to be fun," snapped Pippa. "It's a means to an end."

They shuffled on, hearts in mouths, sweating, despite the chill that emanated from the Lake of Desecration. Keenan, ahead of both Pippa and Franco, was watching Emerald's lithe easy movements and envying her her agility, but then he remembered how she was far from human, and his envy evaporated. Back on Ket, when she had changed, there had been pain there, infinite suffering that spoke of eternal torment, agony, torture, a depth of pain no human could ever appreciate. Keenan gave a cold smile to the sheer wall before him. *Just stick to being human,* he thought, *there's a good lad.*

Eventually, the path widened a little, and Keenan called a stop. Emerald stood, arms folded, saying nothing, but her body-language emanated impatience. Her lethargy and apparent weakness had gone, evaporated. She had slowly become infused with electricity. She almost seemed to hum.

Keenan wiped sweat from his face, and settled his pack into a tighter, comfier position. He glanced at Pippa, who smiled at him, but her grey eyes hinted at an inner fear. This whole place was claustrophobic; it stank of death. Franco made no attempt to hide his fear, and yet he knew the fear was quite an irrational response; there were no charging monsters, no army with yammering machine guns, just a cold, chilled, unwavering silver platter, and a narrow channel of rock to negotiate. He told himself a thousand times he had been in a thousand more terrible and treacherous situations, but for some reason, this seemed a distillation of all those previous occurrences, as if every other moment of threat to his life had become condensed, and surrounded him with an aura of utmost chilling fear.

"I don't want to go on," said Franco, finally, jiggling from one foot to the other.

"We have to go on," said Pippa, and Keenan nodded. "There's no going back."

"I've got a bad feeling about this." Franco scowled; he was the prophet of doom, and he recognised his insecurity.

"Come on," said Keenan, turning his back and following Emerald out onto the narrow ledge of off-camber stone. He didn't admit it out loud, but he shared Franco's sentiment. He felt that something terrible, bone-seeping, soul-crushing had happened, or was about to happen, in this frightening and sinister place. "Let's move out."

"Just damn bloody great," muttered Franco, and followed like a lamb on a string.

"WAIT!" EMERALD HELD up her hand. The ground began to shake, a gentle tremor at first, which they felt as pulses through their hands pressed against rocky walls, but which built and increased in fierceness, in vigour, in pounding rhythmical beats until it seemed the whole wall, the whole cavern was undergoing a serious seismic upheaval. Combat-K clung to the wall, like limpets, parasites, unable to move, unable—even—to pray.

"What's going on?" shouted Keenan over the pounding rumbling of the rock, but Emerald didn't reply. He glanced back at Pippa's ashen face, then down at the Lake of Desecration, which was perfectly still. He blinked. The silver platter remained, unmoved, without ripples: solid. Keenan would have pointed, but instead clung to the wall for life, fingers digging into cracks, cheek pressing against the chilled surface.

And then... it was gone.

"Look down," hissed Franco.

Still, the Lake was calm: not a movement, no murmur, no disturbance whatsoever.

"That's impossible," said Pippa, quietly.

Then there was a *crack* from high above in the darkness, and they all looked up, flinching as a huge section of rock wall detached. They didn't see it at first, just felt a huge vacuum come into creation. A mass of silence moved slowly, but accelerating... and they squeezed tight against the wall as a chunk of rock the size of a house sailed smoothly past, hit the Lake, and was, effortlessly, tugged under. The silver liquid parted, the rock slid from view, then the silver closed neatly behind it: no ripples, no waves, just...

"Silence," breathed Franco. He was panting. Stones and dust trickled down from above in the wake of the breakage, making him blink and scrabble at his face, rubbing the dust away.

"This is a dangerous place," intoned Emerald, then continued along the ledge.

Keenan paused, looking back at Franco and Pippa. They both grinned at him with the sort of madness he had come—years earlier—to know and love. He laughed.

"Fuck it, but by God this is a bad gig."

"Yeah, you're telling us!" squawked Franco. "If I didn't think it'd bring the roof down, I'd shoot you now, and go home for a nice cuppa tea and a handful of Dicks. Keenan mate, this is shit."

"A handful of Dicks?"

"Green pills, used to 'promote a calm and caring understanding in patients'. Stops them, y'know, going mad."

"Ahh. Come on." Keenan laughed, the tension killed. Rubbing dust from his hair, he led his team further across the narrow ledge, and deeper into the jaws of impending desolation.

THE LAKE OF Desolation was huge; an apparently never-ending stretch of placid silver. They crawled along, the narrow ledge their enemy, the lake beneath them a promise of death. Hours rolled by, and still they edged along, muscles burning, sweat stinging eyes, fingertips screaming and red-raw from scraping and clinging to rock, until, finally, with exhaustion claiming all three members of Combat-K, Emerald abruptly halted up ahead.

"Everything OK?" Keenan's voice was a low drawl, weary from the long crawl across the ledge, weary from the never-ending quest for revenge, weary of life.

"We have a problem."

"What kind of problem?"

"There's a break in the ledge; it looks recent, may have been caused by the tremor. It would appear a wall of rock has crashed down, disintegrating the ledge, and leaving us no continuation of path."

"Is the jump big?"

"I would say ten, twelve feet, but the landing is awkward, requiring dexterity; it will be a tough jump. Can you see round me?"

Keenan moved close, pressing against Emerald, leaning around her. The break in the ledge was treacherous, crumbling, dangerous, and definitely would have been difficult to leap, even with a good run. Keenan chewed his lip, scowling.

"We can't go back." He glanced at Pippa and Franco, then gave a resigned shrug. "We'll have to throw our stuff across, and take the jump one at a time. This looks way too dangerous."

They rested for a few minutes, gathering strength. The cool air chilled them, now their exertions had halted. Keenan removed his pack, and shivered as cold air sent ice down his spine. He glanced down at the Lake of Desecration, and again, shivered, only this time with a sense of foreboding. It was waiting to eat them, waiting to draw them down into some dark and inescapable depth.

"You OK?" said Cam, buzzing by his ear.

"No."

"This place is interfering with my internals."

"Have you discovered anything else about this world being a machine?"

"No. I have exhausted the limit of my technical knowledge."

"What about the power source?"

"Again, Keenan, I am at a loss. The power source of this planet does not make sense; it sucks in energy, and gives very little out. Yet it's there, held in check like some huge battery, or even more precisely, a capacitor storing electrons... A planet core isn't like that. This hasn't happened by accident; it's a creation. Like I said, I feel this place is one huge machine. But it's just wrong; even as a machine, it works wrong."

"Why would it store power?"

"For propulsion? Protection? Attack? Like I said, spin and gravity are incorrect. I'm not seeing something, Keenan, something at work here that is awesomely complex."

"Think on it."

"I am. It is torture!"

Keenan grinned, and winked at the little machine. "You're doing well, Cam. You might even get invited on our next adventure."

"Next adventure?"

Keenan grunted, and watched Emerald prepare for the jump. She stood, unfolding, and as she approached the edge slowly and leapt, twisting, her body perfectly parallel with the rock wall, Keenan knew instinctively that she would make the jump. He also realised that a human body shouldn't twist like that. He gave a teeth smile. Shit, he realised, I could die here.

Emerald landed lightly, balanced, and whirled, one hand reaching out to steady herself.

"Throw the packs, and guns. You need to be as unburdened as possible. This will be hard for you people; the wall curves outwards, bulges, so you must try to twist around the curvature mid-jump."

Keenan nodded, and threw his pack across the chasm. Emerald caught it, and laid it safe; then Keenan passed Pippa and Franco's packs, then their weapons. When all their kit was safe, Keenan spent several minutes studying the jump. Emerald had been right; the rocky wall was curved, bowed outwards, a bulge of distension: fine if you were an acrobat, but for normal mortals?

Keenan grunted again, one hand against the wall, his boots shuffling on the ledge. "Shit. Just do it," he muttered, took several steps back, then surged, and launched himself towards the edge.

He leapt, body almost horizontal, arms outstretched, his form elongated, attempting to curve around the wall. He felt it brush his belly, snagging at his clothes, and his teeth were set in a tight fearful grimace as silver flashed beneath him. His boots cracked rock, but touched down, and he scrabbled for purchase, fighting for balance. For one terrible moment he thought he was going headlong backwards into the lake. Emerald grabbed him, hauled him against the wall, and he stood, panting.

"Thanks."

"Don't mention it. You're better to me alive than dead."

"Ditto."

Pippa came next. Without pause she took several steps and leapt, body graceful, spine arching, and landed lightly—in perfect poise—on the opposite ledge. A few loose stones fell, tumbling down, end over end, swallowed. Pippa gave a tight smile, then turned, and gestured to Franco.

"Come on."

"I don't know about this," he grumbled.

"Come on."

"That's a big jump for a little fella like me."

"Just do it, Franco."

Grumbling and mumbling, he back-tracked along the ledge, then turned and narrowed his eyes. He felt his heartbeat quicken. Palpitations thundered through him, through his heart, drumbeats in his veins, in his head, in his soul.

"Bugger."

With sweat-slippery hands he ran, a curious crab-like sideways sprint along the narrow ledge with eyes squinting and lips tight and teeth grating and grinding. He reached the edge, reached out, reached out for life and sanctuary and felt himself detach from the rock path, sail through the air and twist as he had seen the others twist, but he knew as he left the rocky anchor that he wasn't going to make it. Franco's jaw worked, a snarl leapt across his face and he stretched out stretched for life and land and the wonderful beautiful paradise of rock that lay just a few feet in front of him. He watched, wide-eyed, as if in detached stop-motion and saw the look of realisation on Pippa's face. He saw her sprint, leaping, her belly scraping rock as her arms stretched towards him and his twisted disjointed flight and their fingers connected, slid in a mesh of slippery sweat and tight black gloves and *wham* Pippa's hands connected, closing tight. Franco swung down and slammed into the rock wall and rebounded, grunting, all air knocked from him. His face smashed against the rock and stars fluttered in his eyes as he realised—as he felt—the sweat from his hands, bleeding through their contact and...

He started to slide from Pippa's grip.

He gazed up into her eyes.

"Franco!" she hissed, panicked.

"I should have worn my gloves," he scowled.

"Franco! Climb up me!"

But he was sliding, slipping and could feel their bodies and hands moving inexorably apart. Pippa's grip was iron but it was not enough. Franco's boots scrabbled against the rocky wall, body twisting squirming seeking purchase and life but fingers glided and parted and Franco was kicked backwards eyes still connected to Pippa's in an umbilical, forcing them into a final terrifying union. He saw the shock slam her face with realisation and understanding and he smiled. He gave her a final smile, and there were tears in her eyes. His smile said, "It's OK. I'll be OK."

Franco hit the Lake of Desecration. It parted with icy precision and he was sucked down and under and vanished instantly. The silver platter eased lazily together. It knitted perfectly, becoming a solid sheet of glass gloss.

Franco was gone.

CHAPTER 18
THE SENTINELS

"No!" SCREAMED PIPPA, lurching forward with a useless grasp, as Keenan grabbed her belt, and hauled her back. She fell into his arms, head against his chest, eyes closed, weeping. Keenan leant, peered over the side of the chasm. Thirty feet below, the silver gave no indication it had just eaten their friend; complacent light glittered from a blank surface.

"Son of a bitch," snarled Keenan.

"We must move," said Emerald. "There is more seismic activity; I can feel it building. This ledge gets more dangerous with every passing second."

Keenan whirled, eyes meeting those emerald orbs. He saw her lack of empathy, her lack of compassion, and understood her status. She might appear human, but there was no humanity in her alien skull.

Keenan and Pippa moved up and down the ledge, calling out for Franco. Minutes passed, a few minutes ticked over into ten minutes, twenty, and he did not resurface. There was no movement on the Lake of Desecration. It had him, held him, ate him, body and soul.

Eventually, Emerald touched Keenan's shoulder. There was a painful urgency about her, like a junkie needing a fix. "We must go," she said. "He is dead. The Lake has him; there is no escape."

"I can't believe it," said Pippa, her cheeks still wet with tears. "He's gone. He's dead."

Keenan simply nodded. His face was grey, lips cruelly compressed. "Let's go," he said, and crouching, transferred many of Franco's bombs to his own pack. Then, with an exhalation of frustration, of anger, of sadness, of loss, he tossed the flapping, useless sack into the glittering silver below.

He didn't stop to watch it sink.

ANOTHER HALF HOUR of torturous edging along the narrow rocky path saw an end to the Lake of Desecration. The ledge took a sharp drop, which Emerald, Keenan and Pippa leapt, boots cracking against the rocky floor. Then both remaining members of Combat-K glanced back towards the broad plate, shimmering opaquely behind them.

"The bastard," said Keenan.

Pippa nodded, shouldered her stuff, and set off across the narrow platform in pursuit of Emerald. Again the ledge dropped, the roof came down, and walls closed in, until they were in a tunnel large enough to take a FukTruk. Then, suddenly the floor ended, dropping away into darkness. Emerald stepped off the edge, landing lightly ten feet down, and Combat-K followed her down what were, to all intents and purposes, huge steps blasted from the tunnel floor. They descended fifty of these huge steps, each one lurking just beyond the edge of darkness, and testing a person's faith in the unknown, until they finally dropped from the last step into an ankle-deep sludge of viscous fluid. Keenan stooped, and sniffed his fingers.

"Smells like bad oil."

"The Woods of Mekkra," said Emerald, gesturing broadly with her hand. As their eyes adjusted to the gloom, both Keenan and Pippa had a growing awareness of an esoteric scene spread before them. Huge metal trees hugged the edge of vision, twisted sculptures of iron and steel, titanium and lead, their trunks thick slabs gleaming dark with oil, their branches angular and irregular, bone-like titans searing away from severed trunks like the disjointed limbs of diseased alien behemoths. Keenan walked forward, Pippa close behind, their eyes taking in the massive sweep at the edge of the woods. The metal trees hugged their vision, their vista, spreading away in a mammoth tangle of angular wire branches. None of the trees had leaves, but metal detritus covered the synthetic woodland floor, a carpet of needles and splinters, of tangled wire and broken bars. It was a surreal vision, all bathed in a gleam of oil, and Keenan found himself blinking, holding his injured ribs, his mouth a dark crease, as his eyes tried to focus and find a path through this insane jungle of metal. A smell wafted up to greet them. It reminded Keenan of old engines, leaking engines, machinery, factories, black stains on his hands, oil in his hair. It made him shiver, remembering old times, remembering bad times.

Emerald came up behind them; her eyes seemed to glow.

"Our last obstacle," she said, so close her breath tickled Keenan's ear.

"It looks difficult to penetrate."

"There... things living inside."

"What kinds of things?" asked Pippa.

"Creatures of metal, machines. They are sentinels. They protect this place. They will not appreciate intrusion."

"We have to cut through the centre?"

"I know of a path, of sorts. It is a seam through the centre, holding the metal woods together. You need to keep your guns and bombs primed, and your wits about you. To sleep here is to die."

"Will our weapons work against these sentinels?"

"The creatures here are extremely hardy. Let us simply hope bullets are deterrent enough. Follow me."

Shouldering packs, Keenan and Pippa followed Emerald along the edges of the metal woods. Trees spread before them, dark and oozing evil. The smell grew stronger, hot oil, shards and shavings, filling their senses with a cloying aroma that made them sick to their very stomachs.

All the way along this impenetrable smash of woodland they saw things moving, scampering, half-witnessed visions, fleeting glimpses: the shake of a branch, a hollow squeal of twisted tubing, metal claws raking barbed wire, the rhythmical splash of dripping oil.

"Here."

The woods opened, a dark narrow gash winding off into the interior. It was awesomely dark, and a fearsome cold wind blew from deep inside. "It's like a creature," said Pippa, shivering, and pushing close to Keenan. Unconsciously, his arm circled her shoulders, and they stood there, intruders, feeling alien and out of their depth. With the ice wind came doubt, and with the doubt, a loss of self-belief.

"The belly of the beast," agreed Emerald. "You need to focus your strength. This place is not for the faint of heart. Part of the design brief was to instil terror and insecurity into the hearts and minds of any who would come here. After all, it guards a terrible prize."

"Design brief?" Keenan raised his eyebrows.

"Yes. I designed this place. I created it."

"So you will be safe?"

"I never envisaged having to breach it without my powers, without, shall we say, my natural armour. I am not the creature I was; I am weak, and I am frail. They may not be able to kill me, but the sentinels that lurk here could spin webs, entrap me, drag me down into deep metal burrows, and lock me away for a million years. The Woods of Mekkra are a place of suffering, of torture, of torment. Keenan, my advice to you is that anything that looks dangerous, is dangerous. If in doubt, kill it."

Keenan gave a thin smile. He unstrapped a heavy D5 shotgun from his back, and started to fill the chambers with quad-blast compact shells; it could hold eighty. Then, snapping the weapon together and stowing away his MPK, he gave a single discreet nod. "No problem," he said.

THE PATH ALLOWED only single-file movement, and the trees closed in tightly around them, razor branches slicing at faces and WarSuits, which buzzed softly on impact. Tangled wire gathered and squirmed around their ankles, attempting to trip the group. Emerald led the way, with Pippa at the centre, her eyes desolate and filled with an uneasy, growing horror; and Keenan followed at the rear. Cam said he would make himself useful and scout ahead; he zipped up the dark path and, within seconds, had disappeared.

"I hope his sensors and weapons work," said Emerald. She turned, glancing over her shoulder, eyes connecting with Keenan's pale weary face.

"He's a tough cookie," said Keenan.

"Yes, but the machines here: if their hatred is measured on a scale of one to ten, and we are like annoying insects to them, irritants, down near number one: soft flesh merely to be punctured and sheared and parted. Well, machines, other machines, and especially sentient machines intruding will explode from the top of the scale."

"Why?" said Pippa, voice unnaturally quiet.

"It is not something I developed, but something the sentinels here acquired. They seek to protect their self-awareness. They view other sentient machines as a massive threat."

"So, they're likely to attack Cam with a vengeance?"

"I guarantee it," said Emerald.

Darkness flooded the world like blood oil. The metal trees rustled softly, metal on metal, razors on glass; the creaking of branches was the cracking of tubes; the rustle of twigs was like a slow bending of metal panels, a crackling of foil, a denting of armour.

They moved deeper inside, and became aware they were being watched. Sometimes, eyes gleamed within the depths of the woods, pale ovals of silver or steel, unblinking, surveying the group from a modest distance: gauging, watching, evaluating.

"It comes," said Emerald.

They heard it, claws raking the metal pathway, and Keenan whirled, eyes hooded, tongue darting to moisten dry lips as his shotgun came up, and he made ready. It leapt, in huge bone-jarring bounds down the path. It was long and sleek, with scales like ridged metal armour; it resembled a large cat, but with a corrugated body like a caterpillar. Huge jaws dripped black oil. Pale eyes were fixed, and a low rumbling, a growl of engines, preceded it, as it bounded for the attack.

Keenan stood his ground, as the large creature bore down on him, smashing through metal branches, slamming aside razor twigs. Keenan lifted his D5 shotgun, felt Pippa cowering behind him, and pumping the weapon, he stared into metal eyes and saw a reflection of fear in those multi-faceted orbs.

He pulled twin triggers, and saw the creature flinch, veering to one side and stumbling, as the high-velocity shells slammed its head. Keenan sprinted towards it, shotgun still booming as he fired shot after shot into the metal beast, and it squealed, an inhuman sound, rolling to its back and slamming against the trees under the onslaught of violent shells. Legs kicked, the body undulated with a sound of tearing metal, and Keenan was there, his boot on its throat and the shotgun's barrel's against its face. Those eyes stared up at Keenan, pleading. He hesitated. Oil gleamed, dripping from long, slightly curved fangs.

"Keenan!" screamed Pippa, and instinctively he pulled both triggers, jerked back by the recoil, and only then saw a long tail hovering behind him, a sting the size of a fist dripping black-tar toxins. The shells at such close contact slammed a hole through the machine's head. The body started to spasm, twitching, and tiny white sparks of electricity discharged up and down its scales.

Keenan turned, and saw Emerald watching him. She gestured to the trees. Thousands of eyes were watching from the dark confines. Keenan shivered.

"A test?"

"Yes. Come on. We must increase our speed. Can you run?"

"You bet," snarled Keenan, as Pippa placed her hand flat against his cheek and gazed into his eyes.

"You did well."

"I killed it."

"Didn't you feel it? The pull of its eyes? It tried to hypnotise you… it certainly did me. I was immobilised, paralysed. You have a stronger mind than you think, Keenan. It couldn't hook you."

"So their weapons run deeper than simple tooth and claw. I'm beginning to lose my sense of humour with this place."

"I lost mine years ago," said Pippa bleakly.

THE SURREAL EYES in the darkness of the metal foliage stayed on Combat-K as they moved further and further into the Woods of Mekkra. They travelled in silence for a while, with only the sound of their boots clumping the metal pathway as it twisted and turned. Emerald did not speak. She seemed filled with purpose, with a jiggling energy after her previous display of weakness. After a while, sickened by the oppressiveness and claustrophobia of the place, Pippa glanced back at Keenan, his face drawn and grim, both hands gripping his shotgun like a totem.

"Talk to me, Kee."

"What about?"

"Anything. This place is driving me slowly insane."

"I can't believe Franco is dead. He was… more than a brother to me. I've had friends before, you know the score; people come and go, moving in and out of your life; friendships blossom and friendships die. Sometimes you have to be brutal, when somebody close betrays you, attacks you, brutalises you… but Franco, Franco was different.

Franco was a lodestone. Franco was not just the man of the moment, but a man to walk the mountains with." Keenan sank into a sullen silence.

"You know," said Pippa, "on occasions, by God, he wound me up like a spring. He knew exactly which buttons to press, exactly which dials to turn, but I always understood that it was little Franco being the pain in the arse he always was. I think, when I was back on Five Grey Moons, on *Hardcore*, I always knew you guys were alive. I knew you were OK, you could look after yourselves. And, despite our differences, Keenan, I did think about you, did care about you, but now, seeing Franco die like that, it was... shattering."

"You don't realise what you've got until you've lost it." Keenan's voice was quiet. He was picturing, in his mind's eye, a universe in which his little girls hadn't died; they'd grown, matured, gone to university, met fine young men, borne healthy robust children who would call him Grandpa...

Cut short. Cut dead.

"It's funny," said Pippa, "the number of missions we've been on. We've faced terrible odds on a multitude of occasions... and yet, deep down, I knew, knew that we would pull through. I think somehow I developed an immortality complex. We couldn't be beat. We'd dive in, get the job done, get the motherfuck away. Franco's death has... changed me."

"Me too," said Keenan. He sighed. "I feel my whole life has become... pointless. I seek—ultimately—an empty goal. I've considered it, a few times, wondered what drives me, because it can only be something dancing along the edge of sanity."

"I thought revenge meant everything to you," whispered Pippa. She stopped, on the metal path in the metal woods. Eyes blinked at her from a surrounding metal mayhem.

Keenan shrugged. "What will it achieve? Will I feel any better? Will it bring my family back?"

"No," said Pippa. Her voice was a wind-blown whisper. "We could always stop, stop right now, turn away from here, backtrack, and leave this place, this horror, this world. We could go somewhere, somewhere the war didn't touch, somewhere beautiful. We could raise our own family, Keenan. We could begin again."

"No. We've come too far."

"You can never go too far, Keenan."

He shrugged, and grinned, a sudden boyish grin. "Anyway, we're fucked now. There's no easy way out of this shit, and I don't think our ancient friend over there would take kindly to us suddenly reneging on the deal. She says she can give me the name of the killer. Well," he took a deep breath, "despite misgivings, it's something I will have to do."

Pippa touched his arm. "This information, it might get you killed," she said, concern glittering in her grey eyes.

"Then so be it," growled Keenan.

THEY CAUGHT EMERALD up swiftly, just in time to hear the sounds of running water, or, to be more precise, a running but sluggish fluid. The trees stopped on a vicious sharp metal overhang to reveal a wide, fast-flowing tributary of oil. The oil was thick brown, just transparent enough to reveal a menagerie of scattered objects: razors, knives, blades, spikes, on the river bed. Anyone attempting to cross would cut their feet to bloody ribbons.

"You see the stepping stones?" said Emerald.

Both Keenan and Pippa squinted, then picked out the tiny oasis of protruding metal: slick, slippery, but a weaving meandering path across the fast-flowing obstacle.

"Looks dangerous," said Pippa.

"It is, especially the fish."

"Fish?"

Emerald nodded. "Machine piranha, deadly. Can strip you to the bone in about five seconds, consume your bones in ten. If you fall in, you've got a five percent chance of getting out; I advise we proceed with caution."

Keenan and Pippa nodded.

The jagged near-vertical bank was slippery, and they slithered their way down to the edge of the river. Keenan continually looked around for Cam, but the little PopBot hadn't returned.

"You worried about him?"

"The fool got himself filled with explosives the last time he went on a jaunt."

"He'll be OK."

Keenan gave a negative grunt, then stared out at the fifty-foot wide expanse. The oil bubbled and churned, gushing between metal stumps that barely rose above the oil level.

"I'm starting to really hate this place," he said.

"At least you're still alive."

"I will go first," said Emerald. Her black skin seemed to glow, manifest in a vision of human health; even her hair shone, curls filled with a vitality that Combat-K had never before witnessed. Emerald was gradually changing, becoming more powerful, more alive the closer they moved to The Factory. Keenan welcomed the change. In his eyes, the stronger and more powerful Emerald became, the more likely she would be to furnish him with information, with a focus for revenge. Pippa, however, gave an internal shiver. Something about Emerald shimmered at the verge of insanity and suspicion; Emerald gave Pippa just a hint of the creeps.

Emerald stepped out onto the first metal stump. Then, in an incredible show of athleticism, she moved with great speed, her body low and sleek, leaping from one to the other, movements precise until she landed, lightly, on the opposite scooped bank.

Keenan glanced at Pippa.

"You next."

"Cheers."

"You've got more chance of making it across. If I... don't, find out that name for me, and execute the living piece of shit. Can you do that? For me? For one who loves you?"

"I will try my best," said Pippa, voice husky, eyes dropping to the floor. She released his hands, turned, and leapt onto the first stump. She slid with a sickening lurch on the slick greasy surface; and exhaled with a hiss. She half-turned, and grinned at Keenan. "It's damn slippery up here."

"Be careful, girl."

Keenan watched, heart in mouth, as Pippa leapt from one metal stump to the next, her balance refined, arms outstretched a little, her face a Picasso of concentration. She finally made it, touching down on the jagged metal shore, boots sliding, and finally sitting down with a thump. She looked over at Keenan, and he gave her a little wave, but something in her face, an integral horror, made him freeze. She was not looking at him, but behind him, past him and through him.

Without wanting to, Keenan turned.

The metal ridgeline was lined with sentinels, metal wolves, monsters, strange spindly things a hybrid of cockroach and spider. They stood, arraigned in observation, unmoving, except for pale metal eyes that blinked.

Keenan drew in a sharp breath... as the metal horde charged, leaping and howling with metal screams, rampaging down the steep bank as Keenan turned back, stumbled, and leapt out over the fast-flowing oil. His boots hammered from one metal mushroom to the next in a sprint born of panic. He slipped many times, nearly pitching into the oil river, but by some miracle of luck and blind panic he landed next to Pippa, and turned, teeth bared, glaring at the creatures of the woods. They had lined the opposite bank, and seemed almost to be swaying.

"They want you," said Emerald.

"Yeah, well fuck 'em."

"They like you," she said.

Keenan pumped his shotgun. He aimed across the river of oil, and smashed a volley of shells on trajectories of fire. Several machines were caught, hammered backwards, limbs flailing, and slack shattered jaws yapping, armour dented, eyes buckled. Metal screams tore the air, and the machines joined in, tongues flickering: a rising ululating cry that sang and grew in the gloomy subdued vault. It seemed to circle above the group like a live thing: a beast of electric and violence.

Pippa covered her ears, face condensed in pain.

The machines halted their noise, turned, and leapt nimbly back up the torn metal bank. Within a second they were gone.

"What an awful sound," hissed Pippa.

"It is a war cry," said Emerald. She was sombre. Her eyes shone with a new need. "The hunt has been initiated; the game has begun. We need to move and move fast. There are other ways across this torrent."

Keenan clasped his shotgun tight. "Let them come," he said.

THE PATH GREW much wider, and Emerald increased their pace, almost leaping ahead in a loping run. Keenan and Pippa sprinted to keep up, and Keenan was soon coughing and wheezing, sweat bathing him, his snarl a constant on a face of pain and suffering.

"Too many cigarettes," Pippa said.

"Yeah, thanks for the medical advice. If I want a damned nurse I'll visit a hospital."

"Just trying to help."

"Well don't. I know my bad habits and I'm willing to live with them."

They made better time, but the wide path made Keenan uneasy. On a narrow path he could hold back the machines with the animal bark of the shotgun; here, it would be much harder, much easier for an enemy to flank him, not a thought he relished.

Something howled in the distance.

They ran for what seemed like hours, moving through the sweeping smash of metal woodland, and then a hot-oil smell came to them, and Emerald abruptly stopped. There was a circular clearing ahead, and Emerald seemed to pause, wary. Keenan and Pippa readied weapons, primed for trouble. Keenan glanced around the clearing; the floor was a detritus of metal shavings, wafer-thin metal discs and scattered iron rods mingled with the gleam and glint of razor blades. The path ended, then continued on the opposite side of the woodland. Keenan frowned, something had created this space, but for what purpose? The only answer he could think of was that it was a killing ground. It didn't inspire hope.

"We've got to cross it," said Pippa.

"It's a trap," said Keenan. He glanced at Emerald. "Where are they? And what are they?"

Before she could answer, they were there, leaping from hiding places in the dense metal woodland, scuttling and soaring twenty feet into the air with spindly metal legs bending, small oval bodies—battered and dented—pulsing with energy and scatters of light as...

Go on, thought Keenan with a bitter taste in his mouth. *Say it...*

As the *spiders* flew above and around in great leaps, perhaps twenty of the machines, sailing over the group with tiny metal teeth chattering and clashing. Keenan's shotgun *boomed,* smashing a creature from the air in a flail of thin wire limbs and a splash of hot oil. Pippa's MPK roared, bullets whining, tracer flashing and lighting up the dark woodland. A spider landed on Emerald, and she ripped it apart with her hands. The body trailed wires, sparking electricity, as Keenan's D5 boomed again and again. The MPK cut holes through metal and everything seemed to happen so fast, in a confusion of moving metal, bullets, clashing teeth and a metal drone that cut through the scene. Keenan ducked a slash of razor talons, slamming the stock of the shotgun into one of the machines, and as it fell his boot pinned it to the ground. Twin barrels touched its casing. Dark eyes coated in a film of thin oil watched him with dazzling intelligence. The shotgun roared and the spider machine disintegrated in fire and shrapnel as something slammed Keenan's back. He felt legs wrap around him and the shotgun was lifted from him, like sweets from a child, and snapped easily in half as he hit the ground hard. He was smothered by thrashing metal wire, encased in an alloy coffin, and he fought and struggled but there was nothing to punch or kick and it spun him in a web of thin trailing wire which cut into his damaged WarSuit and through the exposed flesh of his wrists, neck and forehead, leaving droplets of blood spattering against the shavings on the ground. Keenan was lifted, then slammed down hard. Jarred, stunned, he was blind for a few moments as unconsciousness teased him. He coughed up phlegm mixed with blood from a broken tooth, and spat into a hazy reflection an inch from his hammered face. He strained, and looking right, he saw Pippa entangled in wires, and Emerald as well. They were all caught and spun and wrapped like wriggling fish on hooks. Keenan spat blood again, and watched the machines moving purposefully around the three cocoons, finally congregating on Emerald. Suddenly, limbs punched out, smashing her head again and again, and again, beating her with sodden solid thumps. Keenan looked away, sure they would crack her skull in half. Instead, her eyes closed and her body shuddered, but she continued to breathe. They were hauled across the clearing and into the close-packed metal trees; bumped along the ground, through tangles of wire and into a frightening stinking darkness.

"Keenan," he heard Pippa cry. There was a *crack,* and she was quiet.

He tried to focus on direction, but it was impossible in the gloom, weaving and bumping through an insane tangle of branches and trunks, through intense brutal metal scenery that added up to nothing less than total confusion. The air grew strong with the stench of hot oil. Keenan found it hard to breathe.

They came to another clearing, larger but more tangled, and filled with perhaps a thousand spidery machines. Their eyes glowed, and they scuttled about purposefully, wiry legs bending and stretching, tiny teeth chattering and filling the air with a sound not unlike rainfall.

Grimly, Keenan realised there was no escape, no way out. Even if he managed to throw off the thin razor wires, which bound him and converted him to an unmoving block of flesh, what then? How could he fight a thousand of the things?

The machines had realised, understood, what Emerald was. The threat she represented, carried in her soul like a disease: the unleashed, unrealised power of a returning, regenerating Kahirrim.

For whatever reason, they had neutralised her.

Keenan shuddered as three of the machines stalked towards him with rhythmical steps, and with glittering eyes, without remorse, without understanding, without empathy, they looked down at him, paused, watching him, and delivered a devastating blow that spun his head and sent him reeling down into darkness, and a world where he would drown in blood and oil.

CHAPTER 19
FACTORY FLOOR

HE SNUGGLED UNDER a fresh duvet, inhaling lavender and the musk of sleep and last night's sex. He turned, cuddling into the welcoming flesh of Freya's back. She mumbled a purr, a growl of awakening necessity, and turned to him, nuzzling him, and rubbing him. Her tongue slid into his mouth, her legs lifting, encircling him, toes teasing down his calf as their bodies pressed hard together and the tease lingered with a tantalising agony. Then the bedroom door burst open in a whirlwind of young girls slamming in, screaming and giggling, "It's Christmas mummy. Daddy it's Christmas get up get up get up!"

KEENAN BLINKED AND tasted blood. His mind clattered like an aged machine. Memories drifted idly as he lay, face down, staring at shards of shattered steel. *Shattered. Just like my past*, he thought. *Just like my life.*

"Keenan."

The voice was a gentle whisper, the tickle of a blade on a victim's neck. Keenan blinked and felt a great and terrible fury rise within him. He would not roll over and die. He would not suffer this indignity, this punishment, this fucking pathetic weakness.

"Keenan!"

He grunted an acknowledgement, eyes burning fire, and strength flooded him. He turned his head. Cam was there, dull black and unmoving. "I thought they'd eaten you."

"Listen very carefully," said Cam. Grey lights flickered. He was silent for a while. Keenan stared at the PopBot. "There is some sort of war raging down here, between the machines, the sentinels: a civil war, a split, a divide; and the others, those hunting you, are about to arrive."

"Cam, I..."

"Wait! We have only seconds. I have spoken to Emerald and Pippa; they are ready. When the avalanche falls, I will cut through your bonds, but the wires are deep, slicing your flesh Keenan. I'll be honest, my friend, it's going to hurt, and hurt bad."

Keenan nodded. "We lost our weapons, but we still have our packs under this... web, wire, whatever: more guns... bombs." He smiled darkly. "I'm feeling the need for some fucking payback."

"Not a time to fight." Cam was agitated. "This is a time to run. Keenan, trust me; if you had seen what I've seen..."

"And what have you seen?"

"This place is huge. It is big, vast, and filled with thousands upon thousands of these damn machines, these sentinels. The creators of this place did not want infiltration."

"It seems an elaborate way to go about stopping unwanted visitors."

"No, Keenan. It's an equilibrium, a balance of metal and machines. It was designed to last a billion years... machines feeding on machines, a constant rejuvenation, fed by the most incredible power source I have ever come across."

"What's at the core?" whispered Keenan.

"Here they come. Brace yourself!"

Gleaming stalks of metal roared through the silence making a sound like a tidal wave hissing and surging. The horizon became a vista filled with charging buzzing chittering metal monsters, insects and lizards. The iron woodland around Keenan teemed with thousands of spider-machines, screeching and clattering, and came alive as the two hosts rushed one another, clashing with a sonic steel boom that reverberated through the ground. Keenan squinted, but saw only a blur of moving metal, as if he was staring down into a whirling turbine. Everything was too fast for him to see; he could only hear and feel a vast ocean flowing over him with a brutal caress.

There was a *buzz*. Keenan bit his tongue on a yelp. Wire glowed and fell away. More buzzes sparked from Cam, and within a few seconds Keenan was rubbing at his wrists, his throat, and his scored and punctured face, hands coming away with flakes of dried blood. Then, Cam was gone, and Keenan crawled after him. Twenty feet away a battle raged. Something hot scythed over Keenan's head making him duck, and rattled off among the trees. Screeches hurt his ears. Metal raped metal, bars hammered bars, gears ground and cogs whirred, and Pippa and Emerald crouched beside him, their faces a hideous criss-cross of wounds. Cam led them, bobbing ahead like a tiny silent ghost, away from the flurry and insanity of battle, down a narrow slope filled with grease, and under exposed metal tree roots as thick as a man's waist. They clambered over serrated knife branches, cursing, and slipping and sliding through a mire of metal waste.

It took them long, long minutes to pick up their previous pathway, but Cam took them through the tangled woodland, his direction unerring, and only when they stepped onto what they perceived as their immediate salvation did they halt, Keenan and Pippa sweating and panting heavily. Emerald was cool, controlled, her eyes fixed with a bright but furious focus.

Keenan un-shouldered his pack, and pulled free a variety of guns and bombs. He also checked his MPK for damage; despite a battering and scratching and scuffing, the weapon was still true. Pippa, however, had lost her automatic weapon. She consoled herself by grasping two powerful Makarov pistols.

"It's not far to the Shrine," said Emerald. "There we can perform the Shift, and the machines won't be able to pursue. They are not designed to enter The Factory."

"Will I be able to follow?" said Cam.

Emerald gave a short shake of her head. "No sentient machines are permitted there; the Shift is an impossibility." Cam remained silent, but Keenan could sense the PopBot's frustration.

"Come on," he growled, then glanced over his shoulder. The cacophony of the warring creatures had dimmed; the metal screeches and bangs had diminished. "When they realise we've escaped—"

"They'll come after us," finished Pippa.

They started to run, sweat pouring down their faces. Emerald and Cam took the lead, and Keenan and Pippa ran side by side, metal trees flashing past them, the air hot, humid, and stinking of hot metal and oil, filling their senses with a cloying perfume of dead machinery. Behind them, the fighting seemed to have ceased; several deafening *booms* echoed across the Woods of Mekkra. Then, at the edge of hearing, a skittering chattering noise could be heard, like the gnashing of billions of teeth, the spinning of heavy gears, and the grinding of metal into paste. The noise increased in pace, growing louder and louder.

Pippa glanced behind, but Keenan grabbed her, forcing her on. "Don't look back," he barked, and they increased their pace down the weaving metal pathway. Suddenly the trees ended and there was a hill, a perfect hummock from a single cast of steel. It rose before them like a giant teardrop from the eye of a metal god, shining softly: a beacon, a promise, a tease.

Emerald bounded easily up the steep incline, and Keenan and Pippa followed, hands and feet scrabbling at the slippery, burnished steel slope. Behind, the noise of the pursuing machines had risen to a crescendo, a clashing jarring mash of metal music... which stopped.

Keenan glanced back. They were at the foot of the hill: thousands upon thousands of sentinels, metal bodies, metal claws, gnashing metal teeth. They bled oil, and salivated grease. Copper smeared their joints, and silver paste glittered on scaled metal tongues. The machines charged as one host. With a scream that built and echoed and boomed, they leapt from the Woods of Mekkra to the foot of the steel hillside. Keenan fired wildly behind him, the MPK spitting fire and glowing bullets. Machines went down, tumbling, trampled by allies. Hot oil spurted into the air. Severed pipes hung like severed arteries, but it made no difference to the mass. They came on with a roar so loud it drowned out Creation.

"I can't go on," wept Pippa, her mad uphill sprint dying.

Keenan dragged her roughly along. Ahead, Emerald and Cam had reached a square, black platform. Keenan glanced back, grunted, and emptied twenty bullets into the face of a reptilian metal cat. Shards of alloy twisted back, peeling open like a flower and the beast tumbled back down the metal hillside, and rolled away, to be trampled under claws.

Pippa stumbled. Keenan whirled, hurling grenades into their midst. Then they were running, and explosions rocked the metal world. Creatures were flung upwards and outwards, living shrapnel, limbs torn and bodies shred. Jaws snapped at heels. Pippa powered alongside Keenan with grim determination, sword in hand, the blade a single gleaming molecule.

Keenan felt the weight of mass behind him, and imagined more than felt hot breath down his collar, knowing that death was a microsecond away. He opened fire again until the MPK clicked with a dead man's bone rattle. *A few more steps,* he thought, *a few more pain-filled steps to sanctuary and haven and...*

Something slammed his back. He went down and rolled, coming up and lashing out to crush metal with hard bone knuckles. He lashed out left and right, smashing fists into metal faces. Beside him, Pippa was hammering her sword in a glittering arc, slicing heads from torsos and limbs from trunks, and for a split second the beasts halted their charge in the face of this joint ferocity. Then, together they sprinted for the platform. New jagged cuts and fresh blood streaked Keenan's face, from razor claws. The two remaining members of Combat-K slumped at Emerald's feet, defeated.

The metal beasts spread out, silently, surrounding the platform. Keenan could smell their hot oil stink like fetid breath. He blinked a lazy blink, reached into a pocket, and with shaking fingers lit a bedraggled home-rolled cigarette. Smoke plumed. He laughed a manic laugh. "Shit," he said.

The creatures bunched, tensed, and Keenan continued to laugh his crazy laugh as Emerald raised pulsing hands above her head.

Electric lightning flickered and discharged in thundering bursts around them, smashing creatures into puddles of molten metal. Keenan and Pippa stared at Emerald, and in the blue flickers and white flashes, beyond the cracks and thumps of raw energy flowing from dark vaults above her tensed body, her frame flickered skeletal and she was, without a shadow of a doubt, inhuman.

With a gathering roar, the sentinels charged.

EVERYTHING SPUN IN great, lazy circles. Colours wafted gently in and out of focus, concentric rings of pastel shades overlapping, interloping, criss-crossing and mixing like smoke. Pain came, pulsing in parallel to the rings of colour, the bands of shade and the cacophony of beauty and agony. He felt his fingers twitch, like the first jolts of electric shock therapy. Spasms made his fingers dance, although he couldn't see them. He felt them, though, jerking and twitching, the tendons in the backs of his hands pulsating and writhing agonisingly like eels in grease. These uncontrollable rhythms moved up his arms and he wanted to scream but couldn't control his lungs. He felt his heartbeat quicken, drumming like thunderous applause in his inner mind, and soon—he had no concept of time, so it could have been seconds, could have been a thousand years—every muscle and tendon in his body was twitching, writhing and coiling, and he was sure his body must be spastically jerking, an epileptic fit without the epilepsy.

His eyes flared open, body shooting up into a sitting position.

Betezh coughed up a ball of phlegm the size of his fist, and watched it roll and nestle greasily in his lap. "Ugh," he muttered, and wriggled from under his own organic produce until it slopped into the footwell of the Buggy. He looked around, head muggy, wondering where he was, what he'd been doing, and... and...

Events flooded back, from the distant drifting memory of Franco's escape from Mount Pleasant, right up to the ejaculation of his mind by the Proton Lake. A wooden tongue probed lead-lined walls, and Betezh spat a few times on the rocky ground outside the Buggy. Then he crawled around until he located a bottle of water. He took one long, long drink, and then another. He emptied the bottle, and tossed it aside. *Where is everybody?* he wondered idly.

Betezh climbed tentatively from the vehicle, his limbs like elastic. He placed his hand on the bonnet, and the engine was still warm, but not hot. So, how long had he been out? And why had they left him? Then he saw the answer, his eye catching the narrow pathway worming its way around the Lake of...

What had they called it?

The Lake of Desecration.

He laughed weakly, glanced at the Buggy, and wondered at his options: ahead, around the narrow path? Or should he take the Buggy and head back through the Lake of Protons? Betezh shuddered. He'd rather eat his own vomit than face that again. In fact, he probably already had.

Anyway, even if he managed to get back, he'd have a lot of obstacles to overcome. And, if he reached the Gunship alive, would he be able to pilot it from the mine-riddled atrocity that was Teller's World?

"Son of a bitch," he muttered. He staggered weakly to the rear of the Buggy, and lifted the boot. He rummaged inside, past all manner of accumulated crap: spare wheel, Buggy jack, a box filled with electronic components trailing wires, an ice axe, a can of WD40. Betezh found a satchel, oil-stained, but still a satchel. "They've bloody left me here with nothing," he moaned. He lifted the ice axe and looked at it: a good weapon, but not exactly a sub-machine gun. Placing the axe to one side, he rummaged again. He found some old tins of what looked like army rations, and again what looked like camping implements. Betezh grimaced, teeth grinding. "Why me?" he asked the silent cavernous vault. "Why do I always get the bum gig? What is it? God's eternal joke? Oh, there's Betezh, he seems to be doing OK, let's fuck his life up in another new and interesting way." He rummaged again, and came out with what could only be described as a sexual implement. He frowned. "Where the hell did this Buggy come from, anyway?"

Betezh salvaged what he could, including a long coil of partially hidden TitaniumII climbing rope—unbreakable!—and picking up the ice axe, wondered how long it would take to catch up the others. He shivered. He didn't want to be stuck down here alone. And he certainly didn't want to end up under attack. He glanced at the axe. It was long and blue-handled, and the blades were chipped. It had seen some use.

Still feeling weak, dehydrated, his head spinning from his altercation with the stuff of stars, Betezh climbed carefully up onto the ridge and looked out across the silver expanse of motionless lake. He shivered, feeling an essence of doom seeping into his bones. "Not good," he muttered, "not good at all!"

TIME SEEMED TO flow without meaning as Betezh followed the narrow pathway, dropping and climbing, undulating and weaving. It could have been minutes or hours, but he finally came to the break in the narrow ledge and peered with a scowl at the jump. He knew he couldn't go back, but to go on meant making what looked like an impossible leap. He stared at his axe, and rope, and glanced up at the rocky expanse, wondering if there was some way he could scale the wall and shimmy across. He tried a few half-hearted attempts at scaling the wall, but a rock climber he was not, and he knew that perseverance would only end in failure and probable death, his death. He put the axe and rope on the rocky floor and shuffled to the edge of the jump. He shook his head, retreated, cursed, and kicked the axe in a fit of temper. The axe scudded along the rock, striking sparks, hit the wall, flipped, and sailed out over the silver lake. It disappeared, was enveloped. Betezh stared in disbelief at his lost axe, his one and only weapon, gone! He danced a little dance of fury on the spot, aware of how ridiculous he looked, but so infuriated that he no longer cared. "I've been punched and smacked, and stapled and poked, and jiggled and broken, and mind-fucked... and now this! Can't go on, can't go back, and I've lost my bloody axe! Ahhhhh!" There was a lot of frustration in that scream. Betezh sat down, legs hanging over the ledge above the lake. He stared down at the silver motionless platter. He blinked. Something seemed to be happening.

Slowly, bubbles emerged. Then, from the depths of silver, rising an inch at a time, glided the axe. Like Arthur's sword emerging from the Lake, proffered by the Lady in some esoteric ritual, the ice axe glooped from the clutching silver fluid, coated as if with a rubber encasing of whatever filled the lake, and it hung there, only partially submerged. Betezh stared at this phenomenon in wonder, mouth open, shaggy brows touching. He watched the ice axe for a few moments, unsure of what to do, and then the axe wiggled, as if wielded by someone with a lack of patience. Betezh frowned harder. The axe wiggled again. "Get me out of here," the axe seemed to be saying. Betezh lifted his coil of rope, tied a loop in one end, and with the finesse of an untrained Rodeo star, lassoed the axehead on the fifth attempt. He pulled. There was resistance, a lot of resistance. Betezh gritted his teeth. *It's my damned axe,* he thought with a stubbornness that would put a mule to shame, *and I'm going to have it back!* He pulled and tugged, and heaved, sweat pouring down his face, and the axe finally moved... and attached to it, was a hand.

"Ugh!" spat Betezh, and immediately stopped his pulling. The hand, and the axe, started sliding back under the silver platter. The axe started to wiggle frantically.

Betezh stood up, looping the rope around his waist and tying it tight. He began to heave, using his considerable strength. The axe and the hand moved across the lake towards him, and then finally started to break the surface. There were a series of *popping* sounds, and a face emerged, unrecognisable, until it broke through the rubbery layers of silver gunk.

Betezh nearly dropped the rope.

It was Franco Haggis.

"It's you!" he squawked, staring down into a face filled with the sort of rage he'd only ever read about. It was animal, primal, a snarling fury with a willingness for genocide.

"Get me the fuck out of here!" roared Franco. He was taking deep panting breaths. His face was beetroot, bulbous and straining. The muscles of his arms writhed as he clung to the axe, as if fighting some terrible force beneath the Lake of Desecration.

Betezh started to pull, and then paused. It was a long pause. It was a pause of careful consideration. He stared down at Franco, and understanding passed between the two men. This did nothing to ease the temper in Franco's furious face.

Betezh hated Franco and wanted him dead. Why, then, would he seek to rescue the psychopathic, insane bastard from a final resting place called the Lake of Desecration? Wasn't that the *one* place Betezh wanted Franco to actually stay?

Betezh gave a shark's grin. "How's it going down there, mate?"

"Pull me out," commanded Franco.

"Actually, I'm considering my delicate position."

Franco glared up from his tenuous grip on the battered ice axe. His ankles were still ensconced in the lake, and small dribbles of silver clung to his clothes, face, and hair. "Your position, Betezh, is one of control. It's up to you whether I live or die. Does that make you feel any better? I am at your mercy."

Betezh nodded.

"Why didn't you drown?"

"Pull me up and I'll tell you."

"What was down there?"

Franco gave a nasty, toothy grin.

"OK. We have a deal." Betezh hauled on the rope, and Franco walked his way up the wall of rock and reached out, grasping Betezh's hand. Betezh hauled him over the final lip, and they both fell back and lay there, not looking at one another.

"I don't know why you did that," said Franco, his voice a caress.

"Neither do I."

"I don't believe you're that curious."

"And you'd be right."

Franco levered himself onto one elbow, and stared at Betezh. "You saved my life. Thank you. You've proved you're still a Combat-K man. I owe you one, mate."

"You owe me nothing."

Franco shrugged, climbed wearily to his feet, and stared down at the lake. He spat, and his spit was silver. "Fucking thing. A fucking curse, that's what it is."

"Franco, why *didn't* you drown?"

"Because it's not a fluid, it's an organism. You can breathe inside it, but believe me, it's not a pleasant experience. It's not somewhere you'd like to take your mother, that's for sure."

"Were there enemies down there?"

"Sort of. The… whatever the fuck it is… has jelly things that come and try to eat your face off. I found a lot of bones." His face looked suddenly grey, weary, old, "Thousands of bones."

"But they didn't… eat you?"

Franco pulled a Kekra quad-barrel machine pistol free. It was scarred like an old warrior. He gave an evil smile. "Let's just say I persuaded them otherwise."

THERE WAS A *crack* like splintering bone like snapping tendon like crushing skull like rock on flesh like steel in bone. Another crack echoed, reverberating hollowly, and Keenan could smell fire and burning, scorched metal, and scorched flesh. He expected to be dead: mashed, pulped, and flattened, but he opened his eyes to find he was in a metal cell, a cube, a room. He blinked, then turned, and saw the confusion in Pippa's eyes. There was a low growling sound, and they both looked through the darkness at the figure of Emerald.

No longer human, she revealed her true form.

Back on Ket, as she twisted and transmogrified, she had shown echoes of her true form, of her alien reality. Now, however, all human flesh, her human disguise, had gone, and she stood as what she was: Kahirrim. Her arms and legs were gone; her body was a simple oval, ridged with black armoured scales, out of which four heavy legs with pointed armoured tips emerged. Her face was a part of the central body, green eyes glowing above armoured mandibles, which clicked softly, rubbing together and gleaming with saliva. When she moved it was with a fluid powerful grace, an insect motion of incredible strength.

Keenan felt his mouth dry. Panic welled in his breast, but he savagely forced it down. He met Emerald's green gaze. He locked onto that gaze, and ground his teeth.

"We are here."

"Yes," said the creature. "I am home. My power has returned. I have been released from thrall, from my curse. You brought me home, Keenan. You have fulfilled your part of the bargain."

"Where are we?" said Pippa, staring around. A ramp led up from the small dark room. Rust streaked the ramp. She heard hisses and thumps in the distance, like... machinery, operating machinery.

"I performed the Shift. Once within range, my power flooded me, wiping away all vestiges of entrapment. I brought you through with me, through to the Second Plane."

"Where did the machines go?"

"There are two planes of reality, of existence, on Teller's World. They are two places, occupying the same physical dimension, and yet they are split, operating at different frequencies, different bandwidths. The machines are not allowed here, in The Factory. No machines are allowed here unless they are part of The Factory. It is against the Law."

Keenan and Pippa were tense, weapons not quite pointing at Emerald. With very slow, deliberate movements, Keenan changed the magazine in his MPK. He allowed the empty mag to hit the metal ground with a booming *thump*.

"You have nothing to fear from me," said Emerald. Her jaws clicked. "I know I attacked you on Ket, but I was controlled, abused, raped, violated. Here I am Whole again, here I am One again. I am a machine: a magician, a prophet, a soothsayer. I am an element from deep beneath The Mountain, and I am Home."

"You made me a promise," said Keenan.

"Yes."

"Will you honour your promise?"

"Yes. I am searching now, tracing the Stems back through a reality curtain. The Threads are long and diverse, and it will take a little time. You must be patient. Come with me."

They moved up the ramp, and The Factory stretched out before them, around them, above them, below them. Every cubic inch appeared to be filled with machinery. Huge towering machines reared off like skyscrapers, each one infinitely complex: parts moving, gears spinning, shafts turning, oil pumping through clear pipes. The floor was a circuit, tiny glimmers of gold flashing through conductive channels. Keenan and Pippa peered at the house-sized machines around them, and hanging above them. They stared with slack-jawed awe at the complexity of the vast, surreal, stunning world into which they had stepped.

Emerald led them forward, four legs *clacking* on the metal floor as they moved between vast towers of machinery. And yet… it was mostly silent, ghostly, eerily quiet. Sometimes bangs or knocks drifted to them, and sometimes the thump of metal on metal, but mostly The Factory ran like a ghost machine.

"What do the machines do?" whispered Pippa.

Keenan shrugged. "Cam would tell us, if he was here, if he could have made the Shift."

"I still don't understand that," said Pippa. She looked pale, white, lost in this vast place.

Keenan nodded. "Physics was never my strong point." He hefted his MPK, and stared at Emerald's gliding, rhythmical body, as it moved ahead of them, leading them down wide boulevards, through a city that was a factory, a machine that was a world.

"She wanted us to help kill her brother, Raze: the one who imprisoned her, and took away her power."

"Yeah. It hadn't escaped my mind." Keenan took out a narrow bedraggled cigarette, put it between his lips and lit it. Smoke plumed. He took a heavy drag, closed his eyes for a moment, then glanced at Pippa. "You want some?"

"Yeah." Like awed kids they followed Emerald through the mammoth metal streets, towers and machines rearing above them kilometre-high. They smoked, and they stared in disbelief, and then they relaxed into a companionable silence.

"This feels like the beginning of the end," said Pippa, finishing the cigarette.

"I wish Franco were here."

"So do I."

They came to a square, surrounded by towers and filled with...

"Ships," said Pippa, her eyes gleaming suddenly. Before them, clustered and cramped, squeezed into every millimetre of available space stood row upon row upon rank upon rank of Hornets, Gunships, Scouts, Hunters, and a myriad of ships on which Pippa had never before laid eyes. They were dull, black, and unmarked with insignia.

"Someone's private airfield," said Keenan, his voice gentle, "a private navy, in fact."

"Why are they here?"

"Maybe The Factory produces warships?"

"No." Pippa shook her head. "I'm not sure what this place creates, but it isn't space vehicles. But don't you see, Keenan? This is our ticket out of this place. A way home."

"We're under the ground," said Keenan. "How could we escape this prison?"

"There'll be a way. There always is."

"They look... old," said Keenan, "despite their lack of use. There's something wrong with them, as if somebody built the damned things, and then left them here for a million years. Can't you see it?"

"All I can see is a one way ticket off this shithole."

Keenan nodded. He didn't argue, there was no point. Maybe Pippa was right. However, their mission was still incomplete, and he still hadn't received his prize.

They moved past the huge gathering of ships, and Emerald remained silent, leading them by a hundred metres, her legs striking the metal ground in rhythmical clacks. Then the ship graveyard was gone, and again they were walking broad avenues, smoking like two condemned criminals sharing their last cigarette.

Suddenly, the metal road came to an end, and a vast chasm fell away before them, into darkness. The chasm was spanned by a wide bridge, ornate, intricate, and ancient. Standing at the start of the bridge, Keenan glanced left, then right. The machines of the Factory stretched for as far as the eye could see, along the ridgeline of this mighty cleft in the world.

Keenan heard Pippa gasp. He looked up, focused.

Somebody was walking towards them.

It was a woman.

FRANCO AND BETEZH lay on their bellies, staring out through the dense tangle of metal trees.

"What is it?" hissed Betezh.

Franco waved him into silence.

Howls and the rending of steel echoed in the distance, and Franco frowned. *This isn't good*, he thought. At first, what looked like a deserted metal forest seemed like an easy bit of trekking, a simple exercise in catch-up. Now, however, there seemed to be other things in the woods, in the dark, and Franco was flung back to childhood, and the monsters under his bed.

"This is an evil place," said Franco.

"I'll agree with you on that."

"OK. What weapons have we got? One working Kekra with a full magazine. One sticky, shite-filled Kekra with half a mag of shite-filled sticky bullets, which no longer work."

"And an ice axe."

"Yeah." Franco grimaced. "Let's not forget the ice axe."

"We're tooled up," said Betezh optimistically.

Franco stared out over the metal woodland. He pointed to the army of machines in the distance. They filled the pathway, the tangled woodland, the air. They moved slowly, distantly, in a wide sweeping line that seemed to be—

"They're searching for something," said Franco uneasily.

"Us?" There was a warble in Betezh's voice.

"How could they possibly know we're here?"

Betezh pointed. A small metal creature with large black eyes sat not ten feet away. It was watching them intently, metal jaws working noiselessly, all six limbs planted firmly on the ground.

"Ahh," said Franco.

The Kekra levelled, there was a *boom* and the creature was blown apart in a tangle of gears, shards and circuitry. In the distance, a metal scream rose over the woodland. Franco and Betezh turned, licked dry lips, and watched, as, like the two flanks of some mammoth distant army, the line of machines started to fold and close, and turn, thousands of integral units acting as a single entity.

"I think we should, like, get moving," said Franco.

"Good idea."

"Which way?"

"Away from them?"

"Sounds good."

"This way?"

"Yep, this way looks just fine."

Their lumbering, accelerating sprint held just a little bit of panic.

THE WOMAN STOPPED, and seemed to be waiting. She was naked, her body slim, athletic, and toned. She carried a black sword in one hand, pointing at the floor. Her stance suggested defiance, an unwillingness to let the group pass.

Keenan heard Emerald hiss. He turned, and looked at the Kahirrim. "You got my answer yet?" he said.

"Soon," said Emerald. Green eyes fixed him. "This is General Kotinevitch, the one who sent the Seed Hunter after you. This is one who colludes with my brother, Raze. He must be nearby." She seemed suddenly tense, nervous, jittery, "You must kill this human, kill her now!"

Keenan nodded. He walked out onto the bridge, Pippa a couple of steps behind him. He eyed Kotinevitch's sword warily as he approached, then looked up into brown eyes, which seemed, at the same, both gently amused and deadly serious.

"Mr. Keenan," said Vitch, ignoring Pippa. Pippa scowled.

"You are General Kotinevitch?"

"I am."

"I keep hearing your name."

"Probably because I keep trying to have you exterminated. It would seem that my best efforts have been thwarted. What did you do with Mr. Max?"

"He died a painful death," spat Pippa. She drew her sword with a slither of snaking steel, and grimaced. Her hatred was real. Kotinevitch, however, remained cool: calm, calculating, almost emotionless.

"A very great shame." She gave a brief smile, green lips parting. "You've done an incredible thing, bringing Emerald home, Mr. Keenan, but nobody will thank you for this act of awesome stupidity."

"Stupidity?" Keenan grinned. "She merely wants to die. Who the fuck are you to stand in her way?"

Vitch shook her head. Her lips compressed. "Is that what she told you? You are so out of your league, little man, it is painful to watch. You know nothing of the devastation you are about to wreak. Look at her," Vitch sneered, "she is still weak, still a victim of the toxins that keep her less than a true Kahirrim. That is why she needs you to do her dirty work. This is why she needs your protection."

"What are you talking about?"

"She would resurrect Leviathan."

Keenan blinked. He heard Emerald approaching from behind, and away beyond Vitch he saw movement. Something huge, black-skinned, the same form as Emerald only larger and heavier; it moved out onto the bridge like a titan, a giant four-legged insect... a monster. Keenan glanced over his shoulder.

Vitch attacked. Pippa hurled herself forward, her sword striking the yukana with a clash and blur of motion. The blades clashed and clattered in a furious exchange of skill. Then Vitch suddenly turned, moving a few steps, her finely chiselled buttocks the focus of Keenan's attention, before gesturing across the bridge to the huge hulking figure of the male Kahirrim.

Raze.

Vitch glared at Keenan. "Leviathan is the Devourer of Worlds. You would doom us all, Combat-K man, for your petty personal revenge. I can tell you who killed your family and your children; it is no great secret in military circles. It was the reason she was condemned to a fucking eternity of imprisonment on the prison circle of Five Grey Moons."

Keenan swallowed, stared into those brown eyes, and watched the moist, green lips smile, a smile filled with malice. "Yes, Mr. Keenan. It was Pippa, the woman by your side, your old lover, your new lover; Pippa, your little gem, your sunshine, your butterfly, who murdered your wife and your family."

Vitch twirled her sword several times, as behind Raze's bulk moved closer, huge heavy legs striking sparks from the ornate metal bridge. Vitch charged, and Pippa gave Keenan a sideways glance. There were tears on her cheeks, and guilt in her eyes, and Keenan stumbled back under the onslaught of the truth.

Pippa and Vitch met at the centre of the bridge, swords hammering and clashing. Pippa fought with fury, with energy, with hatred. Vitch fought with a coolness and skill that was psychologically disarming.

Keenan found himself at the rail of the bridge. He stared down into the yawning chasm. He couldn't believe it, just couldn't believe it. So many questions queued in his mind that his head spun and thundered with pain. It was so unbelievable as to be inhuman, so painful it was like having his heart ripped out by taloned claws, like having his spine torn free with razor teeth. He screamed. He leant over the chasm and screamed, and vomited, and tears fell, and behind him Pippa and Vitch fought with savage ferocity and consummate skill. Vitch's blade cut a line down Pippa's cheek opening a flap that showed teeth. They fought on, Pippa's blood dripping making the metal walkway slippery under slick boots. With a dazzling riposte, Pippa's sword opened a wound across Vitch's left hip, and blood pumped, running down into her pubic mound and dripping, a premature menstruation. They circled warily, both panting, both bathed in sweat and streaked with crimson.

"Keenan," hissed Vitch, "you have to stop this. You have to stop Emerald! She will resurrect Leviathan. He will build an army and the Quad-Gal will never be the same. We will be slaves, as we were slaves before! Listen to me, man! Emerald was one of the Protectors until she turned to the Paths of the Dark Flame... and just as Raze guards the Prison Cell that holds Leviathan... so Emerald seeks to open it!"

"You lie," coughed Keenan.

Emerald leapt forward, over Pippa's head, sharp pointed appendages striking out with insane speed at Vitch, who retreated, yukana sword blurring, fending off the sudden, brutal attack. Then Raze was there, and he was huge, terrifying, his jaws glittering with crystal saliva, his six dark eyes burning with fury. Emerald threw Vitch aside, hammering a blow to her chest that smashed her against the ornate iron rails of the bridge, buckled her, smashed her, bloody and pulped and groaning to the slick ground.

Raze roared, and Pippa stared up in disbelief as he reared above his alien sister. Emerald charged him. They clashed, the bridge rocked, and their limbs hammered at one another, pounding and slashing, jaws tearing and scoring, and biting chunks from armoured flesh. A blow hammered Emerald's head with staggering force and she stumbled, two back legs collapsing. She swayed, as a point missed her eyes by inches and buckled a section of iron railing with screams of twisted metal. Emerald slashed upwards, cutting a line of flesh from Raze's abdomen. He roared again, in pain, jaws yammering in a frenzy as something dark and oil-slick poured from the wound.

Pippa staggered to Keenan. She was bleeding heavily. She did not meet his intense stare.

"It can't be true," he said.

Pippa did not reply.

He grasped her and shook her. "It cannot be true! Tell me it's not fucking true!"

Pippa looked up. Tears rolled down her cheeks. She chewed her lip. Beyond them, the bridge rocked again as the two aliens clashed, beating one another, drawing blood, screaming with hatred and with a rage far surpassing human anger.

"I'm sorry, Keenan."

He staggered back as if struck, and sat heavily on the ground. He stared up, through tears, through panting, through snot. He stared up with confusion acid-etched on his features. "Why, Pippa? In the name of God, why?"

"You betrayed me." Her words were hollow, brittle, as empty as an abortion wracked womb.

Keenan barked a laugh. "I betrayed you? That's a fucking reason to kill my wife, my Rachel, my little sweet Ally? You fucking whore. You fucking disease. How could you do it to them? How could you murder my babes?" He was on his knees. His eyes burned with Hell. His teeth snarled poison. He staggered up, face wild, hands clawing, MPK clattering, forgotten at his hip and, appearing to remember the weapon, he grasped it, solid and real, and stared down at the black alloy, at the drilled barrel, at the elegant gleaming curve of the magazine.

"No." Her voice was little more than the whisper of a confused child.

Keenan stalked forward, gun in fists, and rammed the barrel hard under Pippa's bruised chin. Behind them, the bridge rocked under a terrifying impact. Keenan's eyes met hers. She was crying, but Keenan's tears had gone. A harmattan blew across his soul and all that was left of his sanity was... emptiness.

"No," insisted Pippa. "Keenan, I love you. We can make this right!"

"It can never be right."

"I was mad, with jealousy, and hatred. I was a different person then. I have changed. I am repentant."

"I'm not."

He jabbed at her with the edge of the barrel, which sliced her skin. Blood ran down, over the drilled cooling holes, and Keenan's face was a brutal caricature of human.

Then he was gone, past Pippa, to a heavily wounded Raze who reared above Emerald, cowering and battered and broken on the metal bridge. Keenan straddled Emerald's wounded form and looked up into the six eyes of her enemy. He lifted his MPK and unleashed a payload of bullets into Raze's face. The Kahirrim screamed, squealing as the gun lowered and bullets tore at his soft wounded underbelly. Raze staggered back, and Keenan kept firing, his face neutral his eyes blank plates, lips a line of blood: fifty bullets, a hundred. Still Keenan fired, his gun-barrel glowing white hot. The gun gave a warning beep, and, still striding towards the retreating injured alien, Keenan swiftly switched mags. The roar filled the sky, the air, the world. The gun glowed and Raze was forced back under a hardcore metal onslaught until he stood, cowering at the edge of the bridge, limbs trying to protect his face. Keenan grasped the MPK, willing Raze to die, willing him to be no more. With a final wail the alien reared back, folding, his body a shattered torn marionette, and he tumbled into the darkness of the chasm.

Keenan did not move, did not rush to the edge.

Raze fell in silence and was gone, dead and gone.

Emerald staggered up, lifted something to her face. Energy crackled, in the air, along her limbs, and Keenan turned, frowning, as energy moved out from Emerald's crumpled body in tiny fluttering arcs, discharging across the bridge, and lifting Kotinevitch, bearing her broken body across the ground, and lowering her gently onto a silver disc embedded in the dark steel. Keenan blinked. There were two more discs, the three forming a triangle.

"Emerald?" he said.

Slowly, she heaved and dragged her wounded body into a swaying stance. The energy still poured from her, crackling and fizzing, and with a yelp Keenan dropped his MPK as it bit him.

"Stand on the discs," said Emerald, her voice a dry croak.

As if in a trance, Pippa moved to stand on the silver circle. Keenan eyed the third and felt the pull the need the want the lust. It was more powerful than sex, more needy than lust and, every emotion within him fired him. He knew that the revenge he sought would happen: was a certainty. If he stood on that disc his dreams would be fulfilled and his emptiness and hollowness would fill with purity and love, and everything would be perfect again in a perfect beautiful world.

Keenan moved to the disc.

"No," croaked Vitch.

Keenan felt it, a discord, something shattering the harmony. But he could not move. He was locked, imprisoned without chains, incarcerated without bars. He glanced at Pippa. She was crying

mercury tears. Vitch was twitching spasmodically
on the ground as if in a fit. Then he stared at Emerald, who moved, severely wounded, leaking
oil-blood, to the centre of the three inset discs.

She forced herself to stand tall, then lifted two
limbs into the air. Everything crackled. Black
sparks ran along the metal of the bridge in waves
of screaming energy. A wind blew, thick with the
stench of metal. And Keenan knew, knew with a
sudden, terrible and certain dread that he had
killed the wrong Kahirrim.

Emerald was not a saviour.

Raze had been, as Vitch insisted, a Protector.

Of what? His mind whirled, filled with fallout:
Leviathan? The Dead One? The GodRace?

His eyes lowered, and met Vitch's. She smiled at
him, and he realised that she had wanted him
assassinated, not out of some personal vendetta, or
for some petty financial gain; she had simply
sought to stop this moment coming to fruition. Her
motives, no matter what he thought, had been
good. She understood the bigger picture. While
he...

He smiled sardonically.

Why, he'd just been thinking of petty revenge.

"You must stop this," said Vitch. Keenan did not
hear the words, but could read her smashed lips.

He tried to move, and could not. He tried to
reach his bombs, but could not.

"I am trapped," he mouthed.

Emerald whirled on him, black electric arcs spear-
ing out and smashing him with an agony he would
never have dreamed possible. Energy ran in coursing

rivers down his arms and legs, rippling through his neck and face, brain and heart. He could not scream, could not fall, could not die. His mind became a useless thing; a template of emptiness.

Emerald was speaking in an alien language. Her head lifted. She stared up into the vaults of darkness high above. The world seemed to glow black.

And Keenan became aware of a presence.

He forced his head around, teeth gritted, pain searing him, every nerve on fire with a billion volts of electricity. And there, at the edge of the bridge, stood a man.

He was of medium build, with oiled jet black hair tied back in a bun. His face was plump, cheeks an unhealthy red, and he wore a long black drooping moustache. He looked normal, inconsequential, but Keenan scowled and his face became a broiling pit of seething fury.

"Akeez," he forced between twitching lips.

Akeez nodded, as if acknowledging Keenan's presence at some private dignitaries' function. Then he lifted his dark glittering eyes to a place above Emerald.

Keenan followed his gaze.

Black air was swirling, shimmering, black on black, on black, in different layers of darkness. A roar rushed up from deep below the bridge and blasted into the sky, coalescing and swirling, and glittering with pinpricks of white.

"Leviathan!" screamed Emerald, as spears of black lightning connected her to the resurrection of the Dark God... Leviathan the Eater: the Devourer of Worlds.

Keenan saw it, and it was beyond description. It was terrible— a creature, an entity that coalesced and swirled and was organic and fluid and took a form he would never be able to visualise nor comprehend. Leviathan grew. Then, he reached down with a long narrow limb of slick black metal and plucked Emerald from the bridge, lifting her high into the vault of the underground sky. Slowly, it tore her into pieces, plucking at the shreds with a hundred limbs of oiled black claws and absorbed them into the swirling tornado that was the Resurrection.

Keenan dropped to his knees, coughed blood onto the bridge, and then covered his face with his hands.

Pippa, too, staggered, released, falling to one knee. She stared up, in horror, in fear, in a base antediluvian terror at this God she could barely comprehend. She could feel him, it, inside her, in her head in her mind in her cunt in her heart in her soul. It was terrifying and uncompromising, and lacking in emotion or morals, or empathy, and she knew, she knew it, and it knew her. It was at one with her. It flowed through her veins and spine, and infused her with a part of every atom. She could taste its memories like cold hydrogen corpses on an eternal beach. Leviathan had existed from the dawn of a brittle Galaxy, and its one controlling, absorbing, consuming energy was...

Hate.

Pippa let out a primal scream. Madness took her mind in its fist, and squeezed.

Keenan snarled at Leviathan, saliva spooling from battered lips. He screamed out in defiance at the entity, which spun and gleamed lazily in the sky above him like oiled gold. There was no face, only an idea that it was watching him, but he knew that it was: with contempt, with amusement, with the patience of the infinite. Keenan did not speak, could not speak, but his rage and raw confrontation, and his contempt for that life-taking devourer filled him, and poured out like a river of anguish.

Leviathan coiled about and within itself.

There was a *boom*, subtle and terrifying.

And the very core of Teller's World shuddered.

CHAPTER 20

LEVIATHAN'S SONG

KEENAN SEEMED TO fade from sight. Cam hung, buzzing softly, watching the confusion in the sentinel machines which, having lost their target, milled around. Cam glided lower, surveying the creatures. They looked battered and worn, and not in the best of condition. And he realised they were old, ancient, from another time, another era, from a world when primitive minds had designed machines to be... what? Fearsome? Cam chuckled, revelling in his superiority and with a song in his atomic heart.

Still, the little PopBot was confused. And now, waiting for—hopefully—the return of Keenan and Pippa, he set several spare cores working on the problem of the Shift, which, apparently, he could not make. He journeyed back, over the heads of the whining panting metal sentinels, cruising at speed all the way to the lair of the spidery things, then back, back to the river. Cam paused, staring at the fast-flowing oil. Operations came and went in his tiny casing. He considered the river. What was its purpose? What was oil usually used for? Cooling, but cooling what? Machinery? Machinery used for what?

Cam followed the river, calculating an estimated volume, and increasing his speed until he was a blur. Suddenly the river ended, was funnelled downwards. A huge waterfall was collected at the bottom of a kilometre-deep valley by slick cones leading to thick pipes. Cam considered this. With an internal digital sigh, he dropped like a rock, and was sucked into one of the pipes. Submerged in oil, he checked his seals, and then flowed with the vertical current. The pipes twisted and turned, eventually leading to... a machine: a large machine.

Cam emerged in a shower of oil, punched his way through a sieve of steel mesh, and observed the cooling system stretching off to the horizon. He zoomed, he estimated. The cooling system was six thousand kilometres long by a thousand kilometres wide. More processor cores kicked in. Cam worked, buzzing and vibrating softly, oil dripping from his casing as he calculated and instigated algorithms. He followed the machine, followed the curve that followed the curvature of the planet's hub. And, halting, Cam saw what he needed to see: the machines that serviced the core of the planet, a core that was not molten rock, but... something else.

Impossible, thought the little PopBot.

It cannot be done.

Sensors detected Cam's sentient presence. They emerged from recessed drawers with tiny *zips*, and spun after him, razors spinning and tiny red eyes glittering but Cam accelerated at an awesome rate, back through the mesh, up the oil collectors, and in a burst and flurry of exploding oil, out over the river, the edges of his case glowing.

Cam paused. If he'd had lungs, he would have panted. Instead, digitally controlled coolers extracted and hissed super-iced air over his case until frost sparkled. Suddenly, the tiny red-eyed bots zipped out through the river and surrounded him. They flickered this way and that, unable to keep still, circling him, darting and moving, weighing up his defences... not realising the systems he carried within his miniature hull.

Cam sighed.

Stupidity!

The ten tiny bots attacked, red eyes glowing, and Cam spun as he fired charges, watching them explode with a *crackle* of rapid succession, like a volley of fireworks. Ten bots fell into the river and bobbed away, dead.

Cam rotated again, his conclusion to the problem of the Shift emerging. Ahh, he thought, that's what it is, and that's how you do it. He understood Teller's World, understood it's great secret, and understood the sudden threat facing Combat-K. A threat of which Keenan and Pippa had no idea.

"Oh no," he said.

Something exploded on the horizon. It was gunfire. Cam focused. Injectors *buzzed*, and he accelerated and spun like a bullet across the metal landscape of the Mekkra Woods. He came to a... battle. He could not believe his sensors. It was Betezh... and... Franco?

"I thought you were dead!"

A creature leapt through the air, razor talons nearly disembowelling the small ginger pugilist. He twisted, Kekra roaring in his fist, disintegrating the sentinel, which crumbled around him, huge shards aflame, panels whirring to the ground, buckled and destroyed. He scowled up at Cam.

"No, I'm here, and I could do with some damn bloody help!" More creatures advanced, and Betezh swung at them with the battered ice axe. They circled the two men warily.

This is it, thought Franco. The end!

He scowled in fury. To die in such a way! The shame!

The several hundred strong phalanx of metal sentinels charged, screaming, and the two men, eyes bulging, stood their ground, and began to shoot and swing and growl and curse. Suddenly, above the clearing, a high-pitched noise rattled out a series of wailing and warbling tones, a high-bandwidth transmission of... data.

The sentinels faltered. They stumbled, falling to knees and wings and claws. Franco and Betezh stared at one another in amazement; then clutched one another in a vicious bear-hug.

"That help?"

"What did you do?"

"Random digital noise underplayed with a modest EMP transmission, on an audio frequency. These machines talk to each other via sound.

Primitive, I know. I've just fed their input systems with shit. That should keep them quiet for a little while."

Franco and Betezh were dancing a jig.

"Whoo-hoo!" said Franco. "Still alive!"

"Franco! Keenan and Pippa are in grave danger. I've worked out what this planet is. How it's powered. What the hell's going on. Emerald seeks to resurrect one of the oldest ancient Gods, Leviathan. She was a slave, and he was her master, a million years ago. Leviathan wreaks destruction, dealing death and oblivion to all life. When strong, he will rampage through the Quad-Gal, and those he does not enslave he will consume. He is a parasite, and he was imprisoned."

"How?" said Franco, still panting from the fight and the bear-hug.

"At the centre of Teller's World, which, ironically, is not a world, but a prison, a machine, and, at its basic level, a cage."

"And you worked out how this prison is powered?"

"Yes." Cam's case glittered red. His tone was deadly serious, frightened, even. "The core of this machine—in its entirety—is a chained and harnessed Black Hole."

KEENAN FORCED HIMSELF, with brute willpower, to his feet. He staggered across the trembling bridge. Pippa had dropped her sword, and he picked up the blade, brandishing it in defiance at Leviathan. A sound emerged, and Keenan realised that the swirling oil entity was amused.

"Fuck you," he screamed, and hurled the sword into the swirling darkness.

A limb crashed out from the insanity, plucked Keenan from the bridge and lifted him hundreds of feet into the air. He flew, dizzyingly, the whole of The Factory spreading beneath him. Nausea flooded him. He vomited, and felt death touch him with a subtle caress. His flight halted, abruptly, and he stared down with sour lips at the metal limb that held him, at the talons that cradled him. They were narrow, an approximation of fingers, created by something that had never seen fingers.

Keenan snarled and screamed at the creature without words.

And again, Teller's World trembled.

A scream rent the air. Keenan could smell hot metal, burning oil, the stench of death, rotting flesh, flowers, lavender. And he wept. He wept for the world, and he wept for his wife and for his murdered children. He could see them, their sweet smiling faces, their hands stretching out towards him, Ally brushing crumbs from his shirt, Rachel patting him on the shoulder with child-serious sincerity, Ally climbing nightmare-eyed into his bed and snuggling up close for protection, protection he could always offer them. Oh yeah, protect who? protect what? You offer shit. You can offer no fucking protection. And he hated himself and hated the world. Far below he watched Pippa stir, climb to her feet and glance up with a haunted face filled with empty desolation...

* * *

"WHAT IS IT?"

Franco hefted the huge weapon, and swept it around inside the Lightning APSF—Advanced Prototype Surface Fighter. Cam buzzed a warning, dodged the trajectory, and retreated.

"We have to hurry," snapped the PopBot.

"Calm down, calm down!"

"And stop pointing that damned thing at me!"

"Well, what is it?"

"An RPN."

"You mean an RPG, surely?"

"No. It's a Rocket Propelled Nuke."

"Ahh. I didn't realise they built those anymore." Franco admired the sleek matt green shaft, and peered like a curious kid into the face—the tip—of the nuclear warhead. "Is it dangerous?"

"Of course it's fucking dangerous," spluttered Cam, "and only a madman would build one! Only a bigger madman would use one! A nuke, fired from your shoulder? The daft bastards kept nuking themselves! Insanity! Now put it down, get yourself a sub-machine gun or something, and follow me this instant!"

After an electronic hijacking of the Shift, Cam had led the two dazed men through The Factory, pushing them on faster and faster, urgently, to halt Keenan and Pippa's impending demise. But, as Franco seriously pointed out, he and Betezh were reduced in terms of weaponry. They were hardly in a position to defend themselves, never mind fight and rescue their comrades. If indeed, their comrades needed—or wanted—rescuing.

Cam had reluctantly steered them to the graveyard of ships, and Franco's eyes had lit up.
Realisation dawned. "An escape route!" he blurted, then ran forward, waving his arms.

"You need to find Pippa first," pointed out Cam.

"Good point. You said there were guns?"

"The huge rectangular craft is an Infantry Gun
Carrier."

Franco gave him a thumbs up. "Good lad."

"Just be quick. And Franco?"

"Yes Cam?"

"Let's be sensible about this."

"Aye, Cam."

CAM WATCHED FRANCO stagger from the IGC, bent
almost double under the weight of guns, bombs and
RPNs. He sighed, a silent digital sigh, as the world
around them began to tremble. The Factory shuddered, like an organic beast dying... or coming alive.

"Cam!" shrieked Franco. "What's happening?"

"We have to go. Now!" snarled the PopBot.

Franco dropped several huge bags of guns, and,
followed closely by Betezh—more sensibly
armed—sprinted after the bobbing PopBot. Huge
booms echoed from the sky, and from beneath the
ground. The world was screaming, trembling,
shuddering. They pounded on, and in the blink of
an eye careered from a street to see the world open
before them, then on to a wide bridge above a bottomless chasm. Franco skidded to a halt, eyes
sweeping the scene, taking it in with an educated
eye, used to calculating conflict and the engage-
ment of war in an instant.

Franco stared at the huge swirling mass of Leviathan.

Hmm, he thought. *That has to be bad.*

Then he stared with a frown at the limb holding Keenan several hundred feet above the bridge. Franco ran forward, halting beside Pippa, who was silent, her face a nightmare, her eyes piss-holes leading straight down to Hell. Franco pointed up at Leviathan.

"Oi! You! Dickhead! Put my friend down!"

The limb carrying Keenan swept towards the bridge, and Keenan's rag-doll body sailed past Franco's face with a howl, making him leap back, squawking. High above, a thousand other metal limbed tentacles unfolded from the hub of the swirling chaos that was Leviathan.

Franco scowled. "You cheeky son of a bitch." He shouldered an RPN, smashed the safety cover with the butt of his Kekra, aimed it, and fired.

There was a *whoosh*.

Franco staggered back ten steps, then sat down heavily with a *thump*.

The atomic warhead left a trail of fire through blackness, struck Leviathan, and was absorbed like a stone in a lake of black oil. There was a moment of hiatus, then a deep glow, the ignition of a sun, which blossomed and then went rigid, gloss black, and cold.

A deep groan filled the world. The bridge on which they stood shook. Above, huge rocks fell from the sky, house-sized and jagged, tumbling down past the bridge and disappearing into the chasm.

Franco climbed to his feet.

Betezh nudged him. "I don't think he liked that!"

"Fuck 'im!"

A roar filled the cavern, so deafening it was beyond description. It came from everywhere at once: a blast so devastating it swept those still standing from their feet, and sent Cam scurrying wildly and erratically through the air on random eddies of tornado.

Leviathan's limbs thrashed.

Keenan was swept around, high into the sky, then low skimming the bridge. As the limb came past Pippa, who had regained her sword, she leapt and made a neat vicious diagonal cut—

Talons rattled on steel, like knuckle-dice.

Keenan rolled along the bridge, winded, body and limbs slapping the metal.

The roar echoed again, and the sky rained rocks, several of which crashed against the bridge, making the structure groan. Franco shouldered a second RPN and grinned over at Keenan.

"This is the life, eh lad? Never a boring moment!"

"Fire into the chasm!" screamed Cam. "You cannot kill Leviathan! Fire into the chasm!"

Franco ran to the bridge's rail, leapt, balanced himself, sighted, and standing precariously on the swirling iron above a dark infinity, he unleashed the warhead into the black maw below. A trail of fire cut the tenebrosity in two. The rocket howled, fading from hearing, and the nuke was gone.

Franco's head snapped round. He scowled at Cam. "Nothing happened! You dumb-ass Bot! Anyway, what the hell was I firing at?"

"The chains," whispered Cam.

"Chains?"

"Holding the Black Hole."

Franco's mouth flapped. "What do we do now?"

Keenan sprinted past him. He growled, "We run, idiot."

Keenan slid, stopped, picked up the limp body of Kotinevitch, and flinging her over his shoulder with a wince of agony, sprinted again along the bridge. Behind them, Leviathan roared as somewhere deep deep deep below there was an almost silent explosion. Keenan, Pippa, Franco and Betezh skidded to a halt at the edge of The Factory's broad street. Leviathan swirled and glowed. A terrible silence descended over the scene; calmness, a serenity.

A shaft of black fire a kilometre wide shot from the chasm below, engulfing Leviathan in an instant and blasting a hole through the rock roof above the bridge. The bridge was gone instantly, vaporised. The black fire twisted their eyes around in their heads.

"Run!" screamed Cam, and slammed off in crazy zig-zagging acceleration.

They pounded after the PopBot. Around them, The Factory started to crumble and collapse. Huge towering buildings disintegrated. Mammoth towers collapsed in on themselves. The world descended into a chaos of noise and rumbling destruction. The air filled with waves of smoke and debris, dust and shards of metal.

Combat-K ran for their lives.

Ahead, Cam spun, scanners screaming, analysing the gathered ships in the collection. *There,* he thought. One of the most powerful and brutal ships ever built, known commonly as *No Rest*; it's full moniker was *No Rest For The Wicked*. It was not, reputedly, the safest or most reliable ship ever built, but, by God, it was the fastest.

Cam sped on, communicating with ship Systems and warming engines, bringing subsidiary systems online. The *No Rest* glowed with bright lights, which drew Combat-K like flies to a lantern. Panting, groaning, they sprinted towards the ship, glowing welcomingly through the dust and smoke. They hammered up the corrugated alloy ramp, and Pippa slammed into the pilot's seat, lifting the ship from the ground on a punch of power, before the ramps had even closed. They soared high above the disintegrating Factory, only to discover it wasn't The Factory that was crumbling— but the world.

"What's happening?" screamed Pippa, frantically searching scanners, and dodging a rainfall of crushing rocks as the *No Rest* levelled near the vast cavern's roof, and curled, diving again as she searched for a way out of the planet's interior. Sunburst scans rebounded from the cavern's roof and floors, giving her poor feedback.

"Teller's World is a machine," said Cam, "an impossibility, but one which exists nonetheless. It is powered—and held in check—by a Black Hole at its core. You have heard of a Dyson Sphere?"

Pippa threw him a look. "Encompassing a star with a shell to capture its entire energy output? They tried it. It's impossible. The structure breaks down due to Internal X Pressure Syndrome."

"This is sort of the same, only Teller's World was designed to harness the power of a Black Hole's awesome gravitational pull, while trapping Leviathan at the core. It was a balance, in equilibrium. Now it's breaking down."

"So..." Pippa's eyes were wide.

"This is a race," said Cam. "When the machine stops operating, we need to be beyond the Event Horizon. Otherwise, we will be pulled into the unchained Black Hole with every other atom on this ersatz planet!"

"There," said Keenan. He pointed to the scanners.

"I see it."

The *No Rest* screamed and groaned as Pippa accelerated against an incrementally increasing gravitational pull. The walls of the ship started to vibrate with frightening violence. Pippa slammed controls to the full.

"You're going to have to pull a K Jump."

"Can't do that," said Pippa, teeth gritted. "Way too dangerous, especially from surface-side. It'll spread us all over the fucking galaxy!"

"We'll never out-race the pull," said Cam, "because—and this is the bugger—we're already in it."

"Shit. We've got a one in ten thousand chance of surviving a K."

"If you don't, Pippa, we'll die here. I guarantee it."

Pippa stared at Cam, and gave a single nod.

"What's this all about?" said Franco, face pale and bleak. He pulled out a small bottle, shook free a tiny, rainbow-coloured pill, and swallowed it. His eyes went wide. He coughed. His skin started to vibrate.

"We've got to do a K Jump, but first I need to get out of this shit. Any impurities in our field will throw us off course, and we'll end up inside a fucking star. Everybody! Strap in. This is going to be the bumpiest damn ride of your lives."

The *No Rest* was howling, glowing.

As the cavern collapsed, so Pippa navigated up and out, on a treacherous raining path to the swirling chaos atmosphere of Teller's World. Rocks pounded the ship with raging violence. Below them, as they burst free and soared into the sky, huge chasms opened across the landscape and the world collapsed. In the distance, a range of mountains disappeared in the blink of an eye. Below, the black desert was pouring like sand through an hourglass on a planetary scale.

"Everybody... hold on!"

Pippa's hands clattered across keyboards. Her face was a mask of concentration. Tears soaked her cheeks. Silence swamped the ship. Franco's grumbling, muttering voice was the only sound to be heard under the red glow of emergency lighting.

Pippa hit the boost.

The *No Rest For The Wicked* screamed... and flashed from existence.

It took the K Jump...

And followed a different path.

ABOUT THE AUTHOR

Andy Remic is a young British writer. He has an unhealthy love of martial arts, kickass bikes, mountain climbing and computer hacking. Once a member of an elite Combat-K squad, he has since retired from military service and works as a biomod and weapon engineer at the NANOTEK Corporation.

War Machine is his fourth novel.

You can discover more about Andy Remic at *www.andyremic.com*.

A COMBAT-K NOVEL

ANDY REMIC

The new master of rock-hard military science fiction

BIOHELL

www.solarisbooks.com UK ISBN: 978-1-84416-650-3 US ISBN: 978-1-84416-590-2

The City: a planet filled with corruption, guns, sex, and designer drugs. Zombies roam the streets and are out for blood. The Combat-K squad are dropped into this warzone to uncover what's turned this planet into a wasteland of murder and mutations. Soon their focus is on the Nano-Tek corporation itself...

 SOLARIS SCIENCE FICTION